"Mr. Jones?"

The sound of a voice startled Grant out into the rain. The woman had called him. Immediately, he thought the worst. She was hurt.

He hurriedly swung open the door to her cabin. She literally fell into his arms. Lifting her back inside, he closed the door behind them.

"What's wrong? Are you all right?"

Jacelyn backed up to the cot and sat down before her quaking legs gave out. "I was just . . . w-worried—"

"About what? Did you see something?"

"About you."

He stopped talking and stood dripping in the middle of the room. "Me? You were worried about me?"

"You were wet and cold. It's raining. You could've frozen or caught your death . . . What?" He looked at her like she'd sprouted another eye.

Hell, he thought. "Well, ah . . ." Damn it, he was turning into a stuttering idiot. "I'm surprised. Didn't expect a lady like you to—"

"Ask an outlaw into her room so late at night?"

His brows shot up at her use of the term "outlaw." "That, too."

Jacelyn stared at the scowl marring Grant's features. It was strangely endearing. He must be as shaken by what was happening between them as she. And something was happening. The squirmy feeling in her stomach and the blaze flaming in his eyes told her so.

Grant walked to the foot of the cot. With each step he took toward her, Jacelyn's heartbeat accelerated. He sat on the end of the bed. Jacelyn's lips felt numb as she mumbled, "It's getting chilly. Wh-where will you sleep?"

Thunder rumbled. Grant cocked an eyebrow. "Right here."

JUDITH STEEL

TENDER DECEPTION

ZEBRA BOOKS
KENSINGTON PUBLISHING CORP.

DEDICATION

To Linda Osgood Neff, (or P. S.), whose rare friendship is a treasure I'll always cherish.

The Indian proverb was reproduced with permission from Leanin' Tree, Boulder, Colorado. Many thanks to Mr. Trumble and the friendly, helpful staff.

Nothing is so strong
as gentleness

Nothing so gentle as
real strength

Indian proverb

Chapter One

ARIZONA TERRITORY, 1881

"If you're determined to get yourself killed then, by
all means, go ahead with your damned crazy scheme."

Lieutenant Grant Ward unfolded his lanky form from
one of the two chairs and scrubbed at the back of his
neck. Like a hungry cougar stalking elusive prey, he began to pace the clean, plank floor. A mirthless chuckle
ground from his throat when Colonel Evan Alexander's
lips thinned with impatience.

The Colonel ran rough, chapped fingers through the
sparse hair atop his head and continued to try to talk
some sense into his restless friend. "Just remember,
you'll be on your own." Since the younger man finally
seemed to be paying attention, he rushed on. "When the
atmosphere between the civilians and the Apache is so
volatile, the Army cannot risk becoming involved in
such a questionable situation."

Grant spun around. "Questionable? You know better
than anyone that my scouts aren't responsible for any of
the atrocities they're being blamed for."

"You're right." Colonel Alexander laced his fingers
across his generous belly. "But the Army has to play a
neutral role for now. Get me proof of who *is* responsi-

ble, and I'll do everything in my power to see that justice is done. Until then—"

"Damn it, that's all I'm asking." Grant stopped pacing. He raised his hand to his stubbled chin, a grimace deepening the creases on either side of his mouth. He'd gone two days and nights with only a few hours' rest and even longer than that without shaving. He probably looked deadlier than the hardcases he was so determined to track down.

"You're too valuable to me as Chief of Scouts. If anything were to happen . . . I just wish you'd let the proper authorities check out your suspicions." The Colonel rose from his seat and bumped the polished oak desk, nearly toppling a coal oil lantern from its precarious perch.

Grant reacted quickly, sliding the lantern back to its original position. "I'd be more than happy to do that, if there was one lawman in the area I could trust. The peace officers out of Tucson side with their corrupt politicians. And the lawmen in Tombstone . . . Well, the Earps and their cronies are barely a notch above the outlaws and rustlers they claim to be chasing."

"That could very well be true but . . . what happens if someone recognizes you who knows about your—" He cleared his throat. "Who knew your father and . . . mother?"

Grant stiffened.

The Colonel sighed and sat heavily back in his chair. "There's also the matter of when and where—"

Lifting his broad shoulders in a casual shrug, Grant informed him, "I'll handle everything. We don't want the Army to be accused of knowing too much, do we?"

Suddenly the door slammed open. A young Corporal, attempting to block the forward progress of a very angry-looking woman, saluted awkwardly and stammered, "I'm sorry, sir. I told her you were busy, but—"

Startled by the interruption, the Colonel stood up so quickly his chair rocked precariously.

"Really ... Colonel, did you say?" Her dark navy eyes flared toward the Corporal, who gulped and nodded, then sliced back to the more portly blue-clad figure. "I must speak with you, immediately. It's a matter of ... life and death."

Jacelyn Faith McCaffery came to an abrupt halt in front of the Colonel. From the corner of her eye, she noted another figure—a tall, silent, dark, and imposing figure—but the only person she had time for now was the commander of the fort.

Colonel Alexander winked at Grant before favoring the distraught young woman with a condescending smile. "Now, now, my dear, I'm sure nothing could be so terrible as that."

Jacelyn breathed deeply, unaccustomed to the altitude. The persistent Corporal had once again taken hold of her arm and she shook him off with a glaring frown.

"Please, Colonel. I must find my brother, *now.*"

Taking pity on the attractive, albeit dusty and rumpled, lady, Evan sighed and looked askance at Grant.

Grant shrugged. "We were through."

The Colonel scowled. "Oh, no, we were not. There's more—"

"But ... I really need your help, sir." Jacelyn was prepared to get down on her knees if necessary. She had traveled a long distance—all the way from Richmond—alone. Her purse was nearly empty as most of her available cash had been spent in reaching this godforsaken place.

She was desperate. Finding her brother, James, had literally become a matter of life and death for her.

"Please, ma'am. Don't cause the Colonel no more trouble. Just come along nice an' polite like." The Corporal tentatively reached toward her.

9

She glowered at the young man and threatened, "Unhand me, before I ... I ..." She'd never needed to intimidate anyone before. What deed would be sinister enough to convince the oaf she was serious?

All at once she felt a tug on the collar of her traveling jacket. She was literally lifted and dumped onto the nearest chair.

"Have a seat, lady."

The raspy voice rumbled down her spine. A heavy hand held her in the chair. She turned her head, gave the tall, dark man a quick up and down glance and ordered, "Remove your hand you ... you savage."

Stunned, Grant jerked his hand from her shoulder as if he'd touched a burning ember.

Jacelyn started to rise, but was slammed down again.

Feeling every bit the "savage" she'd just described him, Grant leaned down to stare into her huge, dark blue eyes and grumbled, "If you want to keep that pretty scalp, I suggest you stay put."

Determined to put the man in his place with her acerbic tongue and most withering stare, she instead blinked and found herself speechless. Her first impression of the man had been accurate. Why, she'd never encountered such an uncivilized-looking person in her entire life.

Dressed all in black except for a snow-white shirt, his dark, swarthy features were set off by a black moustache, black sideburns, and uneven coal-black hair swept back beneath a black hat. He was a rogue.

Pale blue eyes sliced into her like the sharp blade of a knife, which at that moment sparkled with layers of frost. She wrapped her arms around her upper body and shivered.

Grant stared into the woman's upturned face. Finally he spied a slight flicker of doubt in her incredible navy eyes. And her full lower lip quivered.

Jacelyn couldn't move her eyes from the man bending so close. His square jaw was as firm and steady as a granite boulder.

Dangerous. The word sent a tremor down her spine. But the dark rogue with the icy eyes continued to study her. At last he released his grip and turned away.

He sauntered over to lean negligently against the near wall, still watching her with the intensity of a lobo wolf regarding its next meal. Those eyes—those blue eyes that seemed to hold the knowledge of a lifetime—held her prisoner. Those eyes—as endless and ageless and mysterious as the terrain the stage had taken her through—continued to impale her. She moistened her lips and scooted forward in her chair.

The Colonel stepped between them. "Let's all calm down, shall we?" He frowned at Grant, then faced the strange woman. "Now, miss, how can I—"

"I have to find my brother, sir. The last time I heard from him, he said he was working out of Fort Huachuca."

Evan Alexander folded his hands behind his back. "Just who is your brother, ma'am?" He cleared his throat. "And who are you?"

"My brother's name is James. James McCaffery." She hurried to explain, "He's a mapmaker."

The Colonel just nodded. When it appeared he was waiting for her to continue, Jacelyn glanced toward the tall, dark man and found him still staring. A wave of heat flooded her face. "And my name is Jacelyn, sir." She implored him, "I must find James right away."

The Colonel nodded again. "Ah, yes . . . Your brother mentioned you, Miss McCaffery."

Forgetting she was already perched on the front edge of the chair, Jacelyn squirmed forward, then had to move her feet quickly to catch her balance. "You know James? Oh, that's wonderful!" She sighed with relief. "So you can tell me where he is?"

11

"Ahem. I'm afraid not."

Jacelyn's brows snapped together. "I don't understand . . ."

Evan Alexander steepled his fingers over his belly and gazed sympathetically upon the young woman. "My dear, I . . . ahem . . . know your brother. I like him. Ahem . . . He's a personable, dedicated young man. He was assigned to map alternative routes to Tombstone and mark the locations of existing ranches in the area when he was tempted to . . . ah . . . Many good men have succumbed to the lure of silver and gold and dreams of fast fortunes—"

"No! Not James. My family's . . ." She hesitated, darting a glance toward the brooding, silent sentry.

Now, beneath that unsteadying regard, was not the time to offer information about the McCaffery fortune. "I mean, ah . . . money has never been that important to James."

She gritted her teeth at the Colonel's implacable features. At least he had referred to her brother in the present tense, unlike that awful little Corporal.

"Perhaps the wealth isn't as important as the search, or even the fame and notoriety that accompany a rich claim," the Colonel persuaded.

"No, I will not . . ." Jacelyn eased back in the worn slick chair. She lowered her eyes and fussed with her skirt. Niggling doubt assailed her. Had James needed to escape the McCaffery name? Had he set out to prove to Uncle Jonathan that he was his own man and could make his own way in the world?

Her brother very well could be trying to do just that. But James wouldn't leave the fort on an assignment, then just disappear.

She lifted her chin and gazed sternly at the Colonel. "Nothing would come between James and his work, Colonel. Not even silver or gold. He is not a deserter."

Though she said the words firmly, a hard knot formed in her stomach. James had deserted her. Left her in Richmond with an uncle she barely knew. Though James had promised to return soon or send for her, he had done neither. She wondered if she really knew her brother as well as she professed.

"I wish that were true, my dear. I surely do."

She tilted her head. "What do you mean?" She entwined her suddenly cold fingers and hid her hands in the folds of her skirt.

Colonel Alexander took out his handkerchief and wiped the sweat from his balding forehead. How he hated dealing with emotional females. Thank God they were few and far between at Fort Huachuca. "Ah, you see ... I loaned your brother a horse. A good horse, since he was traveling into rough country ..."

She narrowed her eyes and stole another look at the dark figure hovering near her side. Although he hadn't moved a muscle, his presence loomed ever larger. She forced her thoughts back to the Colonel's statement. "A horse," she said.

"Ahem, yes. Well, that Appaloosa's my very best horse. Very well trained, if you know what I mean. If, er, something ... say, had happened to your brother ... My horse would've returned. James McCaffery is out there ... somewhere. With my horse."

Like a cork exploding from a bottle of warm champagne, she shot out of her chair. "Pardon me, sir, if I don't believe that a horse is more important than a man's life."

"My dear, that was not at all what I implied."

"I'll pay every cent of what that beast is worth, sir. Just tell me how much." Thinking of her depleted store of cash, her voice trembled.

Evan Alexander flinched. "That's not necessary. Your brother—"

"Don't tell me about my brother, Colonel." She took a deep breath and whispered, "He's all I have left."

Jacelyn sagged back into the chair. Her eyes burned with the threat of tears, but she was determined not to cry. At least not here.

Grant uncrossed his arms and shifted away from the wall, though he continued to watch the woman through slitted eyes. Her uncanny insight, recognizing that he was a "savage," had decided him against her. But the fact that she was desperate to find her brother, and that he was the only family she had, resembled his own situation too closely for him to be completely unsympathetic.

Besides, there was something about the saucy redhead with the challenging navy eyes that ignited unsettling vibrations deep within him. He crossed his arms over his chest again and scowled, despising the way she was affecting him. But right now, he didn't have the time nor the inclination to analyze why.

Before he could move farther away from the woman, the office door opened again.

Jacelyn heard the creaking hinge and turned to see a lovely blonde girl float into the room. As she stepped toward the desk her soft fawn-brown eyes, accentuated by thick, batting lashes, greeted one man, then the other.

"Hello, all."

The soft feminine voice drifted around the office, irritating Jacelyn to no end, especially when the savage's disturbing, sharp blue eyes thawed instantly. Then she mentally chastised herself for even noticing such a trivial detail. This uncivilized country was completely undermining her genteel sensibilities.

Grant heaved a deep sigh of gratitude toward the latest arrival. Maybe, during the confusion, he could make his escape. Stealthily moving toward the door, he paused to tip his hat to the Colonel's daughter, now

14

standing in the middle of the room, looking curiously between himself and the other two occupants.

Colonel Alexander, realizing what Grant was up to, hollered, "Just a damned . . . er, excuse me, ladies. Hold up, Grant." In his haste to stop the younger man, the Colonel forgot to address Grant by his Army rank.

The blonde-haired girl stared at Grant with wistful eyes. "Please don't leave. I was hoping to see you. It's been so long—"

"I beg everyone's pardon," Jacelyn interrupted, "but I need help." Her chest had become so constricted that she had to pause and inhale. She blinked with relief, however, when the tall dark man everyone called Grant mockingly saluted and sidestepped toward the open door.

But the portal slammed shut before Grant reached it. He found himself facing a very angry Colonel.

Evan glared toward the red-haired woman. "I . . . ahem, what was your name again, my dear?" he asked impatiently.

Jacelyn bit the inside of her lower lip to keep from screaming her frustration. No wonder it took so long for the Army to get anything done. She sighed and muttered, "Jacelyn, Colonel. Jacelyn McCaffery."

"Yes, yes. So it is." He herded Grant away from the door and motioned toward the blonde. "Daughter, take Miss McCaffery over to the boarding house and see she gets comfortably settled." He gave Jacelyn a weak smile. "We'll talk again later."

Jacelyn snatched up her reticule. "We most certainly will, sir. Rest assured, this matter is far from finished." Still glowering, she followed the pretty blonde. The only thing that made her leaving more palatable was the fact that the Colonel's daughter was even more distressed by the abrupt dismissal than Jacelyn.

She stalked from the spartan office with as much dignity as she could muster and slammed the door satisfyingly behind her.

Colonel Alexander wiped a trickle of sweat from his neck. He waved Grant back toward the chair the younger man had vacated earlier. "Thank God Shiloh came along when she did. That McCaffery woman is going to be trouble. I just know it."

Grant arched his brow, then slouched in the chair. For once, he and the Colonel were in complete agreement.

Later that evening, just at dusk, Jacelyn stood outside in the cool evening breeze. She'd finished settling herself into an empty room inside a house reserved especially for army guests—at least until another officer, and perhaps his family, was transferred to the fort and commandeered the quarters.

The mid-summer heat had warmed the inside to a stifling degree and she'd found it unbearable. Just like her entire first day at Fort Huachuca.

She leaned against the porch rail and gazed dejectedly at the first star twinkling in the dark heavens. Where was James? Why was everyone assuming the worst of him? And worst of all, why had some of their doubts become hers?

"Excuse me, Miss McCaffery. . . . May I join you for a while?"

Jacelyn started. Self-consciously she smoothed the soft material of her satin damask blouse over her pounding heart as she spied the Colonel's daughter on the bottom step. "C-certainly, Miss Alexander. I'd be pleased. I understand I have you to thank for the use of this house."

Blushing prettily, the other girl smiled. "Well, the boarding houses are either next to the cavalry barracks

16

or half a mile away. Since you're alone and all, I just thought . . ."

"And I appreciate your consideration. Would you care to come inside?"

All at once a low throbbing sound vibrated over the peaceful setting. Jacelyn's eyes rounded as large as saucers as she peered in every direction trying to find the source of the eerie noise. A muffled giggle finally drew her attention back to the Colonel's daughter, who explained, "It's only drums. The Apache scouts are having a war dance tonight."

"W-w-war dance?" The rhythm of Jacelyn's pulse stepped up to match the beat of the drums. "Wh-why doesn't your father do something to stop them?" Jacelyn edged back toward the open door and the inviting glow of the lantern.

"They won't hurt us."

"How do you know that?" A shiver rioted up Jacelyn's spine.

"Grant told me. It's a ritual the Apaches perform whenever they get ready to go on a raid or think they will confront an enemy."

The girl's mellow voice drifted away. Jacelyn glanced to the bottom step. The Colonel's daughter was gone. Finding herself suddenly alone, Jacelyn swept the space illuminated by her lantern with a frightened gaze. There, just at the edge of the shadows, she saw the checked print of a gingham skirt.

The girl called back, "Would you like to come with me to see the horses?"

Just the thought of wandering the fort at night, with the Indians so near, dried Jacelyn's mouth so that she had to swallow twice to speak. "Uh, no, thank you. I don't believe so."

"See you tomorrow, then. I'd like to talk to you about James."

"James? Wait——" She remembered then that she hadn't taken the time to let the Colonel properly introduce them. She didn't even know the girl's first name.

And during the short space of time Jacelyn had hesitated, she'd already disappeared into the blackness.

The farther Jacelyn walked from the light and security of the house, the more quickly her confidence failed in the unknown surroundings. Her chest tightened. Why had she been so quick to say no? What knowledge did the girl have of her brother? But fear halted her steps, no matter how hard she tried to overcome the feeling.

Drat. Hadn't she vowed to take control of her life for a change? Yes. Hadn't she had enough of being pampered and forced into the role of a "lady" with no power to make any decisions of her own? Yes. Now that Uncle Jonathan was gone, she'd decided it was time to show those old codgers back in Richmond that a woman was capable of taking control of McCaffery Textiles. Especially *this* McCaffery woman.

A troubled sigh deflated her lungs. She rubbed her throbbing temples, which seemed to be pounding to the pagan beat of the drums. How was she going to prove herself if she continued to hover in the background of life?

She glanced longingly toward the fire near the corrals. The drumbeats vibrated louder and louder. Dark shapes undulated wildly around the flames. Shrill shrieks stood the hair on the back of her neck on end. Despite the numerous stories she'd read about Indian attacks and mutilated victims, the wild rhythm drew her magically, mystically, forward.

The air around her became charged. Though stars illuminated the blackness, she felt as if a bolt of lightning could strike down at any moment. Footsteps sounded directly behind her. Jacelyn couldn't have jumped any higher if thunder had suddenly rumbled. Spinning, she

18

watched a large, menacing form materialize from the shadows.

She opened her mouth to scream, but covered her lips just in time as she recognized the wicked moustache, daring sideburns, thick black hair, and the features she'd know anywhere. Hatless and shirtless, he appeared every bit the savage she'd first deemed him to be.

He'd stopped and was staring at her. His untamed countenance rooted her to the dusty earth even as a sensation of warmth trickled throughout her insides. She'd never been so near anyone as dangerous and exciting as this man.

"What are you doing here, lady?"

Her mouth opened, but she couldn't utter a sound. It took all of the strength and courage she could muster to shake her head.

"Go back where you belong. This is no place for a woman."

Undecided as to whether he was talking about the particular spot on which she was standing, or Fort Huachuca in general, she was tempted to argue both points. But he'd stepped around her and was walking away.

He'd said what he had to say and gone, as if she were no more important than a spider crawling across a chip of wood. So why was her mind filled with fleeting images of a lightly furred chest and glistening bronzed muscles? And why was she turning and fleeing to the safe haven of the house?

Once she reached the porch, however, she stopped and straightened her shoulders. She'd done it again— allowed a man to intimidate her. Why should she be surprised? Until this trip to Fort Huachuca, hadn't she always been the timid little mouse, following her parents', then James's, then Uncle Jonathan's every order?

Yet look what she had accomplished on her own the

past few weeks, with no help from anyone, let alone a man. She *could* find her brother, persuade James to return with her or get his signature, and then return to Richmond and take over the management of McCaffery Textiles. With James, or without him, no one would intimidate her—ever again.

The next morning, Grant Ward pulled his horse to a stop on a rounded ridge just south of Fort Huachuca. Well, it was actually *Camp* Huachuca, but he figured it wouldn't be long until the compound would officially be recognized as a fort.

His horse snorted, sides heaving from the labored climb. Grant's own chest expanded as he took a deep drought of clean, fresh air and watched the activity below. From his vantage point, the soldiers looked like trails of busy ants as they drilled.

The fort was located where lookouts fielded clear views in three directions of the San Pedro and Santa Cruz valleys. Dust plumes and smoke signals, that might be stirred up by Apache war parties, were visible for miles.

An unconscious grin curved his lips as he thought of the mysterious tales concocted by strangers traveling through this particular area of Apacheria. They described the Huachuca, or "Thunder" Mountains, as the Apache called them, as dark and brooding and filled with eerie frightening noises.

Rubbing the back of his neck, Grant lifted his gaze and scanned the yucca and scrub oak-dotted countryside. Eerie and frightening to some maybe, but he personally loved the foothills. There was just enough green to brighten the earthen browns and grays, and the plants and animal life of both the desert and the mountains coexisted peacefully.

The unfamiliar grin faded as he wondered why, then, couldn't *he* be as easily accepted? Why couldn't the human race learn from Mother Nature? Grant sighed. Damn it, he'd only stopped to enjoy the solitude. Why, all of a sudden, had he dredged up the strife between his two heritages?

Descending the slope into a thick growth of trees and brush, Grant let the horse drink from the stream, then tethered it in the shade for relief from the hot Arizona sun before drinking and resting himself.

Although he tried to think of other things, once he'd settled himself against the rough bark of a large cottonwood tree and tilted his hat over his eyes, Gabriel and Pajarita Ward's faces loomed large and clear beneath his closed lids.

Gabriel Ward. A wonderful, soft-spoken man intent on traveling into Arizona Territory to educate the "heathens." Instead, he'd found the Apache were intelligent people possessing a great love for their family.

He had met a beautiful Apache maiden, whose name in English was Little Bird. The two people, from vastly different cultures, fell in love and married. Less than a year later, Grant Ward entered the world and learned early on of the hatred between his two races.

Grant broke off a blade of grass and stuck it between his teeth. How ironic, he thought, that his father had been struck down by Apache renegades, and his mother murdered by drunk miners incited to revenge by corrupt politicians.

Rising swiftly, Grant swiped bits of grass and dirt from his trousers. A string of bitter oaths floated on the soft breeze as he cursed the feeling of abandonment, the knowledge that he'd never fit in either world, realities that couldn't be shaken away as easily as particles of earth.

A feeling of warmth chased away the chill suffusing

his body as he thought of Colonel Evan Alexander, the man who'd taken a young, confused kid in hand and taught him to survive. In fact, he'd been educated so completely that, unless people remembered him from his younger days, few knew of his Apache heritage.

Into this vision of the Colonel, suddenly intruded a red-maned spitfire. Just as she'd charged into Evan's office, she barged her way into his thoughts. And when he'd seen her last evening, all alone and frightened, she'd chipped away a little of the ice surrounding his heart. He'd known exactly how she felt.

Although he didn't particularly relish that disturbing feeling of tenderness, he couldn't help wondering who she really was. What had lured the pretty desperate-eyed woman to the middle of nowhere? Why did she need her brother so desperately?

He managed to rid himself of any soft emotions, though, when he recalled Colonel Alexander's final order. Hell, didn't Evan understand that he had more important things to do than to keep an eye peeled for the Appaloosa and James McCaffery?

By midmorning, Jacelyn was massaging her tender derriere as the stagecoach rocked and creaked over the rutted road winding away from Fort Huachuca. She sniffed and then sneezed. A small cloud of dust rose from the modest swell of her bosom.

Dust. How could there be so much of it when, after she'd gone to bed last night, thunder rumbled until her ears rang and lightning flashed in her eyes until she couldn't sleep. The sky had literally opened up and poured down rain.

To block out the disturbing commotion, she'd lit the bedside lantern and thumbed through copies of *Harper's Weekly Journal of Civilization* stacked on top of the night stand. When she could no longer hold her eyes open, she blew out the light and tried once again to sleep.

Rest had been intermittent at best. Once during the night she'd heard rocks crumbling from the fireplace in the adobe house. The bedroom roof leaked in three places, but luckily the drips missed her bed. It seemed she'd just dozed when a bugle woke her. She'd turned over, hoping to go back to sleep, but the sun shone through a crack above the window pane directly in her eyes.

She'd given up then and gotten dressed, barely finishing before the Colonel's aide knocked on her door.

Her daydreaming ended abruptly when a stage wheel suddenly dipped into a depression. Her head and pert straw hat nearly bounced against the roof. Setting aside the latest edition of *Harper's Weekly,* which the Colonel's daughter had so thoughtfully pressed into her hand before she'd stepped into the coach, she disgustedly wiped a film of perspiration from her forehead and neck with one of her last clean, embroidered handkerchiefs.

If Colonel Alexander hadn't been so sure someone in Tucson might know of James's whereabouts, she never would have spent the precious ten dollars it cost to climb aboard another filthy stagecoach.

She coughed and glared at the magazine. What a romantic picture it painted of trains and stagecoaches and faraway forts and the Western way of life. Ha!

All she'd experienced so far was soot and dust and heat and more dust. And pale blue eyes. Pale blue. The color of a baby's blanket. But there was nothing quite so innocent in those eyes. She shook her head and quickly picked up the *Harper's Weekly.* Now what had caused her to think of *him?*

After some effort, Jacelyn became absorbed in a gripping tale of a stagecoach and rough roads and an Indian attack. Her heartbeat accelerated and her nails dug into the periodical with each intriguing paragraph. She could almost hear the thunder of horses' hooves and the thunk of arrowheads gouging into the wooden conveyance.

She felt the fear of the story's passengers and experienced the sudden jouncing of the fictional coach. She actually imagined the clatter of wood on wood as arrows slithered off the side of the stage. She even smelled the burning powder from volleying gunshots.

A brave passenger lifted his canvas curtain to peek outside. Indians. Yes. She'd known he would see Indians. But behind the Indians were even more horsemen. *Oh, that poor traveler.*

As her eyes devoured the sentences, the passenger suddenly started waving. The last group of riders were close enough that he could make out their blue uniforms and the banner of the United States Cavalry. The soldiers had driven off the Indians. The passengers were saved.

Jacelyn wiped a happy tear from her cheek and let out a long sigh of relief. The cavalry. What a daring, brave group of soldiers.

She bounced on the hard seat. Something whined through the window draping near her ear. Her eyes widened at the sight of a small, round hole in the curtain. An eerie tingle shot along her spine. Cautiously, she lifted the canvas and peered out. Icy fear shot through her. She screamed and dropped the curtain, hugging her body against the seat as if it could protect her.

In contrast to the *Harper's* story, she didn't think the attackers were Indians. But they were hard-riding, vicious-looking, terrifying men. With guns. And bullets.

"Dear God," she beseeched, "where is the Cavalry?"

She gazed up at Garett. Imust "I beg your pardon"?

Chapter Two

The stage lurched, throwing Jacelyn from the smooth leather seat to the dusty floorboards. More gunshots echoed above the rumble and creaking of the coach. She heard a shout of pain followed by a heavy thump atop the roof. Cowering into a corner, she felt an icy chill replacing the perspiration coating her skin. Her insides knotted.

Swaying and rocking, the stage slowed and finally settled. The oppressive stillness was stifling. She gasped for breath. Her hands shook as she fought to shove her skirt and petticoats away from her face. She looked wildly about the empty interior. What was she supposed to do now?

Her logical mind irrationally focused on the hope that if she remained quiet, perhaps she wouldn't be found. She hunched her shoulders, staying as still as possible, hearing only the rapid thudding of her own heartbeat. Sweat trickled into her eyes and down the back of her neck, but she was too frightened to wipe it away.

Suddenly the *Harper's Weekly* slithered to the floor. She shuddered and her breath hissed softly between her teeth. Just her luck. The Cavalry in Arizona Territory evidently had better things to do than come to *her* rescue.

She waited. And waited. The silence nearly drove her insane. Should she get up and see what was happening? Should she stay down and hope for the best?

She cocked her head. Listen. There it was again. A whisper. The crunch of gravel. The sounds grew louder. Ominous dread intensified the ache in her chest. She couldn't have moved had she wanted to.

The door suddenly swung open. A rush of hot air filled the coach. Sunlight reflected off a pistol barrel. And behind the gun, was a thin, evil-looking face with dark, leering eyes.

"Ah-h-h, que lástima. Only one today. Come out, señorita. Let us see you, íntima." Cruel, narrow lips parted. He called in a high-pitched voice, "Hola, hombres. Venga. Come see."

Jacelyn reached out blindly for something . . . anything . . . Her groping fingers encountered her small, bulky reticule and her limp *Harper's Weekly*. She clutched them both to her breast. Her heels dug into the floor as she curled into a tight ball to evade the dark-skinned man.

Long, bony fingers reached for her. She slapped the filthy hand away.

"No." Jacelyn kicked out. He jerked his hand back.

The door behind her creaked open. She tried to scramble to the center of the narrow coach, but a pair of beefy arms snaked around her waist. Flailing and screaming, she resisted. But the unseen bandit dragged her outside.

Frantically she searched the deep arroyo in which the stage had stopped. The driver. Where was the nice man who had expressed genuine sympathy because she had to ride so far alone? "Help! Someone . . . help me!"

She kicked her feet and swung the magazine until it ripped into harmless scraps as she was lifted even higher in the air. Her head thrashed from side to side.

26

Wide eyed, taking in everything at once, she suddenly stopped fighting. Near the front wheel lay a body. Crumpled. Still. Her heart plummeted to the pit of her stomach.

Even in her panic, she knew it wasn't the blond-haired driver. Only the Wells and Fargo messenger had been wearing a dark blue shirt like that . . . Her gaze shot up to the gorgeous sky. Please, God, don't let him be dead.

Rude hands groped up her rib cage, robbing her of any opportunity of going to the man's aid. She pulled her eyes from the heavens and struggled anew. "Take your hands off me, you—"

She groaned when he did just that and dropped her to the ground. But when he grabbed for her reticule, she regained her balance and yanked it from his hand, squeezing her arms tightly around it. The huge man ogled her again. "It's mine," she hissed.

The bag held every last cent she had to her name. If she lost it, she lost all hope of finding her brother.

"What is thee trouble, Pablo? Thee leetle girl, she ees too strong for one hombre, no?"

The first dark man who'd held the gun had spoken, and Jacelyn turned to get a glimpse of the person who'd taken her from the stage. Still looming behind her, he was taller than the thin man, heavyset with greasy brown hair and tiny black eyes. Her fingers dug into her reticule until her knuckles ached as she backed against the side of the stage.

When the big man followed her retreat, wheezing with each labored step, her lips thinned into a tight line. She could either wilt into a quivering mass right now or follow through with her conviction never to allow another man to intimidate her. She gulped and nearly choked. Of course, when she'd made that vow, she had no idea anything *this* drastic would happen.

The darker-complected man stepped out from behind the larger outlaw. He leaned forward. "The señorita, she don't want nobody taking her bag, Pablo. Why you theenk she be so particular? Maybe she hide some-theeng. No?"

The large man suddenly smiled. Jacelyn recoiled from his foul odor and stared in horror at his bulbous lips pulled back to reveal four crooked, discolored teeth. The rest were rotted stubs or missing completely.

Thinking her attention diverted, the smaller man's clawlike fingers snatched for her reticule. She saw the blurred motion from the corner of her eye and twisted her body. "No-o-o."

"What's the ruckus 'bout? Grab anythin' worth takin' an' let's get outta here."

The little man spun around to face the newcomer. The large man straightened, allowing Jacelyn the room to slip her hand through the bag's drawstrings. They'd have to take off her arm to get her money now.

She also noticed that no one seemed to be paying her much mind, probably sure that she was too terrified to move. Quickly, she dropped to her knees in an attempt to roll under the stage. If she could just get to the other side and run into the thick brush . . .

"Oh, no, you don't." Pablo grabbed her blouse before she'd moved two feet. Rather than risk his ripping it from her back, she allowed him to swing her out and away from the coach.

"Thee señorita, she no part weeth thee . . . valubles, patrón."

Jacelyn flinched when the thin man's cruel eyes bored into her.

"We keel her now, no?"

Terrified, her eyes focused for the first time on the newcomer. Blond hair stuck out in all directions beneath a battered, dirt-encrusted hat. He was stocky and ruddy complected with a gaze so cold and threatening that a shiver raced down her spine. Every nerve ending quivered as she anticipated his next words.

He wanted her reticule and seemed prepared to kill to get it. She swayed, then took a deep breath and lifted her chin. That was the only way he would take it. Over her dead body.

Grant Ward dismounted and felt the cool surface of a horseshoe imprint. Fresh. Very fresh. And he'd found the same track—with the left front shoe having only two nails on the inside rim and three on the outside— around a murdered miner's shack. A miner who'd been scalped and left so that it "appeared" he'd been killed by Apaches.

Grant snorted. Very few Apaches took scalps. They were far too afraid of the ghosts of the dead. And if the Indians rode horses at all, the animals sure weren't shod.

Turning his attention back to the track, Grant decided that the horse he trailed had either lost the nail or it had been purposely left out, maybe due to an injury to the hoof. The reason didn't matter. It was easily identifiable and he very much wanted to have a long chat with the owner.

Mounting his long-legged thoroughbred, Grant followed the trail northward down a sandy arroyo. He rode for nearly two hours before the single set of prints was joined by more tracks, filing into the gully individually or in pairs.

He drew up his horse, dismounted, and squinted from the reflected glare as he walked and led his horse, searching the ground carefully. Six riders. Now, why were that many men meeting in the middle of nowhere and in a depression so deep that you'd have to nearly ride over them to see them?

He mounted his horse and tracked the riders for another hour before he lost the trail on a solid outcropping of rock. He was about to give up when he heard the first round of shots.

He spurred the horse up a slope angling off to his right. Gripping the saddle fenders with his thighs and calves, he leaned forward to give the animal better balance as it fought for footing in the crumbling rock. The main road to Tucson should lie just over the next ridge.

Topping the rise, he heard a woman's angry shouts and frowned. Precious time was wasted as he maneuvered around a dense thicket of mesquite. Finally he reined up where he would be out of sight, yet had a clear view of the arroyo ahead.

At first all he saw was the stage and the backs of several men. Men with guns in their fists. Men wearing their bandanas backwards, yet so confident of their quarry they hadn't bothered covering their faces. Men shoving around a . . .

His eyes widened, then narrowed to mere slits. "Aw, hell." What was *she* doing *here?*

He watched as the saucy woman he'd seen in the Colonel's office yesterday snatched at a small object and spun, protecting it with her body. He silently cursed, then rolled his eyes when he realized it was probably her purse. Damn it, what could she be carrying inside the infernal bit of baggage worth the risk of her life?

He raised his arm and wiped the sweat pooled above his brows on his sleeve. No matter the importance of his own mission, he had to do what he could for the fool woman.

A movement near the front of the stage caught his eye. The late afternoon sun was blinding, but he recognized the outfit of a Wells and Fargo employee on the ground. It appeared the fellow had been unconscious and was just coming around.

Grant held his breath and mentally shouted, *No, you idiot. Stay still. Don't pull that gun.*

The silent warning went for naught.

Ready or not, any decision concerning the most appropriate time to enter the fracas had been taken from his hands. He pulled his own Colt .44 and aimed carefully, keeping a tight rein on his stallion. Before the bullet struck the messenger's gun and sent it spinning from the man's hand, Grant had spurred his horse toward the startled group of men.

His mind raced furiously. He had some fast talking to do. *If* he got the chance.

The outlaw leader recovered quickly from the shock of the gunfire. Pulling his pistol, he spun his horse and ran the animal toward the approaching stranger.

Grant pulled up near the messenger. He noted, thankfully, that the outlaw had noticed the downed man's injured hand and the gun lying several feet away. Grant's stomach muscles knotted. Resting the barrel of his revolver on the saddle horn, he waited to see what the bandit would do. Would he respect the fact that Grant had saved his life? Or would he shoot first and be damned with asking questions?

When the light-haired gent pulled his horse up a few yards away, Grant nodded. "Howdy."

The leader returned the nod. Grant inwardly winced. The fellow wasn't going to make this easy. " 'Peared you could use a little help."

"Didn't need no help a'tall."

Grant cleared his throat and slowly brought up the smoking barrel of his pistol. The blond man's gun pointed directly at Grant's chest. Grant's trigger finger tensed but he merely blew the spiraling smoke from the tip and slipped the gun back into his holster. The leader relaxed.

Grant mentally sighed and inclined his head toward the messenger, who was now secured by two more outlaws. "Didn't see it quite the same as you."

The leader grunted. "Mebbe."

"You need an extra hand?" Grant shifted in the saddle, trying to appear unconcerned whether he was hired on or not. The only plan he'd come up with in such a short space of time was to try to join the gang and wait for an opportunity to steal the woman away. Then he would take her back to the fort and get on with his business.

"Who are ya? Why ya wanna work fer me?"

Grant pointedly ignored the first question, doubting the outlaw really expected an answer. "Because . . . we're both in the same line of work. I'm good. And you need me."

When the leader signaled he should ride ahead toward the coach, Grant slowly released his breath. As he nudged his horse forward, Grant felt the man's eyes boring into his back. Just because he'd made it this far, didn't mean he would automatically be trusted.

A woman's scream rent the air. Grant looked back, read the disinterest on the leader's face, and quickly rode ahead. Dismounting, he stalked up behind a thin Mexican taunting his partner.

"Thee leetle she-cat have sharp claws, no, Pablo? You no careful, you no have cojones."

Pablo growled and pulled a long, thin-bladed knife. "Give me the bag, puta. Now."

"Por favor, amigo. Leave the señorita alive. We soon see what ees beneath all that fine material, no?"

"No," Grant answered. He shouldered past the little weasel and caught Pablo's arm as the Mexican teased the tip of the blade back and forth beneath the woman's quivering chin. Spinning the heavy man around, Grant slugged him in the gut.

Pablo doubled over. Grant's fist connected with the point of the big man's jaw. Grant caught the unconscious outlaw and shoved his body aside. He glanced quickly over his shoulder to make certain none of the others had decided to contest him. Then he faced the woman.

Uh oh. Her eyes were round as china plates, and her mouth had dropped open. Damn it, he'd hoped to have a chance to talk to her before she let on to the gang that they'd met. He threw her off guard by snatching the reticule from her nerveless fingers. He had to jerk twice to get the strings over her wrist.

Dazed, Jacelyn muttered, "You. You're—"

Hell. He swung his fist back, then in a forward arc. He didn't want to hurt her, just give her a light clip on the chin. He needed time. Wincing when his knuckles struck fragile bone, he held his arms out to catch her limp form and gently lowered her to the ground.

He turned and found that the leader had followed him. Grant slapped the damned purse into his hand. "This what you wanted?" Warily glancing around, Grant casually balanced his weight on the balls of his feet. Besides the head man, Grant found himself facing the weasel and the two outlaws who'd bound the messenger. The heavyset one was still on the ground.

The leader took the bag, never once taking his eyes off the new man. "Reckon it is. By the way, ya never did say what handle ya go by."

Grant shifted his eyes toward the woman, who luckily remained unconscious. The groaning Pablo now groggily held his head in his hands. "Folks call me . . . 'Jones.' " He stared the leader directly in the eye.

The balding outlaw laughed, a grating sound that did little to lessen the tension in Grant's gut. "Figured as much. I'm Dick Waddell. You can call me 'boss.' " The curve of his lips was belied by the sternness in his tone.

The leader turned to the thin Mexican. "Eloy, get Pablo on his feet." Then he noted the other two outlaws spread out on his right. "Kid, you an' Bob get busy unhitchin' them hosses. We're losin' daylight."

Bob, a tall, muscular black man, whined, "But, boss, why ya haffa brung in another man now?"

"Ya answered your own question, boy. 'Cause I'm the boss." Dick scratched his chin as he continued to study the man called "Jones." Then, more to himself than to explain his reasoning, he muttered, " 'Cause we're short-handed an' I say he comes."

During the exchange, Grant eyed Bob and the Kid. Bob looked to be tough, with plenty of hard muscles to stretch the worn material of his Cavalry pants and dirty white shirt.

But it was the Kid who captured Grant's attention. He was a thin, pale-skinned albino youngster, sporting a jagged scar that divided the width of his right cheek. He wore a sheepskin vest, though it was hot as blazes, brown twill pants and a double-holstered gun belt tied down to both thighs.

The boy's eyes were so pale as to be colorless and showed absolutely no emotion as they squinted back at Grant. Instinctively Grant knew this was the most dangerous one of the bunch.

The Kid was the first to break the staring contest. He turned to go help his partner and Grant experienced a vague sense of relief to be out from under the spell of those unsettling eyes.

"Eh, patrón, what we do weeth thee señorita?"

Grant quickly shifted his gaze. The woman was sitting up, rubbing her chin. Her eyes appeared glazed and unfocused until she saw Pablo and Eloy and ... himself. His lips thinned at her sudden expression of fear.

Pablo, supported by Eloy, rubbed his sore belly and glared at Grant. "I say we kill her. Eef she gets to any law . . ."

Several long strides carried Grant to the woman's side. His palm hovered over the butt of his pistol. "I handled her when no one else could." His gaze riveted menacingly on Pablo before shooting to Dick Waddell. "I say she's mine."

In an appeal to their greed, he also added, "Look at the clothes she's wearing, and that gold watch around her neck. I'd bet if we took her along, someone would pay to get her back."

Jacelyn instantly reached up to clutch her time piece, silently damning the man for bringing it to the ruffian's attention. She started to shake her head in denial of her worth to anyone, but decided to hold her council. It appeared that . . . what was it the Colonel and his daughter had called the man? Some rugged name—that well suited its owner. Ah, Grant. That was it. At least it seemed . . . Grant . . . was all for keeping her alive. And she definitely supported his decision on *that* matter.

"You gonna let him get away weeth that?" Pablo demanded, although it was easy to see that Waddell's interest had been aroused.

The Kid had sauntered back to observe the confrontation. "I'll take care of the woman, *and* Jones." His fingers reflexively clenched and unclenched as his arms dropped to his sides.

Jacelyn's brows snapped together. Jones? Grant's last name was "Jones"? It didn't seem to *fit*. She cocked her head around to stare at the man, but the sudden movement made her woozy. She winced and rubbed the tip of her chin.

Waddell snorted. "I call the shots 'round here, but if'n any a ya wanna take 'im on, go ahead. I'm haulin' the silver ta the ranch. Think 'bout it. What Jones says makes sense. We can always get rid of the woman if'n we find out she ain't worth nothin'. Let's go, Bob."

For a brief second, Grant looked along with everyone else to where the black man held the stage team. The horses were now loaded with two large sacks apiece, which Grant assumed held the silver.

Then he once again faced down the irate Pablo, sneaky Eloy, and the more dangerous Kid.

Pablo was the first to back down after the outlaw leader turned and headed for his horse. "Well ... Let eet stand. For now. But the puta an' I ... We're not finished yet." His heavy jowls quivered as he smacked his lips and gestured obscenely toward the woman.

An angry retort swelled from deep in Jacelyn's throat. Grant put his left hand on her shoulder, holding her firmly in place. From the side of his mouth, he ordered, "Stay put. And don't say a word."

She debated protesting, but then glanced toward the strange, white-haired man silently regarding both Grant *Jones* and herself. She shuddered. Perhaps this *one* time she'd obey Grant's instructions.

Grant was also watching the Kid. "If you're goin' to draw, cowboy, you'd best do it. Someone's bound to come along soon. If it's just the same to you, I'd like to be a long way away when they do."

The albino's hands slowly eased to rest his palms on his gun butts, but when he flicked his thumbs, it was to secure the leather thongs he kept over the hammers. He grinned, then backed away.

Grant was surprised. He'd figured to have to fight the boy. But just as Pablo had threatened the woman, Grant knew that he and the Kid would meet another time.

Jacelyn waited until everyone was out of earshot before scrambling to her feet. Swaying, and hating her weakness, she clawed at Grant's vest to steady herself.

36

"You barbaric imbecile," she hissed. "Why did you hit me?"

Grant's arms automatically wrapped around the woman. She felt very fragile and very feminine . . . He shook his head to clear away the unwelcome thoughts, then growled, "Because you were about to announce that you and I have met." He looked to see if anyone was watching, then lowered his head. "If you don't keep your voice down, I'll be pleased to do it again."

She backed from his embrace, but found herself trapped by the open door and the stage's huge wheel. She tried to act nonchalant, shaking sand and dirt from her skirt as Grant's big, muscular form closed the space in front of her. Swallowing, she flipped a damp lock of hair out of her eyes.

Her chin rose defiantly, but she kept her voice low. "Yes, I expect you would. You're no better than a heartless savage. Even worse." She felt the sting of tears and blinked rapidly. She would *not* show him how frightened she really was.

"More than you know, lady." Grant's features hardened. His spine stiffened until he felt it might snap if he moved suddenly. "Best you remember that . . . If you value your life."

Before she realized what he was up to, he grabbed her hand and pulled her toward his horse. "Stop. Let go. I won't go with you."

All at once, he did stop. His blue eyes scorched her. She sucked in her breath and quit struggling as she thought about it and realized how much she wanted—needed—to live. For James's sake, she would cooperate. At least until she found a chance to escape. She did not protest when he led her forward again.

Dick Waddell, the Kid, and Pablo were arguing near where Bob and the Kid had tied the messenger. When Grant and Jacelyn approached, the leader called out,

"Hey, Jones. Reckon what ya'd do with this here fella, were ya ta have the say?"

Grant's eyes shifted imperceptibly to those of the frightened messenger. He also felt the daggerlike spears of the woman's eyes gouging his back as she anticipated his answer. For a brief second, he studied the leader's malicious countenance. The man was up to something. But what?

"Well," Grant drawled thoughtfully, "he's injured. You're taking the team. He's not able to give a warnin' unless someone happens along." He twisted the tip of his moustache. "Then again . . . he can identify us . . ."

Jacelyn gasped. She looked at the poor messenger and would have run to his side if she could've freed her hand. The strange sensation of heat rippling through her fingers from the rogue's too-warm grasp reminded her of the devil himself. And she thought of poor Colonel Alexander. The officer had appeared to like this . . . beast . . . of a man. How betrayed the Colonel would feel when he discovered the truth about Grant Jones.

The outlaw leader scratched his stubbled chin as if in deep thought, then waved his hand toward the horses. "Mount up, men. Let's get the hell outta here."

Grant's gaze passed over the wounded man and caught the messenger's look of despair. With a slight shrug of his shoulders, Grant led the woman to his stallion.

Jacelyn balked when she saw he intended for her to ride with him. "Please . . . Can't you just leave me? I can look after that man until help arrives."

Grant looked her up and down. "You ever tended a wounded man before?"

"No, but—"

"Ever even *seen* a man with a bullet in him?"

"Well, no, but—"

"Then what could you *do,* for God's sake?" He cut

38

his eyes toward the outlaws, now arguing over who would get to lead the horses loaded with silver. At least they were too busy to pay the woman any mind.

Jacelyn grabbed his arm. She felt the steel strength beneath her fingers and quickly dropped her hand. "Please . . ." Hearing the whine in her voice, she inhaled deeply. This was no way to assert her new resolve.

"You've taken what money I had. There's nothing else of value." She attempted not to obviously shield her watch, the only possession she'd been allowed to keep. Painful as it was, it was her only reminder of her mother.

Though she fought valiantly against it, a sob welled in her throat. The situation was suddenly overwhelming. Waylaid by bandits. Kidnapped by this . . . this savage.

What if she never saw her brother again? She'd so hoped to persuade him to return to Richmond so they could both have a say in the operation of McCaffery Textiles. What if . . . she never had the opportunity to tell him she was finally beginning to understand his need to find his own way . . . to let him know she was sorry for the hateful things she'd said, accusing him of deserting her the night he left?

"Please, let me stay." A tear trickled down her cheek and she swiped it away before any of the barbarians could see.

But Grant saw the single droplet. He softly answered her question. "You don't want to stay. If you do, you won't have to worry about your damned purse, or watch, or anything else ever again."

Her eyes widened as she realized the import of his words. If she stayed, she'd be dead.

Grant slid his eyes from the woman to the messenger. An uneasy feeling settled in the pit of his stomach. He glanced furtively toward the outlaws, wondering what they had decided to do about the man.

Sensing someone behind him, Grant turned to see the Kid grinning at the woman. "Want I should take her with me? Teach her a few manners?"

Grant shrugged. "Ask her yourself." This was as good a time as any to see if she'd understood his warning.

Jacelyn gulped and quickly shook her head at the albino. "Uhmmm, no-o. I'll ride with ... h-him." She edged closer to Grant.

The Kid's mouth twitched, as if he'd anticipated her refusal. Swinging into the saddle, he looked back and winked. "Perhaps another time."

Staring at the pale-skinned man's back, she suppressed a shiver before glancing at Grant. A glint of what might have been amusement flickered through the depths of his light-blue eyes before he, too, mounted and held out his hand.

Her chest ached as she sighed. What other choice did she have? Trying her best to hide the tremor in her hand, she raised her arm. In less time than it took to gasp in a breath, she was swung roughly before him.

His denim shirt and pants pressed into flesh exposed through rents in her blouse and skirt. She tried to shift forward but the backs of her thighs felt as if they were molded to the fronts of his. She'd thought the intimate contact would feel repulsive. It didn't.

In fact, when he grasped the reins and turned the horse, his muscles contracted, setting off a rippling sensation of heat throughout her body.

A shot vibrated the air around them. Jacelyn jumped. She felt Grant flinch, then shudder. She strained to look back, but he blocked her view.

Behind them, the Kid chuckled. Grant turned her chin

forward. His voice came out more raspy than usual. "Don't. You don't need to see."

"But ... what ... did ..."

Grant's eyes warned her that she could be perilously close to experiencing the same fate as the messenger. She swallowed, finding herself momentarily at a loss for words, or even thought.

Locking eyes with Dick Waddell, Grant clenched his teeth at the sight of the flat-featured outlaw's smug smile. Masking any expression of his own, Grant kneed the stallion and rode up to the rest of the gang to wait until the Kid rejoined them.

Everyone besides himself and the leader held lead ropes to two packed horses. The black man also held the reins to an extra saddle horse. Grant looked closely at the easily recognizable horse and frowned. What was the gang doing with the Colonel's Appaloosa?

As Grant stared at the animal and the empty saddle, Bob sullenly said, "If ya want, take the horse. The Kid don't want it, and Barnes don't need it no more." His brown eyes glanced meaningfully up the arroyo, the direction from which the gang had chased the stagecoach.

Grant shook his head. The intimation was clear. No wonder Dick Waddell had let him join the gang. Robbing stages was a costly business—for everyone.

"Whadda ya think, Jones? The Kid do the right thing?"

Grant knew Waddell was taunting him. However, he just shrugged. "You're the boss."

"Say, boys, we got a right smart fella ridin' with us. Yessirree."

Riding up to the impatient group, the Kid patted his gun butt. "First rule of staying alive, don't leave witnesses."

Jacelyn felt she might be sick. She hated to admit it, but Grant Jones had been right. They would have killed

41

her. She burrowed into the warmth Grant's large body provided, then realized what she was doing. Before she could shift away, his arms tightened, forcing her to remain where she was.

Chapter Three

Streaks of orange and purple blended into a red horizon as Waddell led the gang over rolling, rocky hills and through deep, narrow ravines. Grant and Jacelyn ended up positioned near the center of the group, whether by design or accident, Grant couldn't tell. Grunts and curses echoed ahead and behind as the men battled stage horses unaccustomed to the awkward, heavy packs.

Jacelyn tried to keep her body from touching Grant's, but with each sway of the horse and saddle, she was thrown forward or backward, constantly colliding with him until she finally gave up the exhausting effort. Her muscles ached and throbbed, making her thoroughly miserable.

Once she finally leaned back, she noted that he, too, was tense. He shifted restlessly and, once, when she glanced back, she thought she'd caught him looking into the hills, though it was just a very slight movement of his eyes. When he saw that she was staring, he quickly relaxed, shifted their combined weight to aid the struggling horse and focused his gaze on the trail ahead.

As the minutes turned into hours, she found herself dozing within the circle of his arms. She hated to admit it, but the man's large body and reliable strength were oddly comforting. He'd been almost kind and gentle.

Heat flushed up her neck and into her cheeks. She was beginning to like the security and warmth he projected. Though why she felt such in the ruffian's arms, she couldn't explain. He was, after all, an outlaw himself. A wicked savage.

An uneasy chill ricocheted through her as she recalled their first meeting. What had he been doing in Colonel Alexander's office? Why did he want to hide from the outlaws the fact that he and she had met? Did he have some kind of evil plan in mind involving the innocent inhabitants of the fort?

She stiffened her spine, trying again, albeit futilely, to increase the distance between their bodies, to rid herself of the notion that she could lean on him. He was just another man to fear, to despise, to—

The saddle suddenly dropped out from under her, rose up to support her, then disappeared again. Ground crumbled beneath the horse's hooves as it fought for a solid surface. She grasped Grant Jones's arm, as the horse continued to stumble.

His hot breath puffed in her ear. "Damn. Get ready to jump, lady."

She looked about in stunned confusion. Jump? How?

His arm wrapped about her waist. She heard a snapping sound. A string of curses hissed past her ear. She felt herself being lifted. Suddenly, she was falling and then rolling, over and over inside the curve of his large form.

At last they stopped. Jacelyn gasped for breath.

Grant grimaced. He lay spread-eagled with the woman atop him. Her added weight pressed his back into sharp rocks and prickly weeds. But it was the imprint of her firm breasts that caused him the most pain. Hell, she'd done nothing but wriggle her butt into him for ten torturous miles, and now this. How much more did she expect a man to take?

Jacelyn was afraid to move. Afraid to find out what she'd bruised or broken. But all at once her source of support grunted and rocked beneath her. Awareness of her firm, yet supple cushion, quickened her pulse.

Grant untangled himself and shoved her aside with more force than he'd intended. Climbing unsteadily to his feet, he gazed down at her sprawled form. His breath caught. She was all delicately shaped arms and legs amidst yards of wrinkled and torn material.

And then her wild, frightened eyes lifted to his. The aches and pains he'd suffered while sheltering her during the fall—and those he'd experienced on the ground—miraculously faded as he stared into the deep navy depths.

His horse whinnied, a racking, pitiful sound. He sighed and scrubbed at the back of his neck. Then bending quickly, he placed his hands beneath her arms and hauled her to her feet. "You all right?"

Jacelyn blinked and gazed down ruefully at her filthy, tattered dress. She wriggled her toes and moved her arms. "I-I believe so."

"Hummph."

The thud of approaching hoofbeats and questioning voices encouraged her to hurry and tell him, "Th—thank you. I—I—" But her mouth slowly closed. She curled her hands into fists and rested them on her hips. He'd turned and was walking away.

Walking away. She staggered forward. "Wait." She needed to talk to him. Though, in a way he was partially responsible for her being in this untenable situation, the man had saved her life. Twice. She needed to apologize for the terrible things she'd been thinking. He wasn't the desperado—a word she'd loved and adopted from

Harper's Weekly and hadn't yet had a chance to use—she'd taken him to be.

She held out her hand, but his back was turned. He knelt and ran his hand down the horse's lathered neck. Her heart stopped. The poor animal. It was lying amidst a labyrinth of mounded earth and holes, belly heaving, big brown eyes rolling. Its head lifted as it whickered softly to its master.

Tears blurred Jacelyn's vision. She rushed forward to see if there was something she could do. But before she took two steps, she watched, horrified, as Grant stood and pulled his gun. He aimed the long barrel at the beautiful horse's head.

She gazed imploringly toward the men who'd ridden up and sat watching. Just watching. Surely someone would—"No-o-o!" Her scream echoed the pistol's report. She reached Grant just as he slid the gun into its holster. Pounding his chest, she shouted, "You cruel, vicious monster. Why'd you have to shoot it?"

Grant grabbed her upper arms and shook until she quit raving. "I had no choice. Its leg was broken."

She jerked free and swiped at her eyes. Oh, Lord. She remembered hearing a snap just before she and Grant fell.

Sniffling, she asked more calmly, "You *had* to shoot it?"

"What would you have had me do? Let it suffer?" He took a deep breath, then bent to retrieve his saddle and bags.

Jacelyn stood transfixed, staring at his chiseled features. At the corded muscles flexing beneath his shirt. There was a tension to his movements that she hadn't noticed before. Still, she couldn't understand, if he had to lash out, why he'd chosen *her* to bear the burden of his frustration.

How dare he accuse her of being so cold-hearted as

to enjoy seeing a helpless animal's pain. He just didn't know her. Suddenly, she lifted her chin. No, thank heavens, he didn't. And she quickly shook off the niggling feeling of regret that wormed its way into her head.

She jumped when Bob rode up and threw down the spotted horse's reins.

"Boss s'pected you'd need dis here hoss now."

Grant nodded, grabbed the leather straps and looked at the woman. All he saw was condemnation in her eyes. Damn it. Did she think he'd killed his horse for the fun of it?

The backs of his own eyes burned. He berated himself for the stupid emotions he felt over the loss of the thoroughbred. He should have learned by now that anything, or anyone, he cared about was eventually taken from him.

Dust rose and settled on Grant's boots as the Kid reined near. "You're going to have to stash that saddle," the Kid smirked. "Ain't no room to pack it."

Grant didn't trust his voice. He glanced around until he spotted a slab of rock jutting over a hollow depression. Untying his saddlebags, he slung them over his shoulder then hefted the saddle and carried it to the makeshift shelter where he covered the tooled leather with his blanket.

After returning to the Appaloosa, he tied his bags behind the cantle, mounted and reached his hand out to the woman.

Jacelyn wasn't paying attention. She was still grieving for the horse and wondering if something different couldn't have been done. When she finally did look up, she was met with the offer of Grant's hand—and the Kid's.

As she looked at Grant, all she could see was him shooting his poor faithful horse. The way the animal's body convulsed when the bullet exploded in its brain. She shuddered.

Grant saw the revulsion in her eyes and her violent shiver. If the horrible events of the day could be blamed on any one person, it was damned sure ... Hell, he couldn't even remember the woman's name. He felt a weird sense of relief that she evidently hadn't made much of an impression on him after all, if he couldn't recall a beautiful woman's ... Damn it.

He forced himself to breathe deeply. Jerking his hand away from her, he pretended he'd only wanted to massage the back of his neck. Abruptly, he reined the Colonel's horse around. Instead of inflicting his reprehensible presence on the woman, he'd concentrate on finding out how these hombres came to be in possession of the Appaloosa. The last the Colonel knew, the troublemaking lady's brother had been riding the animal.

Hmmm. Perhaps he'd have a chance to help Evan out after all.

Jacelyn, suddenly faced with only one choice, decided she'd rather not continue on with these ruffians. Hands on her hips, she glared up at the Kid.

The Kid placed his palm on his gun butt. Jacelyn shifted back a step and swallowed. Finally, reluctantly, she extended her hand.

Once she was settled in front of the Kid, she stared longingly after Grant's broad back. When he paused and actually looked back, her heart skipped a beat. She waited, hopeful, wondering why he'd ridden on without her.

But he turned and spurred the unusual-colored horse ahead.

The Kid's right hand rode high on her waist. With his thumb, he stroked the underside of her breast. She slapped his hand. He laughed, but quit annoying her.

Jacelyn rode in stiff silence, trying to avoid comparing the Kid's thin, bony form to the warmth and security she'd felt with Grant. Suddenly, the albino's cold hand covered her breast. He tweaked her nipple. She screamed.

The Kid snickered.

Grant immediately materialized alongside them, and Jacelyn sighed with relief.

"Sorry, Jones." The Kid flashed an evil grin. "You missed your chance."

Grant shrugged. Only his eyes, glinting harder than flint, belied the casual gesture. "Chance? For what?"

The Kid blatantly fondled the woman's breast.

She hissed and raked her nails over the back of his hand.

Grant just arched a dark brow. "What makes you think I missed out?"

Jacelyn gasped.

The Kid frowned. "She didn't make any fuss riding with—"

"That should tell you something, shouldn't it?" Grant's lips twitched beneath the curve of his moustache when the woman leaned forward, lost her balance and nearly tumbled from the Kid's grasp. All the while she stammered, "Why, you . . . you . . . I'll have you know—"

Grant cut in, his gaze never straying from the nervous Kid. "The woman's mine. Best you remember that when your hands get itchy."

The Kid's eyes betrayed as much emotion as a rattler's. "Don't think that I'm afraid of you, Jones. Don't ever think that." But then, with a sudden turnabout, he winked. "Just getting a feel of what I got to look forward to. After you're done with her, of course."

"Of course." Grant inclined his chin, disguising his worry. The Kid was unbalanced. And that made him even more dangerous.

Jacelyn fumed in silence, tempted to slap both their faces. How dare they talk as though she didn't have a say in the matter. And Mr. Grant Jones ... He seemed to be agreeing with this ... this ... centipede. How could a man who'd gone to the trouble to save her life treat her as if she were just a piece of baggage to be passed around and shared ...

She stiffened with outrage. But all of a sudden, the direness of her predicament became startlingly clear. Up to that moment, she'd cavalierly decided to endure the monsters until the opportunity arose to get away. Now she warily gazed into the imposing shadows, at the stark emptiness of the desert and wiped the perspiration from her neck.

The countryside and climate were totally unfamiliar and, with the sun disappearing, night was fast approaching. She was at the mercy, if there was any such thing out here, of these ... bandits. And most especially Grant Jones—who seemed to think he was in charge of her.

She was plagued by mixed emotions about the man. Gratitude for his saving her more than once seemed to outweigh the fact that he had ingratiated himself with the Waddell gang. She sensed there was something going on that she didn't understand, but was it for the good? Or the bad?

Looking suddenly toward where Grant had been, she realized that he'd ridden on—again, leaving her alone and in the dark, in the despicable hands of the Kid. Her skin literally crawled at the thought of being held by the cold-blooded killer. She looked around until she caught a glimpse of his hard jaw and demanded, "Stop. Stop this instant. I will not ride another foot with you."

The Kid sneered. "Oh? That's mighty big talk coming from a puny woman."

When she tried to fight her way off the saddle, he just

tightened his arm. He chuckled, and she shivered at the sound.

But then he stopped his horse. She found herself suddenly free. Elated by the fact that he'd actually obeyed her command, she clambered over the saddle horn. A large tear in her skirt and petticoat caught on the horn. The sound of rending material cut through the silence as she fell and hit the ground hard.

When she finally stood on weak, trembling legs, it dawned on her that everyone else had stopped, too. She scowled as she realized the only reason the Kid had released her was because they had stopped for the night. So much for her newfound authority.

A strange gurgling noise caught her attention. The flare from a fire Bob had just ignited illuminated a small stream. Just across the water, weathered and cracked plank siding blended into the obscure countryside, almost hiding a dilapidated shack.

"Well, here we are." Grant's deep voice so close behind her caused her to jump.

Still a little dazed, she replied, "So we are. But where's 'here'?"

Grant surveyed what he could see of the area. Since leaving the site of the holdup, they'd been traveling east and north. He guessed they were now a few miles north of Tombstone. Given the thick growths of yucca, greasewood, and mesquite, a person would have to know exactly where he was headed to find this small cleared space.

The Kid came up behind Grant and Jacelyn. "Why are you standing around?" He leered openly at Jacelyn. "There's lots to do before supper."

Jacelyn's eyes widened. Do? She looked around in confusion. Just what did one have to *do* to get to eat? For that matter, where would they cook? *How* would

51

they cook? That cabin didn't look like it had been inhabited by anything but rats for years. She shuddered.

And then the thought of food set her empty stomach to growling. Mortified, she crossed her arms over her stomach and ground her jaws together.

Grant stood so close to the woman that he felt her body tremble. His gaze swung reluctantly from the albino to take in her ragged exhaustion. He took hold of her elbow and squeezed until he was certain he had her undivided attention. Pointing toward a flat rock near the fire, he commanded, "Sit down and stay out of the way."

Jacelyn contemplated arguing for all of two seconds. She was just too tired to fight. The toes of her soft leather shoes dragged in the dust as she trudged over to collapse beside the welcoming warmth of the flames.

"Hey, she—"

"Isn't going to do anything tonight," Grant insisted. His eyes bored into the Kid, daring him to say otherwise. As long as the woman was in his custody, he would do his best to see that she was well taken care of.

"We'll just see what Waddell—"

"Has to say about rabbit for supper."

The Kid puffed out his chest and cautiously regarded Grant as his fingers clenched just above his gun. Finally, he relaxed. A grin curved one side of his mouth. "In case you haven't noticed, it's a little late to hunt."

Grant just cocked his brow and set off into the darkness of the desert. Hunger—and pride—demanded that he make good his boast. Besides, a good hot meat would put a little color back in the woman's cheeks.

Over half an hour later, Jacelyn was feeling decidedly uncomfortable as the object of five sets of hostile eyes. The Kid had relished his role in relating the fact that Jones had said she didn't have to do anything to help prepare the food, and that hadn't set well with the others, especially the leader.

She shifted her sore bottom on the cold stone, and glanced uneasily toward the shadows. Where was Grant? Why hadn't he returned? She wound her fingers together, though the nervous reaction was hidden beneath a fold in her skirt.

What if he wasn't coming back? What if he'd decided not to stay with the gang of outlaws? What would happen to her . . . ?

A twig snapped directly behind the Kid. He jumped, grabbed for his gun and spun around to find his only targets were the bodies of three freshly skinned rabbits lying at the edge of the circle of light.

"I killed 'em. Someone else can cook 'em."

Everyone turned to find the owner of the voice towering on the opposite side of the fire from where he'd placed the rabbits. Jacelyn's eyes nearly bugged from their sockets. How had he done that? She hadn't heard a sound. And neither had anyone else, it seemed. She almost smiled at the looks of disbelief contorting the outlaws' faces.

Dick Waddell narrowed his gaze on the new man. "Better watch yore step, Jones."

"That's the idea." Besides hunting, Grant had scouted the area around the campsite. He'd found several routes that he could use to get the woman away and be quickly out of the line of fire from the camp.

But . . . as long as he was already involved with the outlaws . . . and since they seemed to be keeping their distance from the woman, he'd decided to stay with them at least until they reached their hideout. The Colonel would appreciate knowing how and where to rid the area of another gang of fugitives.

And if he were really lucky, Grant hoped he'd also come up with information about the Appaloosa and maybe even discover the whereabouts of James McCaffery. But he didn't like the feeling eating at his gut—that trouble was brewing. Big trouble.

While the rest of the outlaws stonily regarded the slippery "Jones," Pablo grunted, clambered to his feet and walked to the nearest mesquite where he drew his knife and cut three branches. In short order he had the rabbits spitted and roasting over the flames.

The black man dug in a pack until he found a towel-wrapped bundle. Unfolding one corner, he tossed something to each of the men—something that looked suspiciously like biscuits. Jacelyn tried to catch the one he threw to her, but it landed, like a chunk of lead, in her lap.

She picked up the small, hard object and sniffed it. It smelled like flour. Old flour. The others were gnawing off small bits of theirs and, though it was hardly appetizing, her hunger overrode her sense. She bit into the biscuit. Her teeth slid off the hard crust. She bit down harder and flinched when a chunk broke off. At first she wasn't sure whether it was the biscuit that broke or her tooth, but the taste of dry flour soon melted into her mouth.

All at once a prickling sensation lifted the hair along the nape of her neck. She glanced up to find a pair of sky blue eyes staring at her. Disconcerted by the intensity of Grant's gaze, she tried to swallow the mound of hard flour and choked.

A canteen was pushed into her hands. She drank greedily, spilling a few drops of the tepid liquid down her chin. She almost choked again when she looked up and found Grant kneeling beside her, one hand tipping the bottom of the canteen. Sputtering, she pushed his hand away. "E-enough."

She thought she saw sparks of warmth in those unusual eyes, but when she blinked and looked again, any trace of his thawing disappeared as swiftly as wisps of smoke in the wind.

"You all right?"

He sounded irritated and she stiffened. "You don't have to take care of me. I'm fine." There it was again. That hint of amusement. And again it was gone within the space of one blink.

Drippings from the rabbits sizzled in the coals, diverting her attention from Grant. Jacelyn licked her lips. She didn't know when she had smelled anything so good. She leaned forward as the men sliced off hunks of meat. Grant gingerly poked some toward her mouth, but she ducked and reached for it herself.

"Ouch!" She dropped the hot meat in her lap and sucked her blistered fingers. Heat crept up her neck at Grant's mocking expression.

"If you had eaten from my fingers, you wouldn't have been burned."

She grimaced and rolled her eyes. She just . . . didn't want him touching her . . . Or, for her to touch him. The sensations he aroused in her were too disturbing, too pleasant, too . . . unexplainable.

"But then, you can take care of yourself. Right?"

She sniffed and dug through the folds of her skirt until she found the now cooled portion of rabbit. As she greedily stuffed it into her mouth, she hoped he'd revert back to his usual habit of keeping his thoughts and comments to himself.

"Hey, Jones? What you reckon the gal's worth?"

"Sì. The señorita muy bonita." Eloy rubbed his hands together. "Mucho dinero."

The Kid lazily ran the edge of a thin piece of paper down his tongue and stared insolently at Jacelyn while he finished rolling his cigarette. "Personally, I hope no one ransoms her. I'm getting right fond of her company. Aren't you, Jones?"

Jacelyn tried to hide her shudders by wrapping her arms around her legs and resting her forehead on her knees. If they couldn't see her face, maybe they wouldn't notice the fear that must be evident in her expression. Maybe they wouldn't guess that without her brother, there was no one to care what happened to her.

It took Grant a moment to remember that *he* was "Jones." He'd been too absorbed watching the woman's sudden unease and the way she seemed to be trying to make herself invisible. Why was she so nervous about the ransom? Whatever the reason, they'd be gone long before the demand for money could be sent to her family.

He dug his hands into his pockets and casually regarded the gang members. "She'll make ... ahem, us ... all wealthy."

Dick Waddell yawned and stretched. "Don't know 'bout you boys, but reckon I'll dream 'bout what I'm goin' ta do with all that hard-earned money."

Chuckles and muttered comments about what else the men would dream about burned Jacelyn's ears. When she garnered the courage to glance up and see what all the rustling noise was about, her eyes rounded with dismay to find everyone spreading out blankets and preparing to sleep.

She inched a little closer to the dying fire. As soon as the sun had gone down, the night had become quite chilly. But she wasn't going to ask for a blanket or ... anything. Her gaze returned to the dilapidated cabin. Inside she'd be free from the leering stares and might even find her chance to escape.

Her heart pounded against her breast. Sweat beaded her palms. Escape. It was all she could think about.

A large hand covered her shoulder. She jumped.

"You'll be sleeping with me."

She gawked up at Grant Jones. "I beg your pardon?" Surely she hadn't heard him correctly.

"Come over here." Grant paused between each word. She looked exhausted. After all she'd been through today, he couldn't blame her for being slow. But they needed sleep. No telling what tomorrow would bring.

Jacelyn ducked her shoulder from beneath his hand. She leapt to her feet. Panic edged her voice. "I won't. You can't make me sleep—"

Grant bent and shoved his face so close to hers that he could see the shimmering moisture threatening to spill from her eyes. Hell. He growled so that only she could hear, "Shut up." He nodded his head toward the attentive gang members. "Or maybe you'd prefer to sleep with them?"

Jacelyn bit her lip and glanced sideways to see several grinning faces watching their confrontation. Pablo's broken-toothed gape and the memory of his rotten breath caused her to shiver with dread. And the Kid . . . She shook her head.

Grant sighed. "All right, then—"

"Th-the house," she stammered.

"What?"

She swallowed and took a deep breath. "The house, I'll sleep there."

Grant shook his head. The woman was more of a tenderfoot than he'd ever imagined. "Look, lady, it's not safe. Stay here—"

Her chin jutted out. "The house."

He massaged his own aching neck rather than wrapping his fingers around her long, slender throat as he was tempted to do. "Fine." Damn but he'd never met such a hard-headed female in his life. She refused to obey his orders or listen to reason. "Don't blame me if the roof caves in."

"Don't worry. I won't." Jacelyn marched toward the

lopsided house, only to stop at the edge of the stream. The fire had burned so low that it was hard to see how far it was to the other side.

Suddenly, amidst a chorus of snickers and guffaws, she was swept into a pair of hard, yet surprisingly gentle, arms. Three long strides carried them across the water and to the edge of what used to be a porch. She caught her breath when he unceremoniously set her down and a board creaked threateningly beneath her feet.

She resisted a strong urge to throw herself back against his solid chest. Futilely attempting to discern the expression on his face amidst the shadows, she backed slowly toward the door.

Grant tried to read her features, though she was almost hidden beneath the overhang. His chest and arms still sizzled from their contact. She'd felt good in his embrace. And for some silly reason, he yearned to hold her again.

Idiot. He was an idiot. Spinning on his heel, he headed toward the campfire.

Jacelyn pulled on the knob. The door was stuck. She yanked. The wood grated across the width of one board and then jerked from her grasp. She screamed as the door fell from its rotted leather hinge.

Grant turned and ran back just in time to choke on the dust and to wince at the loud crack as the door slammed onto the porch. He watched in silence as the woman uncovered her ears, coughed daintily, and visibly gathered her courage. With a defiant glance in his direction, she stepped boldly into the darkened cabin.

He grinned. He couldn't help himself. The little hoyden had guts. No brains. But guts.

Returning to the campfire, he glared at the grinning outlaws, hoisted up his blanket along with the borrowed, or stolen, Army saddle and recrossed the creek.

Anyone wanting to get to the woman would have to get past him.

He pulled his gun from its holster and rested it on his thigh as he settled down on the ground outside the cabin and waited.

Chapter Four

Jacelyn Faith McCaffery marched into the dark room. As soon as she was out of the aggravating man's sight, her steps faltered. A cobweb clutched at her hair and slithered across her cheek. She choked back a scream as her hands frantically fought off the silken snare.

Standing in the middle of the earthen floor, her chest felt as if she inhaled fire as she gasped for breath. Her eyes burned. Childhood fears of being left alone in the dark threatened to overwhelm her. Wrapping her arms around her waist, she shivered uncontrollably.

An hysterical chuckle whispered past her lips. So, she had won this battle. Just look what her bravado had cost. She was frightened and lost and . . . alone. To her amazement, though, the last thing on her mind was running from the sad shelter.

Something rustled in the debris off to her left. The roof groaned and seemed to sag closer and closer. Lifting her arms over her head, she crumpled like a rag doll as her quaking legs gave out and she fell to her knees.

Heedless of the filthy floor, she lay on her side, curled into a tight ball and gave vent to soundless sobs. For the moment, there was no one to poke or prod or demand her compliance. She could let down her guard and succumb to the fear that she'd fought so hard to hide since the attack on the stagecoach.

The events of the day rolled over and over in her mind. But no matter how she imagined otherwise, she still ended up in the hands of the outlaws, in this horrible rundown shack in the middle of nowhere, no closer to finding James.

Something small and light, but frightening, scurried across her ankle. She gasped and sat up. Gusts of wind moaned and whistled between wide cracks. Shadows crept nearer. A board clattered and fell. Dust swirled in its wake. A chorus of mournful wails sounded from behind the house.

Jacelyn scrambled to her feet. She ran from the room like a kitten with its tail on fire. Stumbling off the porch, she ran awkwardly for several yards until her toe caught something hard, yet yielding—something that cursed loudly.

Arms and legs flailing, she couldn't coordinate her movements as she fell. She panicked and tried to call out. Something cracked against her chin before any sound issued forth.

"Ouch! Get off me, damn it."

She gasped, "I'm not on you. You're on me." When Jacelyn caught her breath enough to focus her eyes, she discovered that she and Grant Jones lay tangled in a heap of arms and legs. The starlight accentuated his flushed features and those stormy blue eyes.

All at once she giggled. And when she started, she couldn't seem to stop. Hot tears trickled down her cold cheeks. She wasn't alone anymore. But she had run after all. Tension gradually seeped from her body, like thick jam from an overturned jar.

And then the hard rib cage beneath her hand quaked. A brief but deep, throaty rumble lifted loose strands of her hair. She realized the warm, rich sound was Grant's chuckle.

Her gaze shot to his face. Sure enough, she clearly saw the white flash of his teeth before his entire body shuddered still. If it weren't for the slight curve molding his lips and the tingling sensation in her palm, she might have imagined his unguarded reaction. But she'd heard it, and felt it.

Grant forced his body to calm. He was lying on the rocky ground, his arms full of curvaceous woman, with portions of those curves pressing into parts of him that responded with a depth of emotion he hadn't felt in ages.

His lips quirked. He'd just happened to be looking toward the cabin when the woman had come rushing out. He'd seen the terror contorting her lovely features and had naturally been worried. Then everything had happened so fast that he had no time to move out of her way. The last thing he remembered thinking as she careened into him was that she appeared half crazed and he had to do something to stop her. When he'd accidentally accomplished that feat, and been prepared to deal with her hysterics, she'd looked directly at him and laughed. A delightful, lilting, extremely pleasing sound tinged with a note of sadness.

He couldn't remember the last time he'd even chuckled. It felt good. Real good.

Now, he had to know. "What're you doing here? Thought you wanted to say in the *house.*"

Jacelyn hiccuped. She took a deep breath and heard a hissed groan. Realizing her limbs were still entwined with Grant's and that she had flattened him on the hard ground, she gasped and hurried to free herself—and him. "Oh, dear. I'm so sorry. I didn't mean to ... It's just ... I didn't see ..."

Her elbow dug into his ribs. He grunted and she tried

harder to get her skirt from beneath his large body. Her knee dug high into his thigh. He cursed and she became even more flustered. "I'm sorry."

Grant raised up and muttered incoherently, he hoped, when the top of his head bumped her chin. He heard the click of her teeth and her indrawn breath of pain. Hell. Finally he grabbed hold of her arms and lifted her until he could free his legs, then set her down by his side.

Though he was glad to get her off him, he had the oddest sensation in his chest, of missing her closeness. He snorted. The soft caress of her breasts aroused him, was all. He swallowed. It had been a long time since he'd been attracted to a woman, and *never* to a city-bred woman. He cleared his throat. "You didn't say why you're here."

"I-I . . ." Jacelyn looked from the dark house to his shadowed face. She didn't know which was the more intimidating. Both hid secrets she was afraid to explore too closely.

In fact, she wondered why she'd been so happy to literally *run into* him. Though he'd mostly protected her from the others, she sensed that Grant Jones was every bit as harsh and dangerous and unforgiving as the Arizona desert.

So, what answer could she give him? What *was* she doing out here—with him? Which was she more frightened of? The creaky old house filled with crawly creatures that could cave in at any moment? Or the man staring at her so intently that her insides felt all quivery and gooey?

"I-I heard a noise."

"A noise?" He looked toward the cabin just as a gust of wind rattled the sideboards. Yeah, he just bet she heard a noise. He turned back to her only to see the long strands of hair that had fallen free from her severe bun were blowing against her cheek and down her back.

"I guess . . . I let it frighten me."

He hated the sudden surge of protectiveness that pooled in his chest, and hated the fact that she'd been frightened. But until they reached the outlaws' hideout and he had a chance to come up with a plan to get her safely away, there wasn't much he could do to ease her fear. "Well," he yawned. "Better get some sleep."

"Y-yes, I suppose." Her gaze darted back and forth between the house and the man. What should she do? Either alone in that . . . that rat trap, or here, with him, she doubted she'd get much sleep.

Grant waited. When all she did was twist and untwist her hands and drag the heel of her shoe back and forth through the dirt, he sighed and got to his knees. Shaking out his blanket, he respread it, lifted his brows and invited, "Offer's still open. You can sleep . . . share . . ." Hell, there wasn't any polite way to put it. "Your virtue'll be safe with me."

But would it really? When she ran her tongue over her bottom lip like that, and breathed so deeply that her breasts strained against the ripped bodice of her dress . . .

Jacelyn ducked her head and mumbled, "All right."

Grant's head snapped up. "All right?" Never in a million years had he thought she'd decide to stay with him. Any fool could see she thought his belly drug the ground with the rest of the snakes. "Why?"

Jacelyn gulped. Why? Why did he have to ask? How could she admit that she'd swallowed her pride rather than face her cowardice? But perhaps she'd made a mistake. Another mistake. Something else she didn't like acknowledging. Gathering what courage she could summon, she decided it was probably best to return to the house.

"Why me?" Grant couldn't believe that he'd repeated the question. He hated to think that it even made a difference, but her earlier rejection, when she'd chosen to ride with the Kid, still stung.

She halted in mid-turn and frowned. This was something else she didn't want to think about. Why had she run to Grant Jones? Deep down, she knew that was exactly what she'd done. She hadn't run *from* the house, she'd run *to* Grant.

A shiver raced up her spine as she peered at him through the thick cover of her lashes. His shadowed features appeared even more craggy and dangerous. When she'd first met him at the fort, he'd been aloof and secretive. Then he'd appeared at the scene of the holdup even harder and colder than she'd remembered.

Yet he'd stepped in to save her. Told the others she was under his protection. He'd treated her . . . kindly. And she felt . . . safe . . . in his arms.

Her emotions were so mixed that she had no idea *why*. "I-I don't know."

Grant shook his head, then ran his fingers through his hair.

She watched the blue-black strands filter back into place like spun silver, only to lift and swirl again in the wind, teasing her senses. She clasped her fingers in her lap to quell an insane urge to smooth the furrows between his brows. Squeezing her eyes closed, she blamed her outrageous inclinations on the fact that she'd never had to camp out of doors at night, or remain so very close to such a virile, provocative man.

"At least you're honest." He sat back on his heels. What in the hell was she staring at? He resisted the urge to run his hands over his face and chest. "Come on." His voice was husky and harsher than usual.

Jacelyn blinked. "What?"

"Come over to the blanket."

A thread of anger at his arrogance coiled through her

before she realized he'd just repeated his offer for her to stay. Gingerly, she sat on one edge. "Ah . . ."

He sighed. "What?"

"There's only one blanket."

Grant stifled a grin. "That's right."

She caught the suspicious twitch of his moustache and narrowed her eyes. "But—"

"There's room for both of us."

Glancing across the creek at the sleeping camp, her shoulders heaved as she exhaled. "All right," she warned, "but I get the outside edge."

"Fine by me." Women! They could be such contrary creatures. He lay down in the center of the blanket and brought the other half over himself. Before he reached across the woman, she snatched the cover from his hand and tugged, trying to stretch it far enough to spread over her body. She tugged again.

"The blanket's small. You'll have to move closer."

She scooted a few inches nearer. It was almost enough, but not quite. She wriggled another few inches. Just right. But she was so close to Grant that she felt the tantalizing, terrifying heat from his large body.

Grant grunted. The woman was so damned tense, she wouldn't be able to move a muscle come morning.

"Ouch." She squirmed uncomfortably.

"Now what?"

"There are rocks under here."

He choked back a chuckle. "What'd you expect? You're on the ground."

She worried her lower lip and turned her head so she could dart a glance at his face. "You seem comfortable."

He couldn't hold back his grin. "I moved the rocks when I made my bed earlier."

"Oh." She got up, fished beneath her side of the blanket and rolled away the largest pebbles. Lying down again, she squirmed and pulled at the blanket, unwittingly tugging Grant closer.

"Aw, hell, lady, lie still. This isn't the Palace Hotel. You'll get used to it." He hoped she was ignorant of the painful images that were forming in his mind as she twisted and moaned.

Coyotes yipped. Jacelyn sucked in her breath. "Wh-what was that?" She edged a little closer to him.

A mischievous quirk tilted his lips. "A coyote. Or . . . maybe Apaches."

"Apaches?" She sat up, stiffer than a pine board.

"Maybe."

"Will . . . will they attack?"

"Hmmmmm, probably not tonight."

She gulped and scanned the dark shadows that appeared to be creeping closer and closer. *"Probably* not?"

"Probably not. Now get some sleep. You'll need to be alert tomorrow."

"T-tomorrow."

"Yep."

Jacelyn lay back and remained as still as a fallen log. She pulled her corner of the blanket up until only her wide eyes and the top of her head stuck out.

Grant felt her tremble and cursed. He hadn't meant to frighten her. Well, maybe he had. But he didn't think she was *that* naive. Then again, he guessed he was dealing with the tenderest tenderfoot he'd ever run across. "Why don't—"

"Hey, Jones," one of the outlaws yelled. "Keep it down over there. Unless . . . you need help with the little woman."

From the surly tone, Grant recognized the Kid. "Thanks, anyway. I think I can handle her."

That statement ignited a chorus of chuckles and catcalls. Jacelyn covered her burning cheeks with her cold palms. It was bad enough that she'd been unable to stay

67

alone in the shack, but then to have those beasts think she might be loose with her favors. Ohhh! And Grant Jones didn't dissuade them of the notion.

"Let them think what they want."

She scrunched down further in the blanket. How dare he read her mind. "But—"

"It's safer for you."

"And what about you?" she hissed.

"What about me?"

"It's rather good for your reputation to let them believe that you and I . . . that we . . ."

Grant reached outside the blanket and patted the ground until he found his hat. He plunked it over his face. Jacelyn had to lean closer to hear his muffled, "Believe me . . ." Suddenly he tilted the hat back and raised his head. He found himself nose to nose with the woman. "What'd you say your name was?"

She puffed up like a horny toad. Evidently she hadn't made much of an impression on the man during their first meeting if he didn't even remember her name. Even more humiliating was the fact that she recalled every little detail about *him*.

Fuming, she leaned forward til the tip of her nose brushed his and whispered, "Jacelyn. Jacelyn Faith McCaffery."

Grant stifled an almost overwhelming urge to run his tongue over her pouting lower lip. She was full of spit and fire and so . . . cute. He must've been too absorbed by her perfectly rounded figure back at the fort, or he wouldn't have forgotten a name that pretty. Jacelyn. Jacelyn Faith. He liked it.

He rolled toward her, barely resisting the temptation to bury his face in the hollow of her throat. "Go to sleep, Jacelyn McCaffery. Tomorrow'll be a long day."

Jacelyn sputtered a few incomprehensible words that he failed even to acknowledge, then snapped her jaws closed. Just like that he'd dismissed her. Go to sleep? She thought not. The ground was too hard. The outlaws were probably over there staring and listening. And she was aggravated. He sounded half asleep already. Well, she'd show him. She ... would ... not ... go ...

Grant pillowed his head on his arm and watched as her eyelids fluttered and then closed. Even as her features relaxed, there was a stubborn tilt to her lips and an air of defiance in the way she clutched the blanket.

It disturbed the hell out of him that he really enjoyed her company.

Jacelyn stretched her cramped muscles. Or tried to. But she found she couldn't move. She blinked, but her vision was blurred. Sniffing, she smelled the pleasant aromas of smoke, leather, and tobacco. She blinked again and saw blue sky. Acres and acres of blue sky.

Where was she? Her insides felt like she'd been turned upside down. Terror held her in its sneaky grip.

All at once everything came back to her. The holdup. Her abduction. Why couldn't she move? Had they bound her? But wait. She could wriggle her fingers. And she was warm. Very, very warm. Only a hairy arm held her down.

Her eyes snapped wide open. She tried to turn her head, but sometime during the night her hair had gotten trapped ... Oh, dear. Trapped by smooth, supple flesh. And hard muscle pillowed her cheek.

Calm down, she ordered herself. *Don't panic. Think.*

She stiffened as images of the Kid, the slimy Eloy, and huge Pablo hurtled through her mind. And another face. A dark, ruggedly handsome face, with pale blue eyes.

She turned her head slightly. Dark, curly hair tickled her nose. Oh, yes, Grant Jones. *His* shoulder trapped her hair. *His* arm weighted her rib cage and *his* fingers curved around her waist. The last she remembered, there'd been a good six inches between them.

"You were shivering."

The deep, rasping voice startled her. "Dear Lord. You must be a mind reader," she mumbled, then scrambled to a sitting position. The jerk to her scalp when her hair finally pulled free brought a tear to her eye.

"Not hardly. Your body tensed. I figured you were awake and probably wondered what had happened." He shifted so he could look into her face. It was a mistake. His body was already going through the fires of hell after lying with her cuddled beside him most of the night, and now her sleepy eyes and mussed hair made her all the more attractive.

"After you went to sleep, your teeth chattered so loud that you kept the rest of us awake," he teased. "We drew straws and I lost. I had to keep you warm."

She gasped with indignation and squirmed a foot or two away. Glancing across the creek, she saw the dead campfire and the other men, who all appeared still to be asleep.

"It's about half an hour till sunrise. I was going to wake you."

She didn't for a moment believe that he and the outlaws had "drawn straws." But she did wonder why he would think to go to the trouble of protecting her sensibilities by waking her before the rest of the camp aroused. What sort of man was this Grant Jones?

Jacelyn sat for some time without speaking, thinking about her situation and what could be done about it. When she happened to glance over at Grant with every intention of confessing that he and the bandits would receive no ransom money, and that keeping her with them was a useless endeavor, his eyes were closed and he appeared to be sleeping.

70

Her eyes darted away, then drifted back to study his peaceful features. Asleep, he didn't seem so intimidating. She assessed his pronounced cheekbones and the nose that was a smidgen too long, and how those features blended with his square jaw and lean cheeks to form the most strongly built face she'd ever seen.

Her pulse accelerated. She quickly averted her eyes. Drat, she admonished her rational self. How could she find her abductor handsome?

Her stomach knotted. Now, it appeared she was the only one awake. Was this the chance she'd been hoping for? Could she escape? Surely, with an entire day stretching before her, she'd be able to find a road or someone to help her.

She took a deep breath and slowly eased from the blanket. Though she was scared silly he would be awake and watching her, caution prompted her to look over her shoulder. Her luck held. His eyes were closed, his arms folded across his chest.

She allowed the time for one final glance at his rugged features and stifled a gasp. She could have sworn his lips had curved into an arrogant grin. Or was it her imagination? She shook her head. His face hardly ever expressed emotion. The last thing he would do was smile in his sleep.

With a slow, relieved sigh she turned and hurried into the desert, praying silently until she was out of his line of vision. Picking her way carefully through spiny yucca and thorny mesquite, she finally found the creek. One of the outlaws had mentioned that he'd picketed the horses near water. It stood to reason that if she followed the creekbed, she could find the animals, pick one to ride and turn the others loose.

Her excitement rose, causing her to become even more impatient as thick stands of brambly oak and tall salt cedar, growing near the water, impeded her progress. Now and then she stopped, looked back and listened. It was too quiet. Any minute she expected to see Grant Jones close on her trail.

Gradually she became more confident.

At last she ducked under a branch and saw the horses. Her brows furrowed as she looked over the huge animals. Which one should she choose?

Several of the horses pricked their ears in her direction. Some rolled their eyes and strained against their ropes. Perspiration dotted her forehead and beaded her upper lip. The closer she stepped, the larger and more frightening they grew.

Summoning her determination, she stepped around a small mesquite tree. Striding forward with her chin held high, she was nearly thrown off balance when a frayed piece of her skirt snagged on a thorn. She stumbled backward into something as solid as a tree trunk, only there were no trees that large anywhere near the campsite. Surprisingly, her elbow buried into something very flexible. A burst of warm air fanned the loose hair around her ear. Startled out of her wits, Jacelyn shouted—into a hard, calloused palm.

"Shut up, lady. You want to wake everyone?"

Jacelyn stomped her foot. She'd been so close. Strength she didn't know she possessed flooded into her fingers as she jerked his hand from her mouth. "You . . . you . . . s-scared me to death."

"That could be arranged, sooner than you think."

Frustrated tears pooled in her eyes. She blinked rapidly to hold them at bay. "Please . . . Please, let me go."

Grant understood how she felt. Yet he hesitated to tell her that he was there for only one reason—to get her away and back to the fort safely. If she knew that, she could say or do something that might put them both in more danger.

"You really think you could get away?"

She tilted her head. "Of course. I would have been gone by now if you—" She happened to look over his shoulder. The Kid stood beside a rock near the creek lighting a long, thin cigar. She gasped. How long had he been there?

Dust swirled as the nervous horses stomped their hooves.

"You folks going somewhere?" the Kid asked as he ground a match into the dirt.

Grant shrugged. "Just looking at the horses. The lady here thinks she could ride by herself the rest of the way."

Dick Waddell pushed between two mesquites, grunting when a thorn gouged his arm. "That wouldn't be smart, Jones. Keep'er with you, 'cause she'll be blindfolded later. Somethin' awful might happen to 'er was she ta ride off by 'er lonesome an' get lost."

"Guess it could at that. I'll be sure to keep her with me." Grant rubbed the back of his neck, grateful that he'd caught up with the flighty Miss McCaffery before the others. He'd almost given her more rope than she needed—more than enough to hang herself.

"But—" When all eyes turned to her, at least all but those of the gaunt Eloy, who was conspicuously absent that morning, Jacelyn swallowed and decided not to argue. No one had mentioned that she *might* have been attempting to escape. Perhaps she'd better let well enough alone.

Waddell wiped a trickle of blood from his arm. "Hope the gal's worth enough ta get us out of this bitchin' desert. Reckon ta spend my best years in San Fransisky."

The Kid grunted. "Sure, and a pig'll fly."

By the time the silent group of riders left the camp, the air was already hot and stifling. Just before mid-day,

73

the rocky yucca and cactus-studded hills gave way to grassy plateaus as they rode due east. Ahead, Jacelyn saw the scalloped edges of dark green mountains and sand-colored cliffs.

Jack rabbits scurried beneath the thistles and horned larks flew from in front of the horses, barely avoiding being trampled by a shod hoof.

For a short time they followed a dry stream bed and enjoyed the cool shade beneath large branches of oaks, walnuts, and sycamores. Several hours later, as they neared the mountain range, junipers and wild flowers sprouted from the difficult terrain.

Jacelyn thought that, under different circumstances, she might have liked riding through the unusual country-side secure in Grant's strong arms. But he made her nervous, the way he kept glancing behind and around them all the time. What *was* he looking for?

Then the outlaw leader reined up beside them, abruptly reminding her of her predicament, as if she could have forgotten.

"Jones, use your bandana and blindfold the gal."

Grant clenched his jaw, but untied his neck scarf. Sarcasm was rife in his voice as he muttered, "Thought you might intend to blindfold me, too."

Waddell's lips curled. "Thought about it. But if'n your gonna be a part of this here outfit, yore gonna need ta know your way around."

Grant didn't miss the leader's inflection on the word *if*. When Jacelyn tried to forestall his tying the scarf around her eyes, he batted her hands down. "Quit fighting me, lady, unless you want your hands bound, too."

"That's tellin' 'er, boy. Maybe you'll do after all." Waddell's grin actually reached his eyes for a split second before he raked long-roweled spurs down his horse's quivering sides and returned to the head of the line of riders.

Aware that he'd unwittingly passed some kind of test, Grant released a long sigh.

Meanwhile, Jacelyn tipped her head back and tilted her chin from side to side but was still unable to see. "You didn't have to tie it so tight, you know," she hissed.

He whispered back, "Yes, I did. Ignorance can save a foolish tenderfoot's life."

Her shoulders slumped. "I'd rather die than be a prisoner forever."

He grinned. She was good. Playing the poor, pitiful, defenseless woman to the hilt, aiming for his sympathy. But he'd been around the woman long enough to know that she had too strong a personality to mean a word she said.

He patted her shoulder, then clenched his teeth to keep from tangling his fingers in her russet mane and trailing them down the silky column of her neck. "I doubt you'll be held *forever*. These thugs wouldn't be able to stand you that long."

Her mouth opened, then snapped shut. How dare he mock her. How dare he pretend to think he knew how badly she might behave. How dare he presume to think he knew her at all.

And he wasn't even trying to talk her out of her glum mood. The ruse had always worked on her uncle. To placate her, he'd finally given in and allowed her to learn the textile business.

All at once, the thought of her uncle weighted her shoulders with depression. She'd tried so hard to prove herself. But he'd never changed his mind about giving a "female" rights to the company's operation.

Grant was grateful for the woman's silence as he forced his gaze from the slender column of her hunched shoulders. He noticed that the valley they'd entered was narrowing. A creek lined with sycamores, oak, and ash bubbled off to the north.

The trail wound around a rocky slope and Grant was surprised to see a farm house and barn and several out-buildings constructed in the middle of another little valley. Beyond this tranquil scene rock spires and pinnacles towered like sentinels over tall pines and more yucca. He shook his head in wonder at the unusual collision of desert and mountain.

He also studied the line of riders for the hundredth time. What had happened to the Mexican bandit, Eloy? Grant had seen the small man saddle up and ride out before the rest of the gang roused that morning. Why hadn't he returned?

As they neared the buildings, a huge man with brown hair and arm muscles as big as Grant's thighs emerged from a long building that Grant assumed to be the bunkhouse. Everywhere Grant looked, the operation seemed to be that of a working ranch. Was this how the outlaws had been able to fool lawmen scouting the area?

The big man called out with a thick German accent, "So, you be back soon."

From the porch of the farm house came another voice. "Waddy, you're back."

Jacelyn couldn't stand it. She jerked off the banana. If they were going to kill her, they'd just have to do it. She squinted through the unaccustomed brightness.

Just as she'd thought. A woman. That last voice belonged to a woman.

Chapter Five

Jacelyn stared at the small, grinning woman casually wiping her hands on a cup towel. Her white-blond hair was tied back, displaying a face wrinkled from weather and a lifetime of hardships, a face that had been beautiful at one time.

Jacelyn's heart skipped a beat. Perhaps, at last, she had found a confidant, a person who would listen and understand her fears and . . . maybe . . . help her escape.

But then the woman hurried over to Dick Waddell, throwing her arms around the thief and killer like she hadn't seen him for a month of Sundays. Jacelyn gulped. The woman acted like she *loved* the outlaw.

Then the woman turned and saw Grant and Jacelyn. Grant saw the hope in Jacelyn's eyes and felt the excitement tensing her body as he lowered her to the ground. His gut tightened and he couldn't help but feel sorry for his charge. Her innocence tugged at his heart. But she would have to learn when and how to give her trust. He knew personally just how hard-learned a lesson it could be.

"Who be them folks, Waddy?"

Jacelyn took a step forward, unable to take her eyes off the silver-haired woman wearing denim britches and pointed-toe boots. A thin, faded flannel shirt stretched across her generous bosom, otherwise Jacelyn couldn't have distinguished her from the other outlaws.

Waddell handed his horse's reins to Bob and sauntered over to stand beside his woman. "The gent here's decided ta join up with us. Calls hisself 'Jones.' The gal we brung along ta ransom off."

Jacelyn expected to see outrage, condemnation, or at least sympathy or pity. She was sadly disappointed. In fact, she found herself blushing profusely while the woman coolly regarded her. Faded blue eyes, that were somehow oddly familiar, seemed to assess and appraise every tattered inch of Jacelyn.

"Reckon she might fetch a good price at that."

Jacelyn bristled. She was tired of being spoken about as if she were some kind of prize heifer at a county fair. She cleared her throat. "I'll have you know—"

"We're pleased to meet you, ma'am," Grant interrupted. He tipped his hat toward the older woman.

Jacelyn sputtered and choked when the *lady,* and she used the term quite loosely, had the effrontery to smile at Grant and push several stray, dingy strands of hair behind her ear.

"Well, ain't he somethin' fancy? Where'd ya find 'im, Waddy?"

Waddy! Jacelyn crossed her arms over her chest. How could anyone with any sense give such a cruel, vicious person a pet name? Waddy. She sighed in disgust.

Waddell frowned at Grant, but told his woman, "Reckon he come along at just the right time, Dory. May've even saved this ole ornery hide."

Before the outlaw pair turned and walked toward the house, the woman favored Grant Jones with such an adoring look that it almost turned Jacelyn's stomach. And that heathen, Grant, had the nerve to appear *proud* of his feat. Her toe tapped the ground, swirling another layer of dirt around her ankles. She could just scream.

In reality, Grant was patting himself on the back. So far, the gang *seemed* to have accepted him—or at least their leader had. He crossed his arms over his chest. If they only knew how much he hated carrying through with this deception.

He inwardly sighed. And there was that look on Jacelyn McCaffery's face again—like he'd just proven for the hundredth time that he was no better than a fresh pile of horse dung. She'd best rid herself of that pious, righteous expression, or he might be tempted to leave her where she was and be damned glad of it.

The Kid came up behind Grant. "Why're you hanging around out here?" He leered openly at Jacelyn. "Wouldn't want our valuable prize to get away before we collect our money, would we?"

Grant itched to smash his fists into the albino's perfect white teeth, but held his temper. *Soon,* he promised himself. *Soon.* Grant glanced over his shoulder to find that the big German had taken the Appaloosa. He took hold of Jacelyn's elbow and guided her toward the porch. The weasel-faced Kid was right. She should be inside and away from this mangy bunch.

Jacelyn winced with her first step. Surprise at seeing another woman had momentarily distracted her thoughts from her aches and pains. But the insides of her legs were nearly raw from so many hours in the uncomfortable and unfamiliar saddle. It had been too long since she'd actually walked. The ground wouldn't hold still.

When Grant seemed to sense her discomfort and paused, she used the time to glance around the bleak setting. The buildings all needed paint. Several poles had collapsed on the corrals. The barn roof had a hole in it. The porch Grant was edging her toward sagged on the far end.

She looked out over the daunting countryside. Defeat

suddenly weighed heavily on her shoulders. How would she ever find her way out of here?

Jacelyn had just taken another step with Grant's support when the woman appeared in the doorway and called, "C'mon. We gotta rustle up some vittles fer the boys. You kin help."

Grant aided Jacelyn up the lopsided steps and backed away. It wasn't that he didn't want to stay and keep an eye on the hard-headed Miss McCaffery. He just figured there were other things—men things—that needed his attention just then.

Jacelyn wrinkled her nose and turned to Grant, but he was halfway to the barn with the Kid trailing behind. Arching her back and struggling to move her throbbing muscles, Jacelyn stumbled after the older woman. She hurt in places she didn't even know she had muscles.

Reluctantly, she walked through the doorway, mulling over the question she'd wanted to ask Grant. Just what were "vittles," and how did one go about "rustling" them?

She hesitated just inside the threshold. The door slammed against her backside. Jacelyn yelped, then flushed with embarrassment and walked on inside.

"Quit yore lollygaggin'. Fetch that chunk o' wood by the chair 'n follow me."

Ignoring the way the woman rattled off orders faster than the morning drill sergeant at Fort Huachuca, Jacelyn stood in the middle of a large room, staring about in utter horror.

A lopsided table stood beneath an open window. Flies buzzed over dirty, cracked plates that had been left for who-knew-how-long. A distasteful odor permeated the room. The hunger that had gnawed at her stomach for the past hour churned into nausea.

Shudders ricocheted down her spine at the sight of a huge cobweb spun between the end legs of a splintered

80

bench. The plump spider itself rested near its latest snared victim.

She stumbled over a footstool draped with a pair of faded trousers with a rip in one knee. As she gingerly picked her way toward the room into which the woman had disappeared, clods of dirt grated and crumbled beneath Jacelyn's feet.

However, a huge moss rock fireplace covering the wall to her left was unexpectedly beautiful. In the middle of the mantel, an embroidered plaque displayed the words *HOME SWEET HOME*. The sentiment brought tears to Jacelyn's eyes. How she wished she'd never left Richmond. She sniffed, then regretted the action as she was nearly overcome again by the odor of the place.

Physically shaking off her desire to wallow in self pity, she picked up a small piece of firewood and hurried through the near doorway—where she stopped, utterly bewildered.

The kitchen, a huge room with a large stove and an indoor pump by the sink, was as spotless as the living/dining room was filthy.

The woman stood with a pan of pea pods in her hands. "What's yore name, girl?"

Faded blue eyes scrutinized her. Jacelyn swallowed her apprehension and replied, "Jacelyn McCaffery."

"McCaffery, ya say?"

Jacelyn nodded.

"Sounds familiar. Don't reckon we've met afore?"

Jacelyn shook her head.

"Didn't think so. Well, ya kin call me Dora. Now don't just stand there with your thumb in your butt. Put that there hunk o' wood by the stove, then snap these here peas."

Jacelyn stiffened her aching spine. She'd just been insulted, yet was too exhausted to think of anything to do in her defense. So, she just dropped the wood and took the pan, vaguely wondering if shelling peas had any connection to "rustling vittles."

Standing there, holding the pan of peas as if it was the only thing supporting her, Jacelyn sighed and asked, "Ah, wh-what am I supposed to do?"

Dora looked Jacelyn up and down reprovingly before spreading her hands on her hips. "My gawd, girl. Don't ya know nuthin'?"

Jacelyn stuck out her chin. "I *know* a lot, ma'am. I'm just *unfamiliar* with your ways." And words. Didn't anyone out here speak plain English?

"Well, now, the mouse has spunk, after all."

"Mouse," Jacelyn squeaked. "I'll have you know—"

"And ya might's well figure ta learn fast. 'Pears we'll be workin' together a spell."

"Oh, no . . ." Jacelyn's mind refused to accept the possibility, but she *knew* enough not to blurt out her plan to escape.

Dora hesitated, but when Jacelyn made it clear she'd said all she intended to say, Dora asked, "Ya do know how ta snap peas?"

Jacelyn gave her a blank look.

Dora sighed. "How 'bout water? Can ya fetch a pail o' water from the well out yonder?"

Jacelyn set the peas on the table and took the proffered pail. She had to concentrate on Dora's directions out the back door to a covered well. She'd never "fetched" anything before in her life, either, but wasn't going to admit that fact and earn another scowl from the woman.

Perhaps, if she could please Dora, she would have an ally when the time came.

Upon reaching the well, though, Jacelyn stood staring at the bucket tied to the end of a long rope. The other end of the rope was wrapped around a crossbar connected to a long handle. For the first time, she regretted the pampering and protection of a wealthy upbringing. There were so many things—things associated with cooking and physical activities—that she'd never had to learn.

After staring at the well for several minutes, Jacelyn finally decided that the bucket had to be lowered into the water and then be raised with the handle. Setting down the pail Dora had given her, Jacelyn reached over the rounded rock partition that caught her at mid-waist and dropped the bucket into the black hole. It seemed to fall forever before striking and splashing the liquid below.

Cranking was easy at first, but the further she raised the full bucket, the harder the handle became to turn. One more turn. Another. Her muscles screamed in pain until she couldn't lift the handle again. In fact, the small half turn she'd just completed threatened to snap from her weary grasp.

She gritted her teeth, bent her knees and put her whole body into finishing the turn. The rope creaked. Below, she heard water slosh over the bucket.

Suddenly tanned fingers closed over her pale hands. The handle lifted easily and began to turn. At last the bucket reached the top and stopped, but swung back and forth over the center of the well. More water spilled onto the rock enclosure and splashed onto her dress, forming small, round spots of mud in the two days worth of collected grime.

She tried to free her hands to swipe at the dirt but, again, brown fingers beat her to the chore.

"What's the matter, lady? Not as strong as you thought? Things not as perfect as they should be for the pampered city girl?" Grant had to keep reminding himself that the woman was responsible for his being here instead of completing his mission. He cursed his feeling of helplessness and guilt at seeing her tired and in pain, along with the complicated crush of confusion and desire that constricted his chest when he looked down into her flushed features and saw the rapid rise and fall of her breasts.

The two top buttons of her blouse had come undone and he was tantalized by the sight of creamy flesh and intricate lace. He closed his eyes and inhaled the faint scent of wildflowers and perspiration. She smelled like a woman—a very enticing woman. Hell.

Jacelyn looked into Grant Jones's mocking blue eyes. She was stung by his low opinion of her, although she couldn't figure out why. Why should she care what he thought? So, she *was* a city girl. She wasn't used to "fetching" water or riding across a desert with outlaws or "rustling" vittles.

The more she thought about it, the more her discouragement turned to indignation. How dare this uncouth barbarian make her feel as if she weren't living up to his standards. Who was he to think she was less of a woman because she couldn't lift a stupid, heavy bucket out of a well?

Jerking her hands from beneath his, she willed them not to shake as she poked him in the chest. "Listen, mister, I've never claimed to be strong *or* perfect." She poked him again, silently acknowledging the disturbing fact that her finger buried happily into dark, damp curls escaping from his open shirt. She stared at the breadth of his chest. Swallowing a clump of cotton, she forced her gaze upward.

Droplets of water sparkled from the ends of his hair. Had he just taken a bath? A bath . . . What she wouldn't do . . . Her anger evaporated like morning dew in summer sunshine. "You've b-bathed, haven't you?"

Grant could hardly keep a straight face. She reminded him of a cocky bantam rooster with the sun highlighting the red in her hair and her cheeks all flushed and rosy.

Her fiery eyes and saucy stance . . . He inhaled and let his breath out in a long hiss. Lord, what a woman!

And he had never encountered anyone whose emotions were so vividly displayed for all to see. Just one look at his damp hair and she'd gone as soft as warm butter. He'd have to remember that.

He wished her resistance would weaken at the mere thought of *him*—as a flesh and blood man—rather than over the idea of cleanliness. The irrational thought momentarily distracted him.

Then he blinked and rubbed the back of his neck. Damn, but he must be losing his mind. Yet, maybe . . . he could use her desire to wash to his advantage. "What does my taking a bath have to do with anything?" he goaded.

She sniffed his fresh, masculine scent and sighed. Oh, to be clean and smell good again. And he looked so good wet and . . . "Ahem, ah, how . . . where . . . could I—"

"Maybe."

She frowned. There he went again, performing his mind reading trick. "You didn't let me finish." She'd show him. "I was wondering . . . if you would carry that pail inside for me."

Grant scowled. "What?"

A mischievous smile teased her lips. "I'm just so weak and all. And you're so big and strong. Could you ple-e-ease carry this to the house?" She handed him the pail. "Please . . ." Aha, she thought. It was worth remaining filthy to shake his confidence.

And from the frown slanting his lips, she'd shaken him like a rag rug in a high wind. She dusted her hands together, highly pleased with herself.

Grant lifted the bucket from the well, filled the pail, and stalked toward the door. He didn't mind hauling the damned water, but grudgingly admitted her request had taken him by surprise. He'd have bet his lucky silver dollar that she'd been going to ask him about taking a bath. What normal woman wouldn't if she had as much grime caked on her as this one?

Jacelyn smiled, all innocence, as she held the back door for Grant.

Dora looked up from snapping the last pea pod. Her eyes widened when she saw the new man. "Glory be, whatcha doin' in here? Ain't supper yet."

Grant set the pail on a shelf and turned to tip his hat. "Just bringing in your water, ma'am. I promise not to get in your way."

Dora flushed a hot pink. "Phsaw. Go on with ya. No need fer ya ta wait on us. There's plenty o' work outside."

"But I asked for his assistance," Jacelyn interrupted. She had to do something to stop Dora's gushing. It was the last thing Jacelyn had expected to see. One would almost think the woman hadn't been around anyone with manners before. Then images of Waddell and the rest of the uncouth gang members flashed through her mind. She supplied her own answer. Poor Dora.

Dora smiled at Grant. "Well, now, ya cain't be doin' such things. Men's work ain't a helpin' 'round no kitchen. Missy here's gonna hafta learn ta—"

Jacelyn's brows shot together. "Men do *so* work in the kitchen. Why, Uncle Jonathan had two chefs and—" Dora's blank expression implied that the woman could not conceive of a male "chef." Jacelyn gave up the argument quickly when she remembered she didn't want anyone knowing about her family situation—or lack of it.

Grant backed quietly out the door. When the two women had been left behind, he took a deep breath. It was enough strain trying to handle one woman at a time. He had no intention of sticking around and being caught between *two* spitting females.

As he strode quickly away, he held out his hand, the one which had covered the two of Jacelyn's over the well handle. He still felt their softness ... and the jolt her touch radiated clear to his gut.

The more he was around her, so feminine and innocent, the more he wondered what was so important as to bring the lady searching for her brother and why she would place herself in such a dangerous position. As he could have predicted, she'd gotten herself in more hot water than a plucked chicken on Sunday.

About an hour later Dora called the men in to eat while Jacelyn made herself useful in the kitchen by stirring a pot of beans. She had completely forgotten the gruesome state of the dining room table. Forgotten—until she carried in the steaming kettle. Then she almost added to the mess by slopping beans over everything as she tried to move aside one of the tin plates.

When Waddell and the others trooped inside and each upended the contents from the nearest dirty plate onto the floor and started spooning food into the same encrusted plate, she thought she'd be sick. And if she had to listen to the slurps, snorts, and grunts much longer ... She retreated to the more pleasant kitchen.

From the doorway, she watched Grant Jones duck through the front entrance. She was amazed when Dora rushed to hand him a clean plate. His smile nearly knocked Jacelyn back on her bottom it was so unexpected, so sudden, and so bright. His features transformed from merely handsome to stunning. All at once the thin air became even more difficult to breathe.

Irritated by her reaction to the man, Jacelyn snatched a piece of cornbread and withdrew deeper into the kitchen. She'd no sooner leaned against the sink to stare at the small chunk of food when Grant sauntered in and approached with a full plate. His hip grazed hers, but she refused to acknowledge his presence.

She fidgeted beneath his watchful gaze. Finally, she snapped, "What are you doing in here? Why aren't you eating with the rest of the . . ."

He arched a thick, dark brow. "Rest of the . . . what?"

Glancing into Grant's face, she watched, fascinated, as the muscles in his jaw flexed with each bite of beans. He ate almost daintily, unlike the gluttons in the other room. She shook her head. "Like the rest of the . . . hogs . . . slopping down their 'vittles.' " At least she'd learned the meaning of the word.

The complete irony of the situation hit her. She almost sounded like Dora, implying that Grant didn't belong in a woman's domain. Then again, he seemed too refined and mannerly to eat with the others.

He grinned. She gritted her teeth and tried to ignore the slight leap in her pulse. But it took too much effort not to notice how incredibly handsome the man was, especially when his moustache tilted just so and the lines on either side of his mouth deepened.

When he swallowed, her eyes followed his Adam's apple down to the dark hair peeking from the "v" of his shirt. She vividly recalled the feel of his broad, muscled chest beneath her cheek—was it only last evening?

She blinked and glanced away, but not before her gaze raked across his, and she saw that he'd watched her watching him. She gulped. He probably knew the reason her skin suddenly felt damp and warm.

Annoyed with herself for feeling any interest in him as a person, and especially for experiencing a slight niggle of attraction, she dredged forth the fact that he'd been the one who had taken her purse and given her money to the outlaw leader, which meant she now had no means to find her brother.

Grant ate another mouthful of beans and admired the agitated rise and fall of her bosom, then allowed himself the pleasure of surveying the rest of her curvaceous figure. It was too bad that he had more pressing things to occupy his mind and time. Pursuing the tenderfoot might be entertaining. Her changeable personality and flammable temper could present a man with a good challenge—if a man had an inclination to accept.

He mentally shook off any notions concerning the woman. He was definitely not attracted to her. Of course not. But the sooner he got her away from here, back to the fort and out of his life, the better. Besides he still remembered her cutting opinion of *savages*. What would her reaction be if she knew the real truth?

His eyes roamed back to her face and he caught her staring longingly out the door. "What're you looking at?"

She wiped her hands down her dusty skirt and cast one last glance outside. "Nothing."

"You were looking at something. What?"

She giggled a little hysterically. "It's stupid, I know, but I thought if I wished hard enough I might hear a bugle, or see a flag and a whole cavalry troop galloping to my rescue."

Grant thought her red cheeks and the shy way she wrung her hands was sweet. He felt a tug in his heart. Again he debated telling her who he was, but decided it was another secret best kept to himself. She plainly wore her feelings on her shirt sleeves. To get them out of the outlaw camp alive, he needed her to appear honestly frightened, even of him.

He reached over and swiped at a smudge on her cheek rather than follow his first instinct to take her in his arms, to give her comfort and calm her fears.

Jacelyn gasped and jerked back. Her eyes widened as she touched her own fingers to her cheek. His touch had been cool and . . . stimulating. Her flesh still tingled where his soft caress had fluttered as softly as a butterfly's wings.

Grant took a deep breath and turned to leave.

"Wait."

His shoulders lifted, then fell. She inhaled at the same time. When he turned around, tilted his head, and lanced her with those eyes, she lost her breath completely. His deep, rumbled, "Yes?" ignited a prairie fire in her stomach.

"I . . ." Why had she stopped him? What on earth did she have to say to this man? She couldn't tell him that he ignited unfamiliar and exciting sensations in her body. She couldn't admit that she didn't want him to leave. She wasn't that foolish—she hoped.

He seemed to stare at her forever before shrugging and sauntering on through the back door. She stomped a foot, then regretted the hurtful action. But then everything she did or said around Grant Jones eventually caused her to feel foolish or childish or stupid.

It was a good thing she didn't care what he thought of her.

A short time later, from her unobtrusive location in the kitchen corner, Jacelyn heard the stomping of booted feet as the remaining outlaws left the house. As she waited for Dick Waddell to come and inform her of her fate, the constriction that had gripped her chest began to ease.

A light tapping of leather soles preceded Dora's arrival. Jacelyn used the few seconds to pat several stray locks of hair into place and to smooth the tattered bodice of her dress. Battling fear and indecision, she strove at least to give the outward appearance of being in control.

"Figured ya was hidin' in here." Dora frowned at the nervous girl. "Dick didn't like it that ya weren't taking your vittles with the rest o' us. But since it t'were your first meal 'n all, I talked 'im inta lettin' ya be." She shook her finger at Jacelyn. "Jest don't make the same mistake again, ya hear?"

Jacelyn gulped and nodded. If things worked out as she planned, she wouldn't have to worry about partaking of more meals with the gang of ruffians.

Dora walked over and pumped water into an empty tin cup, then drank it down in one swallow. Seeing a steaming basin of water on the stove, she narrowed her eyes and glared at Jacelyn. "What's that fer?"

"The dirty dishes, of course."

Slowly and deliberately Dora put down her cup and turned to face Jacelyn. Jacelyn backed up in surprise at the frown of disapproval wrinkling the older woman's face.

"Whatcha tryin' ta prove, Missy, comin' inta my house an' takin' over my chores?"

Jacelyn was stunned. She'd thought the woman would be pleased that she wanted to help. But if condemnation were all the thanks she would get ... She puffed out her chest. "Look, I have no intention of 'taking over' anything of yours." She wrinkled her nose. "Those plates ... And the pots and pans ..."

Before Jacelyn could continue, Dick Waddell strolled into the kitchen and sidled up behind Dora. Jacelyn blinked and backed farther away when the outlaw leader's hands moved up Dora's rib cage and cupped the woman's generous breasts.

Jacelyn turned to leave, but caught the red gleam from the tip of a lit cigar through the door. She hesitated. Someone was out there ... waiting ... watching.

She was tempted to run outside anyway—to run and keep running into the threatening, dark night.

"C'mon, Dory, honey. Got somethin' I wanna show ya."

Dora gasped when Waddell blew in her ear. Jacelyn shuddered and looked desperately around the room in hopes of finding something to occupy her hands—and her mind.

"Can't, Waddy." Dora's speech was thick and deep. "What 'bout the girl?"

"She ain't goin' nowheres. You kin come back later 'n show 'er where ta bunk."

Jacelyn opened her mouth to protest. She wanted to go *now* so she could begin planning her escape. She hadn't thought about the possibility of leaving that very night, but with *Waddy* and *Dory* conveniently occupied . . .

A shiver of anticipation raced down her spine. She glanced toward the now silent couple just in time to see Waddell's lips close over Dora's ear lobe. A niggling coil of heat seared her lower belly. Abruptly, she turned her attention to the water on the stove. Her fingers itched with the need to turn her mind to anything but the disgusting pawing going on in front of her very eyes.

Suddenly, Waddell glanced up and winked. "What's the matter, gal? Ya jealous o' my woman? Wanna come along and make the evenin' interestin'?"

Chapter Six

Jacelyn's mouth dropped open, then snapped shut. She wanted to voice her opinion of Waddell's immoral offer, but she was so incensed, she just sputtered and gaped into Dick and Dora's laughing faces.

For a second, such a brief space of time that she wasn't sure she'd seen it at all, Jacelyn thought Dora's eyes flickered with . . . apology . . . or perhaps, pity.

The back door creaked open. Jacelyn wasn't the least bit surprised to see Grant shouldering into the room.

Waddell slung a beefy arm over Dora's shoulder. "There ya be. Yore slippin', boy. Thought ya were gonna watch this here gal." He gestured toward Jacelyn.

Grant frowned. He wanted to see that Jacelyn McCaffery stayed out of trouble but, damn it, did that mean he had to be saddled with the woman day and night? He had his own business to attend to, not the least of which concerned the Appaloosa and Jacelyn's missing sibling.

The outlaw led a suddenly shy, blushing Dora from the kitchen and called back over his shoulder, "Hang aroun' til we can figger out where ta stash our little gold mine there."

Before Grant could think up a believable argument against staying with the unpredictable Miss McCaffery,

Waddell and his woman disappeared around the corner. A door slammed. Grant found himself uncomfortably alone with Jacelyn, who appeared unaccountably enthralled with a basin of steaming water.

Deciding she couldn't stand around with Grant only a foot away for who-knew-how-long, Jacelyn took a deep breath and marched past Grant and into the living/dining area. Her momentum carried her within two feet of the table before her courage did a sudden dive to the pit of her stomach. Dirty plates. Encrusted pots and pans. Spilled liquor. She swallowed the threat of nausea and bravely continued on.

Filth was one thing she could never abide. And overseeing the housekeeping was one of the few things her Uncle Jonathan had allowed her to do in his huge Richmond mansion. The chore had been easy, for they did little entertaining and Jacelyn had few friends.

Allowed out only in the company of her uncle or one of his hired men, she'd spent most of her time in the big house with nothing to do besides read or sew. Out of boredom, she'd helped the maids whenever they needed her and had become fairly adept with a broom and mop.

But dishwashing? Well, she'd soon find out how accomplished she could become.

Gingerly, she picked up two plates and tried to shake off flies and other ugly-looking insects attracted by flames from the coal-oil lantern sitting in the middle of the table. The action was useless. She returned the dishes to the kitchen, bugs and all.

Grant leaned against the door jamb, arms folded over his chest, watching. She stared at him disdainfully and pushed past his large form, which attractively blocked most of the doorway. After several trips back and forth, brushing against his lean, solid body each and every time, she finally stopped, spread her hands on her hips and scolded, "You could help, you know."

He arched a thick brow. "Why?"

She blinked. Why? Why, indeed. Didn't the man have eyes? Yes. Beautiful but apparently blind eyes? "Because . . . there's a lot to do."

He shrugged.

Blood roiled through her veins. Men! They were all so alike. They wouldn't lift a finger to help a woman with her work. Yet, if a *man* needed something, any little thing, who did he call? A woman.

"Ah, well," she sighed. She set about giving the table a good scrubbing. Arching her aching back, she cast a glance down the hall where "Dory" and "Waddy" had disappeared. She had the strangest need to see the woman.

Glancing toward the implacable Grant Jones and his stoic features, reminded her anew of just how alone and isolated she was.

But, being abducted by the outlaws had proven that she was capable of enduring more physical and emotional upheavals than she'd ever imagined. She had persevered, and it felt good.

She returned to the kitchen and dipped a finger into the basin she'd prepared. The water was still warm. Using a dirty cup towel she'd found under the dining table, she scraped the leftovers off the plates into a rag, to be discarded later. Then she submerged the dishes and scrubbed and scrubbed and scrubbed. They must not have seen warm water in a month of Sundays.

Once she had stacked the plates and cups to dry and emptied the water, she looked around for something to dry her hands. Finding nothing, she reluctantly swiped them up and down the front of her skirt.

Feeling a slight tingle along the nape of her neck, she quickly looked up and caught Grant grinning at her. Grinning? No, it couldn't be. His moustache had just twitched.

She fidgeted beneath his glittering blue gaze. She tilted her head. There was something about the way he looked at her tonight. Something different and even more disconcerting than usual. The contrary sparkle left her feeling hot and cold at the same time and weakened her knees to the consistency of warmed over gravy.

She was the first to glance away, clearing her throat and clutching her bodice together where the buttons were missing. When she darted her glance to Grant again, he was gazing about the living quarters, allowing her a good view of his strong profile. Her pulse quickened. Though she should, by all rights be afraid of him, he only succeeded in making her extremely nervous.

Grant focused his eyes on anything but the woman, trying to shake the strange sensations that rocked his insides every time he looked into those vivid navy-blue eyes. He couldn't figure out Miss Jacelyn McCaffery. In one sense, she seemed as timid and frightened as an inexperienced child. In another, she was as strong and forthright as any seasoned farm wife.

She was holding up well since her abduction. Hadn't once become hysterical. Hadn't acted the swooning female. He admired her subtle strength.

He glanced around the kitchen, marveling at the way she'd pitched in and cleaned up after the meal. Other women in her position would feel content to sit back and let the people who'd taken them prisoner do the work. But not Jacelyn. The city woman pulled her own weight.

He did notice that she favored her tender muscles and rubbed at her back some. But she never uttered a complaint. His mother would've like'd the . . . Damn. He spun toward the door. What the hell was getting into him lately?

"Hold up, handsome."

Grant turned to face Dora, who stood just inside the

kitchen. Her hair had come loose and hung in mussed strands around her shoulders. Her cheeks were flushed, her eyes slightly glazed. She looked like a woman who'd been thoroughly sated.

He darted a glance toward Jacelyn. Her expression of disgust caused him to choke on a stifled chuckle. *That* woman obviously had never experienced a good loving. His groin tightened as he mentally pictured himself introducing the naked Miss McCaffery to every glorious detail.

Dora shoved a blanket into Jacelyn's arms and scornfully eyed the dried dishes. "C'mon, Missy. Jones'n I'll take ya ta where yore gonna bunk a spell."

Jacelyn swallowed her retort at the sight of that look in the woman's eyes again, the one that said Dora didn't believe Jacelyn would be around long.

For the first time, Jacelyn began to wonder if she would leave this place alive. She'd held onto the hope that she *would* escape and find her way back to the fort and her brother.

She blinked. Her chin lifted. Her arms tightened about the rough, wool blanket. She had to think positive thoughts. After all, she'd found the courage to leave Richmond. Had made travel arrangements as far as Fort Huachuca. By golly, she would not give up now.

Jacelyn barreled past Dora, who had pulled a thread-bare robe tightly around her thin frame and started toward the door.

Grant hung back, reluctant to tag along with the ladies, and Jacelyn nearly laughed at the belligerent expression briefly exposed on his face when Dora grabbed his arm and forced him along.

"Don't be shy, Jones. Waddy says your s'posed ta keep watch over the Missy, here."

The outlaw gang was sprawled by the campfire handing around a jug when they passed. The Kid shifted around to see who was coming. At the new man's disgruntled countenance, he called, "What's the matter, Jones? You getting tired of playing nursemaid? Be glad to relieve you . . . for the night."

"An' I'll relieve the Kid." Pablo laughed, then immediately clutched his bruised chin. His eyes bored into Grant as he muttered unintelligible obscenities.

Jacelyn slowed her pace until she walked nearer to Grant. The blanket suddenly became a shield and Grant her haven of safety.

"Mind your business, you two," Dora ordered. "Reckon Jones here is man enough ta handle one slip of a girl."

Jacelyn frowned. No one gave her credit for being anything but a docile little mouse. Well, in a few short hours, she'd show them a thing or two. She'd show them all.

Grant scowled. Every passing moment saddled him more completely with the McCaffery woman. Damn it, he hadn't taken her to raise. Yet, because of Pablo, and especially the Kid, he would have to guard her carefully. And he didn't like the gleam in her eyes whenever she was pressured. Miss McCaffery had something on her mind, and the gnawing in his gut boded trouble.

Dora led them to a small shack set away from the rest of the buildings. She lifted a bar from the hooks on the door, swung it open and motioned Jacelyn inside. "This be your home fer a spell." She winked at Grant. "The maid ain't gotten 'round ta cleanin' fer the new *guest,* but reckon it'll do."

Jacelyn planted her feet outside and hesitantly leaned forward to peer inside.

"Go on. Ain't nuthin' gonna bite ya." Dora pushed Jacelyn inside and slammed the door shut.

Grant, on the outside; Jacelyn, on the inside; both flinched when the bar dropped into place.

Dora nodded toward the shack and told Grant, "Ain't

98

but one winder. Don't reckon ya'll have no trouble watchin' the place. Be coffee in the kitchen should ya hanker fer somethin' warm."

Grant nodded, then flicked the brim of his hat. "Thanks. I'll be all right." To prove he meant what he said, he sat on the edge of a large, flat rock and loosened the bandana choking his neck.

Dora stared at him for a long while, then shrugged. "Suit yourself."

Grant watched the older woman walk back toward her house, then stood and paced the outside perimeter of the small building. Dora had been right. There was only one window and it was a small one. Wide gaps separated a few of the boards, but they seemed to be nailed solid. Nothing much larger than a rat could slip through.

He grinned. Miss McCaffery might be conjuring escape plans, but thinking and planning would be the best she could do. Still, he settled himself on the hard ground and leaned back against the rock to keep a close watch.

Jacelyn stood where she'd stopped, propelled by Dora's shove, in the middle of the room. Her body trembled as she listened to someone move stealthily around the shack. She saw a shadow between the boards, then heard nothing. Only Grant Jones could move that quietly.

Her first breath actually hurt, she'd been holding it so long. There was just enough moonlight filtering into the room for her to make out a cot occupying the full length of the near wall, a table and one chair. And one window. Her heart soared. No glass. No canvas covering. A ray of hope warmed her body.

Placing the blanket on the cot, she ran to the window. It was high. And small. Really small. She dragged the chair over and stood atop it to peer outside. Calculating the window size as compared to her size, she wasn't certain she could fit.

And then she saw him. Settled casually against a boulder. Staring. At her. She gasped and nearly toppled from the chair when she stepped down. Leaning against the wall, she held her galloping heart beneath her hand. Curse words threatened to erupt.

Grant crossed his arms over his chest and stretched out his long legs, highly pleased with himself—and with Jacelyn McCaffery. He'd have been disappointed if she hadn't at least *tried* the window. Maybe now that she knew he was watching, she'd be a good little girl and settle down for the night.

But inside the shack, Jacelyn was searching every nook and cranny, trying to find any weakness, any possible avenue of escape. Over and over, she returned to the window.

Standing beside the table, she wiped a trickle of perspiration from her brow, then shivered when the chill of the evening breeze seeped into her heated body. All at once the remembered image of Grant's clean, wet form made her all the more aware of the granules of dirt gouging her skin. How she wished she'd brought some water from the well.

It was too late to worry about that now. But once the rogue outside dozed and she broke out of this filthy shack, she'd find her way back to Fort Huachuca and soak for twenty-four hours.

She walked over to the cot, pulled the blanket around her shoulders, yawned and sat down. She'd rest for a while and give Grant time to go to sleep. She blinked and rubbed her eyes. Yes, just a little rest and she'd be . . . good as . . .

A loud creak awakened Jacelyn. She sat up quickly. Her muscles protested the sudden stretch after hours of slumping in a cramped position. She groaned.

Sunlight poured through the open door, silhouetting a tall, slender male body. Grant Jones. She blinked to clear her blurred gaze and foggy brain.

She peered through one eye as he stepped forward and set something on the table. Without so much as a "Good morning," or even "Hello," he left, closing the door behind him. She waited, but didn't hear the bar drop.

Sighing, she got up, folded the blanket and replaced it neatly on the cot. So much for waiting until *Grant* went to sleep. She rubbed her eyes and stumbled to the table. Her mouth slowly curved into a genuine smile. Water. He'd brought her a pitcher of water and a tin basin. And a towel.

Her eyes raised heavenward. Unfastening the remainder of the buttons on her blouse, she struggled to free her arms, almost rending the material in her haste to peel it down to her waist. At last she dipped one end of the towel into the liquid. Warm. It was lukewarm, but warm nonetheless, she thought with a smile. Savoring the pleasure, she sponged her face, neck, and what skin she could wash around the lace trim on her silk camisole.

Water dripped from her chin, trickled down her neck and between her breasts. A delighted moan whispered through her parted lips.

Outside the door, Grant stifled his own moan, but his was a sound of frustrated agony rather than pleasure. The soft rustling of material, the sound of dripping water and then the low guttural feminine purrs of delight . . . His fists clenched. Damn.

Several hours later, after Grant had escorted Jacelyn to the main house and left her in Dora's rough but capable hands, he stood in the barn watching the big German shape a piece of hot iron into a horseshoe. So far, the only conversation had been between the rounded metal and the hammer.

At last the big man dipped the heated metal shoe into a barrel of water that spit and hissed, then set the shoe aside. His heavily muscled chest and arms glistened with sweat. Grant tried to think of some way to broach the subject of the Appaloosa, and gratefully smiled to himself when the thickly accented voice broke the silence first.

"You be here a while, ya?"

Grant nodded.

"Be good have help with animals."

"Pardon?"

"The boss say I find work for you." He gestured around the barn area. "There be plenty do. Ya, there is."

Grant's shoulders lifted and lowered on a silent sigh. He should've known the outlaws wouldn't trust him right away. Although he admitted to being disappointed, it would give him the chance he needed to poke around the ranch.

"Guess you noticed I rode that fancy spotted horse yesterday."

The German nodded. "Ya. Too bad about Barnes. He was goot man."

Grant kept his features immobile. "Yeah. Too bad." He leaned his forearms on the top rail of a stall. "Reckon where ole ... Barnes ... got a horse like that?"

The blacksmith snapped his head around and stared at Grant. Grant gave him an innocent expression and continued, "I'd give my next share of a payroll to have a horse like that 'tween my legs." He winked. "That animal rides better'n most women I've had."

The big man grinned and nodded his shaggy head enthusiastically. "Ya. Ya. That's a goot one, that is." He rubbed his square chin. "It must have gotten away from that young fella. But I just take care of it." He picked up the tongs and the horseshoe and hammered the outside rim, still smiling.

Grant flicked his fingers in a quick farewell and left the barn. He didn't want to ask too many questions at once. At least he'd learned two things: a young man, probably James McCaffery, had ridden the horse into the ranch; and one of the outlaws had wanted it.

So . . . had the young man really sold the horse? A horse that didn't belong to him? Grant didn't think so. He'd only been around the McCaffery boy a time or two, but he hadn't seemed to be a horse thief or a man who would go against his word. He'd promised to have the Colonel's horse back within a week. And that had been some time ago.

Grant mulled over this information as he walked back up to the main house. Something else bothered him.

Stepping onto the porch, he was greeted by a face full of dust. Behind the settling dirt he spied Jacelyn McCaffery wielding a broom. When she looked up and saw him, her eyes widened, then narrowed in what he would describe as a satisfied gleam. He coughed and the gleam intensified.

Before either could speak, Waddell shoved past Jacelyn, a saddlebag thrown over one shoulder, spurs jingling. "Jones, just the man I was lookin' fer."

Grant stepped back off the porch and hooked his thumb in his gunbelt. "Were you?"

"Yeah. Me an' the boys is goin' fer a ride. Want ya ta hang 'round an' help Dutch'n watch our little gal." He took out a plug, gnawed off a chunk, and eyed Grant speculatively as he worked the tobacco in his jaws. "Any objections?"

Grant couldn't believe his good luck. Had doubted the big German's account of Waddell's plans. Now

Waddell himself had as good as turned the place over to Grant to explore.

A movement of the broom shot a reminder to him faster than a cactus spine could prick soft flesh. He could explore ... as long as he kept the woman busy and out of his way.

Grant's eyes met Waddell's. "Objections? Should I have?"

Waddell stopped chewing, momentarily taken aback. "Naw, damn right ya shouldn't. I give the orders, ya know." He spat and hitched up his belt.

Grant nodded, then cocked his head, listening, as he said softly, "Right."

From behind Grant, the Kid chided, "You're a smart one all right, gunslinger."

Turning partially around, keeping both men in easy view, Grant affirmed, "Damn right."

The Kid frowned.

Waddell stepped off the porch. "Bob got the hosses saddled?"

"Yes, sir." The albino darted a grin toward Grant, as if saying Grant wasn't the only one who could court the boss's favor.

"Let's get movin' then." Waddell dropped the saddle bags from his shoulders. The bottom one dragged the ground as he headed toward the barn.

The Kid added another, "Yes, sir," for good measure and flicked Grant a cocky salute before following the outlaw leader.

Grant stared after him, then turned to find both Jacelyn and Dora standing on the porch. He tipped his hat to Dora. "Mornin', ma'am."

Dora smiled.

Jacelyn scowled. He hadn't spoken a word to *his* prisoner. But that was all right. She wanted him to keep his distance. Didn't she?

104

Grant tossed out a morsel of bait. "Hope your man has a safe journey, ma'am. Looks to be pretty short-handed."

Dora wrung her hands and sighed. "I told 'im the same thing my own self. Just this mornin'. But that Eloy . . . Don't know what's takin' 'im so long ta get the . . ." Suddenly she blinked and looked between Jacelyn and Grant. "Er, don't know why he's takin' so long."

Grant mentally cursed. She'd almost swallowed the hook. Almost. But he at least knew Eloy was expected back soon.

As the gang rode away from the ranch, Dora turned and went inside. Faced with the choice of following the older woman or standing outside, alone, with Grant, Jacelyn warded off a shiver as his eyes openly and arrogantly scanned up and down her body.

She realized there really was no choice. Inside, she suffered Dora's quiet stares and disapproving frown. Outside, she suffered this man's intimidation and disquieting interest. Tilting up her chin, she took a deep breath, swept her tattered rag of a skirt from her path and regally stalked back into the house.

Once inside and out of sight, she chided herself for her cowardice. As much as she didn't want to stay in Grant Jones's company, the open air was much less confining than the house. Especially after being locked in that disgusting cabin by the very woman she had to face now.

Using the hem of her skirt, Jacelyn dusted off the arm of a chair and a small end table near the fireplace on her way to the kitchen. Her steps quickened, though, when she sniffed the fragrant aroma of cinnamon and apples. Hmmmm . . . Apple pie. Her favorite.

Dora's back was to Jacelyn as she entered the room. On the counter, behind a flour sack, a small knife handle protruded. Jacelyn stared at the carved wood. Her fingers actually ached when she flexed them.

Quickly, before she could talk herself out of taking the risk, she sidled over to the counter and reached out her hand.

"That you, Missy?"

Jacelyn snatched her hand back. "Ah, y-yes."

"Hand me that towel. I dropped a piece o' apple an' it's sticky as hell."

Nibbling her lower lip, Jacelyn darted her eyes between the knife and Dora. The woman knelt on the floor now, her back still turned.

"Ah, sure. I'll get it for you." Again, she stretched out her arm. Her fingers closed over the handle. Her hand shook until she secreted the weapon in the one pocket in her skirt without a hole in the bottom.

With her free hand she grabbed the towel and walked up behind Dora, who picked at tiny bits of fruit wedged in a narrow crack between the boards. Her fingers clenched around the knife. She gazed longingly out the back door.

The gang was gone. Grant had disappeared. Only one threat stood between herself and freedom. Dora.

Chapter Seven

Jacelyn stared at Dora's narrow back, and watched the woman's shoulders lift and fall as she worked, oblivious of the threat behind her.

The tendons in Jacelyn's wrist contracted. Her fingers painfully gripping the knife, she closed her eyes and started to lift her hand from her skirt. Her heart thudded against her breast.

"Ya gonna give me that towel, or ain'tcha?"

Jacelyn blinked her eyes open. Dora stood in front of her, holding out her hand. Whatever thoughts Jacelyn entertained about using the knife evaporated faster than steam from boiling water.

The towel was clinched too tightly in her other hand. Her knuckles ached when Dora forced her to release it. With trembling knees, she sank into the nearest chair, instinctively repositioning the knife so it wouldn't cut into either her skirt or her leg.

Instead of resuming her cleaning, Dora wiped her hands on the towel, then twisted her fingers into the soft material. "Want ta thank ya."

Jacelyn cocked her head. "What?"

"Ahem . . . Thank ya."

Straightening in the chair, Jacelyn drew her brows together as she looked directly into Dora's eyes. "But . . . the towel was right there . . ."

"Naw, that ain't what I'm talkin' 'bout," Dora grumbled. She made a sweeping gesture encompassing the kitchen and the door leading to the living area. "Ya cleaned things up right nice. An' ya didn't have ta."

Speechless, Jacelyn leaned back in her chair. No, she didn't have to. But she needed something to take her mind off being a captive and to keep from counting the minutes of boredom.

Dora turned back to the stove. "Anyways, I 'preciate what ya done."

Faced once again with Dora's slender back, Jacelyn's stomach churned with nausea. She couldn't harm the woman now. Probably couldn't have done it *ever.* She'd gotten this far bluffing her way through her fear. Watching Dora—a hard, proud woman—swallow her pride, touched a familiar chord in Jacelyn.

She took a deep breath and stood. The knife nearly dropped from her cramped fingers as she backed toward the door. "Ah, I need . . . to go . . ."

Dora scraped at the floor and mumbled, "There be a privy near where ya bunk."

"Y-yes, I know." She nearly tripped over her own feet as she fled the house. Once outside, she stopped and breathed deep droughts of piñon and sage scented air. Looking into the blue, blue sky and then around at the rocky bluffs and green-fringed trees, she allowed the pristine beauty and silence of the place to begin to free her bound-up nerves.

Surprised and grateful for the spreading feeling of peace, she leaned against the porch rail and covered her pounding heart with her free hand. Several minutes passed before her breathing returned to normal and she could loosen her grip on the knife.

The knife. What had she come to, to almost use the

weapon against Dora? Just the thought alone was frightening, but she consoled herself by recalling her unusual circumstances. She had reacted—

A sudden movement near the barn diverted her attention. Her gaze focused on the black-clad figure of her tall, dark guardian. Only, for once, he wasn't looking in her direction. His head tilted to one side, as if he were listening for something. Then he moved, slowly, cautiously, away from the barn toward a dense thicket of oak.

Upon reaching the trees, he hesitated and turned. She ducked her head and hurried toward the cabin where she'd been imprisoned. The knife handle seared her palm as she strode rapidly, hoping to secrete away the weapon before her theft was discovered.

A hand clasped her shoulder. She gasped. Spinning around, she was shocked to find that Grant had so quickly and soundlessly pursued her. He stood before her now, a characteristically unreadable expression emblazoned on his features.

She could hardly catch her breath, but her captor wasn't breathing heavily at all.

Grant studied the furrow between Jacelyn's brows and the furtive way she looked toward the cabin where she'd spent the night. "What's your hurry, lady?"

"I-I ... ah ... I'm on my way ... er, have to ..." She finally swallowed and pointed toward the small outhouse several yards away.

Grant squinted one eye as he regarded her. Suddenly he lifted his chin and cocked his head. He'd heard it again. A soft whistle from the trees behind the barn.

Jacelyn glanced in that direction, relieved that something had distracted him. "What's that?"

"Nothing."

"But—"

"A whippoorwill. Just a whippoorwill."

Her face felt like it would crack when she tried to smile. "Oh, I've heard of them. It sounds like they say their own names over and over and over again, doesn't it?" She gulped. Her sweating palm gripped the knife handle so tightly her fingers felt numb.

Grant nodded.

She dug the toe of her shoe into the dust while flexing her fingers. She had to get on about her business. She glanced repeatedly toward the privy. "Well, I guess—"

"Go on," he impatiently commanded. "Just don't stray from the buildings." He narrowed both eyes and warned, "It's dangerous out there."

She raised her chin. "You don't need to threaten me. If you recall, I've experienced the *savagery* of the West and its inhabitants firsthand."

He just stared at her. She exhaled in a huff and spun to leave.

"You haven't seen *savage* yet, lady."

The hair along the nape of her neck stood on end. But she refused to give him the satisfaction of thinking he'd frightened her. Without breaking her stride, she walked toward the privy. Her steps slowed as she passed her cabin and the only window. She glanced from side to side to see if she was truly alone.

Yes. Once again, Grant had disappeared into thin air.

She stopped. The window was almost four feet from the ground and very narrow, but . . . she was fairly thin and there was a good chance she could slip through. Hmmmm. If she could just remove that board at the bottom of the sill . . .

She glanced furtively over her shoulder. No one seemed to be watching. And fortunately, the shack was situated between the privy and the main house.

Returning her attention to the window, she reached up and jerked the board. It felt loose. Her breath hissed from her lips as she smiled and stepped forward to plaster herself against the wall. Hugging her back to the weathered planks, she worked her way to the corner and peeked cautiously around.

A loud hammering came from the barn. Dora was busy hanging wet clothing out to dry. Still no sign of Grant.

Hope crawled up her quivering stomach and aching chest to lodge in her throat. She quickly returned to the window, took the knife from her pocket and pried the blade beneath the board. A small amount of effort was all she expended, but the board creaked loudly as it popped loose and fell to the ground.

She held her breath and listened for several seconds. Nothing.

Hastily she slipped her hand inside the window. Holding the knife against the wall, she released it so it fell only a short distance to the floor.

Tucking loose strands of hair behind her ear, she hurried on to the privy.

Grant carefully threaded his way through a thick copse of Toumey oak. He often stopped and listened. Then, satisfied he wasn't being followed, he continued toward the sound of the whippoorwill.

His thoughts vacillated between his coming meeting and Jacelyn McCaffery. Leaving her a moment ago had been hard. He'd sensed her nervousness and figured she had to be up to something. The illumination in her extraordinary eyes seemed more like determination than desperation, so he wasn't worried she would do anything foolish—yet.

As he climbed upwards, waist-high manzanita blocked his way, forcing him to circle the thicket. Another whippoorwill called from behind a tower of buff-colored pillars. He stepped over clumps of beargrass and around an agave before reaching the rocks.

Finally entering a small cleared area shaded by eerie rock formations, he untied his bandana and took off his hat to wipe sweat from the band.

Sensing he wasn't alone, he looked up to see a short, heavily muscled Apache at the edge of the clearing. The Indian wore blousey cotton trousers, knee-high moccasins, and two gunbelts criss-crossed over his huge, bare chest. A dirty red bandana tied around his forehead held long, dark hair out of his black, glinting eyes.

"Hola, my friend. What took you so long?"

Grant sat on a flat-topped boulder and stretched his aching feet out before him. He glanced at the Apache and shook his head.

The Indian grunted. "White man boots. No wonder you make more noise than two bears fighting."

Grant scowled. No matter how hurtful the comment was to his pride, he couldn't argue the point. He eyed his friend's comfortable moccasins with envy. "Santana exaggerates, as usual. Since it has been many days since we were last together, I will let you get away with it—this time."

"No good to fight with blistered feet, no?" Santana grinned.

"No." Grant returned the grin, then sobered and narrowed his eyes. "I'm on to somethin'. The Colonel's Appaloosa's at the ranch, without the man who rode it from the fort."

Santana nodded once. "What of men we seek? Flat Nose return to Thunder Fort with two holes in leg."

"He was shot?" Grant questioned. Santana nodded and Grant cursed. Flat Nose was one of his best scouts. At the rate the whites attacked his men, soon there would be none left.

Grant met his friend's eyes. "You know who did it?"

"Miners."

"Figures." Grant rubbed the back of his neck. "I found the body of a miner two days ago." His lips whitened with rage as he added, "He'd been scalped."

Santana crossed his arms and waited for Grant to continue.

"I was close, damn it. I know it." He waved his arm in the direction of the ranch. "And then a woman came along . . . I couldn't just go off and leave her."

The Apache stood silent.

"Colonel Alexander asked for my help," Grant tried to explain, though he knew Santana understood he wouldn't delay his mission unless something came up of equal importance.

The Indian lowered himself to squat on his haunches.

Grant picked up a twig and crushed the tip through the dust. "I planned to be gone from here by now, until I saw the horse."

"You think there is connection between miner and these men?"

Grant raised the twig and chewed on the clean end. What about those tracks and the horseshoe? They hadn't been so old. And then the holdup . . . He shook his head. That was something he'd have to think over later. "Tell the scouts to watch their backs more carefully. We've got to try harder to stop the renegades and put an end to this slaughter."

The Apache sighed. "We grateful for this job. Warriors with no battle only old helpless women on reservation."

Grant gazed at his friend with heartfelt compassion. The renegade Apaches would be rounded up eventually. What would his scouts do then? It was another thing he would have to think about later.

"We follow Two Faces trail?"

Grant grinned at Santana's use of his Apache name.

He was a man of Two Faces. One red. One white. And sometimes he felt he had no allegiance to either. He was a man alone. A man who looked after only himself— and maybe a few friends.

"No, don't worry about watchin' my back. I can handle things here. It's more important to concentrate on stopping the killings whenever the Colonel doesn't have other orders for you."

The Apache shrugged.

Grant walked to the end of the pillar. Below he saw the swish of a brown skirt as Jacelyn McCaffery turned the corner of the one-room cabin. He frowned. What was she doing? She should've been back to the main house by now.

He turned to the scout. "I've got to get back. Don't mention the Colonel's Appaloosa just yet. I don't have answers for the questions he's bound to ask."

Santana grinned. "The Colonel is man of *many* questions."

Grant raised one eyebrow. "You could say that."

The Apache lifted his hand in farewell. "Three sunrises. I be back."

Grant nodded and made his way down the hill. He looked across from the rocky-chapparal-covered ground and frowned at a familiar movement near the out buildings. Damn the woman's hide. She'd test the patience of a saint.

She'd better not cause more trouble, he grumbled to himself. One day he might not be around to fish her out of the frying pan.

Jacelyn carefully replaced the board, dusted her hands, and stood back to admire her handiwork. If she didn't know the board had been removed and the nail

114

holes widened for easy slip off, she never would have noticed any difference.

She'd even shoved the table over to the wall beneath the window and crawled through the opening just to make sure she could do it. Getting out had been awkward, and she'd almost landed on her head, but she'd done it with only a few minor scrapes and scratches and another rip or two in her petticoats and skirt.

A smile curved her lips when Grant rounded the corner. But the thunderous expression on his face widened her eyes.

"What are you doing?" he roared.

She calmly crossed her arms under her breasts. "Nothing." Inside, though, her stomach was a mass of fluttering butterflies. He couldn't know what she'd been doing. Could he?

He hesitated, then blustered, "I don't believe you."

She frowned. Tapping the tip of her index finger on her chin, she bluffed, "Have I ever lied to you?"

"You've never had the chance." He scanned the cabin and the surrounding trees. Nothing seemed out of place. Still, he had a feeling . . . "So, what were you doin'?"

"Well . . . I had to . . ." She nodded toward the privy. "You know." Heat flooded her cheeks. She hoped the blush would be enough to convince him.

Grant studied the woman intently, watched the pink color stain her cheeks. But there was something in her eyes. Something that sent a bothersome prickle along his scalp. Dust coated her shoulder. A droplet of blood indicated a prick on her cheek.

Untying his bandana, he closed the distance between them. She tried to shrink away, but he grabbed her arm and held her in place while he blotted the speck of blood. "Hold still, damn it."

"Don't curse at me." She tugged on her arm. He refused to release her. "Unhand me this instant," she ordered imperiously, though her stern voice cracked.

Grant noted her waver and retained his grip and the pressure on the cut. "Do as I say."

"I will not. You have no right—"

"You're bleeding."

She blinked. Resistance seeped from her taut body like thick molasses dripping from a jug. "Oh."

"How'd you cut your face?"

"I . . . don't know." She looked into his eyes and noticed for the first time the incredible length of his long, thick black lashes. With his lids half closed as he peered down at her, he appeared quite . . . well . . . sexy.

Grant frowned as another rush of color tinted her cheeks. Even her nose turned pink. What in the hell was she thinking now? Damned woman. She had to be the most . . . He focused on her full, pouty lower lip, then his gaze traveled over her smooth, ivory complexion and into her deep, deep navy eyes. She had to be the most . . . desirable woman he'd ever seen.

"You should be more . . . careful." He quickly took away the bandana and retied it around his neck. He needed to get as far away from her as possible before he did something really stupid.

Jacelyn found it much easier to breathe once he put space between them. She couldn't help darting questioning glances at his profile, though. She was amazed by her body's heated reaction to his casual touch.

She attempted to calm her fluttering senses by rationalizing that he'd only ministered to her cut. The quick leap of her pulse and her quaking knees were senseless. For heaven's sake, the man was a vicious outlaw, not a drawing room gentleman coming to pay his respects. Why, if he wanted, he could throw her down on the hard ground and . . .

She blinked away visions of those blue eyes slitted as

his mobile lips moved closer and closer to her half naked body, of his corded muscles rippling beneath her fingers as she . . .

Drat! What was she thinking? Was she disappointed that he hadn't ravished her?

Grant watched in stunned amazement as the color of her eyes turned a warm, liquid lavender. Her mouth parted slightly, and her tongue slowly, wetly glided over that inviting bottom lip. He winced and stifled a groan, then shifted his lower body to ease the sudden tightness of his trousers. Why was she looking at him like . . . like . . . a cat who'd spied a floundering trout?

He took a step forward.

Jacelyn backed up, realizing she might have unwittingly invited his advance. "I-I better go back now." She barely finished speaking before she turned and, lifting the longer, tattered pieces of her skirt out of her way, ran toward the house.

Grant pushed his hat forward and scratched the back of his head. Damn. The woman was a constant surprise.

Jacelyn rushed through the back door and into the kitchen as if a pack of wolves nipped at her heels. The room was empty, thank the Lord. Her hand trembled as she pushed a lock of hair from her eyes, then pulled her gaping bodice together.

Her neck and cheeks burned from her embarrassment. What must the man think of her? She'd ogled him in almost the same manner that the Kid and the odious Pablo leered at her. The difference was, Grant had appeared to enjoy it. Ohhhh.

Her lips thinned. With his looks, he was probably used to women staring. What woman *wouldn't* look at a man like him and imagine those long fingers on her skin or . . . She cleared her throat, pumped water into her palm and splashed it on her neck, shivering as the cool liquid trickled down her chest and between her breasts.

"There ya be. I wondered what was takin' ya so long."

Jacelyn jumped and quickly wiped droplets of water from the exposed flesh she could reach. "I-I . . ."

"Don't matter," Dora gruffly continued. "I thought ya might use these." She laid several neatly folded items on the counter.

Jacelyn eyed Dora warily. She didn't know what to think of the woman's sudden turnabout. The rough, complaining woman seemed almost . . . friendly. Jacelyn glanced toward the things. "For me?"

When Dora nodded, but didn't meet her eyes, Jacelyn asked, "Wh-what are they?"

Dora scowled. "Aw, fer Gawd's sake. Ya got eyes. Take a look see."

Jacelyn's curiosity prodded her to take one step, then another. She reached out, then pulled her hand back as if she expected something to jump out and bite her.

Dora turned and left the kitchen, shaking her head as she went.

Feeling slightly foolish, Jacelyn lifted her chin and picked up the top item, a worn flannel shirt. With all of the buttons sewn tightly in place. Soft. Faded. Clean. She shook out the next article. Trousers. Again, the material was worn thin, but they were spotless.

Jacelyn held the clothes up. Though Dora was a small woman, it appeared they wore close to the same size. Her lips twitched. Trousers. She'd never worn anything like them. Uncle Jonathan would have thrown a fit. Did she dare? Her eyes glittered with mischief as a big smile curved her lips.

Glancing down at what was left of her dress, she asked herself if she dared *not* to wear Dora's offerings. She gazed out the window and shuddered. No wonder

118

the outlaws looked at her so . . . so . . . knowingly, as if she had little to hide.

Clutching the garments to her breast, she hurried from the house. Excitement rushed her steps to the cabin. Just think, the prim and proper Jacelyn Faith McCaffery would soon be dressed like a desperado.

She smiled again as she stepped into the small shack and closed the door behind her.

Half an hour later, Jacelyn timidly peered around the door jamb. Seeing no one about, she walked awkwardly into the clearing, swinging her hips stiffly from side to side. The dratted trousers fit all right, so tightly that she couldn't bend her knees. And she was afraid to take a deep breath for fear of popping the buttons or splitting a seam on the shirt.

With each step she took, however, she moved more easily and marveled at the feeling of freedom the men's clothing allowed. No constricting corsets. No heavy petticoats to drag about. It was heavenly.

The only problem she had now were the soft slippers she'd worn while traveling. Holes had already been worn into the soles beneath the balls of her feet. The stitching had broken on one toe, and she scooped sand with every step. She might as well go barefoot.

After scanning the area carefully, she leaned one palm against a nearby tree and used the other hand to remove the kid slippers. She took a step and giggled when green grass squished beneath her tread. Another step and sand oozed between her toes. She laughed. She'd been the only girl at finishing school who'd never gone barefoot but, even then, she'd been afraid to go against her parents' wishes.

She twirled in delight, but stumbled when she stepped on a sticker. The pain was short-lived, however, and she hummed and twirled again, shoes in one hand, her other arm moving like a graceful ballerina.

Grant chose that moment to leave the barn. Turning the south corner, he faced the direction of the cabin. He stopped abruptly at the sight before his eyes. Dora, spinning and singing ... No, not Dora. This person was more voluptuous, had red-gold hair. *Jacelyn Mc-Caffery*—displaying every curve she possessed to full advantage.

He stiffened. His manhood quickened. He licked his lips and walked toward her as if in a trance. But the closer he went, the more effort he expended to control his raging emotions. His eyes narrowed. He yelled, "Damn it, what in the hell do you think you're doing?"

Startled by the loud shout, Jacelyn tripped and dropped her shoes. Her heel landed on another sticker and she yelped with pain.

Grant rushed over, brushed her fumbling hands aside and knelt to take a look. One hand encircled her ankle to hold her foot still. He plucked the goat head from the tender flesh with the other. Very gently he ran his fingers along her delicately arched instep, across the soft ball of her foot to her small, perfect toes. Funny, he'd never noticed that a woman's foot could be so finely shaped ... so beautiful ... and so arousing.

Her ankle was fragile and keenly structured. If he squeezed too hard, it might shatter in his hand.

The sensations coursing up Jacelyn's calf liquified her entire body. She clutched at Grant's shoulders to keep from melting into a bubbling pool at his feet. His fingers traced her arch. She jerked her leg from his grasp.

Grant looked up. Her navy eyes turned that strange shimmering shade of lavender again. "You're ... ahem ... you're ticklish."

Her lips must have moved, though she didn't hear a sound. She thought she nodded, but was too absorbed by the man's unusual blue eyes and those long, long, curling lashes. What woman wouldn't love to have lashes that beautiful, that sensuous.

"Mr. J-Jones . . ."

Grant's eyes never flickered. Even dressed as a man she was adorable, desirable . . .

"Mr. Jones, you mustn't . . ."

She leaned nearer. He reached over and slid his fingers into the thick mass of hair coiled at her nape. Pins scattered in every direction. Red tresses tumbled over her shoulders like a waterfall at dawn.

"Oh," she gasped. "Look what you've done. I'll never be able to find them all." Her breath came in short rasps. No man had ever touched her hair like Grant Jones. His fingers on her scalp felt so good. But she had to find those pins or she would never be able to control her unruly locks. "Please—"

"Leave it." He couldn't take his eyes from the long silky hair and the shorter wisps curling around her ears. Good God, he'd never seen hair so thick; it clung like a frilly cape to her shoulders. "Your hair is much prettier like this. Why wear it like an old maid?"

Jacelyn touched her hair. Pretty? Uncle Jonathan had always said she looked like a heathen when her hair hung loose. And her mother had told her a *lady* never went out in public . . . "Do you *really* think it's pretty?"

Grant leaned back to look into her face. Her voice was soft and tentative, like that of a child seeking reassurance and approval. How could she not know how alluring and gorgeous she looked? "Yes," he said gruffly, "it is very pretty."

Her lips slowly curved into an angelic smile. Grant's manhood throbbed against the tight fit of his trousers.

"No one's ever told me that before."

Grant's eyes widened.

Jacelyn clamped a hand over her mouth. She hadn't

121

meant to say that out loud. Now he'd think she was fishing for compliments, or something.

"No one?" She had to be kidding, Grant thought. A woman that beautiful, and no one . . . What was wrong with the men back East?

"Well, no one that wasn't after my inher . . . ahem, that looked at me the way you just did." Oops. She'd almost slipped and mentioned her family's wealth. Yet, perhaps, if she said something about the money, it would buy her more time, in case she wasn't able to escape.

She shook her head. No. She would not think negatively. She would get away—tonight.

Grant compressed his lips. Damn it, since when had he displayed his emotions on his shirt sleeve? She hadn't seen his desire. She was guessing. If she had run up against wolves before, why pretend to be so innocent and naive?

He uncurled his fingers from her hair. She was just a woman who was more trouble than she was worth. Already he paid her too much attention and expended too little on finding out about the Colonel's horse and discovering the means to get her safely away.

Suddenly he cocked his head and immediately put more distance between them.

"There ya be. Fer a minute, I thought ya might've gone an' done sumpthin' foolish."

Jacelyn spun to face Dora. "F-foolish?" She thought about her unladylike reaction to Grant Jones. Foolish was a mild term compared to her actual feelings. Her knees trembled and she felt quite unsteady without his strong body for support.

Dora nodded toward the corner of the cabin.

Jacelyn shifted her gaze and spied the big German leaning against the wall with a rifle nestled in the crook of his arm. She shot a glance at Grant, but he showed no sign of embarrassment or surprise. He must have heard them coming and that was why he moved away so quickly.

"Don't get any fool notions in yore head, Missy." Dora tilted her head toward Grant. "You neither, handsome. Waddy wouldn't like it none, were ya ta think 'bout leavin' without sayin' adiós."

Grant chuckled.

Dora winked.

Jacelyn frowned. She was being watched by *everyone,* and not just Grant. It meant she needed to be even more cautious when she did make her escape.

"C'mon ta the house. Reckon it's time ta dirty up some o' them clean plates."

A sudden gust of wind rustled the leaves on the trees and swirled dust at their feet. With her eyes still on Dutch, Jacelyn noticed a movement a few feet to the right of the big man's shoulder.

The board at the base of the window jiggled. She sucked in her breath. Evidently she hadn't replaced it as tightly as she thought. Her heart jumped into her throat. She looked frantically around the assembled group. Had she already been found out?

Chapter Eight

Grant, Dora, and Dutch had their eyes trained on a rider approaching the barn. Jacelyn released a silent breath. She'd never have thought it possible, but she was actually glad to see the rat-faced Eloy. Because of his timely arrival, she could continue with her plans.

To make sure their attention remained on Eloy, she started forward and kept a close watch to see that they didn't look back. The wind gusted more forcefully. Her own eyes darted back and forth between the barn and the cabin.

Drat. The big German trailed in behind her. She stifled a curse and forced herself to look straight ahead. All she could do at the moment was trust to God and luck that the board didn't blow off and reveal her deception.

But Grant Ward nodded slightly. He'd seen the sudden fear darkening her eyes. Had followed her eyes when they darted to the window. Noticed the slight movement of the bottom board.

His chest expanded, then deflated as he sighed. He'd known she was up to no good. Now all he had to do was wait and see what her fertile mind had concocted. He was almost proud of the spitfire's gumption. But she sure wreaked havoc with *his* life.

By the time the group reached Eloy, the little man had dismounted and untied the rope lashed around the supplies packed on a mutinous mule who cocked its near hind hoof dangerously close.

As the bags fell to the ground, Eloy gave a swift kick to the animal's flank, then howled in pain when the mule's hoof struck his shin. He reached for his gun, but found his wrist locked in a viselike grip. He looked around and glared at the dark man towering dangerously over him.

"Wouldn't do that, mister. Good mules are hard to find." Grant thought of the trouble Evan had finding enough mules to go around at the fort. But he also admitted to deriving a good deal of satisfaction in thwarting the Mexican.

"How would *you* know, amigo? You have a fondness for these mules?" Eloy's cruel lips lifted in a sneer.

Dora shoved between the two men. "Here now, boys. Eloy, ya know damn well Jones is right. Waddy was jest sayin' the other day how we'uns needed another pack animal. Ain't no need ta get rid o' the only one we got."

Eloy grumbled, but handed the lead rope to Dutch. Dora spread her hands on her hips and eyed the little man intently. "What'd ya find out in Tombstone?"

Eloy looked at Jacelyn and his eyes narrowed in a blatant leer. "Thee Army, they search everywhere for thee señorita. She muy importante."

Dora nodded. "Good. Good. Waddy'll be proud ta hear that. Anythin' else?"

The outlaw rubbed his stubbled chin and winked at Jacelyn. "They say she looking for a man." Eloy's evil gaze shifted to Grant.

Dora turned on Jacelyn. "That right? Ya lookin' fer some'un?"

Jacelyn glared from one curious face to another. Only Grant's held no expression at all. Hot as it was, she rubbed her hands up and down her arms as if chilled. What should she do? Her first instinct was to lie, but what harm could it do to tell the truth? Who knew if some of them had seen James?

"I-I came to Arizona to find my brother." She paused to take a breath. They all continued to stare. "He's employed by the Army . . . making maps."

The German had taken the mule into the barn, but Grant watched both Eloy and Dora closely. He thought he saw a flicker in Eloy's eyes, but Dora's expression never changed.

"That why ya was on that stage? Ya huntin' your brother way out here?"

Jacelyn nodded. "The Colonel at Fort Huachuca thought someone in Tucson might've seen him."

Dora shrugged as if she'd lost interest in the subject. She asked Eloy, "Did ya do what Waddy told ya if'n they be searchin' fer the gal?"

Eloy nodded, his eyes never leaving Jacelyn.

"Good." Dora looked at Jacelyn as if seeing her for the first time in her hand-me-down clothes. She grinned, turned toward the house, then hesitated. "Reckon all we gotta do now is wait."

Jacelyn scowled and made a rude face at Eloy after his back was turned. She "reckon'd" all she had to do now was hurry up and get out of there.

Jacelyn sat on the end of the cot with the blanket wrapped around her shoulders. Tonight she was determined to stay awake. It could be her only chance to get away when she didn't have to contend with the entire gang.

Her worst problem was the wide-eyed Mr. Jones, reclining in his usual place, watching the window. It had to be well past midnight, but he was still awake. The last time she'd peered through the window, he'd had the audacity to wave. Oooohh! He would ruin everything. The later it got, the less time she'd have to put distance between herself and the ranch and the outlaws.

She rubbed her hands together. Wait until Colonel Alexander learned about Mr. Grant Jones and his double life. The next time the rogue dared to show his face at the fort, he'd be arrested and prosecuted for the common criminal he was.

If only she could be there to see it. But by then, she'd have found James and be well on her way back to Richmond. Oh well, from what she'd seen of *Harper's Weekly,* the magazine would probably give a good account of the event sooner or later.

Sighing, she rose and tiptoed to the window. She carefully placed her foot on the rickety chair and eased her weight onto that leg, lifting her body just enough to peek outside. Her heart fluttered erratically. The blanket slid from her shoulders to the floor. At last. His eyes were closed. His chest rose and fell with deep, even breaths. It was now or never.

Slowly, precisely, she took hold of the loose board. Thank heavens it hadn't come completely free and given her away. A nail scraped the wood. Her hand began to shake. Never taking her eyes off Grant's blessedly still form, she breathed deeply until her nerves calmed.

To her relief, the nails came the rest of the way out without making more noise. She debated replacing the board after she was on the other side with the hope of confusing her pursuers, but that would probably be pressing her luck.

She dropped it down with the blanket, dusted her hands and turned to her task. How was she going to crawl through the window without waking the watch dog? At least Dora's clothing would make it a little easier. The first time she'd experimented with the escape, she'd caught her skirt and petticoats on every jagged sliver of wood.

All right, she persuaded herself. *Get on with it.*

Her left leg slipped through easily. The right was harder because she had to hold herself upright with her hands and balance on her bottom. Next she twisted around, but her foot flew out and kicked the plank siding. She froze, wondering if Grant Jones had heard her.

Suddenly, her toes slid several inches down the outside wall. She frantically hooked her arms on the sill, stopping herself. But now the crude wooden sill dug into her stomach, making it hard to breathe. In this position, with only her legs and bottom sticking out, all she could see was the warped cabin floor. She prayed Grant hadn't been awakened by her clumsy efforts. She also prayed her big toe wasn't broken. It hurt like . . . the devil.

Listening for any indication she'd been spotted, she held her breath. Continued silence assured her to go ahead and try to get out. Humping up her rear end, she scooted backward, balancing on her hands and upper torso and bracing her lower body with her throbbing toes.

As quietly as possible, she literally walked down the siding. Her arm muscles burned from the pressure against the boards and she knew her skin would be bruised.

At last, she hung by her hands, mere inches from the ground.

Before she let go, she turned her head until her nose nearly smashed into the wall. Her heart sputtered and thrummed rapidly against her breast. Finally, arching her back, she looked to where Grant had been lying. When she saw he still slept, she released her hold on the sill and dropped the rest of the way to the ground.

Luckily she'd had the foresight to scrape away the dead leaves and grass that had piled up. Only because of the racket they'd made the first time she fell out of the window, she reminded herself.

Taking a last look at the sleeping rogue, and a very deep breath, she eased around the cabin until she turned the back corner. There she leaned back and let her heart settle as she scanned the dark shadows.

That morning she'd tried to pick out a sort of path to follow, but tonight she couldn't see anything that would help her find her way. Jacelyn gazed into the star-studded sky and pushed away from the cabin. Nearing the line of trees, she glanced back at the darkened buildings. A feeling of euphoria filled her being.

She'd done it. She'd really escaped. And all by herself.

Grant rose from his reclining position and held his arms across his stomach. Lord, but his ribs hurt. It had been all he could do to keep from bursting out laughing when the prim Miss McCaffery's derriere had hung so tantalizingly out the window.

He'd been sorely tempted to get up then and there and give her a damned good spanking. But, he decided to wait and see just how far she would go with her hare-brained scheme.

Easing up to the back corner of the cabin, he heard her deep sigh. He waited, listening to her footsteps as she started off toward the trees. At least she'd had sense enough to put her shoes back on, though what good the split scraps of leather would do, he didn't know.

He peered around the corner and watched until he could no longer see her shadow, then stepped out and began to follow. He didn't have to get close, he could discern her direction from the crunch of gravel, snaps of twigs, and muttered oaths.

He grinned. The little lady was learning Western dialect very quickly. He even thought he detected a few of Eloy's favorite phrases, though she couldn't possibly know their English translation—he didn't think.

Now and then she'd stop and Grant assumed she picked up a cache of food or water, but she always went on empty handed. When she started climbing a chaparral-covered hill, he stopped and scratched his head. Why didn't she keep to low ground and follow the valley? This way would just take her deeper into the mountains. Eventually, she might reach Fort Bowie, but it would take days, maybe even a week longer.

The farther he followed, the sooner he gave up trying to think ahead of her. Nothing she did made any sense. In fact, several times she'd walked in circles. Sure, it was dark and the going rough, but this was ridiculous.

Ridiculous! The whole plan was ridiculous, Jacelyn thought. She'd been walking for hours and was dying for a drink. Why hadn't she thought to bring a jug of water? Or even some of Dora's day old biscuits? By sun-up, she'd need something in her stomach. She'd even forgotten to bring the knife she'd stolen and hidden under a loose board beneath the window in her cabin.

She stepped on a sharp rock and bit her lip to keep from crying out. This one cut right through the soft leather sole. And she'd scooped up so much sand into her other shoe that it was heavy to lift. The granules dug into her foot, but she'd emptied the shoe so often she was afraid it cost her too much time.

If she was miserable now, how would she manage to stand it for a day and a half, or even two more days?

That was about how long it had taken the gang to get from the road to the ranch.

Reaching a thicket of waist-high bushes so thick she couldn't walk through, she tried to find a way around. They ended soon enough, but against a rock cliff.

Something slithered along the ground close to her feet. She jumped and closed her eyes, waiting for she didn't know what, but all she heard after that was the rustle of the breeze.

Jacelyn leaned against the sheer face of rock and wiped perspiration from her face and neck. Chill bumps soon dotted her flesh. She began to understand why Grant and most of the men out West wore a bandana and wished she had one with her now.

A coyote yipped nearby and she plastered herself against the rock. Though the moon had risen, it was only a sliver in the black sky and she could barely see three feet ahead of her.

All at once she began to wonder if she would ever find her way out of this horrid desert. What if she just wandered and wandered until those huge black birds with the ugly red heads she'd read about in *Harper's Weekly* decided to swoop down and pick at her flesh and bones?

Fear shuddered through her body. She choked on a sob as she wrapped her arms around her waist. She'd been so certain she could make her way back to the fort. Sniffing, she lifted her chin. She'd escaped the ranch, hadn't she? She'd made it this far. Giving up wasn't an option—yet.

So, taking a deep breath, she pushed away from the rock formation. Perhaps she could go back along the bushes and try to find a way around the other end.

As she started walking, she noticed the sky began to lighten. Dawn fast approached. Too fast. She had no idea how far she was from the ranch, but was afraid it wasn't nearly far enough.

Suddenly she bumped into a solid object she knew hadn't been there before. The shadowy form loomed above her. Terror gripped her, terror far beyond the fear she'd felt earlier. Her mouth opened, but before she could scream, a hard palm pressed her lips into her teeth. An arm encircled her waist like a band of steel.

"Make one sound and I'll let the bears have you for breakfast."

She immediately recognized Grant Jones's deep, raspy voice as his warm breath tickled her ear. A shudder racked her body, either from fright or relief, and she couldn't say which at the moment.

"B-bears?" She sagged against him. Grant. Thank the Lord. She hiccuped and twisted, throwing her arms around his neck. Whimpering like a baby, she realized the man had saved her life—again.

But the wilderness hadn't bested her. Not really. And he had come searching for her, outlaw or not. Deep down he had to have a kind soul.

Grant, surprised that she clung to him rather than fighting off his touch, slowly wrapped his arms around her and held her so close she could've been his second skin.

His hands soothed her trembling body as he tried to fold her inside himself. She was so fragile, so sweet, so . . . womanly. Her breasts cushioned his chest softer than down pillows. Her thighs cupped his manhood as if she'd been made to fit . . .

Thinking became difficult. A raging attack of tenderness charged through him. His chest expanded until he could hardly take a breath. Damn. The last thing he'd ever expected was to feel so strongly for a woman, a very white, very city-bred woman.

A deep sadness chilled his heart. Why had fate determined to place such a lady in his path? Someone he could never hope to have once she discovered his dual heritage?

His fingers curled gently around her upper arms, but it took considerable strength, both physically and mentally, to push her away. He knew what he had to do, but it would be hard—very hard.

"Wh-what kind of fool are you, lady? What possessed you to run into the desert, at night, with no food, no water, no protection for your feet?" He swallowed painfully when he glanced down, and winced at the way she favored first one foot, then the other.

He looked into her eyes. The dark depths swam in tears, though a glint of defiance sparked, and then flared to life. The pitiful urchin was gradually replaced by the firebrand.

"I should leave you to die," he scolded, "except we couldn't collect the ransom."

Jacelyn's knees stiffened. How could she have had charitable thoughts about this horrid savage? He hadn't saved her out of the kindness of his heart. He only wanted to line his pockets with her money.

A fresh flood of tears burned the backs of her eyes. She'd known what he was all along, and had fantasized that his rescuing her time and again was a sign that deep down he had a good heart. What a rotten judge of character she'd turned out to be.

She pulled her arms free from his grasp and retreated until yucca spines poked the backs of her legs. "You . . . you savage beast. Just wait til I find the cavalry and Colonel Alexander. I'll tell him what an awful person you really are, and how he's been a fool to deal with you . . . and . . ."

Covering her face with her hands, Jacelyn could no longer hold the tears at bay. She batted at his hands, but found no strength left to protest when he swung her into his arms and started back to the ranch.

Though she fought against it, she finally rested her head on his shoulder. Why, oh, why, did she have to struggle so hard to keep from liking this rogue of a man? Why, even now, did her body revel at his touch? How could she relish the strength and safety of his arms? What was there about him that continued to attract her, knowing the kind of man he was?

Grant walked briskly, in a hurry to return Jacelyn to her bed, and to leave her there—alone. But she was such a perfect fit in his arms that he had to keep reminding himself that she was trouble. Too much trouble.

All at once a coyote barked nearby. He tipped his head back as she stiffened, then snuggled deeper into his embrace. A guttural chuckle drifted on the wind. Grant gritted his teeth. Damn! Damn Santana for snooping where he wasn't needed. Damn the woman. And damn the feelings he'd inherited from his white father.

The sun had just begun to creep over the eastern horizon as Grant set Jacelyn down inside her cabin. He was sorely tempted to slam the door closed, emphasizing his point, but was reluctant to rouse the inhabitants of the ranch.

So he forced her to sit on the edge of the cot and knelt down to where he could look into her eyes. "I will not warn you to stay put again, lady. Just be grateful it wasn't one of the others who found you."

She leaned forward until their noses almost touched. "And if it weren't for you, and the others, I'd be in Tucson, probably with my brother. Or, perhaps, even on my way home." She poked his chest with her finger. "I refuse to stay here against my will."

He snorted. "You almost got away last night, didn't

you? Are you that anxious to make this country you hate so much your final resting place?"

She thrust out her chin. Why did he have to keep reminding her of the foolishness of her leaving without devising a plan or even taking provisions? Well, she'd learned her lesson. Next time—

"If you *try* to escape again, sweetheart, I promise you *will* be punished."

Jacelyn blinked. He was threatening her, and seemed quite serious. And he'd called her sweetheart. Sweetheart? Was this a facetious attempt on his part to frighten her even more?

She drew in a deep breath and straightened her tired back. For some reason, she didn't feel the fear he probably intended. Now if sleazy Eloy, or the crazy Kid had threatened her, she *would* run for her life. But there was . . . something . . . about this man that elicited her trust—even now, with those blue eyes spitting fire. She had no explanation for her intuition; it was just the way she felt.

"Mr. Jones . . ."

Grant glared, never batting an eyelash.

"Mr. Jones!"

He gritted his teeth. Who in the hell was the woman—Oh, yeah. Him. "What!"

Finally, she had his attention. "Bluster all you wish, but you will not intimidate me. I will do what I have to do. And *that* is *my* promise."

Grant grinned.

Jacelyn leaned back in surprise.

"Your challenge is accepted, lady. But be prepared to face the consequences."

He suddenly leaned forward and kissed the tip of her nose. Her mouth gaped open. Had the man gone completely crazy?

She got up and hobbled after him to the door. "Mr.

Jones." He didn't seem to hear. "Mr. . . ." She shook her head and backed into the room, wondering what had possessed her to call after him. Now who was crazy?

Jacelyn hadn't realized how really tired she was until she sat down on the cot again. Grains of sand ground into every pore whenever she moved. What she wouldn't give to have the empty basin filled with cool water.

Spasms ricocheted down the muscles on her back when she bent down to remove what was left of her shoes. She winced as the cracked leather rubbed over blisters, cuts, and cactus punctures. She had to do something about her feet, whether the rest of her was ever clean again or not.

She had just leaned back on her elbows to lift her legs and wriggle her toes when the door opened and Grant reappeared. Immediately, she sat up, eyeing him with open hostility, until she saw the bucket of water and another small container he carried.

He stepped over and shoved her gently back onto the cot as she tried to rise. "Stay," he ordered.

Jacelyn bristled. Now he was treating her like a common cur.

Placing the bucket and basin on the floor at her feet, he took hold of one ankle and lifted her leg until he could see the sole of her foot. Jacelyn flinched at his first touch, and his grip tightened, setting off a rippling sensation from her calf, up her thigh and all the way to her stomach.

"Hold still," he commanded. She started to protest but he waved his hand in dismissal and dipped a cloth into the water. When he wiped it over the bottom of her foot, she jerked.

"Ouch!"

His eyes dared hers. "This must be done."

She gulped. "I know." The cloth tore away a scab.

136

She hissed. He glanced down to clean the abrasion, but she continued to stare at his bent head. He'd removed his hat and his coal black hair fell in shaggy disarray around his ears and the back of his neck.

As tempting as it was to reach out and smooth the stray strands back into place, she resisted the impulse. Remember, she scolded herself, he's an outlaw. All he's interested in is the money for your ransom.

She hid a smug smile behind her palm. A ransom he would never see. The only ones who would get the message about her disappearance were the old codgers at the Mill. None of them had access to the money without James's signature.

Her eyes narrowed and she glowered at his back. What would happen to her when he found out he was stuck with a prisoner worth nothing because she was a *woman?*

He smoothed something cool and gooey on the bottom of her foot. Her eyes shot wide open. But the burning sting eased almost immediately. "Oh, that feels wonderful. What is it?" She swallowed, wondering if she really wanted to know.

Grant glanced up briefly. "Just an Apac . . . an ointment . . . made from some of the plants that grow in the desert." He accentuated the last few words, to point out that there were a few good things about the arid countryside.

She would have commented, but he quickly looked down again and picked up her other foot. The process started all over again.

Finished at last, he poured fresh water in the basin and set it on the table. Everything else he gathered up and took with him as he headed toward the door.

"Thank you," Jacelyn called softly.

He didn't look at her, but hesitated and nodded. "Dora said breakfast will be ready in an hour. I'll tell her you have a headache or something and won't be up for a while." He then looked her directly in the eyes. "Stay off your feet til then."

Disappearing as quickly as he'd come, Jacelyn was left open-mouthed once again. Trying to figure out that man was definitely going to drive her crazy.

Jacelyn was finishing the breakfast dishes when she heard shouts and the clatter of horses' hooves. Dora's voice drifted into the kitchen as the woman called out to "Waddy." Sighing, Jacelyn wiped her hands on the nearest towel. Like it or not, the gang had to come back sometime.

Walking stiffly through the living room, she tried not to limp. Dora had asked earlier what was wrong, and Grant had shot her a warning glance. She replied that she'd just sprained her ankle. Now, with Waddell back, she especially didn't want anyone questioning or looking at her too closely. She believed Grant when he said they wouldn't look kindly on her attempt to escape.

By the time she reached the porch, most of the men had turned their horses over to the German and Grant. Dora was hurrying back to the house, and Waddell and the Kid headed toward the barn.

Jacelyn's eyes narrowed as she noted the lopsided sway of the Kid's body. Something wasn't right.

Dora ran up the steps. "The Kid's been shot. Get a kettle of hot water and some rags, then meet me at the barn."

Chapter Nine

Dick Waddell helped the Kid inside the barn, cursing every time the Kid's saddlebags bumped him in the rear. "Damn it, Kid, why couldn't ya have left them things on yore saddle?" His eyes narrowed with speculation. "Don't ya trust us?"

The Kid sighed as he sank down on the stack of hay and just grinned. However, as he pulled his bags, one flap fell open and something rolled out. He tried to reach for it, but groaned and caught his side.

"That were a stupid thing ya done, ridin' up ta them Mex's fore we got 'em all corralled. Shoulda knowed one of 'em would have a hog leg."

The Kid just snickered and scooted to where he could get to the object. As he lifted it from the ground, Waddell looked down to see what was so important to the injured, bleeding man. "What the hell!"

Raising the thing in the air, the Kid loudly proclaimed, "The sonuvabitch won't pull another gun—"

Waddell slapped at the grisly object and made a face when drops of blood splattered his hand. "Damn you, boy. Ya've been told time 'n agin not ta take them scalps lessen ya been ordered." His hands clenched into fists as he glared down at the albino. "Yore gonna screw up ever'thin' if'n ya don't use your head."

The Kid's eyes never lowered beneath Waddell's fury. His lips curled. "But the boss hasn't been around in a long time. What he doesn't know—"

"*I'm* the boss."

"Only when *he* isn't here." The Kid managed to get up, grab the bloody piece of dark brown hair and stuff it back into his bulging saddlebags.

As Waddell watched the process, his face turned pale. Dropping the argument, he asked, "How many o' them things ya got?"

"Don't know."

"Ya don't know?" Waddell rubbed his forehead.

"But I haven't lifted one since that fellow rode through a couple of weeks ago."

Waddell sighed. "What's the matter with ya, boy? Weren't no call ta go an' kill that young feller."

The Kid shrugged and pulled out a gold pocket watch. "What's keeping your woman, Dick? I'm bleeding to death and she's up there—"

"Hurry up, Missy, an' don't spill all that water fore ya get here." Dora hustled into the barn, her arms laden with clean cloths, several jars, and rolls of bandages. Her eyes scanned the Kid and settled on the blood-soaked shirt. "Take that thing off," she ordered, while spreading a large cloth on the hay. "Now lean back here an' let me take a look see."

Jacelyn stumbled up to where Dora knelt, wincing when hot water sloshed over the rim of the kettle and onto her feet. Wearily, she set the kettle down, then found her empty hands filled immediately with cloth.

"Soak these an' hand 'em to me when I tell ya."

Jacelyn looked to see what Dora was doing and quickly averted her face from the sight of the ugly red gash along the Kid's white ribs. She'd never seen that much blood before. Her stomach dropped to her knees and surged back up again. She swallowed rapidly.

"Don't ya think 'bout gettin' sick on me, ya hear, Missy? Hand me one o' them rags. Now."

Jacelyn swallowed several more times, dipped a cloth into the water and handed it to Dora, who replaced it with another. As she soaked it in the kettle, a red stain spread over the liquid. Her eyes nearly popped from her head. Blood. It oozed between her fingers when she squeezed the rag.

She swayed. Her lungs refused to function. She felt light-headed.

"If'n ya ain't the most useless female I ever seen . . . Go on an' get outta here," Dora disdainfully commanded. "But first, hand me back that wet cloth."

Jacelyn picked it up and held it out by her fingernails. As soon as Dora had hold of it, she dropped the cloth faster than if it had been a burning match and stumbled toward the barn door. Once outside, she breathed deeply of the fresh, damp air. Glancing up, she was surprised to see dark, roiling clouds gobbling up the blue sky. *Just what this place needs,* she thought, wiping her wet hand off on her pant leg, *a good, cleansing rain.*

Grant led two horses toward the barn door, but stopped when he saw Jacelyn's paler-than-usual features. "What's wrong?"

She looked sideways at him, and found she couldn't pull her eyes away. He'd removed his shirt since she'd seen him last and sweat glistened along the corded muscles on his broad chest. She moistened her suddenly dry lips. "Ummm, it's nothing." But she couldn't ward off a shudder as she imagined a bloody gash like the Kid's on Grant's perfect skin.

For some reason, the thought of Grant's being shot inspired an onslaught of motherly concern. Concern she'd only experienced before for her brother . . . and, perhaps her uncle.

Grant tied the horses to a rail and walked over to take

141

hold of Jacelyn's shoulders. His palms automatically squeezed, then smoothed up and down her arms. "You're as pale as a milkweed blossom. Something happened."

"I-I, ohhh-h-h." She liked it when he touched her so gently, so caringly. "I'm not used to seeing so much . . . b-blood."

He looked her over closely. No, not even the rough garb detracted from her feminine innocence and naivete. The woman was definitely out of place in this country. Just as she'd often assured him. He shook his head sadly and grumbled, "No, don't suppose you have."

Somehow his tone of voice diminished her. She straightened her spine and retorted, "You make it sound like I should be ashamed because I don't swagger and spit, or hold up stagecoaches, or catch bullets between my teeth. I'll have you know that just because I'm a *tenderfoot,* as you've so nastily called me on several occasions, doesn't mean that I'm not as tough as Dora." Her chin jutted forward. "Or *you,* in my own way."

Grant's eyes widened. His moustache quirked suspiciously at the corners of his mouth. He couldn't take his gaze from the stubborn set of her gorgeous features, the proud thrust of her breasts straining the thin cotton blouse with her every irate breath.

At last he held up his hands. "You can stop now. I surrender."

"Don't you dare . . . What did you say?"

"You're right." In fact, the more he thought about it, he recognized a core of steel beneath her fragile exterior.

Jacelyn's bluster crumpled like a folded parasol. "I am? I mean, yes, I am right. And don't you forget it." While she had the upper hand, she thought it a perfect time to take her leave.

But Grant suddenly caught her arm and yanked her

close. He inhaled her special scent and closed his eyes as he whispered in her ear, "Don't go too far, hear?"

She jerked her arm free, hating the warm tingle that remained where his fingers had touched her flesh. Pointing shakily toward her feet, which had begun to ache something fierce, she replied, "Don't worry. It'll be a while before I'm able to try again."

Grant frowned. Again? "Listen, lady—"

At that moment, Waddell strode from the barn, supporting the Kid. "Jones, 'fore ya take them hosses inta the barn, get in there an' clean up any sign o' blood or doctorin' stuff an' burn it."

Grant nodded.

After the outlaws passed, Jacelyn shivered off the leering glance the Kid had given her trouser-clad legs. "Why do you have to *burn* it all?" she asked Grant.

He watched the outlaws and didn't think before he replied, "Probably don't want snoopy lawmen to get the notion this isn't a respectable ranch."

"Lawmen?" A ray of hope brightened her heart. Perhaps she wouldn't have to escape. Perhaps help would come to her.

"Damn," he grumbled beneath his breath. He saw the sparks flare in her eyes and muttered more oaths. "Forget it, lady. All you'll do is get the law and yourself killed. Wouldn't want that, would you?"

"Of course not." What kind of hard-hearted person did he think she was? She wouldn't want to *get* anyone killed. But ... if there was a way she could talk to the man, or the posse, or the cavalry troop, whichever happened along ... There had to be a way ...

He shook his head. The woman's every thought reflected in her eyes and the slant of her lips. "Of course." She was lying, but could he blame her?

Dora bustled out of the barn. She handed the empty

kettle to Jacelyn. "What're ya gawkin' at, Missy? There be a bear or somethin' comin' down the road?"

Jacelyn started. "Ah, no. I was just, ah, thinking how . . . pretty the scenery is around here."

Dora snorted. "Like I said, ya be one useless female." She turned to Grant. "Waddy said ya was to set things right in there. I got it ready fer ya."

He snapped her a two fingered salute. "Get right on it, ma'am."

Dora flushed. "C'mon, Missy. Them boys is hungry as starved lobos."

Jacelyn fell in behind Dora, but glanced longingly down the road one last time. Now that she knew there was a ray of hope, her feet didn't hurt so badly.

Raindrops splattered the dust at her feet and chilled her exposed flesh. She held her arms out and turned her face to the darkened sky. Things were looking up.

Later that evening, Grant finished cleaning the last stall while Dutch repaired a saddle. For the past hour, Grant had fished for information from the huge German, but found out nothing more than that the dead Barnes had wanted to buy the Appaloosa and had later shown up with the horse in his possession. As far as the rider was concerned, Dutch said he didn't know anything about the young man and, damn it, Grant believed him.

Leaning the pitchfork outside the stall, he went to the hay stack to fill the manger. As he reached down, Dick Waddell entered the barn, saw Grant, and hurried over.

From almost beneath Grant's hand he snatched up a pair of saddlebags. He looked suspiciously between Grant and the blacksmith, then held the bags up to see if they'd been opened. When it appeared they hadn't been trifled with, he cleared his throat. "Kid was wantin' these." He turned and rushed out.

Grant cocked his head, wondering why the man acted so nervous. Dutch caught his eye and shrugged. Grant arched one brow and repeated the motion, then returned to the stall. After spreading an arm load of hay in the manger, he retrieved the horse he'd left tied outside.

The horse balked, tugging the lead rope. Grant looked over his shoulder and saw that the animal limped on his left front leg. He led it on into the barn and tied it outside the stall where he had better light. Running his hand down the fine-boned leg, he felt for signs of inflammation or other injury.

As he examined the animal, he congratulated the gang on having one of the finest remudas of strong, swift horseflesh he'd seen. Of course, it was to an outlaw's advantage to ride a horse on which he could lose a posse.

His fingers probed under the fetlock. The horse jerked. Grant spoke softly and reassuringly, gently easing his hand beneath the long hair growing behind the horse's ankle. He frowned, straightened and looked at the sticky blood coating his fingers.

The cut felt long and straight, almost like a bullet wound. He rubbed the back of his neck with his clean hand as he considered the unusual location for a bullet crease. But it certainly wasn't impossible.

"Hey, Dutch. You keep any bacon or meat grease down here?"

The German nodded. "Ya. On the shelf over there. Vat happen to da Kid's horse?"

Grant found the shelf, picked out the jar of grease and headed back to the injured animal. "I'd guess a stray bullet got him. But who knows."

Dutch went back to the bridle strap he was mending.

Grant spoke to the horse when it shifted sideways and rolled its eyes at the unfamiliar object in Grant's hand. Scratching the animal's neck until it settled, he set the

145

jar on the straw-covered floor and picked up the horse's foot so he could get a better look at the cut.

With his back to the horse's head, he bent its leg and drew it between his knees. Cradling the ankle in one palm, he used his thumb to tilt the hoof down, exposing the injury. It wasn't as deep as he'd first thought, and had stopped oozing blood. He dipped the index finger of his free hand into the grease and smeared it into the fleshy crease. He repeated the motion several times until the wound was well coated.

The horse fidgeted and attempted to jerk his hoof away, but Grant held fast, talking softly. At last it quieted. Satisfied that the movement hadn't caused the cut to bleed again, he tilted the foot up and was about to set it down when he glanced at the worn shoe.

His eyes narrowed as he glanced over his shoulder to make sure the German was still busy. He bent closer to the hoof. There were only two nails on the inside rim. Two nails.

Releasing the leg, he straightened and rubbed his hand along the horse's back. The track he'd followed from the murdered miner's claim before he ran onto the Waddell gang and the stage had had only two nails on the inside rim of the left front shoe. Coincidence? Maybe. Maybe not.

He must have squeezed the horse's withers, for it snorted and shifted uneasily. His mind raced with the ramifications of his discovery as he turned the animal into its stall.

Of course he hadn't noticed the track since he'd been at the ranch. It had been relegated to the back of his mind while he concentrated on the woman. Damn. The print would have been obliterated anyway with all of the comings and goings.

Grant waved at Dutch as he left the barn and headed

toward the creek. He needed a place where he could think in private.

When he'd first come across the miner, he'd found that single track leaving the claim. The track had been fresh. But the miner had been dead at least two days. As he'd followed the trail, other riders had joined in.

He squatted next to the water, plucked a thick stalk of green grass from the damp earth and stuck it between his teeth. While he savored the fresh smell of wet pine and enjoyed the cool breeze following the late afternoon shower, questions flooded his mind.

The Kid—just how crazy was he? Was it really the same horse? If it was the Kid's trail, had he also just discovered the miner? Or could he have been there two days earlier and returned to the scene for some reason? What if everything was purely coincidence?

One thing he *did* know—it was worth his time to stay around and find a few answers.

And he'd make damn sure the hard-headed Miss McCaffery stayed put until he was through.

Sure, he could do the Colonel and the woman a favor by checking into the Appaloosa's appearance and gathering information on her brother. Or . . . he could leave now and bring the Army back to take the gang in for holding up the stage and murdering the messenger. But now there was the chance the Waddell gang and his mission were connected.

Did he have the right to jeopardize Miss McCaffery while he conducted his investigation? Yet didn't she have a stake in this, too? He would just have to make sure she stayed at the ranch. And out of trouble. Grant rubbed his eyes. He'd already missed one night's sleep. He needed rest to do his best. Hell, he'd spend every waking minute with her—and even sleep with her if he had to.

Grant's lips twitched when he realized the direction

his thoughts had taken. It wasn't the first time he'd imagined sleeping with her, but it *was* the first time he had no lustful intentions along with the notion.

He yawned. At least she wouldn't be up to making another getaway tonight. He'd take up his post outside her window as usual, but he'd also get some much needed sleep. He hoped.

Several days later, Grant stood in the barn doorway, leaning on a pitchfork. Between rebuilding corrals and working in the barn, he'd been kept busy. Too busy, because he hadn't had a chance to work on his investigation.

From the corner of his eye, he saw Dick Waddell approaching, and from the set of his jaw he had something serious on his mind. Grant silently awaited him.

"Hang up that pitchfork, boy. Yore gonna get a change o' scenery today."

Grant raised a brow.

Waddell walked inside the barn and motioned for Grant to follow. "The Kid ain't ready ta ride, an' we got a job ta do. Want ya ta saddle up. We'll be ridin' out in half an hour."

Grant stopped just inside the door. He glanced toward the ranch house.

"Don't worry none 'bout the gal. Dora an' the Kid'll keep a close watch on 'er."

That was what Grant was afraid of. He didn't care for the way the Kid ogled Jacelyn. As long as Grant was around, the Kid kept his distance, but what would happen when the albino was left alone with her?

While Grant saddled the Appaloosa, he worried about the *job*. How far was he prepared to go to keep up this pretense? But, he had to think of Jacelyn. What kind of chance would she have if he didn't come back with the gang?

He was the first to finish saddling, so he led the horse from the the barn and tethered it to a nearby rail. The other men were still packing supplies, and he used his free time to go up to the house. Quietly opening the back door, he slipped inside.

Jacelyn knew something out of the ordinary was happening. Since she'd come up to help with breakfast, first Dora, then half the gang had been in conference with Waddell. And none of the conversations had been spoken loud enough for her to eavesdrop.

At the moment, the Kid was in the living room talking to the leader; every once in a while the albino raised his voice. She gradually moved so that she pressed against the wall near the door, straining with all her might to hear what was being said.

A hand grasped her shoulder. She jumped and swallowed down a frightened yelp, but nearly smashed her nose on the wall. She spun around and found her face pressed into the open "V" of a white shirt and into the folds of a red bandana.

It was difficult to speak past the constriction in her throat. "You . . . you scared me to d-death."

Grant held a finger to his lips. "Shh-h-h. That's what I want to talk to you about."

Her brows furrowed. "You want to discuss your uncanny ability to frighten me?"

"No. Your death."

Her eyes rounded. He shushed her again and she fisted her hands. "Oo-o-h-h . . . I—"

He tilted her chin, closing her mouth at the same time. He waited until she glowered into his eyes to speak. "I have to leave. Stay close to Dora. If I'm not back by dark, sleep up here on the couch."

"B-but . . ."

A chair scraped in the living room.

Grant took hold of Jacelyn's upper arms and lifted her until they were eye to eye. "For once in your life, follow orders." Suddenly, he leaned forward and kissed her. Then he set her back on the floor, turned, and left as silently as he'd entered.

Jacelyn brushed her fingertips lightly across her mouth, almost as lightly as his lips had done. She followed his path to the door and watched as he mounted the spotted horse and rode away with Waddell, Bob, Eloy, Pablo, and Dutch.

All at once she thought about what he'd said. Her muscles tensed. The dratted man. All she'd done her entire life was follow orders. Her father's, her brother's, her uncle's. Now she was on her own. She didn't have to obey anyone anymore—much less an outlaw—unless she wanted to.

Grant removed his hat and wiped the sweat from his forehead. The gang had ridden south for the first couple of hours, leaving the mountains to stand guard in the distance. They'd stopped on a grassy knoll, overlooking miles of green, rolling hills. Occasionally a yucca or ocotillo reached spindly spines toward the sky, but the rest of the vegetation was too short and clumpy to make out.

Grant couldn't help but love this country. Not only because he'd grown up in southern Arizona Territory, but because of the diversity of nature. From where he sat, in the midst of a grassy plateau, no matter which way he looked he faced the towering, deep purple outline of mountains.

Water was abundant most of the year. Deer, javalina, and antelope provided meat, and in the canyons, if one were lucky, a band of coatimundi might be seen. He smiled to himself as he remembered his father pointing them out once when they'd been hunting. Funny-looking critters, kind of like a cross between a raccoon and possum. He'd watched in fascination as they rooted and foraged, eating anything that wouldn't eat them first.

He was jostled from his reverie when Waddell suddenly rode up beside him.

"Whatcha lookin' at out there?"

Grant shrugged. "I like to keep my eyes open. It's mostly what I *don't* see that bothers me."

Waddell chuckled. "That be right." He started to roll a smoke.

Tipping his hat back, Grant gazed intently at the outlaw leader. "It's been two weeks since we met up. When're we going to send word to the girl's family?"

Waddell lit his cigarette and blew smoke toward the new man. "Why? Ya worried 'bout your share?"

"No. I'm just gettin' tired of riding herd on her all the time. A man doesn't get much sleep around her."

"Hell, boy, I know whatcha mean. Why, if'n it weren't fer my Dory, I'd be hornier'n a crippled bull in a pasture full o' heifers in heat." Waddell reached over and slapped Grant on the back. "Ain't got inside 'er skirts yet, huh?"

Grant kneed his horse, edging it away from Waddell. "That's not what I want from her. Her family might not pay as much if she's returned as soiled goods." He hoped the outlaw took the hint.

Waddell inhaled his cigarette, looked away from Grant and released the smoke slowly. "Ya might got a point there. Don't wanna damage the 'goods,' so ta speak."

Grant caught the smug inflection in the man's voice and tried to look into his eyes. But Waddell continued to glance off. "First," he prodded, "we have to find out where to send word that we have her."

151

"Been taken care of, boy. Ain't no need ya workin' up a sweat worryin' none." Waddell gazed at Grant. Their eyes locked.

Grant finally nodded. "Good. Sooner we collect, the better. I've been a might short lately." His mind chugged faster than a steam engine. Who sent the message? How'd they know *where* to send it? No one had asked Jacelyn, that he knew of. In fact, *he* didn't even know where she was from.

Waddell ground out the butt on his saddle horn and smiled. "Ya do a good job tomorrow, an' I might fatten your pockets some." He spurred his horse forward and called to Grant and the rest of the gang, "Let's ride, ya mule-eared sinners. We got us a collection ta make."

Chapter Ten

Jacelyn glumly looked out the back door at the drizzling rain. For the past few days, in the early afternoon, the sky would darken and a cloudburst drowned the ranch for an hour or so. Then the sun came out and, by evening, dust blew again.

Today, though, it looked like the rain had set in for some time. Because she had nothing else to do during the bad weather, she'd cleaned until the house was spotless. She'd dusted and swept and washed and wiped until her hands were raw and her shoulders felt stooped.

She sighed, returned to a large basin and grimaced at the pieces of rabbit *she'd* cut up. Dora, declaring that there was no sense in a woman being so helpless, had taken her in hand that morning and taught her a few of the "important" things a woman should know—like how to cut up a rabbit and how to cook said rabbit in a "tasty" stew.

Jacelyn sniffed. Well, perhaps Dora was right. The aroma of boiling onions and carrots and potatoes and rabbit made her mouth water.

She could even show Grant, if he ever returned, what she had learned. She snorted at herself. Now why would she want to do that? What would *he* care? All he wanted was her money.

"Well, well. Look who's playing the little cook today."

Jacelyn shuddered and turned to face the Kid. She was afraid to keep her back to the weasel. "What do you want? Supper won't be ready for another hour."

"My side hurts," he whined, and cast her a sneaky leer. "I think someone should look at it."

"Dora's taking care of you." She stepped to the opposite side of a small table, placing it between her and the albino.

He glanced around the room. "But Dora's not here, is she?"

Jacelyn gulped. No, Dora was down at the barn taking care of Dutch's chores while this good-for-nothing clod spent his time aggravating *her*.

"She'll be back in a minute."

"I doubt that."

Jacelyn moistened her lips. "Wh-why do you say that?"

"Seems some horses got out of their corral this morning. Poor Dora's gone to find them."

From the smug tilt on his too-thin lips, Jacelyn knew exactly how the horses had escaped. Ever since the other outlaws had ridden out, the Kid had threatened to get her alone. He had finally done it.

Her heart thudded painfully against her chest as she glanced around the room. The door. She could run to find Dora.

Seeing the direction of her gaze, the Kid moved to block her path. He lifted his lips into an evil grin and began unbuttoning his shirt.

She edged around the table, hoping to throw him off by running through the inside doorway and into the living room. But, again, he blocked her escape.

"You might as well make up your mind to the fact that for the next couple of days you're mine, sweet thing. You'll like me lots better than that gunslinger. I promise."

Compared to this rat, Grant Jones took on the status of a mountain lion, to Jacelyn's way of thinking. "I don't 'like' either of you. Just leave me alone. Please."

She remembered Grant telling her to stay by Dora's side while he was gone. Now she wished she'd taken his warning seriously. She'd asked to go to the barn with Dora—she wanted to figure out how to steal a horse and get away before the others returned—but she'd been told to keep an eye on the stew.

"You just haven't been broken in good, sweet thing. All you need is for me to teach you a few little things about—"

"No. Never." When his shirt was halfway down his arms, she thought she saw her chance and darted toward the back door. But the Kid had a shorter distance to cover. She almost reached the door. Her heart hammered with anticipation. Through the open door she saw freedom.

A thin, but incredibly strong, arm streaked out and snaked around her waist, also capturing her arm. "No," she screamed. A dirty palm covered her mouth, strangling the sound in her throat.

She kicked backward, aiming for his shin. He laughed and his hot breath singed the back of her neck. He caught her leg with one of his and clamped it between his thighs. She twisted, using her elbows and her free hand to jab and try to loosen his grip.

Suddenly he gasped. She felt him flinch. "Damn you, stop struggling."

Realizing she must have struck a tender area, she renewed her efforts. The hand over her mouth squeezed, pinching her lips into her teeth. The arm around her waist tightened, pressuring her lungs. She couldn't breathe. Everything seemed to be happening slowly—too slowly.

Buttons popped from her shirt. A gust of air chilled her perspiring flesh. Tremors ran up and down her spine at the thought of the albino's too-white hands touching her.

The door slammed. "Hand me my gloves, Missy. I fergot ta—Hey, what's goin' on here?"

Jacelyn rolled her eyes. Over the Kid's shoulder, she saw Dora standing in the doorway leading from the living room. Her eyes beseeched Dora to please help.

The Kid turned sideways so that he could see Waddell's woman, while he still held Jacelyn at an angle where she couldn't fully see Dora. "Go on about your business, old woman. This is between me and the little lady."

Dora didn't even blink. She pulled a gun from her holster and shot at the Kid's feet, slicing a quarter-inch of leather from his boot sole.

The Kid hollered, "Cut that out. I'm in charge while Dick's away, and I told you—"

Dora shot again. This time she hit the other boot, clipping leather near the Kid's toe.

He yelped. "All right. All right."

"Let'er go, ya varmint."

The Kid slowly released Jacelyn, but retained enough control to position her body in front of his. "She's not hurt. I never touched—"

"Git on outta here, Kid." Dora motioned the barrel of her gun toward the door.

He held out his hands and backed away. Reaching the door, he stopped and looked back. "What about my wound? Who's going to doctor me?"

"I'll be down ta the bunkhouse in an hour or so," Dora resignedly promised.

The Kid smiled, though it more closely resembled a

crazed sneer. "Some day, old lady, you're going to regret this."

Dora cocked her revolver. He disappeared through the doorway.

Jacelyn stood gasping for breath, afraid she might die of a heart attack then and there. Her eyes brimmed with gratitude as Dora walked on into the room. "Th-thank you."

Dora reloaded her Smith and Wesson and slid it back into its holster like a practiced hand. Jacelyn watched her with envy. "I can't believe you had the courage to use that gun."

Dora shrugged. "The Kid made the mistake of coming off without his. If he hadn't . . ." She shook her finger at Jacelyn. "And don't ya take his threat lightly. Our bein' women don't make a nevermind ta a man like him."

Jacelyn nodded. She walked over to stand near Dora. "Will you teach me?"

The older woman's eyes narrowed. "Teach ya what?"

"How to survive out here. How to shoot. How to ride?"

"Done learned ya ta cut up a rabbit. That's all any lady—"

"I don't care about being a *lady*. I want to be able to take care of myself if something like this happens again." She squinted, staring hard into Dora's eyes. There was that sad look again—like she knew something awful . . . But in a blink it was gone.

"I'll do what I can, Missy. But—" She wagged a finger at Jacelyn. "Ya ain't ta tell a soul. Got that?"

Jacelyn grinned and nodded. "Yes, ma'am." The next time the Kid, or any man, tried to have his way with Jacelyn Faith McCaffery, he'd be in for a big surprise. She refused to lie down like a door mat for their pleasure.

James would be proud of his little sister if . . . when . . . she found him. Her lower lip trembled. It seemed she used the word *if* more and more lately.

Gazing through the kitchen window at the oak leaves shimmering in the wind, she silently cried, *James, where are you? I need you.*

Grant was disappointed when he found out the gang would be away from headquarters several days. After they made camp and settled down for the night, he stared at the quarter moon and worried about Jacelyn.

Would she heed his warning and stay near Dora? Would she try to run away again? Or would she pull some hard-headed stunt and run into trouble with the Kid?

The Kid bothered Grant. The man eluded his usual keen insight. Too many things didn't add up in rationalizing the Kid's behavior. It was like he was crazy, but in an intelligent sort of way.

Grant sighed, stretched out on his bedroll and clasped his hands behind his head. If he found out the albino had done anything—anything at all—to harm Jacelyn when he returned to the ranch, the Kid would be a dead crazy person, and his death would be slow and painful in coming.

Waddell had the gang up and moving before daylight. They were headed in an easterly direction now, toward an area where Grant knew there'd been a lot of new mining. While he'd been riding, he'd been thinking. How had Waddell known there was a shipment of ore on the stage Jacelyn had taken? Why was he taking particular care to be at a certain place at a certain time today? Was Waddell the real leader of the gang? Or was he getting his orders from someone else? Someone privy to secret information.

The rolling hills gradually eroded into one series of arroyos and canyons after another. As the countryside became rougher, Waddell became more nervous, continually shouting at the men to stay together.

Grant nudged his horse to as fast a gait as the rocky terrain would allow, beginning to feel the edge of excitement himself. Whatever was about to happen must be important.

They topped a hill and looked down over a road that wound along the lower, easier traveled flats. The way was clear and Waddell led them down to follow what was more a rutted trail than a road. A mile or two later, they turned a bend into another arroyo.

Summer rains had filled a narrow creek trickling over smooth gravel and around boulders. Salt cedar and cottonwoods grew along the banks.

After watering the horses, they continued through the arroyo until it widened into a grassy meadow. Waddell held up his hand and the gang reined their horses to a stop.

"This'll be a perfect place, boys. They'll let down their guard, thinkin' there won't be no more chance fer a ambush till the next 'royo."

Waddell surveyed the motley group of riders. His glance settled on the new man. "Jones, ya take the hosses through them trees. They be a small rise jest the other side o' the creek. Wait there til I give ya a signal—two shots fired together. Ya understand? Wait there, outta sight, till I call fer ya."

Grant nodded. The other outlaws dismounted and handed him the reins to their horses.

Eloy squinted and asked, "What eef he take thee caballos and leave?"

Waddell scratched his chin. His eyes had never left Grant. "Don't reckon he'll do that. Will ya, Jones?"

Grant replied honestly, "I'm not going anywhere, boss."

"Get on 'bout your business, then. C'mon, boys. We got work ta do."

Grant wasted time searching for a place where he could lead four extra horses through the trees and brush. Water splashed and iron shoes slipped on moss-covered rocks in shaded pools as he forded the creek. The rise was just a plateau of land the creek hadn't eroded over the years, but he crossed to the other side, dismounted and found a spot to picket the horses where he could get to them in a hurry. Then he settled down in the shade to wait.

An hour must have passed before he heard the first gunshot. Sporadic firing reverberated the air, then all was quiet. Grant gathered the horses and mounted the Appaloosa. Excitement and apprehension thickened his blood as it pounded through his veins. Should he follow orders, or go ahead and see if there was anything he could do to help the victims.

Without hesitation he recrossed the creek with the horses and worked his way through the woods until he reached a place where he could see through the limbs and leaves. He was surprised by what he saw.

Instead of a stage or mining company coach, the outlaws, their faces hidden behind bandanas, had stopped an ordinary-looking wagon. The driver and guard were alive, tied securely to the front wheel. He heard Waddell cursing. Pablo was in the bed of the wagon, tossing out boxes and trunks.

"Damn it, where is it?" Waddell stormed over to the bound men. "Tell me where the ore is. Now." He brandished his pistol in front of their faces.

One of the men hurriedly replied, "Don't know nothin' about no ore. Honest. They never tell us what we're gonna be carryin'."

Waddell turned away in disgust. From his location in

the trees, Grant could read the frustration in his expression. Something had gone wrong. Something very unexpected to Waddell.

Grant's attention was drawn to Bob and Eloy as they shot the locks off a small trunk. Eloy quickly threw open the lid, but all he dug out was frilly feminine lace. Several explicit Mexican curses colored the air.

Deciding to make his move, in hopes his intervention would help the two drivers' chances, Grant pulled up his own bandana and exited the trees. He stiffened when Waddell saw him coming.

"What're ya doin' here? I told ya—"

"Heard two shots and thought you'd signaled. I came as quick as I could."

Waddell's mouth opened, but snapped shut when he remembered Eloy and Bob both firing at the locked trunk. "Never mind. You're here, an' we might as well leave. C'mon, boys."

The outlaws hurried to retrieve their horses, but as they mounted, Grant's eyes were drawn to a bright plaid swatch of material dangling from the small trunk. He quickly rode over, dismounted and checked the tag. It was addressed to someone in Tucson, but he decided it would be better appreciated on a small ranch north and east of there.

He closed the lid and hefted the trunk behind the cantle. Hopefully, the Colonel's horse was used to carrying the heavy bedrolls soldiers sometimes used when going on a long march.

He breathed a sigh of relief when the animal accepted the weight. When Waddell shot him a questioning look, Grant shrugged. "Don't want to leave empty-handed. Doesn't appear I'll be gettin' any of that money you promised."

* * *

161

At the ranch, Jacelyn was carefully avoiding being alone with the Kid. She slept in the main house with a chair propped against the doors and the Kid standing guard on the porch. During the day, everywhere Dora went, Jacelyn shadowed her.

So far, Dora had shown her how to "muck" stalls and feed the horses. But the Kid hadn't given them enough time alone for Dora to teach her about a gun or how to ride. Although she knew enough to stay on a horse, she needed better control out in the middle of nowhere.

Dora surprised her once by coming to the cabin with more candles and a remnant of calico just big enough to cover the one window. Though the window was high enough that no one could pass by and casually peek through, the curtain gave her a measure of privacy and added a feminine touch to the place.

Of course, she laughed to herself, Dora didn't know that *she* was the one who used the window the most, looking out at Grant Jones.

A strange sensation pervaded her insides, almost convincing her that she missed the rogue and might even be looking forward to seeing him again—which wasn't true. She could care less about the man. Really. She shrugged off the eerie, empty feeling when she glanced out at his vacant spot beneath a large oak tree. Then she turned her attention back to Dora.

Although the woman was still aloof and uncommunicative most of the time, Jacelyn was starved for any feminine companionship, something she'd sorely missed since losing her mother. Living with Uncle Jonathan, she'd never had a chance to develop lasting friendships.

It wasn't that she intended developing a friendship with Dora, either. She was determined to escape, but it was going to take longer than she'd expected. And she was lonely.

The gang rode into the ranch compound late that afternoon. Jacelyn tried not to appear excited, but ran out onto the porch to watch as the men dismounted. They were quiet and surly. Dust caked the tired lines around their eyes and mouths.

The only one who didn't alight immediately was Grant, and Jacelyn gazed in wonder as he rode past the barn and down to her cabin. She stepped off the porch and wandered in that direction. Drawing close, she saw him lift down a small trunk and carry it inside. Curiosity made her follow.

"What's that?" she queried.

Grant glanced over his shoulder. His chest constricted at the sight of her flowing red hair and rosy cheeks. His dreams the past few nights hadn't done her justice. She appeared more vibrant than he remembered. And more beautiful.

"Don't know what all's in it. But there might be something you can use." He stood back as she walked forward. The faint scent of wildflowers and woman clinched his gut and quickened his manhood.

Jacelyn was drawn to the trunk sitting so invitingly on her cot. It had been a long, long time since anyone had given her anything. And she'd always loved surprises.

She opened the lid, saw the feminine garments, most of which were still neatly folded and packed inside, and drew her hand back as quickly as if she'd been bitten by a deadly scorpion. Turning on Grant, she shouted, "Who do these things belong to?"

His eyes narrowed. He shrugged.

"You stole them, didn't you?"

He displayed no reaction one way or the other. He just stared. That infuriated her. "Sometimes I get to thinking you're different from those . . . those animals,

. . . and then you remind me just how vicious and savage you are by doing something like this."

She didn't know what she'd been expecting when she opened the trunk, but it hurt to see that he'd stolen something that belonged to some other poor woman. Were there things in here the woman would miss? Things that were a part of her life?

Jacelyn slammed the lid. "Well, I want no part of it. Do you hear?"

He turned and left. Jacelyn stood in the middle of the room. Her ire evaporated with the fading clip-clop of his horse's hooves. Damn! She almost blushed just saying the swear word to herself, but couldn't think of a better description for her frame of mind at that moment.

She glared at the trunk, so innocent and yet so *damning*. Tears blurred her vision. Now that she took the time to think about it, the thought had been nice. But what did he think she would do with another woman's stolen clothes?

Jacelyn tried to make excuses, but Dora forced her to sit down at the supper table with the rest of the group. She waited for the usual snorts and slurps as they speared antelope steaks and spooned green peas and fried potatoes onto their plates. However, the unappetizing noises were hardly audible that evening.

Jacelyn glanced up from where she folded her hands in her lap and found the outlaws looking uncertainly from her to each other, to Dora, and back to their plates. Besides Grant, Bob actually used his bandana for a napkin of sorts. Pablo even excused himself when he let wind.

If she hadn't known it to be impossible, she might've thought they were watching their manners.

The Kid was oblivious of the changes taking place

around him. He hollered down the table to Dora, "Pass the gravy, old lady. I—"

Something hard struck the plank table, vibrating the dishes. All eyes jerked toward the head of the table to find Dick Waddell's pistol on the table, barrel end pointed at the Kid.

"Ya know better than ta insult my Dory. Don't know what's gotten inta ya, Kid. Ya've acted strange ever since we got back. But it ain't no excuse. You 'pologize. Now."

The Kid's lips twisted into a pout. Rebellion danced across his features. At last he glanced briefly at Dora, then away. "Sorry," he mumbled.

Waddell fingered the gun. "Didn't hear ya."

"Sorry," the Kid repeated, louder. He peered at Dora. "Didn't mean anything by it."

Dora, her cheeks flushed pink as she lovingly gazed at her husband, inclined her head.

But Dick Waddell wasn't so generous. "That's what ya say ever' time. I'm givin' ya fair warnin', boy. There ain't gonna be no next time. Dory washes your clothes, fixes your vittles. She don't deserve your bad mouthin'."

Jacelyn glanced over to Dora. Their eyes met. Dora's head shook almost imperceptibly. They both knew why the Kid was acting more obnoxious than usual, and Dora evidently didn't want it mentioned.

Barely lifting her shoulders in acknowledgement, Jacelyn dug into the fried potatoes. She just hoped the Kid listened to his boss and took his words to heart.

The dishes were done. "Waddy" and "Dory" had disappeared. The house was still. For the first time in days, Jacelyn was totally alone. She savored the moment and glanced outside at the moonlit night. The kitchen was oppressive with heat and she had an intense desire to go outside to cool off and just relax—alone.

She opened the back door carefully so the hinge barely squealed. Stepping outside, she halfway expected someone to charge around the corner and demand to know what she thought she was doing. But everything remained quiet.

A soft breeze cooled the perspiration on her face and neck as she hefted the thick mass of hair off her back. She meandered aimlessly in back of the house and finally wound up at the creek. In the moonlight, with the reflection off the rippling water, she felt a deep peace settle within her.

It seemed strange to be held a prisoner, with a lunatic threatening her, and yet out here, wearing her men's clothing, in the coolness of the night, with fresh mountain air wisping around her, to feel a sense of *freedom* and self-confidence she'd never experienced before.

Yes, it was *strange,* to feel frightened and exuberant at the same time.

Grant entered the kitchen, ready to walk Jacelyn to her cabin. He searched the empty room, then the living room. Maybe she'd decided to stay up here again tonight ... but ... surely not with Waddell and Dora in the other room.

She was nowhere to be found.

He spun on his heel and reentered the kitchen, but she hadn't magically appeared like he'd hoped. He ran to the barn, but when he opened the door, Pablo and Bob looked up momentarily from their poker game, then returned to eyeing each other's cards warily as Bob resumed dealing.

Jacelyn couldn't have gotten a horse.

He continued on to the cabin, threw open the door,

and was greeted by darkness and the shadow of the trunk still sitting on her cot. Damn it, he'd only been gone from the kitchen five minutes. How could she have disappeared so quickly?

His heart thundered in his ears. God only knew what would happen to her out there all alone. He couldn't search for tracks until daylight.

He'd walk the perimeter of the ranch, just in case. There was always a chance he'd stumble upon a footprint, a piece of clothing, anything to indicate which direction she may have gone.

Reaching the creek, he stopped in mid-stride. In the shadows, he made out a form—a human, feminine form. The wind bent branches overhead, dappling moonlight on a cascade of red hair. He fisted his fingers and moved noiselessly forward.

Her back was to him as she headed toward the water. He stifled a growl of pure disbelief. The little idiot hadn't learned a thing from her previous near disaster.

Frustration curved his fingers into fists, then coiled the muscles in his thighs and calves as he sprang after her.

Chapter Eleven

The peaceful water drew Jacelyn to the edge of the stream. On the silvery surface she spied a leaf shimmering toward her. Concentrating on finding a foothold to try to capture the leaf, she had no idea there was a threat until something rolled into the backs of her legs.

Her knees buckled. She fell forward, landing in the stream. One forearm scraped over a rock. Her other arm buried up to the elbow in the water as her hands slid off the rounded rocks. She opened her mouth to scream for help, but her entire upper body splashed into the cold water, submerging her face in a deeper pool.

Water filled her mouth and throat. She couldn't breathe. Her legs were weighted by something that felt like the trunk of a giant tree. She fought for her life, thrashing and flopping like a sixty pound trout at the end of a line. Water spewed from her mouth as she choked and coughed. Her hands kept slipping off the slick rocks as she frantically tried to secure a handhold.

Suddenly her legs were freed. Using her knees for leverage, she raised herself to a kneeling position and gasped for air.

Something grabbed the back of her collar and a handful of hair. She was jerked to her feet. Hissing a curse and pressing her feet to secure her footing, she curled her fingers into claws and spun to attack whoever or whatever had hold of her.

The last thing Grant expected was for the half-drowned woman to turn and fight like a female grizzly. A rock slipped beneath his foot. With Jacelyn coming at him with her arms waving like the vanes of a windmill in a tornado, he couldn't regain his balance. They both tumbled onto the bank.

Grant took the brunt of the fall. Air whooshed from his lungs. Water dripped onto his face and soaked his shirt and trousers. He raised his arms to protect himself as the woman continued to pummel him.

A fist connected with his cheek. He captured her wrist. Fingernails scraped a button from his shirt. He caught her hand. Her foot connected with his shin, but she was the one to cry out in pain.

As if someone had pricked a hot air balloon, the air and fight simultaneously sighed from Jacelyn's body. She lay atop him, exhausted, hurting, gasping her frustration.

At last she raised her head from his chest and looked into his eyes. "Y-you." She dropped back down, inhaling deeply. A few minutes later, she stirred again. "Are y-you crazy?"

"Me? Crazy?" Grant's chest heaved with each word.

Her eyes again locked with his. "Wh-why'd you do th-that?"

Hell, he thought, she was going to play the innocent again. This time it wasn't going to work. "I caught you sneakin' across the creek, and you accuse *me?*"

She shook her head. Wavy strands of damp hair tickled his cheeks and chin. "I was just picking a pretty leaf from the water." She wriggled her shoulders, tugged a hand from his grasp and reached into her shirt.

Grant, already uncomfortable from the sensations her

squirming aroused, nearly choked at the brief sight of creamy, rounded flesh her movement exposed.

Triumphantly, she produced a crumpled leaf and exclaimed, "See? I caught it after all."

Her breasts molded to his chest when she settled back down. He cleared his throat. "So . . . you weren't tryin' to . . ." One of her legs nestled between his thighs. "Escape."

"Escape?" she croaked. Lifting her forearm to examine a bruise, she dug her elbow into his ribs. "Not tonight. I was just . . ." She winced when he caught her arm to reposition it and his thumb scraped the sore.

He felt her body stiffen. She'd lost the button on the cuff of her sleeve sometime during the scuffle and the material had pushed above her elbow. With his hand wrapped around the bare flesh, he could feel the roughness beneath his fingers. He held her arm to where he could get a better look at it.

While examining the injury, he started her talking again. "You were just . . . what?"

"Ouch." He'd squeezed her other hand and her palm felt bruised. "I, ah, was enjoying the peaceful evening." She sniffed. "Until *you* came along."

She sounded so outraged at his disruption of her free time that he actually believed her. He tried to look at her arm again, feeling suddenly very guilty about tackling her like some desperate bandito. But he couldn't see. The moon had hidden behind a cloud.

He gently caressed her arm. She was too delicate to be treated so roughly. He felt like a heel. "I'm sorry."

Jacelyn's eyes widened in genuine surprise. ''What did you say?"

His eyes lowered to the open "V" of her shirt but shot back up again. Embarrassed by his body's blatant display of desire, he shifted his hips and hoped she was too naive to know what had happened. "I said, I'm sorry. I didn't mean to hurt you. Should've spoken to you first."

Jacelyn hid her face, which she knew had to be beet red, on his shoulder. Although she had been sheltered most of her life, she'd been raised around men. From overhearing conversations between her brother and his young friends, she had a good idea what it was she felt between Grant's legs. She was shocked. And intrigued. And too much of a lady to mention it.

Also realizing she was sprawled in unladylike fashion atop him, she quickly slid off to one side.

"W-well," she conceded, "I'm surprised you admit to being wrong about something." As far as she was concerned, the man was entirely too arrogant and conceited. And feeling his hard, lean form beneath, and now next to hers, created sensations in her body she didn't want to understand.

Rustling leaves on the far side of the creek alerted Grant. He became very still and shushed Jacelyn before she could say more. The faint trill of a whippoorwill drifted across the water and he ground his teeth. Damn it, didn't that Indian have anything better to do than hang around here? The way Santana liked to gossip, every scout and the whole Chiricauhua nation would soon know about the woman.

The wind picked up. Jacelyn shivered when the gust chilled her wet clothing.

Grant also felt the chill and decided it was time they got up. Once he'd regained his footing, he reached down and helped Jacelyn, noting that what was left of her shoes had just about disintegrated from the dunking they'd taken.

He immediately scooped her into his arms. Even wet, she was no heavier than a bedraggled kitten. He set out for the cabin, avoiding the buildings and keeping to the shadows so as not to be seen by the outlaws. She didn't

171

need the added nuisance of the men's obscene remarks if they saw the two of them together, wet and disheveled. Things were hard enough for her as they were.

When he reached the edge of the trees, he set her down, being careful not to land her almost-bare feet in a patch of stickers. Keeping his arms around her, he walked her quickly across the clearing. Though the night was warm, the combination of wet clothing and gusting wind had chilled them both to the bone. Jacelyn's teeth were already chattering.

Inside the cabin, he sat her on the edge of the chair, lit a candle, then walked over to the cot and set the unopened trunk on the floor near the wall. The blanket. Where was the blanket?

Jacelyn wrapped her arms around her waist. She couldn't stop shivering. And watching Grant start toward the blanket beneath the window caused her to shake even harder. The knife. She remembered sliding the knife inside the window and down the wall, but hadn't heard a noise when it fell. It must've landed on the blanket.

She started to get off the chair, but he turned suddenly and frowned. "Stay put."

Why, oh why, hadn't she remembered? It had been so long since she'd spent the night in the cabin, and her mind had been so filled with fear of the Kid, that she hadn't even thought . . .

Grant bent to pick up the blanket. The first thing he saw was the wooden handle and then the silver blade. Now he knew how she'd managed to loosen that damned board, and why it had taken him so long to repair it.

His first thought was to pick the weapon up, brandish it under her nose, and scold her for being such a fool. But his second inclination was to let her keep it for now.

Maybe, if she thought she had some means of self-defense, she wouldn't be in such a hurry to escape.

Beneath his lashes, he glanced in her direction. Her eyes were larger than a full moon and twice as bright. She'd covered her mouth with a trembling hand and looked as frightened as a rabbit coming face to face with a famished wolf. Good God, did she think he would hurt . . .

He sighed. Of course she thought he would be angry. And he was. But not at her. She was only following her instincts to stay alive. He only wished she didn't have to think *he* was the enemy.

Very carefully, he pulled the blanket from under the knife so it slid to the floor and into a crevice between the wall and the floor. Then he straightened and shook out the wrinkled wool. "Here it is."

He strode to her and held it up lengthwise so it blocked her from his view—and he from hers. "Take off those clothes and wrap up in this."

Jacelyn couldn't believe he hadn't found the knife. She let out the breath she'd been holding in one long hiss. With her confidence returning, she considered his demand and stubbornly thrust out her chin. "No."

He lowered the blanket until his narrowed eyes peered over the top. "What?"

She hugged herself tighter. "N-no. Not while you're in the room." She looked away. The way his eyes bored into her, made her extemely nervous. She had an uncanny feeling he knew all her little secrets. But . . . he hadn't found the knife.

"Either shuck those britches or I'll do it for you." He'd had enough of her independent ways. He wasn't leaving until he knew she'd shed the wet clothes—all of them. However, the thought of helping her undress wasn't all that unpleasant, either.

Jacelyn didn't like his attitude that *he* was the only

person who could do anything right. "I think I can handle undressing myself. I've managed to do it alone for a long time."

She made the mistake of meeting his eyes. She could've sworn she saw a red glimmer through the sensual smoky blue. But then he raised the blanket. A warm shudder quaked through her.

"You heard me, lady."

"Oohhh! I've never met a more hard-headed man in my entire life." But she decided she'd probably be a lot more comfortable in the warm blanket than sitting there arguing and freezing for who-knew-how-long.

"Just get on with it," Grant muttered. Just look at who was calling the kettle black. She had to be the most . . . He heard the slither and drip of wet clothing being removed. His fingers clenched into the heavy wool. He remembered clearly his earlier glimpse of a perfect breast, the satin smoothness of her skin. Images of her slow, erotic removal of each piece of clothing tantalized his senses.

He guessed that first she'd take off the flannel shirt and reveal her slender shoulders. She'd peel the camisole one strap at a time. A woman like Jacelyn would, of course, be wearing silk, and it would slither down the mounds of her breasts, catching momentarily on the hard buds of her nipples.

He shifted his feet. It didn't help.

Her trousers would present a more difficult problem, as wet as they were. But they would roll down her generous hips, exposing the soft round globes of her bottom. Her feminine mound would be hidden by curly red hair.

The muscles in his lower belly contracted.

Her thighs would be long and smooth and taper to delicate knees. He'd already had a feel of her calves, and stroked her feet. He'd never known feet to be so . . . arousing.

He stifled a groan and shifted his hips.

Jacelyn jerked several times before she removed the blanket from his grasp. When she had the bulky, cumbersome thing securely wrapped around her shivering body, she looked at Grant. His glazed expression of wonderment confused her, but did more to ignite a fire in her blood than any ten blankets.

Knowing this man for what he was, it was hard to fathom that she was drawn to him—in a physical way. She'd never experienced anything like it before, and had never thought of herself as a woman who could feel pure, sexual lust—like she'd read about in some of James's books.

But the look in his eyes . . . The burning in her body . . . Her fingers tightened on the blanket. She took a deep breath. No, she would not cave in to her body's desires. But, then, why was she reluctant to make him leave? "I-I—"

Grant resisted the damnable urge to take her in his arms and never let her go. He stuffed his hands in his pockets. He had to leave now—now, or he'd lose control of his body and mind. She was too much of a distraction. "I'll be outside . . . if you need . . . anything." He swallowed, then turned and walked to the door.

"Wait." She bit her tongue. Why did she always stop him from doing exactly what she wanted him to do? "I-I'm sure I'll be f-fine."

He shrugged. "Good."

"Well . . . Good night."

"Yeah."

"Ah, are you going to . . . lock the door?" His eyes darted to her. She flinched.

"You'll be safer, if I do."

Her eyes lifted to his. What was he implying? Would he be protecting her from the gang members? Himself? Or her *own* inclinations? She finally nodded. "Perhaps it would be best."

He returned her nod and left the cabin. She waited for the familiar grating of wood as he lowered the bar into place. But she didn't hear it. She didn't know how long she stood there, staring at the door, but her feet finally became so cold that she hurried to crawl into the bed and huddle inside the blanket.

The strangest thing had happened when he left. It was as if he'd taken her sense of well-being. Without his presence filling the room, all of her old insecurities and feelings of being lost and alone mounted again. And her stomach felt . . . empty, though it had only been an hour or two since supper. It was as though he'd walked out and left a void in her life.

She closed her eyes and prayed for her sanity to return. Dear Lord, she beseeched, "Help me, for I know not what I'm doing."

Jacelyn didn't know how long she'd huddled into a lump of human frailty, but she slowly became aware of the tapping of rain on the roof and the west wall. The wind had picked up, rattling the small cabin during one particularly hard gust.

She'd always enjoyed storms at night. She'd lie inside her bedroom, all cozy and warm, cuddled into . . . Inside. Warm. She sat up. Grant was *out* there. He'd already been wet and cold. Now he . . .

Tiptoeing across the cold floor, she peeked out the window. It was too dark and rainy to see anything. Her conscience nagged at her. What should she do? It wasn't proper for a lady to take a man into her home—such as it was—without a chaperone. But since she'd been abducted, nothing she'd done had been *proper.*

She was still alive. Still healthy. All thanks to one man.

Leaning against the closed door, she called, "Mister Jones?"

Grant took off his hat and stood in the cold rain. He needed for the rejuvenating liquid to pound some sense into his head. The woman must possess some sort of evil spirit to cause him to forget who and what he was whenever he was in her presence. He thought and felt things he didn't want to think or feel. And he did *not* want *her.*

When the rain first started, he'd thought to go to the barn to sleep out of the rain and cold. But then he figured that was what she'd be waiting for—a perfect opportunity to escape while everyone was sure to be inside. He didn't believe for a minute that she wouldn't try again when he least expected her to.

His feet carried him to her door instead of the barn. Only to get beneath the eave, he assured himself. He wasn't interested in going inside, or in holding her naked body, or burying himself in her warmth.

"Mr. Jones?"

The sound of a voice startled him out into the rain. It was her spirit, making him think Jacelyn McCaffery wanted him.

"Mr. Jones . . ."

The voice called louder, but was more timorous and uncertain. He frowned. It could not be a spirit then, or his suddenly overactive imagination. The woman had called him. Immediately, he thought the worst. Something had happened. She was hurt.

He hurriedly swung open the door. She literally fell

into his arms. Lifting her back inside, he closed the door behind them before setting her down and scanning what he could see of her sticking out here and there from the folds of the thick blanket.

"What's wrong? Are you all right? Did something happen?"

Jacelyn felt a little hysterical, but confronting his nearly overwhelming masculine aura forced her to gather her wits. "N-no. I'm fine."

She backed up to the cot and sat down before her quaking legs gave out. "I was just . . . w-worried—"

"About what? Did you see something? Has someone—"

"About you."

He stopped talking and stood dripping in the middle of the room. "Me? You were worried about me?"

She nodded and looked raptly at the floor.

He was stunned, hardly daring to believe what she'd said. How long had it been since *anyone,* excepting maybe the Colonel and Santana, gave a damn about Grant Ward?

Yet here was this lovely lady, who'd suffered nothing but grief at his hands, admitting that she'd been worried about him. He spread his arms out. "Why?"

Jacelyn frowned. Why? Where did she begin? "B-because . . . you were wet and cold. It's raining. You could've frozen or caught your death . . . What?" He looked at her like she'd sprouted another eye. ·

Hell, he thought. She'd been sincere. She truly *cared* what happened to him. He began to pace, slapping his arms to stimulate his circulation. On the surface, he was a mass of chill bumps. But inside, he felt warm and secure. Something he hadn't known for a very long time.

"Well, ah . . ." Damn it, he was turning into a stuttering idiot. "I'm surprised. Didn't expect a lady like you to—"

"Ask an outlaw into her room so late at night?"

His brows shot up at her use of the term "outlaw." "That, too."

She pursed her lips, then added, "So am I. But you have saved my life several times. I feel I . . ."

Yeah, he thought, oddly disappointed. That was what this was about. She felt she *owed* it to him to be nice and invite the poor savage in out of the cold.

Good. He could keep things in perspective this way. It wouldn't do to think she actually liked him.

Jacelyn stared at the scowl marring Grant's features. It was the first honest emotion she'd ever clearly read on his usually immobile face. It was strangely endearing. He must be as shaken by what was happening between them as she. And something was happening. The squirmy feeling in her stomach and the blaze flaming in his eyes told her so.

At that moment, she found it very easy to like the man. Because he watched over her, because he'd saved her life, because . . . just because.

All at once she noticed the chill bumps on his forearms. "You're cold. You need to get out of those clothes."

He stopped pacing and slanted her a mischievous grin.

She flushed. "Well, you know what I mean."

"And if I do that . . ." He glanced around the room, but his eyes returned immediately to the blanket. "How would I cover myself?"

Her hands reflexively tightened on *her* blanket. She also looked around the cabin. There were only her wet clothes, or the tattered remains of the dress she'd worn to the ranch, which hung limply from a nail on the wall.

When she gazed back at Grant, his attention was also focused on the dress. He looked back over to her with

179

a strange gleam in his eyes. "You can't wear my dress." She couldn't believe he'd even *think* about it.

He hung his hat on another nail and winked. "I can."

Her chin dropped, but she met his stare. Finally she repeated one of his favorite responses and shrugged. "Go ahead. I can hardly wait to see if it looks better on you than me."

Grant nodded and began to unbutton his shirt. "Close your eyes."

She did better than that by lying down and pulling a corner of the blanket up to cover her face. Her "Let me know when, or if, I should look," was a muffled indication of her skepticism.

Jacelyn moistened her lips as she listened to the rustle and scrape of clothes being removed. In her mind's eye, she pictured the sculpted muscles of his chest and back, and wondered if the rest of his body was as beautiful. And she wondered what justice a *dress* would do his male perfection.

Bare feet padded across the floor. Her ears were attuned to every sound and she heard the whisper of material as he lifted down the dress. A loud rip almost caused her to peek. It wasn't that she cared about the dress, but her curiosity was getting the best of her.

"You may look."

She sat up quickly, grabbing at one side of the cover as it threatened to slide from her shoulder. Her gaze froze on Grant. Her body went numb. The rogue had the audacity to stand there, almost naked, looking at her.

His bare chest, illuminated by the lightning, was a muscled expanse of flawless, sensuously shadowed skin. He wore her dress, fashioned into an Indian garment she recognized from the *Harper's Weekly*—a breechcloth. A long piece of skirt material ran between his legs—long, tapered, nicely proportioned legs—and was held up by a belt around the waist and hung down in front and back to his strong-looking knees.

Every other inch of flesh on the man was bare for Jacelyn Faith McCaffery to appreciate. And as much as she wanted to turn her head, or close her eyes, she could do neither. Lord, he was perfect. He looked like a statue she'd seen in a museum once. Too good to be a mere man.

"Well?" he prodded. She was quiet—too quiet.

Jacelyn licked her lips. She opened her mouth, but rather than look like a gaping trout, snapped it closed. He was all *too* real.

Impatient, Grant quipped, "Who looks better in the dress?"

"No question about it. You." Her cheeks felt scalding hot. Her gaze slid down to his toes.

His chest expanded. Of course, *he* would have insisted *she* did, if asked. He turned and spread his damp clothes on the table beside hers.

Jacelyn sucked in her breath at the sight of his lean, powerful thighs and the curving hint of buttock. "H-how did you learn to do that?" She started to point at his . . . loincloth, but quickly snatched at the drooping blanket.

Grant hesitated before giving his answer. "I . . . lived with the Apache." His breath caught when her eyes widened even further but refused to meet his.

"Really?" She was horrified to think he'd been in such close proximity with the heathens, but was also impressed. For a man to live with the Indians and come back alive . . . No wonder he was so hard and tough. *Harper*'s would love to hear his story.

Grant longed to read the expression in her eyes, to see her true reaction to his confession. But her gaze seemed attached to his navel. Finally, the tension in his shoulders eased. He was pleased with her calm acceptance of his relationship with the Apache, for she had seemed terrified of the Indians whenever they were mentioned. Perhaps she was more understanding than he first thought.

When he continued to stand in the center of the room, Jacelyn glanced from the clothes-covered chair, to the table, to the hard, filthy floor. Now that she had invited him in and he had changed out of his wet garments, what was she going to do with him?

As if reading her mind, Grant's eyes also surveyed the room. He shrugged and walked to the foot of the cot.

With each step he took toward her, Jacelyn's heartbeat accelerated. By the time he reached the bed, she was sure the whole cabin resounded from the pounding in her ears. He only sat on the end of the bed, but it didn't help her predicament. Tonight, with both of them nearly naked, and the cozy atmosphere of the place, and the rain beating a primitive rhythm outside, she seemed even more affected by him than usual.

Her every nerve ending was attuned to his every movement. Her blood ran hot and thick through her veins whenever he looked her way.

Now, as she watched him, she noted goosebumps dotting his smooth flesh. He was cold, but would never admit it. Her own lips felt numb as she mumbled, "It's getting chilly. Wh-where will you sleep?"

Thunder rumbled. Lightning struck nearby with a threatening roar and a brilliant flash that highlighted his powerful physique. Jacelyn jumped. The raging storm reflected in his eyes. She shuddered.

Grant cocked an eyebrow. "Right here."

Chapter Twelve

Jacelyn scrunched into a tight ball with only her eyes and the top of her head peeping above the blanket. Her throat felt like she'd swallowed a bucket of sand when she rasped, "H-here? You're g-going to sleep h-here?"

Reaching beneath the blanket, Grant grabbed hold of her feet, relishing the feel of soft feminine flesh against the backs of his knuckles. He gently eased her body straight. In a heartbeat, he lay beside her and scooped her blanket-clad form into his arms. "Now we can both be warm."

"B-but . . ." She felt his big body tremble and knew she wouldn't turn him out. And she had to admit, it was definitely warm. So warm that a new heat prickled her skin wherever his body touched hers, even through a layer of thick wool.

Grant sighed. Cold as he was, if she had protested, he would've left the bed. Snuggling closer, with her head nestled beneath his chin, he thought again how perfectly she suited him. If he was looking for a woman, she would . . .

He mentally shook himself. Damn it, he was *not* looking for a woman. Didn't need the aggravation in his life. And she'd only asked him inside to repay a debt.

Though she had readily accepted the fact that he had

lived with the Apache, she still didn't know the whole truth. Besides, Jacelyn McCaffery was too refined, too fragile to live in his country, and he could never survive anyplace else. The Apache needed him now and he needed them . . . and he always would.

He didn't realize that his arms were tightening around Jacelyn.

The casual embrace in which he held her, closed to trap her against him. She tilted her head to look into his face. His brows were deeply furrowed. His eyes were closed. She swallowed the questions she wanted to ask about his capture by the Indians and how he managed to escape. They could wait till another time.

It felt good just to lie in his arms. So safe. So warm.

Consecutive claps of thunder rumbled across the heavens like the heavy wheels of a stagecoach, startling Jacelyn from her dreams. Flashes of lightning illuminated the room as briefly and quickly as bullets fired from a pistol.

A storm, she thought, through the fog of sleep that was again enveloping her.

She tried to move, but couldn't. The holdup. The outlaws. They had her tied down. She wouldn't let them take her. They couldn't have her purse or her watch. It was all she had. No!

Images of the Kid and Eloy, grinning, reaching out for her, filled her mind. She had to get away. Run. Run for her life. She struggled. One arm came away free. Something still held her down. She couldn't breathe. They were smothering her.

She couldn't move her legs. No matter how hard she tried, she couldn't run. Help. Help me!

"Jacelyn. Wake up, sugar."

184

Hands gripped her arms. She swung her free arm and winced when her knuckles connected with bone.

"Damn it, lady. Wake up."

Her arm was captured. A heavy weight pressed her down and down ... She was helpless. Yet, something familiar in the raspy voice echoed through her head. Something that told her she was safe now. She blinked and stopped fighting.

Gradually she opened her eyes and focused on the face hovering above her. Dark hair and a moustache. Thin lips. High cheekbones. Blue eyes. Blue eyes and incredibly long, black lashes. A beautiful face.

Suddenly she stiffened. Groggily, her memory sifted through the events of the past few days. Grant Jones. Her nemesis. Her savior.

Grant released her hand and placed his palms on either side of her cheeks, holding her face so she had no recourse but to look into his eyes. "You had a nightmare."

Her eyes searched his. She was scared. What would happen to her? And what might have happened to her already if it hadn't been for this man?

She threw her arms around him—or tried to. One arm was still tangled in a blanket. Squirming, she freed herself and *then* wrapped her arms around his broad shoulders and hung on for dear life. He might be an outlaw, but he was also a gentleman. He'd looked after her and taken care of her like ... like James would have.

Except ... the supple flesh beneath her fingers surely didn't belong to James. The woodsy scent of smoke and leather could never be James's. And James would throw a fit if he thought his little sister physically yearned for a man, or knew of the desire she felt to have that man hold her and touch her and ... love her?

Grant couldn't believe it. She hugged him harder than a lonely widow. "Jacelyn ... What're you doing?" Her blanket had spread out during the night. Her bare leg lay across his. The satin feel of her skin sent a red hot spasm directly to his groin.

What was she doing?, Jacelyn wondered. She wished she knew. Her nose nuzzled into his chest, so solid and big. He felt good, made her feel good to be held so gently, as if he truly cared. She could almost forget where she was and why. For a little while she would like to put her worries aside and enjoy a few minutes of peace and quiet in this man's arms.

Lightning flashed. A pop and sizzle sounded near the cabin. She chuckled. So much for the quiet.

Grant reached down to adjust his breechcloth and inhaled quickly when his hand grazed the bare flesh at her waist. He raised his head and looked down. The blanket had twisted during her nightmare, freeing her legs. No longer did it come together in front.

Skin as delicate as porcelain and pale as ivory was exposed to his view. He swallowed. Unable to resist, he laid his palm on the indention of her waist. Her flesh quivered. His body quickened in response. He stared into midnight blue eyes wide with question.

"Wh-what are *you* doing?"

He cleared his throat. The minx had heard him after all. He whispered, "You're so beautiful. I've wanted to touch you like this almost from the first moment I saw you."

A teasing glint challenged the pleasure in her eyes. "All you wanted to do when we first met was bully and intimidate me."

"I said *almost*. Besides, someone had to take you in hand. You had an experienced Colonel quaking in his boots. I couldn't let you do that to Evan."

"I did not." Her brows drew together. If he and the Colonel were first name friends, why didn't Colonel Alexander stop Grant's lawless way of life?

186

"You were rude." He rolled so that he lay half on top of her. Their flesh melded at thigh and hip. Her expressive eyes glittered with both innocent desire and trepidation.

But Jacelyn still had breath enough to quip, "You were rough and ill-tempered."

"You called me a savage." He laced one hand into her thick mass of hair. The other moved in smooth circles up her rib cage as he waited tensely for her reply.

"Y-you still remind me of one, sometimes."

"You're a smart lady."

Jacelyn was so alive with feeling and emotion as his fingers caressed her body that she could hardly follow the conversation. She really should tell him to stop. All of her years of strict upbringing combined into a surge of guilt for enjoying the way he was touching her.

Before she moved her lips to speak, his mouth covered hers. Gently. Very gently. He nipped and nibbled until she responded, then placed powder puff soft kisses on her chin, cheeks, forehead, eyelids, and nose.

When he reached the tip of her nose, Jacelyn impatiently moved her head so he touched her lips. She wanted him to kiss her on the mouth again. Only this time more satisfyingly, longer, harder, so she could savor the sensation.

He willingly accommodated her. His tongue glided hot and moist over her bottom lip. She moaned as delicious tingles spiraled through her body to concentrate in one heavy, aching need in her lower belly.

He tilted her head until her mouth parted beneath his coaxing pressure. He eased his tongue slowly between her lips. She stiffened. With Apache patience, his hands massaged and gentled her like a flighty filly.

A shudder ricocheted down his length when she instinctively molded her body more closely to his.

Jacelyn felt his reaction. A coil of pleasure unwound

through her. She was amazed to discover that she—mousy, timid Jacelyn McCaffery—could cause a rogue like Grant Jones to tremble. Her confidence blossomed more fully than prairie flowers after a warm summer rain.

One of his hands skimmed her hip. She thought his calloused palms were a lot like the man himself. Powerful. Rough. Yet possessed of a quiet gentleness.

Her body became as pliable as dough, yielding and flexing as she returned his kiss. Her tongue tasted his lips and delved between his teeth. He opened his mouth more fully, inviting her exploration. Her pulse ran wild.

Her arms tentatively circled his shoulders. Her fingers danced lightly along the ridges of his spine. His back arched and she swallowed his groan of pure delight.

Grant thought he must've died and gone to heaven. No woman had ever taken the time to do to him the things Jacelyn did. He wanted to give her the same pleasure, and smoothed his palm over her rounded hip, to her small waist and along her rib cage until his fingers stroked the underside of her breast. The sensitive flesh quivered from his touch.

When his palm moved to cover her breast, he gently eased aside the gold watch, whose lucky case was slick and warm from contact with her skin. He captured her protest with his mouth, kissing her over and over, teasing, tantalizing, until she once again reciprocated his caresses.

He raised his head only high enough to let his lips brush hers as he whispered, "Let me touch you, sugar." His flattened palm moved in quick circles over her nipple. Her eyes darkened. Her chest rose and fell in jerky breaths. His own breathing became ragged. As he'd suspected, she was as fiery in body as in mind. And, Lord, but she set him ablaze, too.

He also sensed her hesitation and fear. She wanted

him, he could tell from her body's responses. But she was frightened of what she didn't know.

"Let me show you how good it feels." He waited. He would not continue without her willing consent.

"I-I don't know what to do." Tears burned her eyes. She didn't want to seem lacking, but she'd never done anything like this before. She'd been raised to believe that a woman saved herself for marriage, and then only gave herself because it was her duty.

She knew what she should do, but her words rang true in more ways than one. She'd never been informed that being with a man felt . . . good. Or that sometimes a woman's body took control of her emotions.

She was naturally shy and hesitant. No matter her own feelings, a man like Grant must've had many women. It amazed her to think that he was taken with *her*.

A choked chuckle escaped her to tease against his lips. Of course, out here, he didn't have much choice. It was either her, or Dora.

Grant sensed her self-doubt. He nibbled her ear and asked, "Has no man ever told you how beautiful you are?"

She shook her head, then nodded. "My brother."

"Brothers don't count." His teeth grazed her lobe, then his tongue. She shivered and he warmed her in his arms. Again, he captured her breast.

"You are a beautiful woman, Jacelyn McCaffery. You have a body made for loving." What he could see of it, he grumbled silently. Damn that blanket, anyway.

"You mean it?" Uncle Jonathan had told her to beware of men, that they would only want her for her money. Her words became stuck in her throat. Her uncle had known what he was talking about. That was the very reason Grant had brought her here—to get her money.

He watched the change in her eyes. She was resisting

189

her feelings—rejecting him. He cupped her face in his hands and stared earnestly into her eyes. "I do not lie."

She swallowed.

"You'd do well to remember that."

She nodded.

"And, yes, I do mean what I say about your beauty." He suddenly raised his upper body and tugged the blanket. The wool fell back, exposing her lush body to his hungry eyes.

Jacelyn gasped and tried to cover herself. "No."

Grant eased down, resting his chest on hers, effectively blocking her efforts. Damn, but she was soft. "The Great Spirit blessed you with a wonderful body. Do not hide it."

She was so busy trying to find something to do with her hands and some place to focus her eyes that she paid little attention to his words. "This isn't right. You don't really want me."

He lowered his head and trapped her lips with his. He kissed her long and hard and deep until her arms instinctively wrapped around his back. Their tongues met and mated. His plunged into her honeyed recess, pulled back and plunged again. She tasted sweet, so sweet.

Jacelyn understood there was something very erotic and elemental about the rhythm of his movements. It excited her. And that terrified her.

Grant ended the kiss and rolled to his side. He pulled the edges of the blanket together and just held her. It was painful, but he felt rewarded by the look of relief on her face.

Secretly, he promised, *next time, sugar . . . you won't want me to stop.*

Grant watched the dawning light creep through the window. Regretfully, he left a sleeping Jacelyn, tucked the blanket around her body to take temptation from his mind, and went over to check their clothes. Everything was still damp, but body heat and sunshine would dry them in no time.

"Jones, where ya be?"

Jacelyn yawned and rolled over to see Grant standing by the table in his breechcloth. Today she didn't feel so shy looking at his finely sculpted form. She had actually touched a lot of that tanned, taut skin.

She yawned and stretched. "Did you say something?"

Her trousers and undergarments sailed through the air and landed on her head. Before she could pick them off, an iron band wrapped around her wrist. "Get dressed."

She looked up in confusion. "But—"

He shushed her. "Don't argue. Hurry."

The hard line of his jaw and the steel glint in his eyes warned her to do as he said. What had happened to put the "savage" expression on his face again?

"All right, but turn your back." She pulled her undergarments under the blanket and glanced at Grant beneath her lashes. Her camisole slithered from numb fingers. Her mouth gaped open.

Grant had his back to her. He'd removed the breechcloth and was stepping into his pants. He was naked. Beautifully, shockingly naked. Except for the bandana knotted around his neck. And he was gloriously breathtaking.

"Jones, ya in there?"

Jacelyn jumped at the sound of Waddell's voice so close to the cabin.

Grant buttoned his pants, threw on his shirt and quickly set the chair by the door. With a last glance over his shoulder, he ordered, "Finish dressing, then cover up and pretend you're still asleep."

He opened the door, stepped through, and closed it behind him. For some reason, she didn't even think to

191

disobey. She was beginning to realize that unlike most of the men she'd known, when Grant gave an order, it was to her benefit to follow through.

Grant stopped outside the door and ran his fingers through his touseled hair. He stretched and casually scanned the surrounding area. Waddell approached from the direction of the barn and was only a few yards away. Grant scratched his stomach through the gap in his unbuttoned shirt.

"Jones, why didn't ya answer me? I've been huntin' ya an' ya weren't in your usual place."

Yawning, Grant mumbled, "Slept in there." He tilted his head toward the cabin.

Waddell looked at the door and then back to Grant. He winked. "Finally got inside, did ya?"

Grant knew what he was asking. "Naw. Just moved in when it started raining." He seethed at the innuendo. Taking a deep breath, he realized he'd never felt protective of a woman's reputation before. In fact, back at the fort, he'd kidded a young corporal in much the same manner Waddell was joking now.

"Aw, hell, boy. Mean ya didn't sleep—"

"Sure, I slept some." He winked. "But I wasn't going to let her catch me at it." He could've laughed at the outlaw's expression—incredulous, disbelieving. Grant refused to satisfy his curiosity. Let the man think what he wanted.

"She still in there?"

"Yeah."

"Well, you're doin' a good job." There was a measure of surprise in his voice. "Shouldn't be long 'fore we know what she's gonna be worth ta us," he added in confidence.

"Oh?" Grant leaned back against the cabin. "Who's gatherin' the information?"

Waddell's eyes became hooded as he pulled a plug of

tobacco from his back pocket. He offered it to Grant, who turned it down. "We got someone who can do the job. An' Eloy dug up a few things in Tombstone." He worked the big chunk of tobacco around in his mouth. "That brother o' hers was s'posed ta be makin' maps o' some sort. We figgered he were a spy."

Grant's muscles tensed. "What'd make you think that? You see him?"

"Mebbe."

Grant kept his own features from registering disappointment that the outlaw had now decided to keep his council. But he kept prying. "Dutch says that Appaloosa I ride belonged to a young fella that came through a couple of weeks ago. Think that was her brother?"

Waddell chewed and spat. "Mebbe."

"The girl might be easier to handle if we tell her something about her brother."

"We ain't gonna tell 'er nothin', ya hear?" Waddell stepped in close to Grant. "Not til we get the dough. Then we might do what we can ta see she meets up with 'im."

Grant shrugged as if whatever they decided to do with her made little difference to him. But he didn't appreciate the sly look in the outlaw's eyes. Waddell knew something about Jacelyn's brother, and Grant had a sickening feeling that it wasn't good news. He also had a gut feeling that he better stick even closer to the woman.

Waddell spat a mouthful of tobacco juice, blocking a lizard's hurried path, then shifted his gaze to Grant. "We got us another job. This 'uns a sure thing. Gonna give ya a chance ta earn your keep."

Grant nodded.

"Grab ya a bite o' breakfast. We'll head out in an hour."

* * *

193

Forty-five minutes later, Grant pulled the cinch tight on the Appaloosa and led it from the barn.

The Kid tied his own horse to the rail as Grant approached. "You did a good job tending my horse, Jones. Appreciate it," he grudgingly added.

"It's a good horse." Grant curiously watched the albino tie a bedroll behind the cantle on his saddle. "Didn't think you'd be able to ride for a while."

"Getting cabin fever." He finished tying the leather strings and turned to face Grant. "Eloy's feeling a might poorly. He's going to hang around this time."

Grant's eyes narrowed. Leaving Jacelyn alone with the Kid had made him uneasy, but . . . Eloy? His stomach felt like a hill of ants was nibbling away the lining.

The Mexican had made no secret that he wanted Jacelyn and would eventually have her. Leaving him alone on the ranch with her was tantamount to setting a beehive full of honey in front of a hungry bear.

Rubbing the back of his neck, Grant started toward the ranch house, stopped in mid-stride and spun back to the horse. Pulling his knife from its scabbard, he bent and picked up the Appaloosa's left front hoof. Using the blade, he cleaned particles of dirt and straw from the frog. He worked his way around the animal, doing the same with each hoof.

When he reached the right front hoof, he fumbled and dropped the knife. Picking it back up, he scooped a small pebble into his palm and hid it beneath the handle.

Silently apologizing to the horse, he pried a small space between the hoof and shoe. Glancing through his lowered lashes, he searched the area close by to be sure no one was watching. Seeing none of the men paid him any particular attention, he quickly poked in the piece of gravel.

He set the foot down, straightened, resheathed the knife, and dusted off his hands. Without a backward glance at the horse, he again set off toward the house. As he reached the porch steps, his prisoner came through the front door.

Jacelyn smiled, surprised and delighted to find Grant right in front of her. Dora had informed her the men were leaving soon, and she had hoped to catch a glimpse of him.

"How long will you be gone?" She twisted her fingers together to keep from clutching onto him. Why did he have to go? As frightened as she was of the outlaw gang, knowing Grant was somewhere around the ranch gave her a sense of security. But now he was leaving . . .

"I don't know." He wished he could confess "not long," but he again figured that what she didn't know couldn't hurt her. Her emotions played across her face for all to see. He wouldn't risk telling her that thanks to a soon-to-be-lame horse, he'd be back to look after her. So, he just shrugged.

Dora joined them on the porch at the same time Waddell sauntered up from the bunkhouse. Dora glanced toward the barn and commented, " 'Pears the Kid's saddling up." She slanted a knowing look at Jacelyn, who returned the look and heaved an exaggerated sigh of relief.

Waddell spun the ammunition cylinder of his pistol and fingered the bullets on his holster. Satisfied, he finally glanced over at the Kid. "Said he feels up ta ridin'." He looked back to his woman. "Eloy's feelin' poorly, so he'll be stayin' 'round ta see after ya women folk."

Grant didn't miss the slight widening of Jacelyn's eyes, or the brief flash of fear across her face. The look disappeared in an instant though, and she didn't make a fuss or complain. His chest tightened. She was some trooper.

Jacelyn felt like winter had blown in. The mention of rat-faced Eloy chilled her. The Kid was overtly repulsive and Pablo was vengeful, but Eloy possessed an evil determination for which her bravado and small stature were no match.

She glanced at Grant, but knew there was nothing she could say or do to change things. He was, after all, a member of the gang. Though he'd promised her protection, he still had to follow Waddell's orders.

She gulped and swayed nearer to Dora. The older woman had helped her fend off the Kid, perhaps she could influence Eloy. Of course, she rationalized, she might be worrying for nothing. She was probably the last thing on Eloy's mind *if* he was ill.

Grant reluctantly trailed Waddell to the barn after sending Jacelyn a stern glance. He hoped she would recall and obey the instructions he'd given her the last time he had to leave. If so, she would probably be fine until he returned.

After the men had ridden out, Jacelyn and Dora went to the kitchen. The older woman folded a cup towel and frowned. "Wish I had somethin' ta cut up ta make more o' these here towels. Shoulda asked Waddy ta fetch a yard or two o' muslin."

Jacelyn leaned against the counter and regarded Dora thoughtfully. "Is there a general store in Tombstone?"

Dora glanced at the floor. "Don't know, but I reckon so."

Jacelyn's brows furrowed. "You mean you've never been to Tombstone? Where do you shop?" From what she'd overheard, Tucson was days away and Tombstone was the closest town.

Dora stepped on an ant who dared to cross her clean floor. "I don't."

"What? You don't? Not at all?" But then she remembered the living room and other areas of the house she'd seen. There were few frills or knickknacks, the kinds of things a woman might buy when she went to town for supplies and necessities and found some little item to splurge on.

"Ain't been in no town fer years. Waddy, or one o' the boys does all the shoppin' I need."

Jacelyn's heart went out to the woman. No wonder she was so hard and calloused. She probably hadn't had another woman for company in ages. How Jacelyn wished she had something to give Dora to use for towels, or some little feminine something.

All she'd had was the torn dress, which Grant had completely destroyed last night. She had nothing else . . . Her eyes rounded. Yes, she did. The trunk. Hadn't Grant said it contained clothing? And who knew what else?

Although *she* refused to wear pilfered property, as long as it was there anyway, Dora might find something she needed.

"You know, we could go to my cabin . . ."

"Naw, there ain't nothin' worth nothin' in that old shack. I done seen. That's why I had ta give ya the blanket."

"But, remember when the gan . . . boys came back last time? Grant brought a trunk. I haven't looked inside, but . . ." She suddenly recalled how pleased he'd been to give it to her, and how hateful she'd acted. He hadn't *had* to bring it all that way.

She sniffed. But he'd thought there might be something she could use. Something to make her life easier. Had she totally overreacted in refusing to accept "stolen" articles?

Looking at Dora, she smiled. "Let's go see what's in the trunk." It might even be fun, she thought.

Dora seemed hesitant, but soon caught some of

Jacelyn's excitement. She grinned back. "All right by me. It's still a while 'fore time ta start supper."

They walked down to the cabin and went inside. Jacelyn nervously glanced around to see if Grant had left anything that might show that he'd spent the night with her. The only thing was her torn dress, but that wouldn't mean anything to Dora.

All at once, her eyes darted to the floor beneath the window. The knife. Grant hadn't found it, but it was there somewhere. She would have to keep Dora's attention directed away from the window. And at her next opportunity, she'd have to find and hide the weapon.

She herded Dora to the trunk, which was still against the wall near the foot of her bed. Jacelyn grabbed a leather handle and tugged, intent on moving it to the center of the room. The trunk didn't budge. Her eyes rounded. Grant had lifted the bulky weight to his shoulder and easily carried it. With a sigh of appreciation for the power of the muscles she'd caressed the night before, she gestured for Dora to take the other leather handle. Together they succeeded.

The women looked at each other and smiled, like two little girls about to open something forbidden.

With a thrill of naughty expectation, Jacelyn slowly raised the lid.

Chapter Thirteen

Behind Jacelyn, Dora gasped and reached into the trunk. She pulled out a red and green plaid shawl that Jacelyn thought had probably been thrown in at the last minute to keep dust from sifting into the rest of the clothing.

It appeared old and worn to Jacelyn, but she didn't say a word when she saw the awe and delight in Dora's eyes as she gazed longingly at the garment.

"Lawdy be . . . Ain't it the most beauteous thing ya ever did see?" Wrinkles seemed to fade magically from Dora's face. A rosy blush tinted her pale cheeks. Her light eyes sparkled.

"Yes," Jacelyn agreed. "It's lovely."

Dora ran her hands over the finely woven wool. "It's soft as a newborn lamb."

"Try it on," Jacelyn urged.

"Oh . . . oh, I mustn't."

"Why not?"

"Well, it don't belong ta me."

Jacelyn shook her head in wonderment. The woman lived with a pack of thieves and murderers, but didn't want to wear something that didn't belong to her. Dora was proving to be quite a contradiction.

"But . . ." she argued, "Grant said that I, ah, we . . .

were to use whatever we needed. That's why he ...
went to the trouble to ... bring it." Again she thought
about what prompted him to do such a thing. None of
the other outlaws gave a hoot about the *womenfolk*.

Now if the trunk had been filled with guns and ammunition, or gloves or belts or something useful to
them, it would've been a different matter. The more she
learned about Grant Jones, the less she understood him.

"Well, mebbe I can jest see what it looks like ..."
Dora drew the shawl lovingly across her shoulders. She
couldn't keep her hands still as she continued to stroke
the soft material. "Lawdy, ain't it somethin'?"

Jacelyn spotted a moth hole and a few shiny spots
where it had been worn thin. But then she scolded herself. She'd been fortunate enough never to have to wear
clothing that was too old or too small or too—anything.
Now, in her situation, and Dora's, they should be grateful for whatever they had, in whatever condition.

"Dora, I think you should keep the shawl. It looks
wonderful on you."

Dora spun around. "Ya really think so?"

"I do."

"Wel-l-l-l ... Reckon I might at that. Lessen *you*
want it." Her fingers dug into the colorful wool.

Jacelyn smiled and shook her head.

As hot as the August day had turned out to be, Dora
kept the shawl on and peered over Jacelyn's shoulder.
"What else be in that thing?"

The next few items were lace undergarments—
camisoles, pantalettes, and several pairs of stockings.
Jacelyn was sorely tempted to take a pair of each. She
had yet to have a bath, other than that offered by the
rain last night, and she was almost to the point of steal-
ing to get fresh underthings—almost.

"Aw, my Gawd, looky at them fancy things, would
ya." Dora carefully picked up a camisole with a wide

piece of lace around the top and an embroidered rose on the bust. "I ain't never seen anything like this afore in my life."

"Take that, too. There's several in here." Jacelyn gnawed on her lower lip. Funny that she could be so generous with someone else's clothes. And she was thoroughly enjoying Dora's pleasure. Her brows wrinkled. Perhaps she and Grant had more in common than she thought. Perhaps she was being unduly stubborn about the matter.

Dora shook her head. "Nope, ya ain't took nothin' yet. You pick, then I'll take somethin'.'"

Jacelyn sighed and picked one of each from amongst the undergarments. She could always put them back later. Besides, whoever owned this trunk was obviously wealthy and could probably easily replace the items. And the possibility was slim that the rightful owner would come to claim the trunk—or want clothing back that had been in the hands of outlaws. Dora needed the clothes . . . and if Jacelyn was honest, she did too.

Next were two satin night dresses and one serviceable linen robe. Several cotton and worsted day dresses followed. Dora fondled each item as it was unpacked and laid everything aside. "I ain't got much use fer such fripperies."

Jacelyn pulled out thread and needles, a mirror, and a tortoise shell brush and comb set. She felt a light touch on her hand.

"You need them things, Missy."

She reached up and felt the rats in her hair and flushed. She was afraid to pick up the mirror and decided against doing so until she was alone. But . . . if Dora thought she looked that bad . . .

Dora's indrawn breath caught her attention. The woman's eyes wide with awe, her mouth slightly ajar, drew Jacelyn's eyes to the trunk. She reached in and shook out a short-sleeved gown of silver-gray velvet. It was simple, yet elegantly styled with a scooped neckline, capped sleeves and a full gathered skirt that earned "oohs" and "aahs" from both women. Stunning was the only word she could think of to describe the gown.

She held it up to Dora. At first she'd thought the color would be too bland on the wan Dora, but it accentuated her silver hair, pale eyes, and high cheekbones.

"Oh, Dora, you've got to have this."

Dora backed away. "No. No, I cain't."

Jacelyn looked puzzled. "Why?"

"Don't got no use fer nothin' that pretty." Adamant about the matter, she added, " 'Sides, it's too big. It'd fit you better'n me."

Jacelyn thought Dora acted scared of the dress. As if she wasn't good enough to have something so fine. But as Jacelyn eyed the dress and then Dora, she made mental notes on the tucks she could make to fit the dress to the older woman.

Thinking it would be a wonderful surprise, Jacelyn quickly folded the dress and laid it in the lid. She then reached into the trunk again and pulled out several pairs of shoes. Once again she was tempted to take something. She might as well go barefoot for the little good her own shoes did her anymore. She sniffed. All right, just one pair. But she would hide them under the bed and only wear them when the opportunity arose to escape.

The next items were a baby blanket, knit caps, and booties, and tiny gowns. She laid them with the gray dress and dug back into the trunk.

Dora sighed and sat back weakly on the cot.

Jacelyn turned, holding up yet another baby blanket. "These would make good towels. We could . . . Dora? What's wrong?"

Tears trickled down the woman's face. The sight was so unexpected that it frightened Jacelyn. "Are you sick?

Can I get you something?" She was nearly frantic. Dora was so still, and seemed to be staring into a different world.

Finally, Dora held up her hand. "Don't worry none 'bout me. I'll be all right."

Jacelyn was on her knees, looking up into the woman's chalk white features and red-rimmed eyes. "You're *not* all right. I'll go get Eloy." She shuddered at the thought. "Perhaps he can catch up with the—"

"No!" Dora took hold of Jacelyn's shoulders. "Don't mention this ta no one. Understand?"

Jacelyn cowered back and nodded, but she didn't understand. Not at all. What had upset Dora so?

Dora sighed again. A deep, hurtful sigh. "It's jest . . . I ain't never told no one . . ." Her sad eyes found Jacelyn's questioning ones. "I had me a baby once. A baby girl. The most precious thing in my life."

When Dora paused, Jacelyn couldn't control her curiosity. "What happened to her?"

There was a long silence. Jacelyn had just about decided that Dora wasn't going to answer.

"I had ta give 'er up."

Jacelyn rocked back on her heels. "Oh, no."

"Didn't want ta do it. Was the hardest thing . . ."

"How terrible. Why did you have to do it?"

"Had no choice." Dora's voice cracked. "I were afraid the boys was gonna hurt her, an' me, too, if'n I didn't."

"The boys? You mean the gang?" Jacelyn was flabbergasted. Outrage contorted her voice. "The *gang* made you give up your child? How could they? How dare they do such a despicable thing?" Phrases like *lowdown scum* came to mind, but Jacelyn was so appalled she found herself speechless.

"It were the right thing ta do. She bawled all the time and slowed 'em down. An' tweren't no life fer a young'un." Tears still rolled down Dora's cheeks, dripping into the shawl. When she noticed, Dora sniffled and moved the wool from her lap.

"Did someone adopt her?" Jacelyn was fascinated. This woman was more than she'd ever expected.

"No. I jest found a woman what looked like a good mother . . . an' I give Shiloh ta her."

"Shiloh," Jacelyn repeated. "What a beautiful name."

Dora smiled. "An' she looked jest like me."

"Oh, Dora. Do you have any idea where she might be?"

"Naw. Waddy said he's looked in the towns around. But he ain't never seen 'er."

"Is that why you don't go into town? Are you afraid you'll see Shiloh somewhere and—"

"No, Missy. It's cause the law got ta recognizin' our bunch, with a woman an' all riding along. Waddy says it's safer fer everyone if'n I jest stay put."

"How long has it been since you've been to a town?"

Dora thought, and shook her head. "Been so many years now I don't rightly recollect."

"You don't mind? You don't get lonesome?" Jacelyn couldn't imagine never going to town—for years.

"I can't afford ta, it jest makes me miserable," Dora replied defensively. " 'Sides, I got everything I need."

Jacelyn was getting used to reading expressions. She could tell from the stubborn set of Dora's chin and her compressed lips that she had better stop pushing for answers.

"Well, I wonder what else is in the trunk?" When she received no response from Dora, she shrugged and added with a forced smile, "Let's see, shall we?"

Waddell seemed in no hurry to reach their destination as they rode west from the ranch. The sedate pace was easier on the horses, but Grant was grinding his teeth like he could chew the sights off his six-gun by the time the Appaloosa began to limp. They'd ridden farther than he had planned. It would be well after dark before he could make it back to the ranch.

Grant hollered, pulled his horse to a stop and dismounted. He was running his hand down the animal's leg when Waddell rode up.

"What's the hold up, Jones?"

Grant continued to feel the Appaloosa's leg. "My horse went lame."

"Damn it, what happened?" Waddell scowled and scratched his belly.

"Don't know. How much farther we got to go?"

"Too far fer a three-legged horse. Reckon your outta luck again."

Disappointed that Waddell was so tight-lipped about their destination, Grant tilted his hat back and rubbed his forehead. "Damn. I didn't join up to sit back at the ranch," he lied, and hooded his eyes. It didn't sound like Waddell would force him to continue.

The Kid rode up. "What's going on?"

"Jones's hoss went lame."

"Hell, we need him. What if the mill sends out guards?"

Waddell's eyes narrowed. "Shut up. I'm sick o' your whining. We'll manage."

Grant showed no emotion whatsoever as he looked at the two men. "I could go back and change horses and meet you somewhere."

"Naw, won't be no time fer that." Waddell looked back the way they'd come and then over to Grant. "Long as yore gonna go back, might's well ride north o' the house an' see if the rain filled the tanks."

"If I have to." Grant shook his head slightly. The outlaw would probably make a good rancher if he'd put aside his life of crime. What a waste.

Waddell pointed to the Appaloosa. "Take it slow on that hoss. Don't want him crippled permanent."

"Neither do I," Grant agreed.

The Kid glared at Grant. "I don't like this, Dick. That horse never showed any signs of being lame before."

Waddell snorted. "Neither did yours 'fore it were shot. Think he crippled his horse on purpose?"

The albino squinted one eye. "Maybe."

"Jus' so's he could bitch 'bout bein' sent back? We gotta get goin'. You comin', or stayin' ta argue?"

"If I don't come, you for sure won't have enough men for the job."

"So get your butt gone."

Grant mounted and watched the outlaws ride off. His mind worked furiously as he tried to figure out what mill the Kid had been talking about. There were several in the direction they were headed.

He was suddenly torn by indecision. He felt it his duty to warn the mills about a possible outlaw attack, yet he couldn't bear to think what might happen to Jacelyn if he didn't return. Damn. He could be worrying for nothing, but his gut instinct warned him that Eloy wouldn't wait too long.

He rode into an arroyo and around a bend. Stopping the horse, he dismounted, picked up its hoof and dislodged the stone. "Sorry, boy."

Grant patted the animal's neck and walked around to check the cinch before swinging back into the saddle. A shadow fell over his shoulder. As he turned, something hurtled from the top of a boulder and slammed him to the ground. He struggled, but his right arm was twisted behind his back.

A knife blade pricked his neck. He stopped moving, silently cursing his stupidity for not checking the arroyo more closely. His negligence was about to cost him his life.

A low, guttural voice ground in his ear, "My brother has lived too many moons among the white eyes. He is soft and weak and rides with his head in the sky."

Grant closed his eyes, then reopened them. "Head in the *clouds*, Santana. And you are only a half-brother. A lucky half-brother, this time." Yet he had to admit that Santana was right. He'd been so concerned about getting back to the ranch and the woman that he hadn't paid attention. *He'd* had luck on his side lately with all the renegades and bandits roaming the country.

The Apache chuckled and helped Grant up. "Santana does not know meaning of this word, luck."

"Santana is a boastful braggart today, too." Grant grinned, but knew what the Indian said was true. His brother would never have survived this long on luck alone. His skill and cunning had been developed from the time he was first able to walk.

Squatting on his thickly muscled legs, Santana gestured in the direction the rest of the gang had ridden. "Why you leave the other white eyes?"

Grant hunkered down next to the Apache. "I'm worried about the woman. The Mexican left to watch her has an evil heart. She is not safe."

The Indian nodded.

Grant scrubbed the back of his neck. "You must do something for me."

Santana stared into Grant's eyes, waiting to hear what his brother had to say.

"The other men are on their way to rob a mill wagon. Probably a shipment of silver bars. I figure they're headed to either Charleston or Contention. Ride to the fort and tell Colonel Alexander. Maybe he can send a troop, or at least telegraph a warning."

Santana nodded. "It is done. I go thunder fort." He rose gracefully to his feet. "You ride to woman?"

"Yes. I just hope I get there in time."

The two men clasped each others' forearms. Santana faded into the hills. Grant mounted and kicked the Appaloosa into a lope. As the sun sank lower on the horizon, his desperation and sense of urgency increased.

Jacelyn and Dora prepared supper that evening with a new air of camaraderie. Earlier, they had cut a baby blanket into fourths and the soft towels now lay neatly folded in the cupboard.

They were carrying venison stew and fresh-baked bread to the table when Eloy walked in. He'd been hanging around outside all day and though Dora paid him little mind, Jacelyn's skin crawled every time he looked at her. His sharp, beady eyes seemed to rip the clothes right off her body.

Conversation was minimal during the meal, though it was apparent Eloy had something on his mind. Whenever Jacelyn darted a glance in his direction, he had a smirk on his face, like he was privy to something she and Dora didn't know.

A long silence was broken when Dora slammed her fork on the table. "Gawd damn it, Eloy. Whatcha sittin' there grinnin' like a bloated ass about?"

Eloy frowned. He stuffed a chunk of buttered bread in his mouth. Shaking his head, he just kept eating.

Jacelyn sighed and gave up her attempt to eat. Her appetite had disappeared with Eloy's first leer.

"Thought ya was hungry, Missy. Ya ain't done nothin' but push yore vittles 'round the plate."

Jacelyn tucked her hands in her lap. "I'm sorry."

Dora took the last bite of her stew and scooted her chair back. "Well, don't know 'bout you folks, but I'm done." She picked up Jacelyn's plate and plucked Eloy's stew-filled fork right out of his hand.

"Eloy, your job's done fer the day. Me an' the girl'll do right fine til mornin'." Dora eyed Eloy critically and with a hint of wary speculation. "Ya still ain't lookin' too pert. I'd get a good night's shut eye, was I you."

The man's eyes glinted with malice. His nostrils flared. But to Jacelyn's relief, he didn't say a word or offer resistance to Dora's command. Yet he still had that nasty smirk on his lips. Jacelyn shuddered.

When Eloy was gone, Dora stacked his plate on top of hers. "Don't know why Waddy keeps that slimy bastard . . ." She glanced quickly to Jacelyn, then back to the table. "That feller 'round. Gives me the willies, he does."

Jacelyn smiled weakly. "I couldn't agree more."

They cleared the table and went into the kitchen. Dora scraped the dishes and set them in a basin. "Ain't 'nough o' these ta worry 'bout tonight. What say we turn in?" She pointed at Jacelyn. "An' you're gonna sleep up here."

"Thank you, Dora." Jacelyn had been afraid to walk down to her cabin with Eloy lurking about, but hadn't wanted to admit it to Dora. "But I need my blanket."

"What the hell, then. Since I don't got another'un, we'll jest go get it." She patted her full belly. "Could use the exercise."

"No, no. You don't need to—"

"If'n we get goin', we'll be back 'fore ya can quit your arguing."

Jacelyn grinned. Her protest had been weak, at best. "You're probably right."

Stars twinkled from the cloudless sky. The half moon illuminated their way along the path. Jacelyn looked up, remembering the hours James had spent studying the stars, using navigation maps a family friend had given him when he was just a child. He'd plot out faraway destinations and play "pirate" in a tree house in the backyard. It was not surprising to Jacelyn that he'd ended up a mapmaker.

James. James, please find me. Please.

The women had just reached the cabin when Eloy stepped from the shadows. He winked at Jacelyn. "Ah, lady, I hoped you would come."

"Eloy, what the devil ya doin' here? Thought I done told ya ta hit the hay."

The Mexican shook his head. "I had hoped you stay in su casa, señora." He leered at Jacelyn. "I only want theese one."

Dora spread her hands on her hips. "I'm warnin' ya, Eloy, ya better go on 'bout your—"

Eloy's arm shot out. He caught Dora across the mouth with the back of his hand. When she went for her pistol, he smashed his fist into her chin. She dropped to the ground, unconscious.

Jacelyn screamed. "Dora! Dora, are you all right?"

The Mexican grabbed her around the waist and pulled her back against his bony body.

"Thee old ladee, she no hurt bad. Now you must make me mucho happy, or I kill her, no?"

"No." Jacelyn kicked out and caught him on the shin with her heel. Her other foot hit his other shin. He released her, but stood right behind her, blocking all escape routes except the way into the cabin.

She tried to slam the door, but his foot blocked her efforts. Too late, she realized she'd run into a trap.

Her heart sank as her terror rose. She glanced to the window, but remembered Grant had repaired it. Besides, the beast would be on top of her before she got one leg through the opening.

The knife. Why hadn't she gone to the trouble of finding it before now? She scurried behind the table and kept it between herself and the Mexican who entered right behind her.

His movements, slow and measured, were that of an evil reptile tracking its prey. He smelled of sweat and manure. Her stomach churned. She tried to gulp down her fear, to think rationally.

Edging around the table away from him, she darted a look over her shoulder. *Where was the knife?* He slithered closer. She couldn't breathe. She clutched at the table and glanced below the window. *Where was the knife?* He snarled a chuckle of anticipation. *Could she beg?* The hard glare in his eyes told her that would be useless.

She prayed.

He grabbed the table and jerked it, jarring her arms, enjoying the depraved game.

Please, Lord, this would be a good time for the Cavalry to ride to the rescue.

He jerked the table again. She hung on, then responded by shoving it into his thighs. He cursed and swung out to hit her, but caught only air when she ducked to search for the knife.

Please let me get away.

He stalked around the corner of the table.

On her hands and knees, she frantically hunted for her weapon as he loomed over her.

Please, give me the strength to survive ...

She scrambled to her feet and ran for the door.

He grabbed the back of her shirt. Loose threads gave way. She screamed. The shirt ripped away from her shoulders. In a new frenzy of fear, she lunged for her freedom.

Clutching scraps of empty flannel, Eloy shook his fist and roared.

She reached the door. Her heart thundered. She could make it.

Eloy made a flying dive. Her feet rolled out from under her. He pinned her to the floor. His hands were everywhere, pinching, prying, tearing. She rolled to scratch at his face.

He cursed and slapped her.

She wedged her knee against his chest and pushed, futilely.

His fingers clawed her camisole. He yanked until the flimsy material tore from her body.

She pummeled his face and shoulders. Kicked any place she could reach. Rabid now, he growled and slammed his fist into her chin. Stars blazed behind her eyes. Everything spun out of control.

He grunted and groped her soft breasts. Panting, he yanked at the waistband of her trousers.

Conscious enough to feel what he was doing, through a gray fog she struggled anew. Her nails gouged the tender skin beneath his eyes.

"Bitch. I will hurt you for that." He hit her with the back of his hand.

Jacelyn tasted blood. Pain flooded her. She couldn't think. Couldn't react. Reality seemed far away as new sensations assailed her. Cool air teased her skin. Rough hands hurt her. She tried to lift her arm, but it was heavy. Too heavy. Her mind was fuzzy. But she felt the pain.

Hot breath hit her lips before they were crushed against her teeth. A thick, wet tongue forced its way into her mouth. She gagged.

"Now you weell be mine, bitch. The gringo no be so hot a shot, no?" He twisted her nipple until tears rolled from her eyes. "No?"

She rolled her head from side to side, trying to escape the horror.

"Be muy bueno por Eloy. Maybe Eloy keep you. You like that, eh?" Again he cruelly twisted her nipple.

"No. No!" From somewhere, she found the strength to open her eyes. All thought and feeling fled, leaving her on the other side of terror. He was above her, grinning, drooling. He held a knife. A huge knife. The blade pointed at her chest.

Oh, Grant. Moonlight glinted off the blade. With primal fear, she screamed.

Chapter Fourteen

Grant rode into the ranch headquarters well after dusk. Looping the Appaloosa's reins on a rail near the barn, he ran toward the house where a lantern burned. He was probably going to make an ass of himself by bursting in on the women and scaring them half to death, but he didn't give a damn as long as they were safe.

He slammed open the front door and hurried into the living room. Everything looked normal. He rushed to the kitchen. Dirty dishes were stacked in the basin, but all else was in its place. Nevertheless, the foreboding burning inside him became a roaring blaze.

Where were they? "Jacelyn? Dora?" He went down the hall. The bedroom was empty. His heart pounded in time with the throbbing in his temples as he ran from the house and back to the barn. Throwing open the door, he stopped and listened, but heard only the stomp of a hoof and a muffled snort.

He backed from the barn and looked toward the bunkhouse. There was a light, but he wasn't drawn in that direction. Instinct turned him toward the cabin. He took his first step and heard the scream.

Panic lent wings to his feet. He recognized Dora before he reached her, moaning and holding her chin as she leaned against the cabin.

Dora saw Grant and motioned him inside. "Hurry!"

Grant didn't need any extra urging. He nodded and shouldered through the doorway as Jacelyn screamed again. Eloy kneeled over Jacelyn's half-naked body. Blood surged through Grant's veins as all of his protective instincts collected into one raging roar. "No!"

He grabbed the Mexican by the shoulders, picking him up and shaking him as if he were little more than a field mouse.

Eloy twisted and jerked free of Grant's grasp. He landed with his knees bent and fumbled on the floor. When he stood, he held a double-edged knife in his hand.

Grant grinned. He pulled his own thin-bladed knife from its sheath. Balancing on the balls of his feet, he passed the knife from one hand to the other, enticing, taunting, and gradually backing up to lure the outlaw away from Jacelyn.

Eloy feinted to the left, then shifted back and struck out. Grant dodged, spun and kicked, catching Eloy in the stomach with the toe of his boot. Eloy hissed and doubled over, but he still managed to slice Grant's thigh with his knife. The Mexican's eyes took on a crazed glare at the sight of first blood.

Jacelyn groaned and rolled to her side. She was nauseated. And humiliated. And cold. Cold to the depths of her soul. But little by little she realized one of her prayers had been answered.

She knew she needed to move to get out of danger. She focused on the cot and her blanket. She had to get the blanket. So cold. Her hand shook as she reached out. A hard body bumped into her, knocking her against the wall. Weak and dizzy, unable to think clearly, she huddled into a ball where she'd fallen.

Grant's hand contracted on the knife handle. His eyes spit fire as he faced the outlaw. Eloy charged and Grant

215

blocked the thrust, raising his own blade to take a chunk of flesh from a gaunt cheek before his hand was knocked off target.

Eloy yowled. Grant bent his knees and shifted his weight. "Come on, you sonofabitch. I'm goin' to take you a piece at a time."

The Mexican's lips curled. "We weell see, eh, gringo?"

While Eloy gloated over his barb, Grant stepped forward, slit the arm out of the outlaw's shirt, and quickly moved out of reach. Eloy shouted his frustration and thrust out awkwardly. Grant grimaced, sensing victory was near.

Jacelyn heard Eloy's yell. With dread she lifted her head to see Grant spin and nimbly leap away from the tip of Eloy's knife. The hard, dangerous gleam in Grant's eyes and the catlike grace and quickness of his movements reassured her.

Grant baited the Mexican, trying to anger and frustrate him into letting down his guard. At the right moment, Grant swung his arm upward. The tip of his knife grated along the outlaw's rib cage.

Eloy darted away and stopped, looking at the blood soaking his shirt with amazement and confusion. His eyes glazed and he breathed deeply, like a man who'd held his breath a moment too long. His eyes focused on Grant, who was only mildly winded and was grinning like a lobo wolf sure of his next meal.

Suddenly, Eloy glanced at Jacelyn. She cringed closer to the wall. The outlaw's eyes narrowed and flickered around the room that had turned into a trap.

Grant's gaze never wavered from Eloy's. He saw the man's eyes widen and his pupils contract as he made a decision. *The fool.*

When Eloy made his move, Grant moved, too. What he didn't see was the chair, which had been moved during the scuffle. His foot hooked the chair leg. Cursing, he fought to untangle himself. Eloy was within two feet of Jacelyn. Whimpering, she scooted farther down the wall. Grant's gut contracted.

Finally free, he dove forward and tackled the outlaw. His momentum careened them both into the cot.

Grant allowed himself one quick glance at Jacelyn.

Eloy kicked Grant on his injured thigh. Grant turned his full attention back to the struggling outlaw, determined to end the threat against Jacelyn.

During Grant's brief distraction, Eloy had shifted his knife to his other hand. His lips pulled back in a feral sneer. "Now, gringo, you die."

Grant heard the hissed warning. Reflexively, he raised his right arm when the knife came unexpectedly from his left side. Their blades clashed. The hilts clanged together. Their eyes locked in angry determination. Eloy's wavered first. His arm trembled beneath the pressure of Grant's weight. Eloy bent his knees and kicked the suddenly daunting man aside.

Their knives parted. Grant was tossed backward, but didn't fall. He was there to meet Eloy when he came off the cot snarling, his knife poised to thrust. But the outlaw's foot slipped on several drops of blood. His momentum carried him forward, but threw his arms back as he fought for balance. He crashed into Grant, impaling himself on Grant's long, thin blade.

Surprise registered on both men's faces. Disbelief mingled with pain on Eloy's. Grant felt grim satisfaction. He yanked his knife from Eloy's chest and let him sink slowly to the floor.

Grant started to turn away, but talonlike fingers gripped his ankle. He looked down to see Eloy's mouth working and knelt.

"Y-you no . . . have win . . . yet . . . *gringo.*" He spit the word with his last breath of life.

Grant just stared as the outlaw died. He wiped the blood from his blade on the man's pant leg. Then he rose and turned to Jacelyn.

She was where he'd last seen her, eyes glued to Eloy's body, while her own form shook uncontrollably. He snatched the blanket and knelt down beside her. Gently, he nestled the watch, which had swung around to her back and miraculously survived the attack, back between her breasts, then drew the wool across her shoulders and tucked it around her trembling body. Crooning soft encouragement, he untied his bandana and dabbed at the blood on her chin before taking her in his arms.

Jacelyn couldn't seem to take her eyes off the man who'd beaten and forced himself on her. Although she'd seen everything, even watched him die, she expected him to rise and come at her with fire burning from his eyes, teeth bared and blood dripping from his fangs. She still felt his hands on her, hurting and degrading her. A sob tore from her throat.

"Jacelyn . . . sugar . . . He's not going to hurt you, or anyone, ever again. I promise."

She hiccuped and finally nodded her head. Gradually, she became aware of warmth seeping into her chilled flesh. Of gentle arms holding and rocking her. Of soothing hands rubbing up and down her back.

She buried her face in Grant's chest and coiled her fists into his shirt, holding on to him as if her life depended on him. Which it had. Several times.

Suddenly she remembered Dora and how brutally Eloy had struck her. "Grant, please . . . See about Dora. Sh-she might've been k-killed." She choked on another sob.

A solid thump nearby drew their gazes. Dora had righted the chair and sat slumped in it. The left side of her face was swollen and discolored, her eye slitted. Her lower lip was spit and bleeding. But the other eye settled on Jacelyn, unerringly bright.

"My Gawd, would ya listen ta that? The gal looks like she's been stuffed through a wringer, an' she be askin' after me."

Grant wasn't surprised, but he could tell Dora certainly was. Of course, he guessed the older woman hadn't had many friends.

Jacelyn sniffed and rasped, "Dora, are you all right?"

"I will be, Missy. Been banged up worser'n this afore." She stood a bit unsteadily, but motioned Grant to follow her. "Bring 'er on up ta the house. No need ta hang 'round here." She glanced briefly at the body and shuddered.

Grant was grateful for Dora's invitation. It couldn't be good for Jacelyn to have to keep looking at the bloody body. He gathered her close to his chest and rose, carrying her as if she were the most precious thing in the world. Stepping over the outlaw, he squeezed her tightly so she couldn't look down and really see the gory mess.

Once outside, Dora waited and took hold of his arm as they walked up to the house in the early morning darkness.

Jacelyn reached out and covered Dora's hand with her own. Though it was difficult to move her jaw, she mumbled, "Sure you're all right?"

Dora snorted, then winced. "Lawd, yes, child," she insisted as she hurried up the steps to open the door. "Now we need ta see 'bout you."

Grant laid Jacelyn on the sofa. When she struggled to rise to a sitting position, he pushed her back down. "Stay," he ordered.

She peeked up at him. "I've heard that before."

A slight grin curved one side of his mouth, but he quickly sobered. How could she tease him after all that had happened? Didn't she realize she could have died in that cabin? Didn't she know that he'd almost lost his mind when he saw her lying half-naked and fighting for her life beneath that piece of filth? Didn't she realize it hurt him just to look at her—into her pain-dulled eyes, one cheek swollen to twice its normal size, with the cut on her mouth, and the bruises that were beginning to appear—and know how close he'd come to losing her?

"Grant? What's wrong?"

He closed his eyes. If she hadn't already guessed those truths, she was perceptive enough to pick up on them from his actions. He was grateful to be spared from having to make a response when Dora bustled into the room carrying a basin of warm water, rags, and a tin container.

"Move outta my way, boy." She set the water and other items down, then knelt beside the sofa. Dipping a towel into the water, she patted the dirt and blood from Jacelyn's face. When Jacelyn tensed and tried to turn her head away, Dora sympathized. "Shore wish I had somethin' fer the pain, Missy, but used it all on the Kid, damn 'im."

"I've got something."

Dora and Jacelyn both looked at Grant as he untied a pouch from his gun belt. From inside, he took out several smaller pouches. He took one and went into the kitchen. When he returned, he carried a cup of water. Lifting Jacelyn's head, he held the cup to her lips and commanded, "Drink."

She shrank back. "I, ah . . ."

"Drink."

She blinked and drank. She had no strength of will to argue with her bossy savior.

Dora stared at his pouches, then at his face. She frowned.

Jacelyn sipped the last of the concoction and gurgled, "What is it?"

He held her chin up until she swallowed the last drop. "Indian pipe."

She narrowed her eyes. That didn't tell her much. "What's it for?"

"It will ease your pain." Sitting back on his heels, he made room for Dora to continue her ministrations. He didn't tell her that it was sometimes used as a replacement for opium and that it would also enable her to sleep.

Dora finished sponging Jacelyn's face and took the lid off the tin. She scooped some of the contents onto her fingers and smeared it over Jacelyn's worst bruises.

Again Jacelyn tried to push away. "Now what's that stuff?"

"Mashed milkweed roots," Dora said, matter of factly going on about her business. "It will heal the swelling." Her eyes happened to meet Grant's, and when he nodded at her, she frowned again.

He was the first gunman she'd ever run across who carried doctoring potions around like some Indian warrior. She studied him closely, noting the dark hair and high cheekbones. But then he had those blue eyes ... and moustache and sideburns. No Indians she'd ever seen had that much hair on them. No, he was just smarter than the average outlaw. Didn't believe he was forever invincible.

Jacelyn held still while Dora finished working on her face, all the while wondering what her physician in Richmond would think of the backwoods remedies. She would've grinned, if it hadn't hurt so much, at the image of old Dr. Hammond throwing up his hands in disgust, then sliding his spectacles back up his nose. More than likely he would rant and rave about country quacks.

Dora tugged at the blanket. "Let me see if you need tending anyplace else, Missy."

Jacelyn whimpered and held the ends adamantly closed.

Seeing Jacelyn's shy glance toward Jones, Dora nodded and told him, "Run down ta the cabin an' fetch back one o' them night dresses in the trunk."

Grant ground his teeth at the way Jacelyn retreated into herself when she glanced at him. Damn it, he wanted to shout, it wasn't as if he hadn't seen her naked, or even felt some of that creamy flesh. Worst of all, though, was his dread that her encounter with Eloy would ruin her feelings toward men—men in general, him in particular. She had too passionate a nature for her to bury it forever.

Inwardly cursing, he turned without a word and left the house.

After he'd gone, Dora insisted on looking over the rest of Jacelyn's battered body, though the younger woman protested and blushed profusely. Clicking her tongue at all the bruises on Jacelyn's breasts and thighs, Dora concluded, "Killin' was too good fer that bastard. Shoulda let the 'Paches have 'im." And with that said, she glanced questioningly after Jones and shook her head.

Jacelyn's lids drooped. She sat up enough for Dora to slip the blanket from around her shoulders to spread it over her length, then slumped back down. She was so sleepy she could hardly summon the strength to form words to answer Dora's questions and to thank her for helping.

Surprisingly, she felt pretty good. Her face and body didn't throb with pain, though she still felt a dull ache. Whatever Grant had given her worked.

Through a fog, she thought she heard his voice. But then it was Dora who urged her to sit up and don a

222

night dress. As the cool material slithered over her feverish flesh, she realized she hadn't worn anything so soft for a long, long time. Was she back home? No, there was that voice again, that deep, husky voice that brought visions of strength and gentleness and blue, blue eyes.

She sighed and let herself drift. So tired. Sleep ...

Grant stood beside the mound of earth and wiped the sweat from his brow. He decided to go ahead and bury the outlaw and clean up the cabin that night. Might as well do something; he sure couldn't sleep. He was too keyed up from the fight and too concerned about Jacelyn to rest. Chores. A well-known cure-all for what ails a body. So, why wasn't it working?

Returning the shovel to the barn, he decided to curry and grain the Appaloosa. He'd forgotten about the animal until he went to the cabin to hunt up a nightgown.

The horse whinnied and Grant scratched its forehead. "Wish you could talk, big fella. Then maybe I could find out what happened to James McCaffery." If only he could rid himself of the feeling McCaffery's fate wasn't good.

Grant tossed the horse some hay, blew out the lantern, and walked from the barn. As if from their own volition, his feet carried him toward the house. He wanted to check one last time on the women. He'd finally talked Dora into drinking some of his Indian pipe and had put a poultice of her milkweed on her cheek and chin. But only after he'd promised to keep a close watch on Jacelyn had she given up and gone to bed.

Strangely enough, Dora had turned out to be different than his first impression had led him to believe. There was no question that she was intensely loyal to her man, but she had taken Jacelyn under her wing, and Grant would be forever grateful to the woman for standing up for Jacelyn when it counted. He liked Dora, and was glad he didn't feel it necessary to put on an act around her anymore.

He quietly opened the front door and let himself inside. Noiselessly, he crossed the floor to the sofa. Jacelyn lay like an angel, albeit a battered one, with her red-gold hair spread about her and her hands folded across her chest. No black and blue marks or swollen cheek could detract from her beauty. He cleared his throat. Good Lord, he was getting maudlin with emotion.

He took a deep breath and bent over to light the candle on the side table before he sat down on the edge of the sofa. A wisp of hair dangled across her forehead and he gently brushed it aside. Now that he'd seen for himself that she was resting peacefully, he probably should leave.

He trailed his finger down her uninjured cheek and along her delicate jaw. Fury roiled in his gut when he thought about how easily Eloy could've broken her bones. He cursed, wishing he'd drawn the bastard's death out, made him suffer the way he'd tortured Jacelyn. He sighed and started to rise.

Jacelyn was awake, but she didn't want to do or say anything to startle the owner of those cool, gentle fingers. When the tender touch stopped and she felt the sofa tilt, she reached out. "Don't go."

Grant's heart flip-flopped. He sucked in his breath at the sight of dark, navy eyes staring lucidly back at him. "I, ah, didn't mean to wake you. Just wanted to make sure you were resting."

Her lips twitched and she winced. "Ow. I was."

He cleared his throat. "Well, I'd better leave so you can go back to sleep." He started to get up, but her fingers tightened their grip on his arm.

"No ... please ... stay." Her voice trembled. "W-would you hold me? Please?"

"Ahh-h-h. Are you sure?" He'd seen her look of terror after her encounter with Eloy. He couldn't blame her if she had no use for men, period. But, how could he refuse to do something he'd ached to do all along?

Jacelyn looked deep into his eyes, sensing his turmoil ... and his tenderness. She was still frightened, warily searching the shadows, afraid one of them would turn into Eloy's spirit and swoop down upon her. But as soon as she'd seen Grant, the fear had dissipated.

She didn't want to be alone. She needed him to hold her and reassure her that he'd never leave her alone again. "Please?"

He lifted her shoulders and slipped beneath her so that her upper body rested across his lap. Cradling her against his chest, he smiled when she laid her head on his shoulder and snuggled into him.

"Promise me something," she said.

He scooted down to lay his head against the back of the sofa and lifted his feet onto a low table in front of the couch. Once he was comfortable, he drawled, "Hmmmm-m-m?"

"Tomorrow ... show me where you bathe."

"Bathe?"

She nodded.

Then he remembered how at one time he'd thought to use her desire for cleanliness against her as a means of bending her to his will. What an ass he'd been. "Sure. If you're up to it."

Her lids drooped again as his warmth comforted her. "I've dreamed of a bath. Ever since I saw you ... with water dripping from your hair ... rolling over your muscles." She yawned. "I mean ... your chest." Her nose nestled into the hollow at the base of his throat. "You have a beautiful . . . body . . ."

His brows slashed together. "What? Jacelyn . . ." He listened, but all he heard was her even breathing. Her voice had been soft and low and fading, but he thought she'd said something about liking his body. Damn. Had he just imagined it? Or had she really said it?

He sighed and leaned his head back. He'd let her sleep a while and then leave. Just a while.

A board creaked. Grant awakened instantly. Something shuffled across the floor. He slowly unwrapped his arm from Jacelyn and inched it to his side. His fingers curled around his pistol butt.

"Jones?" Dora whispered. "Jones, ya awake?"

Grant released his breath. "Yeah."

"How's the gal?"

He blinked, amazed that the sun was up and he'd overslept. He'd *never* done that before. He looked down at the precious bundle resting against his chest. Then again, he'd never had someone like Jacelyn ask to be held all night, either.

He blinked again and discovered those intriguing eyes looking back at him, half-lidded and a little unfocused, but she was smiling. His heart thundered in his ears. He glanced quickly to Dora, hoping she didn't hear it clear across the room.

When the older woman regarded him innocently, he beckoned, "See for yourself."

Dora came to stand in front of them. First she frowned at the ugly marks on Jacelyn's face, then smiled, too, when Jacelyn tried to grin. She touched a hand to her own distorted features. "We're a coupla sights, ain't we?" Then she sobered and informed them, "Got grits an' bacon. Come fill your bellies."

Grant helped Jacelyn to the table. While he ate with gusto, he sympathetically watched the two women mangle their food with sore teeth and bruised faces.

He soon became aware of Jacelyn casting surreptitious glances his direction. Every time he'd look her way, she'd quickly avert her eyes. He kept watch through his lowered lashes, and when she glanced at him again, he raised his head and said, "You wanted something?"

Jacelyn felt her cheeks flood with heat and shivered at the tingle of pain the action caused. But she nodded.

Grant tapped his fingers on the table. What could be so frightening that she was this leary of asking? "Come on, sugar, out with it."

Dora leaned her elbows on the table and licked bacon grease from her fingers, raptly taking in the evolving scene.

Jacelyn took a deep breath. "Remember what you promised last night?"

He frowned. So much had happened last night. He'd made several promises. Which one did she . . . "Ah, the bath."

She nodded enthusiastically, then closed her eyes and gingerly rested her chin in her palm.

He sat forward, instantly concerned. "I don't think you're up to it today. We better wait—"

Her eyes shot open. "You promised."

"But—"

"Aw, shucks, Jones, go on an' take 'er. There be a pool 'bout half mile down the crick. Might make 'er feel better."

He stubbornly shook his head. "It's not a good idea."

Jacelyn's face, the side where he could see her expression, fell. He gritted his teeth, then shrugged. "If that's what you want . . ."

The grateful light in her eyes made his chest swell. Hell, he might as well admit it, if she asked him to carry her across Death Valley, he'd damn well do it.

Chapter Fifteen

Grumbling beneath his breath about mule-headed women and their contrary ways, Grant helped Jacelyn along the creek bank to the pool. While he muttered, she expounded about obstinate men who thought their way of doing things was the only way.

By the time they reached the pool, both Jacelyn and Grant were flushed and silent, looking anywhere but at each other.

"See, I told you I could walk on my own," Jacelyn triumphed. "My legs weren't hurt, you know?"

His lips thinned. "Yes, I know. But I thought carrying you would keep you from tiring."

She darted a glance at his angry features. "It was very thoughtful, but I am capable of doing a fews things on my own." Men! Why couldn't they accept the fact that some women liked their independence and didn't always need a man to do for them.

A guilty thought niggled into her mind. So far, she hadn't set a very good example for her arguments. What if Grant hadn't come back to the ranch last night? She certainly hadn't refused his help then, had she?

Grant handed her soap and a towel.

She took them, then met his eyes. "I want you to know, though, how grateful I am . . ." She choked, unable to say the words without dredging up painful memories.

He looked away first, unable to gaze into those dark navy eyes without losing a part of himself in their fathomless depths. At that moment, his thoughts were anything but moral and upstanding.

And the last feeling he wanted from her was gratitude.

He stared into the rippling water. "I'm no hero. Just did what had to be done." He stuffed his hands in his pockets and looked up. A squirrel crouched on an overhead branch, turning a pine cone between its front paws.

Jacelyn's mouth dropped open. "No hero? Who else in the Waddell gang would have come to my rescue?" All at once the image of Grant Jones leading a charging Calvary troop galloped through her mind. She quickly shook her head at the absurd picture.

"Go on and take your bath while the sun's shining on the pool." It wasn't the desire to be labeled a hero that had driven him to kill the Mexican, but he wasn't about to examine too closely what had.

She looked at him questioningly.

"It'll be warmer."

"Oh." Deciding the bath took priority over the stupid argument, she sat down and removed the scraps of leather that barely protected the bottoms of her feet. When that was done, she looked over at Grant, who stood as straight and majestic as an Arizona cypress.

She glanced toward the pool and back to Grant.

He hunched his shoulders when he felt her eyes on him. "What?"

Exasperation thickened her voice. "You don't plan to stay here while I bathe, do you?"

He grinned. "Of course. You don't think I'd leave you out here alone, do you?" He repeated the last two words with her same inflection of incredulity.

"No. I mean, yes. You can't stay here."

"I can." He spread his legs and folded his arms across his chest. "A prisoner might try to escape out here."

She thrust out her chin, but blanched at the strain on her sore muscles. She gathered up her shoes and stood. "Then I won't take a bath."

He nodded and took two steps back the way they'd come. "Good."

She frowned, and regretted the action. Drat. Every facial movement she made hurt. She looked ruefully from the arrogant rogue to the swirling water. Why give him the satisfaction of doing exactly what he'd wanted all along? Besides, she desperately needed to scrub last night away.

If he insisted on staying and watching, then he'd better get an eyeful now, because as soon as she could, she was leaving this miserable place behind.

Smiling sweetly, she inwardly cringed from the sudden pain in her cheek and the embarrassment heating her flesh as she began to unbutton the night dress. Of course, underneath, she'd donned a fresh camisole and pantalettes Dora had fetched from the trunk, so her modesty wouldn't be completely vilified, but . . .

She gazed longingly at the water. Sinful as it sounded, she had hoped to dunk herself without having to wear *any* clothing. Sighing, she decided that bathing in any form was better than no bathing at all.

Grant watched her fingers fumble over the buttons, saw the red tint work its way up her neck to flood her cheeks. His conscience bothered him, but he'd be damned if he would leave her here unguarded.

Outlaws and renegades roamed the area and he wasn't that familiar with this part of the mountains. No telling what wild animal might decide to join her in the creek.

Having made his decision, he stalked over and

shoved her hands aside as he deftly took over the task. Unnerved by the feel of her satiny skin teasing the backs of his fingers, he felt his own face heat and quickly stepped away when he finished.

Jacelyn was also shaken from the warm feelings his touch provoked. After the horrible things that had happened last night, the nasty things that Eloy had . . . Well, she hadn't expected to enjoy a man's touch for a long time—if ever again. But Grant had disproved that notion last night and again just now. The briefest brush of his hands set her flesh atingle.

She looked up in wonderment. What did she do now? Thank him for undressing her? That hardly seemed appropriate. But . . .

"If you need me, I'll be up the creek a ways."

She gazed in the direction he pointed. The creek turned to the right around a mass of boulders and disappeared behind a tree trunk whose roots had been washed bare over the years and angled down into the water like long, gnarled fingers.

Grant turned and walked away along the grassy bank. Incredulous, she watched him. What about the possibility of his *prisoner* trying to get away? Instead of feeling relief, she found herself staring longingly at his back with a sense of abandonment and loss.

Soon the soothing sound of the water became more than she could resist. Stepping out of the night dress, she debated taking off her undergarments since Grant had left her alone. But a quick glance around and the scary notion that eyes watched her settled her dilemma. She'd wear the underclothes and wash them at the same time.

She picked up the soap and stepped carefully over slippery pebbles and stones. When the water first lapped over her toes, she started and almost yanked her foot out. As Grant had predicted, the water was *cold.*

Her hand brushed something small and hard on her chest. She gasped. The watch. She clutched it in her hand, thanking Heaven that she hadn't gotten it wet. It still amazed her that Eloy hadn't ripped it from her neck when . . .

She took it off and sloshed over to the bank where she laid it carefully on top of her night dress. Then, unable to resist the urge, she returned to the water.

The pool wasn't deep, flowing to just above her knees, but through the clear water she could see a flat rock worn smooth of moss. She could sit on that and douse her whole body. Her skin prickled with chill bumps as she lowered herself.

The rock was steady, and though it took several seconds to get her breath back after sitting in the cold water, she enjoyed the feel of the cool liquid, reveled in the cleansing, healing properties as it washed over her injuries. She took a deep breath and leaned back, immersing herself, hair and all.

Grant was right. When she raised back up, the overhead sun heated the air and the water and her body so she didn't chill. She felt fresh, like a little girl whose only fear was of being scolded when she got home for playing in the water.

Home. For once, she didn't experience the severe ache of longing usually associated with her thoughts of Richmond. It had been days since she'd worried about what was happening at the mill. After Uncle Jonathan's death, and during the months she battled for control, the business had continued to produce. She supposed it would continue to do so now. Her presence, or *absence,* never affected the output.

She soaped her hair and rinsed it, then reached inside the camisole and scrubbed her upper body, all the while planning the changes she would make one day soon.

233

Brighter colors. New designs. Women didn't always need "serviceable" fabrics.

Finally she sighed and decided to quit worrying about things she could do nothing about and enjoy her bath. The water was invigorating once she'd gotten used to it, and she was tempted to lean over and dunk her face, too.

That was the way Grant saw her when he crept up through the trees. He'd come because she was too quiet. Her first gasp was all he'd heard and he was worried that something might have happened to her.

But there she was, floating face down in the water, holding onto the rock and kicking her feet. Her hair skimmed out over the surface like an orange cape, swirling, drifting . . . He shook his head. He mustn't become so entranced that she would catch him watching. She'd probably think the sight of those baggy drawers and revealing camisole would lead him astray.

Hell, she'd be exactly right. Look at her. Her long, shapely limbs were displayed in front of God and every creature in the forest, including himself. Wet, those silly, feminine clothes just tantalized him more.

He tore his eyes away. If he didn't walk away now, he might embarrass himself.

A few steps into the trees, he heard a whippoorwill call from about the same location he'd impatiently waited only moments earlier. He picked up his pace until he reached a thick stand of salt cedar near the creek bank and returned the call.

A sudden movement to his right revealed one of the younger scouts. No more than a teenager, the short, thinly muscled boy had proven himself to be very valuable to Grant.

"Hello, Timmy B." Grant surprised himself by using the name the soldiers had given the boy. His Apache name, hard to pronounce for most Anglo tongues, sounded similar to Timmy B, so that was his name around the fort.

The youngster smiled. "Hola, Two Faces. Or should I call you by your white name? Maybe you no longer Apache, so long you have been away."

Grant playfully cuffed the lad. "I should never have talked your family into sending you to school. You learn too fast, boy."

Timmy B. straightened his already arrow-straight spine. "I am no longer a boy. Otherwise, Santana would not have sent me with an important message."

Grant chuckled, then remembered how easily his own pride had been hurt at the young man's age. "You're right. Scouts enlisted with the United States Cavalry are not *boys.*" Yet there were a few young lieutenants he could name who were still too wet behind the ears to command a troop. Sometimes he wondered about the intelligence of the military.

"What is Santana's message?"

"He say, *it is done.*"

Grant nodded. "Good." Santana had gotten the message to the cavalry. Now, if they could get a troop there in time, or at least notify the mills, the Waddell gang could be in for a surprise.

The boy turned to leave and was about to wade into the creek. A splash downstream reminded Grant of Jacelyn and something else that had been in the back of his mind several days. He called out and Timmy B. turned. Grant's eyes traveled down the small Apache's breechcloth-clad form to his feet. All in all, the boy was about Jacelyn's size, though she might be an inch or two taller. But their feet . . .

"What would you trade me for my boots?"

The scout looked puzzled. "Trade? I have nothing of value, except my knife, or pistol." But his eyes strayed wistfully toward the shiny black, tall-topped boots.

235

Grant rubbed his chin. Of course he wouldn't ask the scout for his weapons, and he felt a little guilty about his next request because he knew the boy had always longed for a pair of white-eyes boots. Though why anyone would *want* to wear the stiff, toe-pinching things, Grant couldn't fathom.

"How about trading your moccasins, right now, for my boots, when I get back to the fort?"

Timmy B. shook his head. "Is not a fair trade."

Grant sighed. Only a conscientious youngster fresh out of school would quibble, especially if he were getting the best of the deal. "Your sister worked all day making your moccasins, didn't she?"

The scout nodded.

"She spent hours on the beadwork."

Again the boy nodded.

"They look almost new. My boots are old and worn." He could see the kid was thinking, and he didn't want him to think long enough not to make the deal. Grant held out his hand. "Trade?"

Timmy B. eagerly clasped Grant's forearm. He couldn't hide the excitement in his eyes, though at first he tilted his head and said, "Maybe I am one getting short end of branch." But he grinned. "Trade."

The Apache pulled off his moccasins and set them down beside Grant. He hastily pointed out, "The moccasins will not fit you."

Grant raised one eye brow. "The boots will not fit you."

The boy shrugged as if that did not matter, but gave Grant, and then the moccasins, one last curious glance as he crossed the creek and disappeared.

Grant laughed to himself as he picked up the moccasins. No doubt as soon as the scout returned to the fort, he'd pick out some likely looking soldier about his size to engage in a game of monte. He'd wager the boots once he had them in hand. As many soldiers discovered, to their chagrin, Apaches were excellent gamblers.

He looked downstream. Surely the woman was through with her bath by now. He grinned. Ready or not, he would join her.

"Drat. Oh, drat." Jacelyn tripped over the slick rocks. She reached down and righted herself, and gratefully sighed. At least she hadn't made another loud splash. Looking over her shoulder as she tried to hurry, she half expected to see Grant charge around the bend like a snarling lobo. But, so far, so good.

She stopped to catch her breath. Her heart thundered so loud her ears rang. What had Grant been doing, talking to that Indian? Just thinking about what she'd seen caused her knees to shake.

She had finished bathing and wondered why Grant hadn't yet returned. He'd seemed perturbed earlier, and she'd been sure he would only let her stay a few minutes. Anyway, she'd decided to wade up the creek and surprise him. At first she hadn't seen him, had almost panicked, thinking he'd become impatient and gone on without her.

But she'd noticed the briefest flicker of movement on the right bank at the edge of the trees. Wading closer, she was about to call out when she recognized his black vest and red bandana. Then the sun reflected off a bronzed chest just behind Grant. She'd thought her imagination was running wild, but the closer she went, the more of the fellow she could see: the breechcloth; long brown-black hair held back with a leather headband; dark, flat features. An Indian. A real live Indian.

And he was talking and gesturing to Grant as if they were old friends. She had panicked. What if they saw her? What if Grant didn't want her to know about his assignation? He might even think she'd been spying on him.

She didn't know *what* to think. Or what *he'd* think. So, she'd run. Or sloshed through the water as quickly and quietly as she could. Of course, she'd fallen and made more noise than a volley of gunfire. But he hadn't come after her.

Something suddenly constricted her chest. Something that sat her back down on the rock. She began to feel angry. *Why* hadn't he come? What if she'd fallen and hurt herself? What if she were drowning? If she was under his protection, as he kept spouting to everyone, why wasn't he rushing to see if she was all right?

What ludicrous thinking, she scolded herself. She was turning into a complete idiot. She didn't want his protection.

And drat it, ever since she'd awakened in his arms this morning, she'd found herself focusing more and more on how she'd felt with Grant rather than on the abuse meted her by Eloy. Maybe it was better, though, to think of good things.

Those good things were creating warm tingles in her body again, too. She felt flushed and a little light-headed and . . . very weak. Perhaps she'd better get out of the water and put on the night dress. If Grant hadn't returned by the time she was ready, she knew her way back to the ranch. And she wasn't about to go searching for him again. No telling who, or what, he'd be talking to by now.

She staggered over the rocks to the bank. A hand reached out and took hold of her elbow. She yelped and jerked her head up. Grant. Thank heavens he was alone and not trailed by a horde of savage Indians. Sighing with relief, she let him help her out of the creek.

Grant studied her taut features. "What's wrong, sugar?"

Jacelyn blinked and tried to calm her jittery nerves. She didn't think she would tell him what she'd seen. "Ah, I . . . I'm just a little weary. You, ah, might have been right about my overdoing things today." She kept her eyes on the folded night dress, slightly embarrassed by his casual use of the word, *sugar*. As much as she was beginning to like the endearment, she knew it meant nothing to him.

Grant was surprised to hear the woman admit *he* was right about *anything*. He looked at her closely, wondering what she was up to. Something wasn't right and damped his desire to gloat. He followed the direction of her gaze and picked up the night dress before she reached it.

Something fell from the folds. He bent to retrieve it and discovered her watch. Picking it up, he handed it to her and waited until she'd put it around her neck before indicating the gown again. "I'll help you."

She stepped closer and started to take the night dress, but noted the determination in his eyes. Obediently, she held up her arms so he could slip it over her head.

Grant raised the gown, hesitated, and gawked down at the exposed flesh thrust together by her upraised arms. Dear God, but she was lush and beautiful. The swells of her breasts looked like smooth cream, awaiting his pleasure to taste and enjoy.

His hands shook. Heat licked through his body straight to his groin.

"Grant? Is something wrong?"

"N-no. I, ahem, just had to find the arm holes." Still, he fumbled putting the gown over her head until she finally took it from him.

"I see you're more accomplished at *undressing* women," she snapped, as the night dress slid down her body.

Grant hardly heard a word as he watched the soft material adhere to her damp undergarments, accentuating her puckered nipples.

"Excuse me."

"Huh?"

"Would you hand me my shoes, please? They're right behind you."

He reluctantly looked away from her breasts to the shreds of her shoes. With distaste, he picked them up. Glancing from the shoes to Jacelyn, who stretched out her hand, he cocked his brow and tossed them into the creek.

"No. My shoes," she wailed, and started after them.

He quickly stopped her. Pointing to a rounded boulder, he commanded, "Sit."

She pursed her lips, then held up her fingertips to soothe a tender cut at the corner of her mouth. She sat.

Grant backed up a few steps and plucked something from the ground.

Jacelyn cocked her head. "What's that?"

He slowly came forward, suddenly uncertain of her reaction to his gift.

Jacelyn warily eyed the pieces of leather in his hands. She shied back when he held one out and explained, "These are moccasins. You need something to protect your feet."

She opened her mouth, closed it, and asked, "For me?" Was that what he'd been doing with the Indian? Getting something for her? Now, certainly, she'd never mention that she'd seen them.

Moccasins. What unusual-looking things. They had curled toes, kind of like she'd seen in drawings of elves or clowns. When they were unfolded, the tops were taller than those of her lace-up shoes left behind at the stage holdup.

Grant was pleased with the interest he saw in her eyes. At least she wasn't outright refusing the footwear.

240

He picked up her foot, one dainty foot, and slipped it into the moccasin. He'd folded down the top to make putting it on easier, then rolled it up her leg. His hand moved up her slender calf.

He heard her quick intake of breath and glanced up. She was staring not at the footwear, but at his hand. Her tongue darted out to moisten her lower lip and his belly sank to his knees.

"How does that feel?" he asked, reluctantly setting her foot on the ground.

"Wonderful," she sighed, eyes half closed. Suddenly she stiffened. She made a great show of standing up and exclaiming how the supple leather conformed to her foot. "It really does feel wonderful." Surprise was evident in her voice.

She reached for the other moccasin at the same time he did. "I can put it on." Her breath came out deep and husky.

"Let me." He sounded hoarse and out of breath, as if he'd just run ten miles through the desert with no water.

They spoke at once. Their eyes met. The moccasin lay between them, all but unnoticed.

Grant cleared his throat and quickly grabbed it up. "I'll do it."

She gulped and closed her eyes, steeling herself for the sparks his touch ignited wherever he put his hands. Even preparing herself, she flinched when he ran his thumb along her arch. Her breath caught as his fingers circled her ankle. Butterflies flitted in her stomach when his palm glided up her leg.

He frowned at the scratches on her calf. "The moccasins will protect your legs, too."

She nodded. As soon as the second moccasin was on her foot, she leapt to her feet. Her lips trembled as she smiled. "Th-they're perfect."

His eyes devoured her. "Yes."

They swayed toward each other. Grant placed his palms on either side of her cheeks and with exquisite care smoothed his thumb along her bruised jaw.

She sighed. "Thank you." She had no idea whether she was thanking him for the moccasins, for coming to her rescue last night, for his tender caresses, or for making her feel desirable at her ugliest moment. Each reason was as important as the other.

Grant touched his lips to hers, a soft and floating kiss that wouldn't cause her pain. But she suddenly leaned into him, wrapping her arms around his waist. He sucked in his breath and helplessly held her. Just held her . . . until she snuggled her nose into the "v" of his shirt and lightly kissed his chest.

"Lord, lady," he groaned. Her fingers dug into his back. His hips instinctively ground against her. He wanted to crush her in his arms, to tumble her to the ground and bury himself in her moist warmth.

"Love me, Grant."

He tilted his head and kissed her neck, nibbled her ear lobe and nipped the tip of her nose. His hands ran over her shoulders and down her back, caressing, molding, until he reached her hips.

"Please, love me."

His heart thundered more loudly than a herd of running horses. He had to be sure his imagination hadn't gone wild. "Lord, I want to," he whispered.

She pressed closer.

He couldn't breathe. His manhood pulsed and swelled. He kissed her lips, wanting to probe the honeyed depths beyond but afraid to do something that might hurt her.

Hurt her. He gasped and inhaled deeply. The air hissed slowly through his teeth as he lifted his head. He couldn't do it. Not now. Not after what she'd just gone through. He knew exactly what she felt. After facing death, she needed to reassure herself that she was capable of feeling, that she was alive.

No, this wasn't the time. When they made love, he wanted it to be right, wanted her to want *him*.

It took every ounce of strength he could summon to set her away. "I can't, sugar."

Jacelyn recoiled. Her eyes burned. Her chest felt like it would explode. She'd swallowed her pride and offered him the most precious gift she possessed, and he'd rejected her.

She put a hand to her face. Was it because she was ugly? Because another man had handled her body?

Grant held onto her shoulders. He saw her touch her bruises and knew immediately he'd made a grave mistake. "No, sugar. You're wrong. You're beautiful."

She shook her head. He lied. She'd seen her reflection in the water. Her face was grotesque. She repulsed herself, so how could she not repulse him?

"Sugar—"

"Stop it!" She jerked from his grasp and covered her ears. Her eyes widened when it dawned on her that she'd laid her heart on the ground and he'd trampled it. Could she have fallen in love with a rogue like Grant Jones?

Unable to bear the discovery of her true feelings and his denouncement at the same time, she turned and fled.

"Wait," he yelled. "Jacelyn, come back. Please . . ."

Chapter Sixteen

Jacelyn stopped before reaching the ranch headquarters and sat down to rest in the shade of a spreading oak. She had shamed herself by running. It would have been better just to acknowledge her lapse of sense. He would have understood if she explained that she hadn't known what she was saying. That she hadn't meant the words quite the way he'd taken them.

She should've thanked him for behaving so sensibly.

So, if she truly believed all that, why did she feel so devastated? Why, at that particular moment, had she realized she was in love with the man? But was she really? How had it happened? Why? He was a rogue, an outlaw. Would eventually be killed or imprisoned.

Then what? Would she slink back to Richmond, the wronged-woman in a story in *Harper's Weekly?* She could imagine the title now: "Good Virginia Girl Goes Bad."

Tossing a pebble into a thick cluster of manzanita, she sighed and tried to convince herself that she had no reason to be upset. Grant had ignored her foolish outburst. She still had her honor. Soon, she would escape and find James. Everything would be all right then. Her thoughts and emotions would return to normal. Of course they would.

Just because the man was handsome and kind and thoughtful didn't mean she loved him. Just because he had saved her life over and over again didn't mean she should feel so grateful as to lose her heart.

Her situation was unfamiliar and frightening. She'd found someone to depend and rely upon and had allowed her feelings to get out of hand.

She mentally congratulated herself on getting her muddled mind straightened out.

"Jacelyn?"

The deep, resonant voice ignited sparks in every nerve ending. A need to throw herself into arms she knew to be strong and secure almost unraveled the common sense she'd just worked so hard to weave together.

But she composed her features, rose to her feet, and faced the most masculine, attractive man it had been her misfortune to meet.

"Jacelyn . . . Are you all right?" Grant hesitated, unsure of what to say to keep her from running away again.

She nodded. "Fine."

"That's . . . good. Look, I'm sorry—"

"No," she choked. "No. I'm sorry, and I owe you an apology. Please forgive me for acting so foolishly." She looked down at her new footwear and her heart turned somersaults. "I don't know . . . what came over me."

Grant shrugged. He was sorry, too. Sorry that she'd misunderstood his intentions. Sorry that his fondest wish would never come true. Narrowing his eyes, he made a firm resolve. There *would* be another time. She *would* invite him to love her. He would see to it. Just as soon as Miss Jacelyn McCaffery had put Eloy—and a few other things—behind her.

She shifted from one foot to the other. She didn't know what to think of the strange light in his eyes.

"Ahem, well, Dora probably needs help with supper. It's best I go back."

He glanced skyward, surprised at how quickly the time had passed. Taking hold of her elbow, he guided her back to the path.

She glanced at him through the thick fringe of her lashes, praying he hadn't felt the leap in her pulse. "Th-thank you again for the moccasins. I can't believe how comfortable they are."

He nodded and looked with envy at her leather-gloved feet. He'd like to dig his own moccasins out of his bedroll and wear them instead of the toe-cramping, Army issue boots.

Before they reached the headquarters, he stopped and stared into her eyes. "Friends?"

Relief washed over her. He wasn't going to make a big deal of her silliness. She smiled, and at the same time inwardly tamped down the thrill of knowing he'd still be near. "Friends."

As they passed the cabin, Jacelyn stopped, then turned and walked to the door. She hesitated. Her hand shook. But she pushed it open and stepped quickly inside. Her eyes widened. Behind her, she heard Grant mutter an exclamation.

Someone had scrubbed the blood from the floor and righted the chair and everything that had been knocked over during the fighting. A fresh bouquet of wild flowers decorated the table. Laid out on the cot next to the folded blanket were more undergarments from the trunk. Another worn, but clean, shirt lay next to her trousers, which also appeared to have been brushed clean. Someone had worked hard to put things to right. Someone. Someone who knew her need for everything to be *clean* after her trek to the creek. Someone who'd chosen the silkiest, most feminine garments available. Dora.

Jacelyn turned to Grant. "Did you know she intended to do this?"

He shook his head.

As much as she'd dreaded coming back inside the place, thanks to Dora, it wasn't nearly as bad as she'd thought it would be.

Grant was also grateful to the older woman. Although he'd removed the body, and had planned to clean up some, he just hadn't had the time. He studied Jacelyn intently and saw that she seemed to be all right, before he glanced toward the clothing and said, "I'll wait outside."

She just nodded, stunned by the miracle Dora had wrought. Without Grant distracting her attention, she managed to unbutton the night dress by herself. She shed her underclothing that, though fresh from the trunk, had touched her filthy body before the cleansing soak in the stream, and picked up a dainty, frilly camisole. It had only been a few weeks ago that she had taken things like lacy lingerie for granted. Her circumstances had changed, but she'd changed, too.

Once she'd donned the fresh camisole and a pair of dry pantalettes, she allowed herself a moment to revel in the sensuous feel of the garments. They felt good against her skin. Like Grant's hands. Heat suffused her body. She halted that thought before it could do further damage to her self control. Quickly, she pulled on the trousers and shirt.

Recalling the comb and brush she'd set aside, she gasped with delight when she found a fragment of mirror had been placed beside them. She had a lot for which to thank Dora.

A piece of wood used to even the legs on the cot served to prop up the mirror. Unpinning her long, red tresses, she began to comb deftly through the damp tangles. The bristles stimulated her scalp and she closed her eyes.

Minutes later, a calloused hand covered hers on the handle. She nearly jumped from the chair, but was gently pushed back down.

"You missed a tangle," Grant huskily explained as he coaxed the brush from her fingers and began to stroke it through her hair.

Jacelyn automatically bent her head forward and sighed with contentment. No one, excepting her mother, had ever done anything so intimate, and certainly never a man. His long, gentle motions felt wonderful, shooting a delicious riot of bone-tingling shivers up and down her spine.

Grant, too, enjoyed numerous sensations as he eased the brush through the thick mass of red-gold hair. The more he brushed, the faster her hair dried. Becoming softer. Shinier. Sifting through his fingers like fine strands of silk.

He inhaled the scent of soap and wild flowers and briefly closed his eyes, savoring the quiet peace of doing this small chore for her. He'd never brushed a woman's hair, though he'd had many an opportunity. He might have tried it sooner had he known it was so arousing.

When he finished, they were both as still as owls in the midday heat, listening, waiting, seemingly afraid to break the soothing silence.

Jacelyn swallowed and shifted in the chair. Her breasts felt oddly heavy and her nipples pulsed with each brush against the new camisole. His hand hung lifeless as she pried the brush from his fingers. She found it hard to meet his eyes. "Thank you."

"Ahem, my pleasure." Once his brain regained the

ability to send orders to his limbs, he walked stiffly to the door, mindful of keeping his back toward her.

She rose unsteadily from the chair, waited for her knees to stop trembling, and followed after him.

They had almost reached the barn when Dora walked out on the porch and called to them. "There ya be. Thought mebbe ya mighta wallowed down in that there pool an' drowned."

"Not hardly." Grant smiled and tipped his hat. Outlaw, or no, he'd come to like the woman, if only because of her kindnesses toward Jacelyn. Jacelyn needed a woman's companionship, especially after what had happened with Eloy.

Jacelyn and Dora's eyes met. Although Jacelyn sensed it was unnecessary, she admonished, "Dora, you shouldn't have gone to so much trouble on my account. But ... I appreciate it. Thank you for cleaning the cabin."

Dora's pale cheeks flushed pink. She shrugged. "T'weren't nothin'." To Grant, she ordered, "Wash up. Vittles be near done."

Grant nodded and walked around to the back where Dora kept a basin of fresh water, soap, and a towel. By the time he entered the kitchen, the women were carrying antelope steaks, fried potatoes, and fresh bread to the table.

During the meal, he glanced at Dora and wondered for the hundredth time what it was about her that seemed so familiar. When a slice of green apple pie was placed in front of him, though, he completely forgot everything but the tart-sweet taste of apple and cinnamon.

Jacelyn devoured her dessert to the last crumb. "Dora? Where did you get apples way out here?"

Dora hooked her thumb over her shoulder toward the kitchen. "Ya know them trees on the other side of the well?"

Jacelyn nodded. Oh, yes, she knew the well. Her arms had finally strengthened until she could haul up a full bucket of water now. She even went to the well sometimes when she could just as easily pump water in the kitchen.

Dora continued, "Through them trees be another clearin'. Whoever homesteaded here first musta planted 'em a bunch of pear an' apple an' cherry trees. Some of 'em is still alive."

Grant patted his flat stomach. "Sure am glad. That was mighty fine, ma'am. Waddell's a lucky man."

Dora's face turned crimson. Jacelyn also agreed that the outlaw was indeed lucky to have such a loyal woman. Maybe Dora was a bit frightened, too, of everything that was going on, but she had to love the man to have given up all that was precious to stay with the outlaw leader.

Jacelyn remembered the gown they'd found in the trunk. Now, more than before, she was determined to repay Dora for her kindnesses by altering the dress to fit. Dora would be so thrilled and surprised.

"What do you think, Jacelyn?" Grant interrupted.

"Ah, what?" She'd been so lost in thought over the gown, she hadn't known anyone was talking to her.

Dora repeated, "I was a wonderin' if'n ya wanted ta stay here in the house at night til the boys get back."

Several answers entered Jacelyn's mind. Yes, for safety's sake. No, she'd have a better chance of escaping if she stayed in the cabin. She slanted a glance in Grant's direction. *If* she could figure a way past *him*.

Finally she shook her head. "Since you worked so hard to clean up the cabin, I think I'll go ahead and sleep there."

Two pairs of eyes looked askance at her.

She sniffed. "All right, I admit I'll probably be scared to death. But I'll still be just as scared if I wait two, or even three, more nights." Her chin jutted out. She winced, but forcefully added, "I can do it. I have to do it."

Grant stared at her for a long time. The little city girl never ceased to amaze him. She had gumption.

Dora nodded. "Good fer you, Missy. Ya got more guts than ya can hang on a fence."

Jacelyn's meal turned upside down in her stomach. "Th-thanks." *I think,* she added to herself, swallowing several times.

Before Jacelyn retired, however, Dora smeared her face with the milkweed concoction and Grant made her drink more of his healing liquid. By the time they were finished, she was cranky and tired of being poked and bullied, even if they were well-meaning.

She finally said good night and started toward the cabin. She noticed how bright the night was, though, and hesitated. Everything was visible. The spiny shapes of the yucca, the tall trees, the path ahead. The full moon and twinkling stars were beautiful. The heavens seemed so close, like she could stand on tiptoe and become a part of it all.

This was such a *big* country. She seemed insignificant in comparison. At first she'd been intimidated, in a hurry to find James and leave for familiar homelands as quickly as possible. Yet, in some ways, she wouldn't have traded this adventure for anything. Her lesson in independence had certainly taken sudden and extreme twists and turns.

She heard footsteps behind her, but was becoming so accustomed to the light, stealthy movement that she immediately recognized who it was.

Grant stepped up beside her as she started walking again and accompanied her as far as the barn. When he stopped, he canted his head toward her. "Arizona is not such a terrible place, is it?"

251

She blinked. "Stop that."

He grinned. "Stop what?"

"Reading my mind. It's nerve racking. And I want you to stop right now." To keep her train of thought, she had to look away when his smile broadened. She didn't know which was more irritating, his reading her thoughts, or mocking her.

"All right," Grant readily complied.

She exhaled. "All right? That means you'll stop?"

He nodded, still smiling.

When he twirled the tip of his moustache, she began to fidget. "Fine."

His eyes bored into her. "You're satisfied now?"

She nodded and slowly headed toward the cabin. Looking back over her shoulder, she found him staring after her. She quickly turned her head and moved more briskly, only to dart one more glance back. But he was gone. In just that brief space of time, he'd disappeared. As quickly and quietly as the savage she'd seen him with by the stream.

Entering the cabin, she pushed the door closed and wished there was some way to lock it from the inside. She looked around the room. Her eyes settled on the trunk. It wasn't big enough to be any real protection, but it was all she had. And now that several items had been removed, she might manage to slide it across the floor to block the door. Pushing and pulling and panting, she finally succeeded, though it took several minutes. Then she straightened and proudly dusted off her hands.

Two steps away from the door, she heard a thump. The trunk rattled. She spun around just in time to see Grant trip over the thing and almost fall. Oops! What had she been thinking? The door opened to the outside, not the inside. All the trouble she'd gone to had been for naught.

She put a hand over her mouth. Grant's shadowy figure loomed ominously on the threshold.

"What in the hell were you doing?" he thundered.

Quivering slightly beneath his glowering presence, she nevertheless held her ground. She fisted her hands on her hips. "Trying to lock my door. Why?"

He stalked into the room until he stood only inches away. Bending his head, he looked her in the eye. "Don't ever lock your door against *me*. I'm the one who does the locking. Understand?"

"No. It's my life you're supposedly protecting."

"I don't need help."

She felt daunted by the total confidence in his eyes, steeling his features and gravelling his voice. But she was also perplexed. "Ever? You don't *ever* need someone, for anything?" For one who'd never had independence, it was an eye-opening experience to come face to face with someone who was completely self-governing.

Grant shook his head, went back, and slammed the door closed, then went over to the table and set down a bundle. Without saying a word, he lit the new candle Dora had left.

Jacelyn puffed out her chest. He was obviously ignoring her question. She asked another. "What's that?" and pointed to the long, round thing.

"My bedroll."

Her eyes narrowed. "What's it doing here?"

He untied the leather strips holding it together. "I'm going to sleep in it."

"Not in here, you're not."

He cocked his brow.

She realized the foolishness of trying to argue with him and plopped wearily on the bed.

He spread the bedroll in front of the door.

Twisting her hands together, she choked, "You're really serious."

He just stared.

"Wh-what are you looking at?" Although she hated giving him the satisfaction of knowing he'd unnerved her—again—she hastily glanced down to make sure all of her buttons were fastened.

Grant was fascinated. He could sit and watch her changing facial expressions forever. He blinked. What had prompted him to lose control?

But as he looked at her battered features, he didn't see the bruises. Instead, he imagined the fire in her eyes when she looked at him, or the small lines deepening the grooves of her mouth when she smiled, or the soft streaks of gray that would eventually highlight her hair.

Jacelyn crossed her arms over her chest, feeling as though she'd sprouted an extra eye or something. "Do you mind?" she whispered. "I'd like to put on my night dress."

He sat on the trunk to pull off his boots. "Go ahead."

"I can't change with you here," she insisted.

"Sugar, I've seen or felt most of everything you're so desperate to hide."

Her mouth dropped open. She snapped it closed so fast her teeth clicked. "Why, you . . ." She was too outraged to speak. "I've never—"

"I know," he said with a smug grin.

She shot to her feet. "How dare you!"

"But I haven't dared . . . yet."

Her face began to ache. "This is pointless," she sighed, not realizing she'd spoken aloud until she saw his moustache twitch. "Go ahead and be a . . . smart ass." She flinched as she said the curse word, but then actually felt better when he gave her a startled look.

Feeling suddenly like a butterfly about to shed her cocoon, she turned her back and began to unbutton her shirt. All right, if this was what he wanted, she'd change right in front of him. A little tingle of anticipation ricocheted down her spine.

Grant suddenly regretted his teasing as she reversed the blanket on him. But if she was daring him to watch, he would accept the challenge, and gladly. Yet when she cast a glance over her shoulder, he quickly focused his attention on his other boot. Damn it, what had gotten into him? He felt like some young boy getting his first peek at a half-naked woman.

It became clear to Jacelyn, as she pulled the night dress over her head, that Grant Jones was truly a gentleman. No matter his bravado, he respected her desire for privacy, even in the middle of nowhere, with no one to care one way or the other what happened to one "city" woman.

As she blew out the candle and crawled under the blanket, she shivered. In the shadows, she could almost see Eloy's face, feel his evil breath and hear his foul words. She froze, momentarily paralyzed by fear. But Grant's even breathing chased away the imagined terror. His presence allowed her to feel secure again.

He was there to keep the ghosts at bay. Whatever happened, he would protect her. He had told her so, and she believed he'd keep his promise.

She went to sleep with a slight curve to her lips.

Grant was not quite so lucky. He was plagued with a sense of having lost a part of himself to the unpredictable woman.

The next morning, Jacelyn awoke to find herself alone in the cabin. She experienced a moment of panic until she noticed Grant's bedroll neatly folded and placed out of the way beneath the table. She smiled. Evidently, he planned to make sleeping inside a habit.

The smile gradually faded as she thought how quickly

he was becoming a habit with her. A habit she needed to break immediately, or risk humiliating herself again.

She dressed and headed for the main house. The headquarters was so quiet that she began to think perhaps her time to escape could be during the daylight when it was least expected and when she could actually see where she was going.

She changed direction and walked to the barn. It took her eyes a while to adjust to the dark interior. Slowly, she proceeded down the center aisle, noting the saddles and bridles hanging to her left, and the horses kept in the corrals. At least it would be easy to catch one.

"Morning."

She jumped a foot, then held her hand over her pounding heart.

Grant leaned out of a stall. "What's the matter, sugar? Guilty conscience?"

She took a deep breath and stammered, "Wh-what would I have to f-feel guilty about?"

He shrugged, but continued to pin her with his eyes.

She meandered over to the spotted horse and patted its nose when it came to the front of the stall. "I just came in to see the horses." That was no lie. And she wasn't proud. She needed the gentlest horse she could find to make her escape.

"So I see." Grant rested his forearms on the top rail.

"Well ... I was on my way to see if I could help Dora." It was a lame, but plausible, excuse to escape the flint-eyed rogue. And was also true—until she'd gotten her hopes up and been sidetracked.

"I'll go with you," he offered.

She used one of his favorite gestures and shrugged.

They entered the house through the back door and found Dora stoking the stove with wood. The woman was sleepy-eyed and moving slow.

"Morning, folks. Cain't believe I slept past sunup.

256

These last few days been the easiest I've had in near twenty years."

Grant didn't seem to understand what she was talking about, but Jacelyn knew the past few days Dora had been free—free from watching her back, free to express kindness and generosity to a prisoner, free to be treated like any decent lady. Probably for the first time since her marriage to Waddell. Jacelyn sent Dora a reassuring smile and rolled up her sleeves. "What can I do?"

Dora blearily eyed Jacelyn's feet. "Ya can start by tellin' me where ya got them fancy moccasins. Ain't seen nothin' like 'em around here."

Jacelyn wriggled her toes and grinned. "Grant . . . got them for me." She couldn't explain it, but she wasn't ready to share the fact, with either Grant or Dora, that she'd seen Grant with an Indian.

Dora, her eyes rapidly clearing, looked immediately at Grant.

He shrugged. "When do you expect Waddell and the boys back?"

Dora frowned at Grant's back as he pumped water into a basin. "Don't rightly know. But reckon it won't be more'n a day or so."

"Good." He grabbed a towel and walked out the door.

She looked at Jacelyn, who was suddenly engrossed over a bowl of flour, then sighed and poured herself a cup of coffee.

Half an hour later they munched on biscuits, eggs, bacon, and gravy. Grant glanced at both women and announced, "I've got orders to check the water in the tanks. Dora, will you be all right while we're gone?"

He watched Jacelyn's expression intently, waiting to see the light dawn.

Jacelyn sat stone still. She twisted her hands in her lap. "Taking me along to serve you a picnic lunch? Or don't you trust me to stay here with Dora?" she demanded, thinking it would give her time to become better acquainted with the horses.

Dora reached over and patted Jacelyn's arm before glancing thoughtfully at Grant. "Reckon you two'll mosey back by suppertime?"

Grant leaned back in his chair and emptied his coffee cup. "What's the matter, ma'am. Don't trust me?"

Dora grinned. "Ain't never met a man yet I'd trust. Don't figure ya put your pants on any different than the rest."

Glancing at Jacelyn's profile as she stared out the window, Grant wondered if this might not be the perfect time to spirit her away. Yet confidence in his ability to keep her safe, at least for the time being, allowed him to consider two important reasons for staying: the need to find out more about her brother, and his determination to see if there might be evidence to link this gang to the scalpings and murders being blamed on the Apaches.

There was also a purely selfish motive to think about. The longer they remained at the ranch, the more time he had to spend with Jacelyn.

He looked Dora in the eyes. "We'll be back."

While he and Dora talked, Jacelyn surreptitiously glanced at Grant. Like the older woman, she wasn't all that sure he could be trusted. After all, what reason did he have to take her along? He had to have an ulterior motive. But what?

Chapter Seventeen

Grant rose to his feet. "If I'm goin' to check those tanks, I have to go. Are you coming?" He held his hand out to Jacelyn.

Even as she wondered if he was giving her a chance to make a choice, her fingers, of their own volition, wrapped around his and he helped her to her feet. She looked down at Dora, who sat contentedly finishing her coffee. "Won't you come, too?" Her eyes pleaded for the older woman to join them.

"Gawd, no, Missy. Since ya done started cleanin' up this ole place, now I gotta keep after it." She waved her hand, indicating the living room.

"But—"

"You heard the lady." Grant tugged Jacelyn through the door.

The spotted horse was already saddled when Grant led it from the barn. She glanced behind him and asked, "Where's mine?"

Grant frowned at the excitement ringing in her voice. The damned woman was up to something. "Right here. You get to ride with me."

She tried not to show her disappointment. "Oh, well, fine." Drat. She had hoped to ride by herself, to practice before making her getaway.

He lifted her into the saddle, then swung up behind her. When he slid into the seat, Jacelyn was chagrined to find that she sat more on his lap than in the saddle. She wriggled forward, but the swells dug into her thighs.

"Hold still, damn it."

"But this is very uncomfortable," she complained, then gasped when his arm snaked around her waist and held her even closer to his hot body.

"Better?"

"Not really." The top of his forearm teased the underside of her breasts. The backs of her thighs rode the tops of his. His chest caressed her spine every time he leaned forward. She swallowed and her throat felt as scratchy as if she'd downed a mouthful of Arizona sand.

Grant reached for the reins with his free hand and turned the horse in a northeasterly direction.

"How far do we have to go?" She'd been blindfolded originally coming into the headquarters. Now she studied the countryside with wide, watchful eyes, taking in every detail.

"A couple of miles."

"Oh, look," she exclaimed, as they rode deeper into the mountains. "Pine trees." She sniffed the air and sighed. "They smell so good."

Grant had been in these mountains as a child, when Cochise had made them his stronghold. It had been a long while since he'd taken the time to appreciate the great diversity of nature found here. The mingling of cliffs and ridges and boulder piles, broad and narrow canyons, supported diverse and useful vegetation. He could think of no other mountain range where he could see oaks, buckbrush locust, pines, yucca, and agave all growing together.

He also sniffed the clean, cool air. Seeing the mountains through Jacelyn's eyes was like seeing them for the first time himself.

A noisy chattering in the treetops drew Jacelyn's gaze to a gray-breasted jay, hopping from branch to branch as if following along with them.

Grant held out his hand to keep a limb from smacking the distracted woman in the face. When the same limb swayed back, he nearly lost his hat and cursed.

He reined the horse to a stop atop the next ridge and looked down on a series of shorter ridges leading to another rise of mountains miles in the distance. Jacelyn sucked in her breath at the contrast of greens and browns outlined by brilliant blue sky and white puffy clouds. She turned her head to see if Grant was as taken by the sight.

She stared into eyes even more bright and beautiful than the sky. At last she turned away, having forgotten what she wanted to say, and released the air in her lungs with a long, slow breath. "Wh-what are you looking for?"

He pointed down. Besides the green tree tops, she saw a stream and, to the left of the stream, a pond.

Grant told her, "When it rains hard enough that the water runs instead of soaking into the soil, it collects in depressions that ranchers sometimes deepen and line with rocks to hold an extra water supply for their cattle."

"But there's water in the stream," she pointed out. "Why go to all that trouble?"

"During a dry year, the creeks disappear. Tanks can be the only water for miles." He remembered a spring where his mother had drawn water that he didn't think was too far from where they were now. Curious as to whether it was still there, he rode in that direction.

They faced toward a cliff of rock towers and pinnacles of such odd formations that Jacelyn was tempted to give them human names. Others had boulders perched on top of boulders. She couldn't understand what kept them from toppling down at the slightest gust of wind.

Grant pulled the horse to a stop and dismounted. Holding out his hand, he helped Jacelyn down, hugging her a little closer than was necessary for a little longer than was necessary.

She supported herself on his shoulders as he let her body glide down his tall frame. Her blood thickened. She languidly enjoyed the sensations of his hard muscles molding her soft flesh. She whispered, "Why did you stop here?"

He set her down, though he did so reluctantly. After tying the horse, he took her hand and led her around a boulder and through a growth of vines. When he stopped, she looked over his shoulder.

"Oh . . . It's gorgeous."

Water tumbled right out of the rocks and spilled down onto a boulder eroded into the shape of a bowl. Below that was another almost like it. The water trickled in a stair-step fashion into a larger pool surrounded by a grassy bank at the base of the slope.

"How did you know this was here?" Her eyes shone as she clambered down the rocks toward the pool.

Grant followed close behind. "The Apache know every water hole."

She turned and looked at him. "And you saw it when you were . . . with . . . them?" She had horrible visions of the poor man being bound and the Indians torturing him. What tremendous strength he'd had to survive such an ordeal. Her heart went out to him.

He marveled anew at how readily she accepted his Apache heritage. Most white women were terrified of anything or anyone remotely connected with the "savage" Indians. Jacelyn herself had used the term fairly often, and he doubted she'd meant it as a compliment. She must have had a change of heart for some reason.

Women. He'd never yet met a man of any race who could figure out a female mind.

Upon reaching the pool, Jacelyn sat down and removed her moccasins. Her face alive with delight, she dangled her feet in the water.

Grant grinned at the childlike expression of glee transforming her features. It was the first time he'd seen her truly happy and carefree. His heart warmed. Once he had her away from the outlaws, he'd do everything in his power to see she stayed that way the rest of her life.

Hell. He shook his head. Who was he kidding? As soon as she was away from here, she'd be on the fastest stage out of town and headed home. He sighed. It would be just as well. What did a halfbreed Chief of Scouts have to offer a woman like her?

He had money. His father's family had been very wealthy. But the money was in a bank in St. Louis because he didn't have much use for it here. A man was judged by what he accomplished, not by the size of his bank account.

He hunkered down and plucked a blade of grass. Water splashed on his arm. Jacelyn screamed. He looked up just as she hurled herself at him. Her momentum toppled him backward, and they ended up in a tangle on the ground.

She had her arms wrapped so tightly around his neck that Grant, on the bottom of the heap, could hardly breathe.

"Sugar, what's wrong? Are you hurt?" He managed to wedge his arms between them and shove her back enough to see her face. Concern furrowed his own brows as he searched her thoroughly. No blood. All he found were the same bruises she'd had before they started the trip.

Jacelyn's chest heaved as she gasped for breath. She tilted her head toward the pond. "B-bear!"

With Jacelyn still molded to his chest, he unscrambled his legs and scooted up to a sitting position. He scanned the area around the pool and glanced toward the Appaloosa. The horse stood peacefully munching weeds. "Sugar, I don't think you saw a bear."

"Yes," she said quickly. "It had beady little eyes. And claws. And a long tail ... and—"

Grant chuckled, then broke into a full-throated, rumble from the chest, laugh.

Jacelyn hiccuped and held on for dear life as his guffaws nearly vibrated her from his lap. For a moment, she stared open-mouthed, not believing what she was hearing. How dare he laugh at her. Of all the nerve ...

But as she calmed down, she looked—really looked—at the expression on his face. Soft. Vulnerable. Boyish. Her heart melted.

Tears of mirth trickled from his eyes. Indignation stole over her features. She punched his shoulder. "What's so dratted funny?"

"B-b-bears ..." he choked.

"There's nothing funny about them," she huffed.

"H-how b-big?"

She let go of his neck long enough to hold her hand up indicting about four feet.

He broke into another spasm of guffaws. "Ha. Ha. H-o-ow tall?"

Her eyes shifted to his bandana. She lowered her hand.

He cocked a brow.

She made a face. Her hand fell even lower. "All right. But if it wasn't a bear ... What was it, Mr. Smarty?"

A grin continued to curve his lips. She thought he looked absolutely charming. Roguish, but charming.

"It was a coatimundi."

She frowned. "A what?"

"Coatimundi. Looks like a cross between a racoon and a possum." He held his hand to a height of about eighteen inches.

She looked toward the water and shrugged.

"Uh oh, it's coming after you."

She shrieked and buried her face in his shoulder, pressing her body against his so hard he toppled over again.

He started to laugh again, but suddenly felt guilty that his teasing had frightened her. Wrapping his arms around her, he shifted his body until she lay atop him. Soft. Sweet. His hands smoothed up and down her back. Her breasts molded to his chest and he felt the gradual hardening of her nipples as he continued to caress her.

Jacelyn raised her head and looked into his eyes. "You . . . I . . ." What was it she'd wanted to say? The smoky passion in his gaze completely robbed her of thought. Every nerve ending on her body anticipated his touch. A prairie fire raged from the roots of her hair to the tips of her toes.

She'd tried to talk herself out of these feelings for days, but it was impossible to deny that she enjoyed the feel of his hard body next to her softness, liked the way he tenderly touched her, adored his manly scent and loved how his eyes made her feel like the most desirous woman on earth.

Grant felt a difference in her body, a yielding that had never been there before. His heart raced. He lifted his head. She lowered hers. Their lips met briefly and parted. Sky blue eyes delved into a pair of deep violet.

Jacelyn waited, afraid to say anything, afraid to move. The last time she'd been in this situation, she'd asked him to love her and he'd turned her away. She didn't know what to do. She was tempted to get up and be the one to do the rejecting, but there was something about their being together, touching, tasting, that seemed fated. She didn't know why she sensed it so strongly, but she did.

As crazy as it seemed, she'd lost her heart to the rogue. Since she'd never thought to let it get away in the first place, and had no intention of reclaiming it and handing it over to another, why shouldn't she take advantage of this opportunity? Instinctively she tested his resistance and wriggled her hips to fit even closer to his body. Her eyes rounded at what she felt. Exultation swelled her heart.

Grant also sensed that something momentous was happening, something fated from their first confrontation in Colonel Alexander's office. His jaw clenched in a last battle with his conscience. If he were any kind of gentleman, he'd get up right now, take her back to the ranch, and lock her in that damned cabin—alone. But, hell, no one had ever accused him of being a gentleman. And from the glint in her eyes, she'd be devastated if he tried to act like one.

He slid the fingers of one hand into the thick mass of her hair and pulled her head down. His lips took hers in a sizzling mating of flesh. With the other hand, he cupped her bottom and pressed her against his arousal. Her mouth opened. His tongue gratefully explored what she offered. He teased. She skittered back. He tantalized. She shyly tasted him. He enticed. She responded by anticipating his next move and parried his thrust, then advanced her own.

His toes curled uncomfortably inside his boots.

Delicious shivers ran up and down Jacelyn's spine. Her nails dug into his shoulder blades.

He groaned and swiftly turned, rolling her beneath him and onto the tall, springy grass.

Their lips parted. She sighed and moved her hands over his shoulders and around to his chest. Her fingers deftly unbuttoned the top two buttons on his shirt, but as her hands delved lower, her confidence waned. His flesh rippled against the backs of her knuckles. She inhaled his masculine scent. Her insides burned hotter than desert sand at midday. Her fingers worked loose another button.

Grant wound his hands through the hair curling at her temples and held her head still as he placed kisses from her fluttering eyelids to the tip of her chin before once again devouring her lips. When he raised his head, he studied her intently.

"Are you sure, sugar?" His lips brushed hers with each word.

She nodded, creating a slight friction between their mouths. She backed up her conviction by running her hands inside his shirt and weaving her fingers through his wiry curls.

Grant sucked in his breath. Flames of desire licked through his body.

Jacelyn felt as if they were the first, only, and last people on earth here in the beautiful little oasis in the desert. The only thoughts that mattered at this moment were those of Grant and what he did to make her feel so wonderfully feminine.

By mutual, silent agreement they helped each other out of their clothing. But, suddenly feeling very shy and vulnerable with nothing on but the watch around her neck, Jacelyn ducked her head and tried to cover herself with her hands and arms.

Grant would not allow that. Facing her, each of them on their knees, he twined his fingers with hers and drew her arms around his neck, forcing her body against his.

Her eyes widened at the softness of his skin. He grinned. Then leaving her arms around his shoulders, he began a gentle exploration of the flesh contouring her different body parts.

She arched beneath his knowing caress and gasped when the naked evidence of his desire nudged her belly. His lips trailed after his hands as far as her shoulders. His tongue traced wetly into the hollow at the base of her throat. She moaned with pleasure as her skin sizzled and begged for more attention.

Her body felt as if it could float to the heavens and soar like an eagle. She hardly noticed as he bent her backward and lay her once again on the cool, spongy grass. His knees spread her thighs. She stiffened, experiencing a moment of panic.

Stretching atop her, Grant rested most of his weight on his elbows. His eyes caught hers and he noted the uncertainty mirrored there. Tenderly, he stroked her russet hair behind her ears.

"Has anyone told you how beautiful you are?" He hoped if they had, she would keep the names to herself, otherwise he'd have to hunt them down and do away with them. He wanted to be the only man in her life, the only one to whisper in her ear, to murmur words of . . . love.

Relief flooded his chest when she shook her head. "Good." He kissed one corner of her mouth and then the other until her head turned with each movement and her lips sought full contact. He grazed her lower lip with his teeth. "I will tell you. Jacelyn McCaffery, you are the loveliest woman I have ever held in my arms."

She blushed and touched her bruised cheek. He kissed the back of her hand, then nuzzled her fingers aside and lightly brushed his lips across the discoloration.

Jacelyn thought it the sweetest gesture he could have

made. It almost wiped away the visions of hundreds of other women lying in his arms, just as she did now. "H-how many women—"

"Hush." He took her mouth in a long, deep kiss that made sweat break out on his forehead. "Only enough to make my loving you all the better." Invading her mouth with his tongue, he taunted and teased until she eagerly responded.

He slid one hand to her rib cage and smoothed his palm down her velvety skin. Blood rushed to his groin until he thought he might die from the pleasurable pain. Breathing deeply, he tamped down his desire. He wanted . . . needed . . . to erase the doubt from her eyes. She had to want . . . need . . . him, too.

"Touch me, sugar."

She blinked and reflexively dug her nails into his flesh. "I am."

"No. Really touch me."

Like a child exploring a new doll, she carefully eased her fingers over his body. Again she was surprised by how soft his masculine skin felt, though beneath it ran the iron hardness of corded muscles and a reassuring warmth that left her fingertips burning as they trailed down his spine to the gentle rise of his buttocks.

Again he whispered, "Touch me."

She instinctively moved her hands lower. His muscles bunched beneath her palms. He buried his face in her neck and nipped the top of her shoulder. A surge of supreme power rippled through her. Her barest touch had elicited a primitive reaction from the strongest man she'd ever known.

Along with the power emerged a new bravery. She loved the feel of him, reveled in the undulating flow of his tendons and flesh. Her heart sang with the pure sensation of *love* for Grant Jones. It wasn't gratitude, or a sense of owing him. She wanted to give herself, her trust, and willingly risked her soul.

Grant raised his head. Every muscle in his body tensed with the need to bury himself within her feminine depths. He looked into her eyes and his chest swelled. The doubt was gone, replaced by a longing intensity as great as his own.

He rotated his hips, teasing himself between her thighs. Her eyes rounded as her legs instantly spread and he took full advantage of her openness. The tip of his manhood probed into her warmth. She was tight, but wet and slick and ready—for him.

To make sure he didn't hurt her, he slid a hand between them and teased her with his fingers until her hips arched and perspiration beaded her perfect body. He captured her eyes and waited, watching the fire flaring in the navy depths.

Jacelyn's breath was ragged. She rasped, "Please."

"Please, what, sugar?" he growled.

She swallowed. "Please ... put out the ... fire ... burning inside me."

"God knows, it'll be my pleasure." He inched inside her. Her hips rose to meet him. He entered slowly, one short thrust at a time. She wet her lips, and he immediately bent his head to taste her.

Jacelyn's lower body moved to an age-old rhythm. Each of his movements intensified the sensations in her lower belly until she thought she would explode. Her body came alive, separating itself from her mind, taking them both on a ride that was wilder than anything she could ever have imagined.

Sparks flickered behind her closed eyelids. Her chest tightened. Her hips bucked. Muscles she never knew she had strained.

She held on to Grant as if her life depended on him. Surely she wouldn't shatter into a million pieces if she gripped him tight. But his skin was slippery and she was afraid she'd lose her grasp. She ground her nails into his back. Bit into his shoulder to keep from screaming out loud.

Grant thrust long and hard. He'd been taken by surprise when she began to undulate wildly beneath him, but it was a wonderful surprise and he gladly adjusted to her. Hell, what a woman. She had more passion in her little finger than any ten women he'd had before. He'd known . . . but never experienced, anything like this . . .

Her heels pounded his buttocks. He plunged one last time, shooting his seed into her. He gasped as she contracted around him again and again, draining him until he was weak and his body felt as limp as damp denim. "Damn," he drawled, collapsing to one side to keep from crushing her with his weight.

Jacelyn looked into the blue sky, gasping, wondering how she'd come back to earth so quickly. For a time, she'd thought Grant had taken her as high as the clouds. She closed her eyes, but kept her arms wrapped tightly around him. He was her anchor, her security, her love.

Without thinking, Grant murmured an endearment in Apache. He snuggled her close, wondering what she would look like, lying in a wickiup, on a bed of soft hides, her hair tousled and her eyes soft and dreamy— like now.

But the time was past for lazy days spent hunting and fishing and loving with his Apache relatives. Most of them had already been herded to the San Carlos reservation or had fled to the Sierra Madres in Mexico. The few of them left were either scouts with the Cavalry or about to flee because of the persecution directed their way by whoever was causing the most recent problems.

He shook away those depressing thoughts, for the time being. But it was just another reminder that he needed to finish his business at the ranch and get on his way.

Still, for now, he tightened his arms around Jacelyn. All he wanted to do this minute was hold this warm, loving woman.

Jacelyn thought about the strange words Grant had spoken. She placed a hand on his chest and felt the rapid beat of his heart. "What did you just say?"

He yawned. "I don't know. When?"

"Just a minute ago." She nuzzled her nose into the soft hair on his chest. "It sounded funny. Was it something you learned from the Apache?"

He tensed. He hadn't realized he'd spoken his thoughts aloud. What would she have done if he'd called her "his love" in English? Run for her life? Probably. "I can speak Apache."

Poor Grant. How awful his experience must have been. "How long did you . . . stay . . . with them?"

He thought about his years at boarding school, and then with the Cavalry. "I was fifteen or sixteen when I left."

Oh, she thought. He'd been captured when just a child. Just think of all he'd missed not growing up with his family. "How did you escape?" She circled his nipple with her index finger and watched it harden. He was such a beautiful man, physically as well as in his manners. At least being with the Indians hadn't done any permanent damage.

"Pardon me?" Grant frowned. Escape? What was she talking about?

"I was just wondering how you managed to get away from the Indians after you were captured. You must've been very brave."

His heart contracted. Somehow, she'd misunderstood. His gut roiled. No wonder she'd been so understanding. What would she do when she found out the truth? He drew in a deep breath. Might as well find out now as later.

He turned his head so he could look her directly in her eyes. This time there would be no question. "I told you I lived with the Apache, didn't I?"

She felt the muscles in his body tighten and sensed something was wrong. "Yes . . . but—"

"And I did live with them, sugar. My mother was a Chiricauhua Apache. My father was a missionary and dedicated his life to teaching and helping my mother's band."

Jacelyn's eyes narrowed as she began to comprehend that Grant Jones was a halfbreed. One of those characters *Harper's Weekly* described as a lawless renegade accepted by neither whites nor Indians.

And a halfbreed Apache. The fiercest, most hostile tribe on the continent. And he was one of them. An outlaw. And she'd just made love to him.

Realizing all at once that their bodies were still joined, she tried to push him away, but his arms were like thick ropes, binding, restricting, imprisoning.

"Let go, you savage. You lied to me," she sobbed. "You lied."

Chapter Eighteen

Grant held his temper as best he could. This was exactly the reaction he'd expected the first time he'd mentioned his association with the Apache. Though always prepared, this time he thought the horror on her face and the accusation in her voice would rend his heart in two.

"I never lied to you, lady."

For some reason, as angry as she was, his reverting to "lady" rather than "sugar" pricked her heart. "Yes, you did." She continued to push at him, but he just held her tighter. She could even feel the part of him inside her pulse and harden again and it sent a white-hot spasm of fire through her.

"You heard what you wanted to hear." His own anger grew, despite the fact he tried to control it. Damned city woman. She knew nothing about the Apache, nothing about *him*, but believed every word of condemnation she'd heard or read.

He wondered what she'd read about the Apache's capability of making love. Had he passed muster? His manhood pulsated, thickening as her body contracted around him. Her body liked what they'd done, and that she couldn't deny. And she'd like it again.

Jacelyn panicked when her body began to betray her.

"Let me go. You can't do this," she hissed, and pushed harder against his boulder-solid body.

His teeth nipped the lobe of her ear as he growled, "Oh, but I can. And you want me to." He filled his hand with her breast and felt the nipple harden in his palm.

"I hate you." She nearly sobbed out loud. He was right. No matter what else had happened, her heart belonged to him. As illogical as it seemed, she felt like she would wither and blow away if he *didn't* make love to her again.

"I don't believe you." His breath teased her ear and he exulted at her answering shiver.

He moved inside her and she met his thrusts with an urgency that frightened her and startled Grant. Their eyes locked and dueled as their bodies engaged in motions of attack and retreat, joined in combat to a climax so sweet it brought tears to her eyes.

Grant saw a tear brim over and trickle into the already damp hair at her temple. He caught the next droplet on his tongue. Then there were too many to try to stop. He held her while she sobbed, and grimaced as a single Apache tear mingled with hers.

Once she started to cry, it was impossible for her to stop. She cried over her uncle's attempt to keep her away from the business by willing it to James. She cried over a brother who had promised to come back. Over a brother who was missing. Over Colonel Alexander's accusations. The stage holdup. Being taken prisoner and held for ransom. Dora's misery over her sacrificed child. The attempted rape and Eloy's gruesome death.

But mostly she cried over love found . . . and suddenly lost.

Grant's Apache blood wasn't the issue—a fact that surprised even her. He couldn't have treated her better, under the circumstances. But he hadn't been honest with her. He'd allowed her to believe something simply to elicit her sympathy.

Why did men manipulate her? Why hadn't he told her the truth before he took the precious gift of her total trust?

Now that fragile confidence was broken.

Gulping back more sobs, she looked into the sky and saw bright-colored birds flitting merrily from tree to tree. Leaves rustled and a red squirrel scampered toward the pool. How could life go on so normally when her whole world had just turned upside down?

Grant sensed from the bleak hopelessness in her eyes that whatever they had found together was over. His fears had been well founded. He didn't know why it hurt worse this time than other times before, but it did—much, much worse.

He swallowed. It was just as well. If she couldn't stand the fact that he had Apache blood, then he wanted nothing to do with her. He'd thought, though, that she was different.

As their breathing returned to a semblance of regularity, Grant heard the tinkling sound of water spilling into the pool. He narrowed his eyes. If she was so ashamed of making love to an Indian, he'd help her get rid of any damning evidence.

Rolling off her, he gathered her in his arms and rose before Jacelyn knew what he had in mind. Three long strides carried him to the edge of the water where he at least had the foresight to remove her watch and toss it toward the pile of clothing.

Jacelyn kicked and screamed when she realized his intent. "No!" She grabbed for his neck, but too late. The next thing she knew, she was sailing toward the water. "I can't swim," she yelled as she landed bottom first and sent a spray of water in all directions.

She came up sputtering and splashing, only to be met

with another face full of water as Grant jumped in beside her. She tried to twist from his reach, but he caught her under the arms and lifted until she found her feet.

"You all right?"

She spit water from her mouth. "No, I'm not." Swiping hair from her eyes, she demanded, "Why'd you do that?"

He shrugged. "You'd worked up a sweat."

She grimaced. Of all the uncouth things to say to a woman. "Well . . . so had you," she reminded him, then regretted the memory of the wonderful feelings he'd elicited in her own body.

"That's why I'm here." He dunked himself and stretched to float flat on his back, appearing as nonchalant as possible so she wouldn't think he'd come in after her for fear his hasty action would cause her harm. "Why didn't you ever learn to swim?"

She edged away from him, trying to keep tender feelings of comradery from overwhelming her.

"I-I don't know." She didn't want to tell him that her parents had traveled extensively, and the people left in charge of James and herself had usually been older. There'd really been no one to teach them, or actually to care one way or the other about them.

"I'll teach you." Grant crossed his arms, cursing himself for his foolish, impulsive offer.

She studied the ripples in the water. "Maybe some other time." Of course, she knew there would never be another time. And it surprised her how much that knowledge hurt, how empty she felt inside. But it was the way it had to be. He wasn't the man she'd thought him to be.

He stilled his features. Certainly she would refuse. After all, he might try to scalp her when she wasn't looking. Or, better yet, torture her. According to most whites, Indians were no better than animals and the only

277

good Indian was a dead Indian. Since he was probably the *only* Indian she'd known firsthand, he must symbolize the worst there could be.

He inhaled, then let the air out in a long, defeated sigh. He was tempted to ask her not to mention his Apache ancestors to the Waddell gang, but to say something might encourage her to do just the opposite. If he let things be, maybe she wouldn't think to use the information against him.

Jacelyn waded toward the bank, each step heavy, embarrassed now for him to see her naked.

Grant shook his head and stalked boldly from the water. He could never figure out why white people were so ashamed of their bodies that they covered themselves in layer upon layer of clothing.

He picked up her watch and undergarments, disdainfully examining the flimsy scraps of cloth, then the shirt, trousers, and moccasins. He dumped them at the edge of the water and stepped back, casually crossing his arms over his chest as he waited for her to come out.

Jacelyn tried not to look at his blatant display of masculinity, but couldn't drag her eyes away from his broad chest, lean torso, tapered legs and ... Her eyes darted up to that part of him that had made her feel things she'd never imagined *ever* to feel.

She swiftly glanced to his face. His male beauty literally stole her breath away. That is, until she noticed the smug glint in his eyes. He was daring her to come out, knowing she would refuse.

Her chin jutted forward. She took a deep breath. She stepped out of the water. A few unsteady steps more carried her to the pile of clothing. She gave him a defiant glare and was gratified when he was the one to back away. Just to prove she could do it, she even sat down and then stretched out on the grass to let the sun dry her body before she dressed.

Grant swallowed when she started toward him. He hadn't thought she'd be brave enough to come out. But there she stood, water trickling in rivulets over her shoulders and between her breasts, down her tummy and into the thatch of red curls at the juncture of her creamy thighs.

Damn, she was a beautiful woman. His heart ached at the thought of finding her and losing her, all within the space of a heartbeat.

When she draped her nakedness on the grass, he cleared his throat and scolded, "Your skin is too fair to be exposed to the sun this long."

She flipped a lock of wet hair from her shoulder. It was all she could do to turn her head and meet his eyes. She gulped at the sight of his hungry gaze devouring her. Mustering the courage to sniff haughtily, she said, "I can take care of myself, thank you. Besides, the sun feels good."

He arched a thick brow and left her to find his own clothes. By the time he'd dressed and returned, she was sound asleep. He forced his eyes away from her lush body, bent to pick up her garments and watch, and tossed them none too gently onto her pinkening chest and stomach.

Jacelyn started. Her eyes shot open, and she found him towering over her, a fierce glower shooting from his stormy eyes.

"You have five minutes. If you're not ready, I'll leave without you."

She sputtered and fumed, but to no avail, as he'd already turned and headed up the rocky slope to the tethered horse. Tempted to let him go on, she nevertheless looked at the rugged terrain surrounding her and scrambled to her feet. She was dressed and up the hill in three minutes.

Grant was already mounted. She thought there was

disappointment in his eyes that she'd made it on time, and proudly held out her hand for him to lift her up in front of him on the saddle. She might be a tenderfoot city girl, but she learned fast.

Once she was settled, Grant nudged the horse down the ridge and into the next arroyo. He was disappointed all right, disappointed that instead of wrapping his arms around her and cupping her firm breasts in his palms, or nuzzling the soft underside of her ear, he instead sat stiff and straight in the saddle. There was an adobe wall erected between them, though they touched in a dozen tantalizing places. It was a damned shame.

They rode in silence for half an hour, following a faint trail that Grant assumed would lead to the next water. The countryside became steeper and rougher, until he finally pulled the Appaloosa beneath the shade of a tall pine to rest.

He lowered Jacelyn to the ground, dismounted himself, and pulled the saddle off the sweating animal. Fidgeting beneath the woman's intense stare, he pointed to a shorter, long-needled tree. "If you're hungry, gather some of those piñon nuts. They're good."

Grateful to have something to do, she turned, albeit more reluctantly than she was comfortable with, toward the sweet-smelling pine. Close to the base of the tree, she saw small, oval seeds on the ground. She picked one up and looked back to Grant, who nodded his head. She shook hers. He'd called these teeny little things nuts? They weren't like any nut with which she was familiar. Walnuts and pecans. Now *those* were nuts.

Warily she tested the shell and winced when her teeth slid off the tough, thick coating. She tried again, worried that it was her front tooth cracking when the shell finally gave. But only a small piece fell off. She bit down again. Another little portion broke away. She tried to pick it open, but the shell, tiny as it was, was too thick to break with her nails.

By the time she managed to get to the meat, it was in tiny pieces that she could hardly grind in her teeth. But what she tasted was pretty good. She just couldn't imagine going to so much trouble for so little in return. However, the bushy-tailed squirrel, that stared at her for a second with its cheeks stuffed full before it bounded up the tree, seemed to think they were worth the effort.

She picked up a few more of the nuts and wandered through the trees. The warm day brought out the fragrance of the pines and wild flowers. Despite the ugliness that now overlay what should have been a beautiful memory, the day was gorgeous. She decided to enjoy being outside and away from the confines of the ranch.

Ahead, she saw a small clearing. At the far end were rock tailings. Someone must've tried to mine the area. Eagerly she approached the mine. She'd seen pictures and read about the miners in *Harper's,* but she'd never seen a real, true-to-life mine.

Off to the left was a partially constructed building. Beneath a board she saw rounded handles that were probably connected to some sort of tools. She moved around the pile to get a better view and picked up the end of a long board.

Her eyes rounded at the sight of a pair of leather boots. Tucked into the tops were denim trousers, filled out with a man's legs.

She screamed and dropped the board, backing away as quickly as she could. Her heels caught on a root and she plopped down on her bottom, screaming again as she tried to clamber back to her feet.

Gentle hands clasped her shoulders and helped her up. "What's wrong? Are you hurt?"

She danced sideways as Grant knelt and hurriedly felt

her legs and arms, trying to hold her still so he cold find out what was wrong.

"No." She slapped at the hand near her breast. "Not me," she breathlessly rasped, the pointed toward the boards. "Th-there!"

Seeing that she was nearly hysterical with fear, Grant pulled his gun and slowly stalked toward the mine. He placed each foot carefully, expecting to find a rattler close by. He jumped and started to spin around when he felt a slight touch on his arm.

"Damn it, lady, don't come up behind a man like that. You could get yourself killed."

She shrank back. "I'm sorry. B-but he's over there." Again, she gestured toward the stack of boards.

Grant nodded and changed direction. "He?"

"I-I th-think so," she whispered. "And I think h-he's d-dead."

A breeze wafted through the clearing. Grant wrinkled his nose. Something was dead, all right, and if he were any judge, it had been that way for some time.

He peered through the lumber and saw a boot. He glanced back at Jacelyn. Her rounded eyes never blinked as she nodded. He walked up to the top end of the board and stepped over a wide growth of chapparal. Holding one hand over his nose, he moved aside several branches with the gun barrel and found the upper portion of a body. A blue shirt covered the man's back and . . . Grant's stomach turned. He'd been scalped.

His fingers clenched on the gun butt until he decided it would be safer to put the gun up. He sensed Jacelyn coming up behind him and grimaced when she gasped.

He reholstered the pistol and turned to take her elbow. Her face was deathly pale, but she still had enough spunk to jerk away from him.

Cursing her stubbornness, he ordered, "Go back to the horse and wait. This's no place for a woman."

Her eyes felt like they were full of sand when she blinked. "Wh-what're you going to do?"

"I'm going to drag him out of there and bury him. Why?"

She shrugged, keeping her eyes diverted toward the small black hole that was the mine entrance. "I was hoping you'd do that."

My God, Grant thought, she really must think he was some kind of barbarian. "Go on and get out of here. No need for you to watch." She'd really have a fit if she saw that the body had been scalped.

"No! I mean, I want to stay. I found him." What she didn't want to admit was that she was afraid to go back alone. No matter what she thought of Grant, she felt safer with him than without him.

"Have it your way." He tore out some weeds, grabbed the blue shirt at the shoulders and dragged the body into the open.

Jacelyn sniffed, gagged, and turned her back. She wouldn't leave, but she didn't have to look.

Grant pulled the dead man to a mound of earth near the mine where it wouldn't be hard to cover the body. As hard as the ground was, it would take a day to dig a grave with a pickaxe. He walked back to the partial building and pulled a broken handle, an axe, and finally a shovel from under the boards.

Ever curious, Jacelyn held her breath and strolled around the place where he'd removed the body. Something dark, lying on the bent, yellowed grass, caught her eye. She looked first to Grant, who was busy shoveling dirt over the dead man, and back to the object.

She kicked a piece of gravel, paced in a circle, but couldn't stand it. She *had* to see what it was. Turning her head aside to take a deep breath, she walked over and picked up . . . a leather pouch. She turned it over several times, looking at it closely. Her heart stopped beating. Her fingers went numb. She walked to the center of the clearing in a trance.

She held out her hand. In the bright sunlight, the embossed gold initials "J M" shone from the flap. Her knees shook so badly she couldn't support herself. She sank to the ground, clutching James's mapping tools to her chest.

"No!" The scream burst from within her, rending her apart. "No! Stop!" She leaped to her feet and ran to Grant, grabbing his arm as he held another shovel full of dirt and stared, bewildered, at her.

As she slid down beside the body, she could see only patches of the blue shirt and denims. Frantically she clawed through loose earth and gravel.

Grant tossed down the shovel and grabbed the crazy woman. Hell, her eyes were glazed and she could hardly catch her breath. She moaned and showed all the signs of going out of her mind. He tried to pull her off the poor, dead soul.

"No! Let me go," she cried, as he dragged her away.

He turned her to face him, but she struggled like a truly mad woman. Shaking her until her hair tangled around both their shoulders, he shouted, "What's gotten into you, lady?"

Tears rolled down her dusty cheeks. Her breasts heaved. She couldn't focus on him. Finally, he pulled her against his chest and held her until she exhausted herself. Perplexed, he cupped her head to his shoulder as she ceased to fight and cried like she'd lost her last friend.

Her hands were at his waist. He felt something catch his belt. Gently, he released her, caught and steadied her when she sagged against him, and took her hand in his, prying her stiff fingers off a strange pouch.

The initials and their significance struck him like a kick in the gut. He looked from the partially exposed body to Jacelyn. "Aw, hell, sugar." Remembering the condition of James McCaffery, he coaxed her away from the body and over to a rickety bench. "Sit down."

She did, and wiped her face with the tail of her shirt.

He opened the pouch. Inside were several hasty, but very precise maps, showing the locations of mines and ranches and even available water sources. Grant whistled. The man had known his business.

Behind the maps he found a sealed letter addressed to Miss Jacelyn McCaffery, Richmond, Virginia. It appeared the young man intended to be in town very soon after he'd written the missive.

Grant looked at Jacelyn's red-rimmed eyes and tear-streaked cheeks, hoping that whatever was inside the letter wouldn't distress her further. Hesitantly, he handed it to her. "This is yours," he said gruffly.

She blinked. Her hand shook as she took the letter and traced her name with her fingertip. A letter from James. After all the years of waiting, he'd finally written her a letter. Her heart throbbed painfully fast as she ripped into the envelope.

Grant watched her, thinking how she didn't fit any mold he'd tried to fit her into. He'd thought she would be very meticulous and careful not to tear the paper. Instead, she was like a child at Christmas, mindful only of getting to the important things.

Though she'd ceased to sob, tears trickled anew down Jacelyn's face as she read James's letter. The further she read, the more distraught she became.

James wrote that he wondered why she hadn't come to him, or at least written to let him know she'd received the money he'd sent. He had waited and waited. And she could tell from the tone of his words that he'd been hurt and disappointed.

Damn, Uncle Jonathan. She angrily swiped at a tear.

She hoped the old man had gone to hell and was burning there even now.

She clutched the letter to her breast and bowed her head. James hadn't deserted her. He'd done exactly as he promised. But Uncle Jonathan had intercepted James's letters. All those kindly pats of condolence as she worried and wondered about her brother . . . They'd been a lie. He'd been a selfish old man bent on manipulating her life.

She shot to her feet. "Damn him!" Now, more than ever, she was determined to go back and run that company. She *deserved* that position, it was her right, after all that her uncle had taken from her.

Slowly, she walked toward James. Why? Why had someone killed him before she could explain and set things right?

Grant moved in front of her. "No, sugar. Don't look at him now."

She stepped around him. "I-I have to be sure. And I . . . need to say goodbye."

He tried to block her, but she outmaneuvered him and ran the last few feet to the body. "I have to know . . ." she tried to explain. "What if someone just stole his things?" She turned pleading eyes on Grant. "Would you roll him over so I can see his f-face? Please?"

Grant shrugged, even as his stomach coiled into knots. The only way he could get her away would be to knock her on the head and carry her. Even then, he suspected she'd find her way back. One way or another, she would see for herself what had been done to her brother.

If he could just have a chance to explain. But . . . no. He couldn't risk telling her who he was or what he was doing. As close as Jacelyn had gotten to Dora, no telling what she might blurt out. His shoulders sagged as he picked up the shovel and began uncovering the body.

Jacelyn couldn't watch as Grant worked. She kept trying to convince herself that maybe . . . just maybe . . . someone *had* stolen James's things. But if they had, her rational mind intruded, wouldn't the outcome be just as bad? She gulped and pressed her hand to her heart, praying for a miracle.

Grant grimaced when he turned the body over. Surprisingly, though, given how long the man had been dead, the varmints hadn't done too much damage. You could still see the patrician features, wide-set eyes and pointed chin. He and Jacelyn had probably resembled one another a great deal.

A sudden, wrenching gasp behind him confirmed the identity of the body. Grant turned to take Jacelyn into his arms, to comfort and console her. His arms remained at his sides when he saw the horrified expression of revulsion on her face.

Jacelyn had prepared herself for a shocking sight, but when she saw the ugly gap atop her dead brother's head, she couldn't describe the sickening sensation that roiled through her.

Her arms wrapped around her stomach. "He-he's been scalped." Her eyes dragged to Grant. "Hasn't he?"

Grant stared into those accusing navy eyes and nodded once.

Suddenly, something snapped inside her. The strain from learning Grant had not been honest, that he had Apache blood in his veins, and then to find James dead, *scalped* . . .

Her eyes stabbed into him. "Who . . . Who did this?"

Chapter Nineteen

Jacelyn ran backward to get out of Grant's reach. Her voice quavered. "You know who killed my brother. Maybe you were a part of it. Maybe you did this."

Grant shook his head. He'd known she'd be upset at the sight of her scalped brother, but he'd never considered that she would turn on him. He wedged his hands into his pockets and frowned when his left hand encountered his lucky silver dollar. Somehow, its magic was failing him.

Taking several gulps of air, Jacelyn shook her head as if she couldn't quite bring herself to believe what she was thinking, but she said the words anyway. "You brought me here on purpose, didn't you? You knew I'd find him . . ." She recalled Grant talking to the Indian. The moccasins. They'd just been an excuse.

And there'd been other times when he'd conveniently disappeared. No telling what heinous plots they'd planned for the poor miners who'd begun work here and—

Grant took advantage of her preoccupation to step forward and grab her upper arms. When she resisted, he squeezed tighter. "Now, you listen, lady. No self-respecting Apache would've left this good leather pouch and these pretty pictures." He shook out a very artistically drawn map.

Suddenly he remembered an object he'd almost tripped over when he'd moved the body. He grabbed Jacelyn's hand and pulled her over to the shrubs. Leaning down, he used his free hand to move branches until he found what he was looking for.

"See this?" He held up a telescope.

A mutinous frown marred her features, but she nodded.

"This would be a treasure in any Apache warrior's wickiup."

"So, what are you implying?" She finally jerked her hand free and crossed her arms over her breasts. No matter what he said, how could she believe him? The man was a liar.

He scowled at the haughty, disbelieving glare in her eyes. Damned woman. He was butting his head against a stone wall, but he'd explain it anyway. "Apaches did not kill your brother." He said each word very slowly and succinctly.

She threw her arms in the air. "How stupid do you think I am? I may be a tenderfoot, but I know well enough that Indians take scalps."

"That proves you're just an ignorant city girl," he rumbled, baring his teeth in his anger.

Her eyes rounded.

"You've read some of those 'true' stories about the West. Whites introduced the *admirable*," the word dripped sarcastically from his lips, "custom of scalping to the Indians years ago. Indians just made an art of it. But . . .," again he spoke very slowly, "few Apaches believe in taking scalps." He pointed to her brother's body. "That's why I know my people are not responsible for this."

While she appeared to be mulling over the believability of that fact, he cautioned himself that there were always a few renegades who'd take scalps, but most of those Apaches were either in the Sierra Madres or avoiding his scouts and Fort Huachuca and escaping into Mexico further east.

Jacelyn pursed her lips. "No . . . I don't believe you. How else could you know James was here?"

"Damn it, lady." He cringed and darted a glance at the body. Apaches didn't talk about the dead or repeat their names for fear of death and the spirits, but he didn't guess this was a good time to convince Jacelyn McCaffery of the value of Apache beliefs. "What makes you think I *knew* anything? I'm just as surprised as you to find him . . . anyone . . . here. I know the Appaloosa's—"

"What? What about an Appaloosa?" She remembered the Colonel's saying her brother had been riding his good Appaloosa horse. Glancing around the clearing, she could see no sign of a horse. "What is an Appaloosa, anyway?" She speared Grant with her eyes. Again, he must think he was dealing with an idiot. He *knew* something, all right; and *she* knew he did.

Grant shrugged. "It's just a horse." Hell, why couldn't he learn to keep his mouth shut around this woman? She already held his life in her hands. He only hoped she didn't realize how important her silence would be.

Jacelyn stomped the ground. She could tell he wasn't going to tell her anything. Her shoulders sagged as she walked back to look down at her brother. Poor James. He'd been too young and vital to die like this. Her fists clenched. Some how, some way, she'd find out who was responsible, whether he be Apache, or white, or even . . . Grant Jones, in whom flowed the blood of both.

The ride back to the ranch was made in a silence as deep as the lengthening shadows. Grant was bone tired from burying Jacelyn's kin and carrying rocks to cover the grave. Jacelyn was heartsick, grieving over the loss of her brother who, until two hours ago, she believed had betrayed her, and the loss of her first and, she vowed, her only love.

When they entered the headquarters and stopped in front of the barn, a numb sensation settled over her as Grant set her on the ground. In the dusky light, she didn't even see Dora come out on the porch as she walked in a daze to the cabin.

Closing the door, she scuffed over to the water pitcher and dampened a rag to hold over her puffy, scratchy eyes. She wet the rag again and flopped into the chair.

The door opened, but she refused to look up. Evidently, nothing she said could keep Grant from doing what he pleased. And the last thing she wanted right then was another argument. She was simply too worn out to engage in a verbal battle with the man.

"Here ya go, Missy. Eat this here stew. Ya need ta put somethin' in that tiny belly."

Jacelyn dropped the rag and looked into Dora's sympathetic face.

The older woman placed a bowl on the table and leaned her hip against the corner. "Yore man told me about your brother."

Jacelyn frowned at Dora's choice of words. She doubted Grant would ever belong to any woman, and this woman certainly wasn't interested in him. But she didn't have the energy to refute the point. She lifted her shoulders in a half-hearted shrug. "I still can't believe it, Dora. He's *dead.*" She choked on the word.

"Yeah, I lost my family a long time ago. Didn't know my pa at all. Ma, she run off when I's ten. Reckon when I met my first husband an' had my Shiloh, I didn't know much about motherin' my own self."

Regret for many things tugged at Jacelyn's heart. Even with her own pain so fresh, she felt compassion for the young woman Dora must've been, forced to give up her child, yet thinking it was for the best. "I'm really sorry, Dora. Your life hasn't been easy."

"Pshaw, it ain't been all that bad, neither. Waddy's been good ta me."

Jacelyn shuddered at the thought of the outlaw. Good? Sure. What man wouldn't stand by and watch the woman he loved give up her daughter? Yet, Jacelyn thought, compared to the life Dora had known before she met Waddell, maybe it was "good." She shuddered again with that terrible thought. "He wasn't the father of your child, then?"

"Darby, my husband, turned up 'is toes directly after we'd come West ta start our new life. Left me'n Shiloh in the middle of Tucson without a lick of money, no family, nothin'. Then I met Waddy."

"But ... how could he have let you give up your daughter? Surely he knew how much she meant to you."

"Course he did." Dora spread out one arm, palm up. "What kind of life would this've been fer a kid? Least mebbe she had a chance ta learn some readin' an' writin' and such."

Jacelyn reached out and took Dora's hand. "I just don't know how you can stand not knowing for sure what happened to her."

Dora swiped the back of her free hand under her nose. "Well, Waddy says he's been lookin' around. Mebbe ... one day he'll see 'er, or hear somethin' about 'er."

"I hope so." But Jacelyn doubted it. Waddell had more important things to think about—like the next stage to rob. And he seemed to Jacelyn to be the type of man who needed to be the center of things. He probably hadn't wanted to share Dora's affection with another soul, even her daughter.

"Well . . ." Dora squeezed Jacelyn's hand then slipped away from the table. "Guess I'd better get on up ta the house and rustle up some vittles fer your man."

"But, he's not—"

"It were real thoughtful of 'im ta be concerned fer ya. Kinda reminded me o' my Waddy, back when we first come together."

Jacelyn leaned her elbows on the table and buried her face in her hands.

"Now ya eat that there stew while it's hot, ya hear?" Dora left the door open when she left.

Jacelyn nodded, though she was still reeling from Dora's high praise of Grant Jones. Thoughtful? Concerned? What a laugh. The man had single-handedly destroyed her life. The last two words she would use to describe him right now were thoughtful and considerate. Lying. Deceitful. Those were more appropriate.

Feeling somewhat better as she thought of all the vile words she could apply to Grant, she sniffed disdainfully. Her mouth watered at the savory aroma of the stew. She hadn't eaten more than a few piñon nuts since breakfast. And she did need to conserve her energy. Her chance to escape could come at any time.

She was almost through eating when the hair along the nape of her neck prickled. Only one person ever caused her nerve endings to tingle so that she knew immediately whenever he was near.

She lifted her head and turned to find Grant standing in the doorway staring at her. "Go away."

"Sorry. Can't do that." He stalked into the room, carrying the mapmaker's pouch and telescope in one hand, a bucket of water in the other.

She thought he looked entirely too predatory. "I don't want you here."

"Sorry about that, too. But I'm here." He placed the pouch and telescope under the cot—as close to the wall as possible—then went over and grabbed his bedroll and spread it out.

She shot to her feet. "Then I'll leave."

He reached over and slammed the door shut before she'd taken two steps. "You'll stay right where you are."

Her eyes narrowed. "But . . . I have to . . . use the facilities."

He straightened from unfolding his blanket. "Fine. I'll go with you."

She stomped her foot. "You hard-headed savage." The significance of her words caused her to pause, but only briefly. "Don't you understand? I don't want anything to do with you."

He shrugged, keeping his face turned away. "I understand all right." He hunkered down between her and the door.

"Then get out of here."

"Sorry."

"Oh-h-h!" She threw up her hands and collapsed onto the cot. Running her hand down the side of her face, she flinched when her fingers touched her tender cheek, the one that hadn't been injured in the melee with Eloy. She grinned carefully, maliciously, and informed him, "You need a shave." It gave a tremendous boost to her confidence to find some flaw in the man's perfection.

Grant ran a hand over his moustache, scraggly beard and stubbled cheek, but refused to dignify her comment with a retort. She was right. He couldn't remember going so long without at least shaving his beard. "Done."

Mischief tilted one corner of his lips. "The beard'll be gone the next time we make love."

She gasped. "I never—"

"Yes, you have."

"I meant . . ." she declared loudly, "there'll never *be* a next time." She rolled over to glare at him.

He arched a brow.

"I mean it."

The other brow arched.

She cursed and turned onto her back where she could stare at the ceiling instead of his insolent features. But even then she felt him looking at her and remembered how his eyes had roved so appreciatively over her body. Her flesh suddenly felt warm and tingly.

Grant chuckled as if he knew exactly what was going through her mind, but he was actually laughing at himself. Just the mention of making love to her again had him as ready as if he were a stud confined in a stall next to a mare in heat. Damn.

"Do you still need to go . . . outside?" he asked.

"No."

"You said—"

"I don't have to go any more. All right?"

"Fine."

"Fine." Jacelyn closed her eyes, but tossed restlessly. Grant moved his bedroll closer to the door and slept with one eye open.

Grant rose with the sun the next morning. After folding and storing his bedroll, he soundlessly walked over to peer down at Jacelyn, lying curled in a tight ball, still wearing her clothes.

She looked so innocent and childlike in her sleep, that Grant's arms ached to hold her. He was sorry for the pain she'd suffered at his hands, but she'd hurt him, too.

He'd never planned to lose his heart so quickly and thoroughly, and then have it broken in an even shorter period of time.

Sighing with deep regret, he shook out her blanket

and laid it over her before leaning down to brush her cheek with a kiss. He didn't know what would happen when this was all over but, maybe, if the spirits allowed, they would have a chance to talk and set things right.

He left the cabin and was headed toward the barn when he saw a light shining in the kitchen and veered in that direction.

Dora stood in her robe, watching a pot of coffee boil. She spun in surprise as the door opened and Grant entered. "Watcha doin' up at this hour, Jones? Reckoned y'all would sleep in a while after the day ya put in."

Grant yawned. "Jacelyn's still sleeping, but I need to go around and check the rest of the waters. Thought I'd let you know so you can . . ." He cocked his head back the way he'd come. "So you can . . . you know . . ."

Dora moved the pot off the fire and filled a cup for Grant. "Don't worry none. I'll keep an eye on 'er." She eyed Grant intently. "Reckon the gal's some important to ya, huh?"

He shrugged and blew on the hot liquid before taking a sip.

Dora grinned. "I like her. It'd be good ta have another woman around here." Then the grin became a frown. "Hope it don't cause no trouble with Waddy and the boys. They's hopin' fer a big ransom." As she spoke, she turned to wrap several biscuits and a thick slice of beef in a towel. "Here, take this with ya if'n ya ain't gonna hang around long enough fer a meal."

Taking the food, he set the coffee down and started for the door. "Thanks, Dora. See you later."

She watched him go with a knowing expression on her face. "Yep, reckon ya will."

Several hours later, Grant rode from the foothills and looked over a rolling, grassy plateau. In the distance he saw a herd of cattle and, nearer, three mounted cowboys. From the looks of the men, with their chaps, rifles, and knives, they were the real thing.

He thought it a shame the true cowboys had such a bad reputation in these parts. Although not all cowboys were outlaws, all outlaws were referred to as cowboys because of the expert way they tended to drive stolen cattle across the desert.

As the riders came closer, he lowered his right hand to his thigh, near his revolver. One of the cowboys had drawn his rifle and held it across his lap, probably with his trigger finger already engaged.

They stopped a few yards apart, regarding each other in silence. The trio was a scraggly group, Grant thought, all looking enough alike to be from the same family. They rode thin mustangs that appeared to have been "rode hard and put up wet" too many nights.

Finally, one of the men nodded toward the mountain range behind Grant. "You work for that outfit back in the foothills?"

Grant lifted his shoulders and lowered them slowly. "I reckon."

A skinny, buck-toothed youngster pushed his hat back and scratched his forehead. *"Reckon,"* he drawled, "how Waddell's calf crop is this year?"

"Haven't seen all that many cows," Grant said warily. "Just been checking the waters."

The oldest-looking boy rested his hands on the horn and shifted in the saddle. The smile on his lips failed to reach his eyes as he said, "Ole Waddell has the best set of cows this side of Texas. Yessirree. Ever one of his herd comes up with twins, and sometimes even triplets, every darn year."

The gent with the rifle just nodded his head.

"Wouldn't know, boys. I just been there a few weeks."

The buck-toothed one looked at his friends. "Mebbe he's all right, Danny. Least he's out doing his job."

Grant watched Danny, the oldest, consider the youngster's words as he studied Grant. "Mebbe." He warned Grant, "Just be careful you don't let that rope down too close to that herd yonder. Them calves done been branded."

Grant flicked the brim of his hat. "Don't have no intention of riding that far, gents. Y'all take care now."

He kept his eyes on the silent member of the trio as he reined his horse around, and breathed easier when all three of the cowboys turned their mustangs and rode back the way they'd come.

Well, he'd learned something else about the Waddell gang. Besides robbing stages and silver wagons, they were suspected cattle rustlers. He'd gotten involved with a busy bunch of men. Colonel Alexander would be glad to see the Waddell gang put out of business.

Spurring the Appaloosa into a ground-eating lope, he headed back to the ranch. All of a sudden, he had a strong feeling that something was wrong.

Back at the ranch, Jacelyn had a hard time waking. Her eyes were scratchy and her temples throbbed. She ached all over from sleeping uncovered all night. And she was tender between her thighs from . . . Well, she didn't want to think about from *what* right now.

She stretched and was surprised to find a blanket covering her. She didn't remember pulling it up.

Slowly lifting her head, she glanced toward the door. The floor was empty. Craning her neck, she saw the bedroll packed neatly in the corner. Grant was gone. The throbbing in her head subsided slightly.

Someone tapped on the door. She stiffened and tentatively called, "Come in."

298

Dora pushed the door open and brought in a plate of fresh, buttered biscuits. "You feelin' all right, Missy?"

Jacelyn yawned and sat up on the side of the bed, smoothing some of the wrinkles from her clothes. "I think so." She noticed the concern on Dora's face and felt a new warmth in her heart. "You have more important things to do than bring me food, Dora."

"Pshaw. Ain't neither. Now when them boys get back ... that's different." She smiled sheepishly. "Been kinda nice having ya around, Missy. Ya've made things easier fer me."

Jacelyn's cheeks flushed with heat. "I needed something to do, too."

"Your man seems ta be keeping ya busy now." Dora winked suggestively.

Tears burned the backs of Jacelyn's eyes. She'd almost conquered her emotions, she thought. Until Dora reminded her, and she recalled anew her intense feelings for the man, and remembered the wondrous things he'd done to her body and the love she'd felt before and after it was over.

To think she would never feel that again hurt more than she could say. For the rest of her life all she would have were memories, and even those would be marred forever by the events that followed.

"Here, here, child. What's all them tears fer?"

Jacelyn sniffed. She hadn't realized she was crying. "Nothing, really."

"Still feelin' bad 'bout your brother, ain't ya?" Dora awkwardly patted her shoulder.

Gulping, Jacelyn nodded, feeling a little guilty that her thoughts had centered on that awful savage rather than poor James.

"It'll pass." Dora shoved the plate in Jacelyn's hands. "Go ahead and eat, then come on ta the house when ya feel up ta it."

"I-I will."

As soon as Dora left, Jacelyn wiped her face, managed to eat part of a biscuit, then found her gaze drawn more and more to the gray gown she wanted to alter for the woman. Dora had been so kind . . . It was the least Jacelyn could do before she left.

Jacelyn had gone to the house and visited with Dora a while before borrowing a needle and thread. Pretending she needed to mend something of her own, she returned to the cabin and set to work on the gown. It was early afternoon before she finished, and she also repaired her torn camisole and pantalettes. The items were too hard to come by, though the thought of wearing them again did cause her to shiver.

Sighing, she walked to the door and looked around the headquarters. Except for the chirping of a few birds, everything was still. Her stomach knotted. This would be the perfect time to leave, when no one expected it.

When she left the cabin, besides the gown, she carried a towel folded around the leftover biscuits and a canteen, which she'd found in the barn, already filled with water. This time, she was better prepared. She also had Grant's bedroll. It was bulky and heavy, but once she had a horse, she didn't think it would be any trouble.

Her heart thudded painfully every time she thought of Grant. In fact, she was beginning to wonder if the urgency of her need to leave didn't have more to do with her getting away from *him* than any other reason.

She just couldn't trust herself around the man. She behaved so irrationally, her body reacted so violently, that she hardly recognized herself. Even knowing better, knowing the kind of man he was, she still loved him. Bewildered and aggravated, she shook her head.

A frown quirked her lips downward as she tiptoed up the front steps. Leaving all but the gown on the porch, she slowly opened the door. She prayed the hinges wouldn't creak and alert Dora, who'd said she would be spending the afternoon baking a peach cobbler with fresh fruit gathered from the orchard.

Jacelyn's mouth watered at the thought of fresh peaches, but she wouldn't miss the treat if she made good her escape. Glancing hastily around the front end of the house, she heaved a sigh of grateful relief upon finding it empty. She didn't know what to say to Dora.

Spreading the gown across the back of a small sofa so Dora would be sure to find it, she hesitated long enough to smooth some wrinkles from the soft material before heading back toward the door. She walked softly, her eyes focused out the window. She thought she'd seen a movement by the barn, but must've been mistaken.

"My Gawd, Missy, what ya gone and done?"

Jacelyn stopped abruptly. She spun to find Dora, wide-eyed and open-mouthed, reaching tentatively toward the gown. "I-I thought you sh-should have that." She glanced longingly over her shoulder at the door. She'd been so close.

"Oh, my . . . Ya didn't need ta go and do that." But Dora held the dress up, then clutched it to her breast. "Ain't it the most beautiful thing ya ever did see?"

Jacelyn couldn't help but smile. "Yes, it is beautiful. And it will look even more beautiful on you." She began to edge toward the door.

"Reckon I should try it on?"

Jacelyn's fingers curled around the knob. "Oh, ah . . . sure. Why don't you do that right now?"

Dora dragged her eyes from the gown to regard Jacelyn. At the sight of the younger girl's nervous shuffling, she frowned. "Where ya goin', Missy?"

301

"I, ah, forgot the needle and thread. I-I'll go and get it while you change. Might need to take another tuck . . . or something."

"Yeah, ya might at that." Dora's fingers dug into the gown.

Jacelyn's mouth worked. "G-goodbye, Dora."

"Bye, Missy." Dora watched the girl scoot through the door and close it quickly behind her. She heard scraping and fumbling on the porch and walked to the window with a heavy heart.

It came as no surprise to Dora to see Jacelyn loaded down and heading toward the barn. She'd suspected for a long time that the nice young man, Jones, had had his hands full keeping the gal in line.

She laid the gown on the table and stood undecided as to what to do. It wasn't right that the men held the girl against her will, but . . .

Dora's eyes narrowed. Someone was riding down the road. She ran to the door and threw it open. At the same time she saw Bob come from the trees behind the barn. The boys were back. Missy didn't know it and was headed right for them.

"Stop," Dora yelled. "Stop her."

Chapter Twenty

Jacelyn stiffened when she heard Dora scream. She ran toward the barn, but saw the black outlaw coming toward her. Spinning, her mind racing, she nearly choked on her flip-flopping heart.

Suddenly she caught sight of a horseman nearing the ranch. She remembered someone saying that lawmen sometimes checked on the ranches. Her feet sprouted wings as she ran down the road. Shouts from behind her spurred her on.

"Help! Help me!"

The rider kicked his horse into a gallop and hurried toward her. Excitement strained her muscles to their fastest pace. The bedroll jiggled from her arms. Biscuits dropped in her wake. Only the canteen slowed her down, but it was looped over her neck and shoulder and she couldn't discard it.

The closer the man rode, the more hopeful she became. He appeared to be olive-skinned and his attire was black and fancy. This was definitely not an outlaw. With her eyes glued to the man, she failed to see a rut in the road and stumbled. She fell to her knees just as he pulled up beside her.

"H-help. Please . . ." she gasped.

"Señorita?"

Running feet pounded close behind her. The stranger had dismounted and she clutched at his short jacket. Gulping for breath, she stammered, "Th-these men, they're outlaws. Th-they're keeping me prison—"

"Damn, Felipe. Ya showed up at just the right time, boy."

Jacelyn jerked her head up to stare at the man bending over her. He was dark-haired and dapper and clean-shaven and was grinning at her. Not evilly, just grinning. It sank in that Waddell had called him by his first name.

Defeated, her eyes dropped to his shiny black boots. So, he was an outlaw, too. Her body sagged, but the man grasped her arms and helped her to her feet. She felt Waddell's heavy hand on her shoulder and was shocked when the fancy fellow pulled her to his side.

"What is the matter, Ricardo? Do you have to chase your women down now, eh?"

"Ya don't know what the hell your jawin' about, Felipe. This here's the gal we done told ya about. An' she was tryin' ta get away."

Felipe nudged Jacelyn and started walking toward the headquarters, leading his horse behind. "Surely this beautiful young lady could not be so hard to manage."

Waddell limped alongside and grumbled, "Don't know. Jones's been watchin' after 'er."

"Jones?" Felipe questioned.

"Yeah, ya know, the new feller."

"Hmmmm. I think I remember."

Jacelyn listened intently to the conversation. She kept her eyes lowered to the ground, darting surreptitious glances toward the men when the opportunity allowed. There was something about the two that puzzled her, but she couldn't put her finger on what it was exactly.

As they approached Dora and Bob, Waddell called

out, "Where's that Jones? Thought he was supposed ta be keepin' this gal."

Jacelyn glared at the older woman. She couldn't believe the time and trouble she'd wasted on that gown, only to have Dora betray her at the first opportunity.

Dora wouldn't meet Jacelyn's eyes. She muttered, "Jones is out checking them waters like ya told him. I said I'd keep my eye on Mis . . . her."

"Well, what about Eloy? Why isn't he helpin' out?"

Silence fell over the gathered group of people. Dora met Jacelyn's eyes. "Ya know he weren't feelin' up ta snuff when ya left."

Waddell nodded.

"He jest got sicker 'n sicker 'n turned up 'is toes right sudden." She swallowed and rolled a rock around with the sole of her boot.

"Always thought he'd go from lead poisoning myself," the Kid contributed as he sauntered up to join them.

Jacelyn's mouth gaped open at Dora's lie, but snapped shut when the Kid blatantly ogled her. The man called Felipe's arm dropped around her shoulder and she felt like a centipede had crawled up her spine. Tempted to shake him off, but afraid of what that action might precipitate, she held her council to see what would happen next. She had a nasty notion that her foiled attempt to escape put her in a most precarious position. Her wonderful plan had deteriorated into a major mess.

Dora hurriedly changed the subject, looking around as she asked, "Ain't seen Pablo 'n Dutch. Ya leave 'em in town?"

Waddell glowered at Felipe. "Pablo 'n Dutch ain't comin' back." He took off his hat and swiped his shirtsleeve across his sweaty forehead. "There were a Cavalry detail close behind the wagons. We never had no chance."

Jacelyn felt the fancy man's arm stiffen and used the opportunity to step away from him.

"There have never been Cavalry guarding silver before," Felipe mused.

"Damn right," Waddell agreed.

The Kid looked up from cleaning his fingernails with the tip of his knife. "I reckoned that someone must have tipped them off we were coming."

Felipe scratched his chin. "Possibly. But who?"

"Couldn't have been anyone but Jones. He was the only one who wasn't with us the whole time ... but you," the Kid amended as he snuck a sly glance at Felipe.

"Watch it, Kid," Waddell ordered. "Ya know if'n it weren't fer Felipe ..." He looked at Jacelyn and suddenly switched topics by asking Dora, "Jest when did Jones show back up?"

Dora casually stuffed her hands into her pocket and leaned against a hitch rail. "Well, let me see ... Y'all left about mid-morning, and reckon he got back here a hour er two before midnight." She dared Jacelyn with a quick glance. "Ain't that right, Missy?"

Jacelyn couldn't help but shudder at the memory of that night. And, yes, it had been about that time when Grant made his timely entrance. She gulped and nodded. "Th-that's right. He came back that very night."

Realizing she was still nodding, she stopped. Why was she so worried about defending him when he and his Indian friends probably murdered her brother? No matter what he said, she couldn't imagine anyone but an Indian being vicious enough to take a scalp.

Waddell looked back and forth between the two women. "Didn't figure he'd get back til the next mornin', with a crippled hoss and all. Ain't no way he coulda taken off and warned no soldiers."

His shoulders hunched and he sounded disappointed.

Jacelyn barely took note of the fact, though, as she was busy watching Dora, wondering why she hadn't told the men the truth about Eloy and what he tried to do.

She finally shook her head. Dora was a hard person to understand. But was she a friend, or not? A real friend wouldn't have betrayed her, yet only a true friend would save her embarrassment and humiliation in front of the gang.

The Kid argued Waddell's estimation of Grant. "Couldn't have been anyone *but* Jones."

Waddell scowled. "How'd he do it, then?"

"I don't know."

"Then shut up and go hang up the saddles before the rats get at them cinches." Waddell looked at Felipe. "Let's go on inside an' palaver a spell."

Felipe took off his hat and bowed to Jacelyn. "Only if the pretty señorita promises she will join us for supper."

Jacelyn sputtered.

Waddell frowned. "Don'tcha think we better lock her up in that cabin?"

"And deprive ourselves of a beautiful woman's ..." He glanced toward Dora, who frowned, and added, "Two beautiful women's company?" He looked into Jacelyn's eyes. "You will promise not to do such a foolish thing again, won't you, señorita?"

Jacelyn saw the warning in his eyes and felt it in the grip of his fingers when he took her hand.

"Won't you?"

She swallowed and had to moisten her lips before she could answer. "I-I promise."

Felipe smiled. "Ah, see? That was not so hard." He turned to Waddell. "And there are many fine, brave hombres to see she keeps her word, no?"

Jacelyn shivered, but with one last bit of defiance, added silently, "I promise, until I get another chance."

Waddell called out to the Kid. "Keep your eyes on her. No call ta take chances."

The Kid grinned. "My pleasure . . . boss." His grin widened when both Waddell and Felipe stopped midway up the stairs to glance back at him.

Jacelyn thought the albino looked mighty pleased with himself as he swaggered toward the barn and she wondered why.

Dora fiddled with the top button on her shirt. Her voice was hardly more than a whisper when she said, "Ya watch yourself, child. Don't ya let that Felipe sweet talk ya none."

Jacelyn's spine stiffened. "You mean don't let him fool me into thinking he's a friend? Like you did?"

Dora's head snapped back as if Jacelyn had slapped her. "Yeah," she said sadly. "Just like that."

Although Jacelyn had thought it would make her feel better to let out her feelings toward Dora, it didn't. It was all she could do not to call Dora back when the woman turned and walked rigidly into the house.

Jacelyn started toward the cabin, but remembered Grant's bedroll lying up the road. She decided to retrieve it, and felt a prickling sensation down her spine. Looking over her shoulder, she saw the Kid trailing along behind her, with his knife still in his hand.

Refusing to let him intimidate her, she went on and picked up the bedroll, then stalked haughtily past him on her way back. When he opened his mouth as if to speak, she just glared. A feeling of supreme satisfaction stole over her when he quietly fell in behind her.

It was mid-afternoon and Grant was within five miles of the ranch headquarters, when he heard a bobwhite call from the chapparal ahead and to the right of the trail. Veering in that direction, he chuckled to himself when he flushed a covey of quail. It wouldn't do to let Santana know he'd been fooled by the real thing. Though his chest would puff out for a mile, the Apache would never let him live down his mistake.

Grant's feeling that something was amiss increased the closer he came to the ranch. His gut clenched as he imagined the trouble Jacelyn could have made for herself.

He was thinking about her when he heard the quail call again. He cocked his head, but continued down the trail. Entering a growth of oak, he started when Santana stepped from out of nowhere and blocked the path directly in front of him.

"Hola, my brother. You are floating in the clouds again, no?"

"No," Grant lied. "I've known you were there for some time."

The Apache arched his brows.

Grant reined his horse around the Apache and continued on. Santana disappeared again and returned several minutes later mounted on his mustang. When Grant reached a creek, he stopped and dismounted to let his horse drink. Santana did the same.

"Timmy B. told me you were able to warn the Colonel in time."

The Apache nodded.

"Did he catch the gang?"

"Two dead. Rest fly away."

Grant scowled. He hadn't really expected them all to be rounded up, but he'd hoped. "The Colonel didn't mention anything about Miss McCaffery, did he?"

Santana hunkered down and picked up a twig. He drew circles in the mud. "He knows where she is."

Grant studied Santana. "What else has happened?"

"The white eyes, they think the Apaches have taken the woman."

"What? Why?"

Santana shrugged. "Another stage stopped near where the woman was taken. Driver and messenger killed and . . . scalped."

"And so everyone thinks that Apaches are responsible for both?"

The Indian jabbed the stick into the earth. "Yes."

Grant sighed. "Damn it, we've got to find who's behind the rotten shenanigans." Resentment coiled in his gut at his preoccupation with Jacelyn McCaffery. If he hadn't become involved with her, he might've already found the bastards. Well, it was time now to get on with it, especially since all he'd accomplished was to thoroughly convince her he was the savage she'd thought all along.

Santana nodded toward the Appaloosa. "The Colonel still talks about the horse. He will be glad to have it returned."

Grant realized Santana didn't know about the body they'd found. "Part of the mystery is solved. We found the woman's brother. He'd been dead a couple of weeks. And he'd been scalped."

Santana cursed.

"You might tell the Colonel next time you see him."

The Apache grunted. "I go to Thunder Fort soon."

Grant mounted the Ap. "Be careful. I wouldn't want to lose my best quail caller." When Santana just stared at him, unaware of the joke, Grant shook his head and rode on toward the ranch.

Half an hour later, he pulled up on the edge of the clearing. Lanterns burned in the barn and bunkhouse as well as the house. He nudged the horse forward, knowing now why he'd had the feeling that something was about to happen. It had. The gang had returned.

The Kid walked out of the barn just as Grant rode up.

310

"Wondered if you were going to show up anytime soon, Jones."

Grant narrowed one eye. "Why wouldn't I?"

"Oh, thought you might feel guilty."

"Guilty? Me? Why?" Grant dismounted and tied the Appaloosa.

"Guess you wouldn't know anything about our running into trouble, would you?"

Pretending surprise, Grant queried, "Trouble? What kind of trouble? Get more silver than you could carry?"

The Kid hesitated, but for just an instant. "Seems someone ratted on us. Cavalry showed up. We lost Pablo and Dutch."

Grant rubbed the back of his neck. He was truly sorry about the big German. He'd been a hell of a blacksmith. "How could that have happened? Waddell didn't seem too worried when I left. Thought things were pretty well taken for granted."

"That's what we wondered. *How* it happened."

Grant turned to the Appaloosa and loosened the cinch. "Who else knew where you were headed?"

"Only one other person. And he wouldn't have had anything to gain."

Being purposely obtuse, Grant innocently stared the man down. "You think that one of *us* might've gone to the Cavalry?"

"Maybe." The Kid gritted his teeth as he moved closer. "'Course, don't guess poor ole Eloy can be suspected anymore."

Grant tensed. So, they knew about Eloy.

"Yes, poor Eloy. He was more ill than any of us realized."

Grant and the Kid both spun toward the husky, feminine voice.

Jacelyn moved into the light. She twisted her hands together, hoping Grant would take her hint.

The Kid leaned against the barn door. "Just when did *poor* Eloy die?"

Grant opened his mouth, but Jacelyn quickly spoke up. "Why, the very night you left. All day he'd felt worse and worse. Dora and I did all we could." And that was the truth, she told herself. But "all they could do" hadn't been near enough. The outlaw had been too much for the two of them to handle.

Grant's mind reeled. Evidently Jacelyn and Dora had told the gang Eloy died of natural causes. For Jacelyn's sake, he hoped they believed it.

The Kid looked long and hard at Grant. "You see him, Jones?"

"Yep."

Great. Jacelyn nearly smiled. Grant would take care of the questions now.

The albino snarled at Grant. "So what was the matter with him?"

"I'm no doctor, but I'd say he stopped breathing and died."

"Damn it, gunslinger, I've had enough of your smart mouth." The Kid moved away from the building, holding his hands above his pistols.

Jacelyn turned gratefully at the sound of approaching footsteps.

The Kid cursed. His fingers twitched.

Grant kept his eyes riveted on the albino, who he still perceived to be the greater threat since whoever approached had purposely made himself heard.

"Gentlemen, gentlemen. How rude of you to forget your manners in front of a lady." Felipe stopped beside Jacelyn.

Grant's hand eased down to rest on his hip, just above his own revolver. His features turned to marble as he regarded the good-looking stranger standing so possessively next to Jacelyn.

Felipe took note of Grant with hard, assessing eyes. "You must be Jones."

Grant nonchalantly shifted his weight and widened his stance. "And who're you?"

Silence stretched between the two as they studied one another. Finally Felipe said, "I am Felipe Barraza."

The Kid relaxed back against the barn, hooking his thumbs in his gun belt. "Ole Felipe don't think much of us peons. He doesn't come to the backwoods too often."

Grant noticed the way Felipe's eyes hardened as he turned his gaze on the albino. There appeared to be no love lost between the two men. It was a fact to remember.

Felipe put his hand beneath Jacelyn's elbow. "Shall we dine? Dora was wondering what was keeping everyone."

Jacelyn covered her mouth. She'd been sent to the barn in the first place to call the Kid to supper. Interrupting the conversation between the Kid and Grant had completely wiped away any thought of her original intent.

Grant remained where he stood as the others turned to leave. "I'll be up as soon as I put my horse in the stall."

Jacelyn hesitated, thinking to walk up with Grant so she could explain all that had happened since he'd been gone, but Felipe's grip on her arm prevented her from doing so. For the moment, she was scared to be the cause of another upheaval. Waddell had been watching her with a strange expression on his face all afternoon.

Watching them leave, with the nattily dressed dandy's hand on Jacelyn, set Grant's gut to heaving. A white hot rage shot through him, settling in the fingers curling close to his gun. He clenched his hand and turned away from the sight to lead the Appaloosa into the barn.

Damn it. Since when had he ever allowed his feelings

for another person to cloud his judgment? He'd learned years ago that it was safer to live his life alone. Sure, he had friends, and even family besides Santana with the Chiricauhuas, but he kept himself distant, even with his scouts. Few emotional entanglements caused fewer problems for a white Apache.

But then along came Jacelyn McCaffery, who, in a few short weeks, turned his well-ordered existence upside down and around. If he'd had to lose his heart, why couldn't it have been to a woman forgiving enough not to care about his Apache heritage—something he could do nothing to change.

He let go of some of his frustration forking hay to the horse. When there was nothing left for him to do for the animal, his grumbling stomach persuaded him to go to the house, whether he wanted to or not.

He rubbed the back of his aching neck. There had been something about Jacelyn, a certain tension, that bothered him. Somehow, he had to get her alone to find out what she and Dora had told Waddell concerning the departed Eloy.

Sighing, he trudged to the house.

Everyone was seated at the table when he walked in, with Waddell and Felipe occupying the two end chairs. Jacelyn sat to Felipe's right, with the Kid across from her. To her right was Bob. There were vacant chairs across from Bob, and between Dora and the Kid. He chose to sit between Dora and the Kid since the seat was closer to Jacelyn. He wanted to be able to watch her face.

The Kid started to reach for the boiled potatoes, but Felipe cleared his throat. "We will pass the food. No need to grab like barbarians."

"Aw, hell, ever since that damned woman's been here, everyone's acting like she's visiting royalty," the

Kid pouted. "When the hell are we going to get rid of her?"

Rather than responding, Felipe just excused himself and disappeared into the kitchen. When he returned, he carried several folded cup towels. He handed one to Jacelyn. Taking one for himself, he held out the others. "Napkins?"

Grant reached for the remaining two towels and handed the extra one to Dora. Like Jacelyn, he spread his across his lap. Dora and Felipe tucked theirs in the collars of their shirts, and Grant smothered a grin at the incongruous sight the dandy presented. So smooth and well-mannered, exceptionally dressed, with a towel dangling down his chest.

Grant heaped his plate with potatoes, gravy, beans, and fried chicken. He had cut his first piece of meat and forked it into his mouth when Waddell mumbled around a mouthful of beans, "What we gonna do about the gal, Felipe?"

Felipe looked irritated as he swallowed. "What do you mean?"

"I mean, what if'n she tries ta get away again—and makes it? Our cover's gonna be blown fer good. We can't let that happen." He gulped down the food. "What you heard from her folks?"

Get away? Again? Grant nearly choked on the tender chicken. His eyes shot to Jacelyn. The truth was evident in her flushed cheeks and downcast eyes. Holy hell! His gut feeling this afternoon had been right on target. The woman had been in trouble up to her precious little ear lobes.

When she refused even to look at him, Grant reluctantly turned his attention to the dandy. Waddell was asking guidance from Felipe, which immediately answered some of Grant's questions. For instance, how could Waddell be smart enough to know when silver

315

shipments were sent and payrolls delivered by stage? And who had been in charge of Jacelyn's ransom? Gazing at the dapper Felipe Barraza, he knew.

Felipe dabbed the towel to his mouth. "As yet, I have heard nothing." He solicitously patted Jacelyn's trembling hand. "I see no reason why things cannot continue as they have for a few more days."

The Kid scooted his chair back. "Damn it, Felipe. She's bad luck. Someone's sicced the Cavalry on us. First we lose Barnes, then Pablo and Dutch, and—" He glared at Dora and Jacelyn and turned to include Grant. "And then *something* happened to Eloy."

He jabbed his finger at Jacelyn.

She scooted back in her chair. The knife she'd finally found in the cabin and slipped into a hidden sheath in the moccasin tingled against her calf.

Grant's right hand inched up his thigh.

"She . . . she's going to ruin us if we don't take care of her . . . now." He made a move to rise as he reached for his gun.

Grant already had his pistol in his hand. He put the tip of the cold barrel beneath the Kid's ear and slowly cocked the hammer. "Just sit quiet."

The Kid growled an oath, but settled back in his seat.

Waddell sucked gravy from his fingers. "Hell, Kid, ya ain't helped us a damned bit by pullin' some of *your* fool stunts, neither."

Felipe sliced his gaze to Waddell, who cleared his throat and found something fascinating about his potatoes.

"What are you talking about, brother?"

Jacelyn gasped and stared between the two men who looked absolutely nothing alike.

Felipe smiled and softly explained. "Forgive me. Our mother was not discriminating in her choice of lovers. Our relationship," he cocked his head toward Waddell

316

and grimaced, "is more of a business arrangement than an accident of birth."

"Now," Felipe waved Grant's gun away, nodded when Grant complied and reholstered the weapon, then speared the albino with his cold, black eyes. "What have you done, cousin?"

Grant leaned back in his chair. He'd been hit with more surprises tonight than a kid watching a magician pulling tricks from a silk hat. The Waddell gang seemed to be a *family* affair.

The Kid squirmed in his chair and darted pleading glances to Waddell, who now found something wondrous in his beans. "Ah, I haven't done anything. Honest." He reached in his pocket and pulled out a watch. Fumbling it in his hands, he finally flipped open the lid.

Jacelyn stared at the watch. She swayed in her chair and grasped at the watch around her neck. The smooth back dug into her palm. The watch that matched hers. Her father's watch. Then her brother's.

And now the Kid held it in his slimy hand.

Chapter Twenty-One

Jacelyn's eyes were glued to the Kid's hand. She felt numb, yet a murderous anger exploded inside her chest.

What if Grant had been right? What if the Waddell gang, or even the Kid on his own, had killed James and not the Apaches? Or, what if, as horrible as the Kid was, he'd just found the watch?

Her firm resolve to escape withered and died. She was suddenly just as determined to stay and find out the truth, whatever it might be, about James's death.

Then, she would exact her revenge.

Darting a glance to Grant, she sucked in her breath to find him staring directly at her with a strange expression on his face. Usually, his features were devoid of emotion whatsoever, so to actually see him thinking, and evidently about her, was worrisome.

She released her watch, being careful to let it fall beneath her shirt before someone noticed.

But Grant had noticed. And having held her watch himself, he remembered it was similar to the timepiece the Kid had just snapped shut and shoved back into his pocket.

Listening to the Kid, and seeing the animosity between the other members of this disreputable family, finally pushed Grant to decide on his next move. He had to get Jacelyn out of here. Her life was too precious for him to endanger her while he continued to snoop around.

He already had enough on the gang to convict them of several robberies. Though it would be nice to get solid evidence that someone here knew something about the mapmaker's murder and scalping, and he eyed the Kid with definite suspicion, it might take longer than would be healthy for both Jacelyn and himself.

No, he'd get her away as soon as possible.

As he looked around the table, at the exhausted gang members and the yawning dandy, he didn't rule out leaving that very night. This might be the only occasion when their guard would be down.

Suddenly, someone pounded the table. Dinnerware rattled. Everyone looked to see who'd caused the ruckus.

Dora stood with her hand still flattened on the planking. Her eyes shimmered as she glared at the male occupants of the room. "Enough, damn ya. I worked hard fixin' them vittles and I ain't gonna put up with yer caterwaulin'. If ya wanna eat, eat. If'n ya wanna jabber and fight, go out ta the pig pen where ya belong."

As if it had taken all of her courage to call such attention to herself, she sank back into her chair.

The Kid looked at Grant with a "we'll settle this later" glower then, seeming grateful to have Waddell and Felipe off his back, dug into his food with gusto.

Bob, who'd been eating during the entire confrontation, asked Dora to pass the gravy.

No one wanted to leave the food.

Dora sighed and cut another piece of chicken.

When Jacelyn bent forward to take a bite of beans, the watch dangled between her breasts. All at once she recalled Grant picking her up and taking the time to remove her precious possession before dumping her in the pool. She also recalled the heat generated on her skin from just the bare brush of his knuckles.

She glanced in his direction, but his gaze was on Felipe.

While he ate, Grant sensed someone watching him. He looked up on several occasions and caught the dandy darting furtive glances toward him.

Near the end of the meal, their eyes locked. Felipe wiped his mouth and leaned back in his chair. "Mr. Jones . . ."

Grant's brows slashed together.

"You seem very familiar. Perhaps we have met before."

His ability to compose his features stood Grant in good stead as he studied Felipe more intently. There was always the chance he'd run into the man somewhere, but it most probably would have been at the fort. He would have been dressed in his moccasins and leather breeches. He doubted the man could recognize him now in his *white man's* clothing, but . . .

He shrugged. "Maybe. Maybe not."

Felipe scratched his chin. "Where have you spent most of your time?"

"Wherever my business takes me at the time." Grant narrowed his eyes.

Taking the warning, Felipe steepled his fingers and started slightly when Dora came up behind him from the kitchen. Grant, too, scolded himself for not even noticing that the woman had left the room when she'd been sitting right next to him.

"Pass your plates if ya want peach cobbler," she announced. The air was suddenly filled with empty plates. Dora chuckled. "One at a time, mind ya. One at a time."

The only good thing about being at the ranch this evening, Jacelyn decided, was that she hadn't missed Dora's cobbler.

Once the meal was finished and Dora and Jacelyn were clearing the table, Grant followed them into the kitchen. It didn't take him long to notice the cool shoulder Jacelyn turned to Dora.

When Jacelyn would have passed him going back for more dirty dishes, he blocked her way. Nodding toward Dora, he asked, "What's going on between the two of you?"

Jacelyn sniffed and slanted a glance at Dora, who sheepishly averted her gaze. "All I have to say is, that woman is a traitor." She pushed past him and stalked on into the living room.

Grant looked at Dora. She nodded and began filling a basin with water. "She's right."

He held his arms out to his sides. "I don't understand." It was a state he was becoming familiar with since meeting Jacelyn McCaffery.

Dora sighed. "When she tried to run off this afternoon, I called the coyotes on her."

"That surprised her?" Hell, he'd gone after her and brought her back before. Surely she didn't expect them, even Dora, to just watch her go and do nothing. She was a prisoner, after all.

A tear rolled down Dora's cheek and Grant frowned. He felt uneasy around crying females. Didn't know what to do. "Ah . . ."

"I would've let her go, too." Dora glanced through the window, looking for a sign of Waddell or one of the men. "But I saw Bob down by the barn. The boys had come home and we hadn't heard 'em." She swiped her shirtsleeve beneath her nose. "And then I seen Felipe ridin' in. Any one of 'em coulda . . . Well, ya know." She dunked a plate into the basin, splashing water onto the floor.

Grant just nodded. Yeah, he knew. Dora had saved

Jacelyn's life. Without thinking, he walked over and swiftly placed a kiss on Dora's cheek.

Dora flushed a bright pink. "Aw, pshaw . . . What'd ya go and do that fer?"

"Yes, why'd you do that, Mr. Jones?"

Grant spun to find Jacelyn standing in the doorway, a look of jealous outrage distorting her lovely features. By damn, the woman cared. She might not realize it, or even admit it—yet—but she damned sure cared enough to get riled when he kissed another woman.

He just grinned and shrugged and left the kitchen whistling.

Dora also gave Jacelyn a knowing glance, then quickly went back to washing the dishes.

Jacelyn stood where she'd first stopped upon finding Grant kissing Dora, who was, after all, a married woman. And he'd had the nerve to ignore her question and walk out on her. Why . . . the heathen.

Close to an hour later, the Kid and Bob were in the bunkhouse playing poker. Grant was in the barn currying the Appaloosa. The women were still in the kitchen. Felipe and Waddell stood talking in the moonlight near the orchard.

"Gawd, Felipe, we ain't hardly got no men left. How're we gonna pull off somethin' like that?" Waddell scowled and scratched his belly.

"When the time comes, we will find more men if we have to, but this is one deal that is too good to pass up." Felipe brushed dust from his sleeve. "And our cousin will get to do what he does best."

Waddell grimaced.

"Don't get squeamish now, brother. The more animosity we create between our Mexican and Apache friends, the more money we make. The Mexicans blame

322

the Apaches. The Apaches go after the Mexicans. The Cavalry chases shadows. And we have the silver and gold at our fingertips." He kissed his fingertips to make his point. "The Kid does his part very well. It could not be sweeter."

"Yeah, but jest look what happens when a dab o' vinegar seeps into all that sugar. Half our men are gone. The Kid gets carried away doing his *part.*"

"So, we have a little trouble now and then. Lady Fortune has smiled on us for a long while, and will again." He looked back toward the ranch house. "And collecting for our little guest will be easier than skimming cream from the milk. I have discovered she is heir to McCaffery Textiles, a very wealthy manufacturing company. Our Mr. Jones was very wise when he suggested offering her for ransom."

Waddell snorted. "He's an odd one, that Jones. But so far, he's done his job. Jest don't reckon I trust him much."

Felipe waved his hand. "As soon as his usefulness is over, get rid of him. The same with the girl. But for now, we will keep them both. He seems to be good help. And Miss McCaffery's family might need proof we have the right woman." He folded his hands behind his back. "Besides, she is a very beautiful woman. I think she might like me, no?"

"I don't know . . ."

"I have spoken. You will do as I say, won't you, Ricardo?" He leaned closer to Waddell, smiling an evil little smile.

"Yeah. Sure."

"Good. Now, let us go see what is keeping the ladies."

Waddell fell in behind Felipe, maliciously eyeing the younger man's back. "Yeah. Sure."

* * *

Jacelyn wiped her hands on a towel, arched her aching back and started to leave the kitchen.

Dora glanced at her and took a deep breath. "It fit."

"What?" Jacelyn paused by the door.

"The dress. Ya done a fine job a fixin' it up." Dora opened the oven door and banked the fire.

"Well . . . I'm glad." Jacelyn put her hand out to push the door open, but hesitated.

"Want some coffee?" The older woman took down two cups and offered one to Jacelyn.

"Ah, I don't think so." A wan smile momentarily curved Jacelyn's lips as she went outside, closing the door softly behind her. She wasn't nearly as angry at Dora as she had been, but she couldn't quite forgive her either.

Dora had dashed her dream of escape, although now she was grateful that she'd been here to see the Kid with her brother's watch. Actually, she thought, dragging her moccasined feet through the dust, she was too confused to know how she felt or what she thought about *anything* just now.

"Good evening, señorita. May I walk you to wherever you are going?" Felipe smiled the smile that had charmed many women out of their finest dresses. He ogled her long legs in the form-fitting trousers. Surely this one would take only a few smiles and flattering words.

Goose flesh prickled Jacelyn's skin when the fancy man joined her. "No, I, ah, am just going to . . ." She saw Grant in the barn and angled in that direction. "To the barn."

"But it is a lovely evening. Why don't you stay out here with me and watch the moon? It is full and will rise any moment," he wheedled.

"Go ahead. It's a little chilly for me." She scurried

through the barn doorway and breathed a sigh of relief when Grant hurried toward her.

Grant had heard their voices as they approached and had quickly hidden the bedrolls and supplies he'd managed to secrete in the end stall, under a sheaf of hay. However, he couldn't take the chance of anyone looking too close.

"Mr. Jones," Felipe commented irritably, "Do you always spend so much time with the horses?"

Grant tipped his hat to the side of his head and slouched against the near stall railing. "Yep."

Felipe squinted as he studied Grant's face. "I'll remember soon where I've seen you."

Grant shrugged. "Can't imagine it would be that important."

Jacelyn stepped away from Felipe, who seemed glued to her side. "Maybe you saw him at Fort—"

"Miss McCaffery—'' Grant lunged from his leaning position and inserted himself between Jacelyn and the dandy. "I think it's past your bedtime. If you will excuse us . . ." He steered her past Felipe.

Felipe stepped forward. "I will gladly escort—"

"No need." Grant put his arm around Jacelyn's shoulder and started through the doorway. "She's my responsibility and I take it very seriously. Why, if I had been here this afternoon, she would never have tried such a stupid stunt."

Jacelyn set her heels, but it didn't begin to slow him down. She twisted her shoulders, but he increased the pressure of his grasp. His hot breath teased her ear as he growled, "Say good night, sugar."

She hissed, "No. I don't want—"

"Say good night," he repeated in a deep whisper.

She turned her head. His eyes bore into her like sharp yucca spines. She gulped. "G-good night, Mr. Barraza. Thank you for—" She was whisked into the darkness before she could finish. In fact, she was hurried to the cabin so quickly she hardly felt her feet move.

At last, they were inside with the door closed. Grant released his grip, then had to steady her.

She inhaled deeply. "Oh-h-h, you ... you ... barbaric savage. How dare—"

Grant bent his head and commanded, "Lower your voice."

Her jaw worked, but she finally closed her mouth and refused to utter another word.

He glided silently to the door and cocked his head, listening.

Crossing her arms over her chest, Jacelyn tapped her toe impatiently. Her bravado wavered slightly, though, when he turned his dark, brooding gaze on her. "Wh-who do you think you are? You have no right to manhandle me."

A scuffing footstep sounded from outside, near the door. He scowled, then loudly told her, "You're right. But it's high time you quit wandering around. You caused enough trouble for one day."

Her amazement that he'd admitted she was right was shortlived. How dare he criticize her. "I'm tired of being held a prisoner." The backs of her eyes burned even as she thrust out her chin. "I want my freedom. I want to go ... home."

She blinked, surprised that her image of home seemed muted and hazy, whereas a week ago, she'd dreamed about big, soft beds and fluffy pillows and an armoire filled with clean, feminine clothing.

Grant was shocked at how badly the thought of her leaving hurt. He hunched his shoulders and cleared his throat. "You've been treated good enough. And you heard Mr. Barraza. A few more days and you'll be on your way ... home."

He leaned toward the door and heard another scuff, farther away this time.

Jacelyn stared into Grant's eyes. "Do you believe that? Do you really think I'll be allowed to leave?"

He made a swift decision to wait a few hours to get her away. The outlaws needed time to settle and fall asleep. He needed time to adjust to a few changes. And Jacelyn needed rest. He'd wait until just before they left to tell her of his plan.

He fell into the huge, dark pools of her eyes and stated firmly, "Yes. You're going to leave here."

His conviction made her feel better. She sighed and sat back on the bed. When Grant continued to stand near the door, she frowned and looked to where he kept his bedroll. He usually had it spread out by now.

Her heart thudded. She quickly scanned the small room. Where was it? She was certain she'd returned it. Things had gone so crazy that afternoon, she honestly couldn't remember. She darted her eyes to Grant. He also had a puzzled expression on his face.

"I-I'm sorry."

His eyes followed hers as they scoured the room, wondering what she was searching for. As far as he could see, everything was as they'd left it that morning, except for the bedroll he'd hidden in the barn. Completely baffled, he asked, "Sorry about what?"

"Y-your bedroll."

His brows lifted. Hell, how'd she know about that? "What about the bedroll?"

"I t-took it." She twisted her fingers. "I guess I l-lost it."

He mentally relaxed. So that's why it had been so dusty. "You mean you stole it."

She nodded, then scooted back on the bed when he stared at her with a strange glint in his eyes.

Grant figured out with satisfaction that she must have

forgotten what she'd done with it during the confusion of her "escape" attempt. And now she felt guilty. Good.

With everything quiet outside, he stuffed his hands in his pockets and shuffled to the middle of the room. "What am I going to sleep in? Sure is cold."

Sweat beaded her brow. Cold? He had to be joking. Wasn't he? But when she looked at him carefully, she could have sworn he shivered. "You can have my blanket."

"No, I couldn't do that. You'll need it before morning."

"I don't think so." It was the warmest night she could remember since her arrival at the ranch. "Besides, it's my fault—"

"No. I won't take a woman's only cover." He paced the length of the cot and back.

"For heaven's sake," she snapped, "Will you sit down? You're driving me—"

He immediately plopped on the foot of her bed.

"No," she yelped. "Not there. I meant—"

"Sure is comfortable. Sleeping on the floor without a bedroll'll hurt my old back injury."

Her lips thinned. He'd never mentioned a back injury when he'd been picking her up and tossing her around like a sack of flour.

He shifted until he leaned his back against the wall. "Yep, this is nice. No wonder you snore so loud."

Her eyes rounded. "Snore? Me?" She leaned toward him, shaking her finger in his face. "I do not snore."

He grabbed her wrist. Off balance, she tumbled into his lap.

"Oh-h-h, you—"

Grant bent his head and tasted her lips.

She beat her fist against his shoulder. "Let me go. I don't want—"

His lips took hers again. His tongue explored the ridges of her teeth.

"No ... please ..." She tried to remember all of the things he'd done to make her hate him, but they suddenly didn't seem all that important. His arms felt too good around her. He tantalized and invited. Her tongue pursued its own expedition into remembered territory.

"Please ... what?" he whispered huskily, just before sucking the lobe of her ear into his mouth.

She moaned. "Don't ..."

He pulled her shirt tail loose and ran his hands up her back, rubbing her chest against his. "Don't?" he prodded.

"Don't ..." Suddenly she was lying on her back on the bed, his heavy weight pressing into her. His mouth was wet and warm as he kissed her jaw and the underside of her chin. His hands were everywhere, teasing and exciting her body. "Don't ... remember."

His laugh was short and sweet and rumbled through his whole body. She wrapped her arms tightly around him, absorbing, memorizing. As much as she hated that he'd lied to her about other things, the chances were good he'd told the truth about her brother. And she did love him. God help her ... She did.

Perhaps this night he would love her, too, for just a while. She would have these memories to hold her and keep her warm through the rest of her days.

Grant had only intended to hold her until it was time to awaken her and leave. He'd never thought she would return his ardor or kiss him until she stole his breath away. But he was nothing if not pleased. He would joyfully take whatever she offered.

It was hell, loving an unpredictable woman.

And it was hell, what she was doing to his body. The brazen hussy already had his shirt unbuttoned and was working on his trousers. He sucked in his breath when her knuckles brushed his manhood. "Lord, sugar," he gasped. "Don't . . . don't stop now."

The sound of his voice brought Jacelyn back to some sense of sanity. But the feel of his warm, vibrant flesh pulsing in her palm lent her the self-confidence to continue what she'd started. A throaty giggle burst from her lips. "This isn't real. It isn't me. I'm dreaming."

Grant quickly helped her out of her clothes and finished removing his own. "Sugar, you're the most *real* woman I've ever felt." He nuzzled his face between her generous breasts. "And I'm the one who's dreaming."

Jacelyn wriggled until she cradled his narrow hips between her thighs. His hard body felt wonderful against her and her fingers couldn't travel fast enough over his ridged muscles. She wanted . . . needed . . . to touch and feel him. Everywhere.

He flinched when her fingers traced his ribs. She felt it and tickled him again. The next thing he knew, they'd rolled and he found himself encased in drapes of long, red-gold hair and warmed by soft, very feminine flesh.

"What are you doing to me, lady?" He filled his palms with her breasts. They swelled and her nipples puckered to hard little nubbins. He tugged gently on the soft globes, urging her down until he could suckle to his heart's delight.

Jacelyn inhaled sharply. The sensation of his mouth pulling at her breast shot liquid fire straight to her loins. Her inner muscles contracted as she rotated her hips, instinctively seeking the part of him that was so distinctly male.

His moist tip nudged against her. She spread her legs to fully accommodate him. Slowly, surely, she lifted her hips up and down, gradually taking his length inside her.

Grant tried to remain still, to allow her the enjoyment of every nuance of feeling. But when she began to pump up and down, up and down, slowly—inch by warm, wet inch—he lost control. His hands flew to her hips. He held her tightly as he lifted to meet her downward motions.

She moaned and opened her mouth. He took her lips in a kiss that matched the heat their writhing bodies created. Her lower body bucked. He rode with her. She spasmed around him, clutching, draining his seed as his heels dug into the bed and he arched one last, urgent time.

Jacelyn collapsed on top of him and fought to regain her breath. Ripples of sensation coursed from the center of her being, leaving her spent but aware of every perspiration-slicked movement.

Snuggling her head in the hollow of his shoulder, she kissed the side of his neck. The tendon strained under her lips. She smiled. Winding her fingers through the dark curls on his belly, she reveled in the feel of hard muscles bunching at her slightest touch.

But soon, the pleasure turned to pain. Amidst the joy, intruded sadness. Tears welled in her eyes and spilled over.

Grant grabbed her hand, then raised it to place a lingering kiss in her palm. There were so many things he'd like to say to her, but was afraid to. Intuitively, he knew she was thinking of her brother and probably . . . other . . . discomforting memories.

His voice was rough as he persuaded, "Tell me about your . . ." Apache superstitions or no, it was important that he say the name. "Tell me about James."

Jacelyn stiffened, yet after what they'd just shared, it seemed ridiculous not to talk to him. Besides, it was suddenly very important that he understand why she'd come to Arizona Territory and why James's death was doubly devastating.

As she told him everything, a cleansing feeling settled over her and she snuggled even closer to Grant's warmth.

Grant allowed her to speak without interruption. His heart went out to the extraordinary young woman who'd risked everything to venture into the wilds of the West. He suffered her anxiety and shared her misfortune. It was good that she set free her emotions. And he was reluctant to break the pleasant spell that seemed to have settled tenuously around them. Enjoying the closeness of their joined bodies, his lips curved.

Breathlessly ending her tale, the last thing Jacelyn saw was Grant's lazy smile before she blinked, yawned, and dozed.

Grant's nose itched. He turned his head. It still itched. He tried to lift his hand, but was surprised when he couldn't. His whole arm was numb. Rolling his head, he found Jacelyn McCaffery curled against his side.

He hated to disturb her, but ... Suddenly, he jerked his head toward the window. Thank God it was still dark. How long had they slept?

Regretfully, wishing they could lie together so peacefully the rest of their lives, he shook her smooth, bare shoulder. "Sugar? Wake up."

Jacelyn moaned and stretched. Someone kissed her. She smiled and opened her eyes to find Grant poised above her. She lifted her arms around his neck and pulled his head down for another kiss. "Is it morning already?"

"'Fraid not." He savored the opportunity to join their lips again while she was groggy and pliable from sleep. He had no doubt her mood would change drastically when she fully awoke and started to *think* about the happenings of the past few days.

But he had to stop, though his body ached to continue. Swinging his legs from the bed, he winced when his feet struck the cold floorboards. He quickly untangled their clothing from the blanket and tossed over her pantalettes and camisole.

"Put these on, then hurry and finish dressing."

"Why?" She pulled the blanket back over her head, snuggling deeper into the warmth left from his body.

He buttoned his pants and slipped his arms into his shirt. Leaning over, he grabbed a corner of the blanket and jerked it off of her. He drank in the sight of her nakedness. "C'mon, lazy woman. We have to go."

She lifted up on one elbow and squinted at him. "What did you say?"

He buckled on his gun belt. "I'm gettin' you out of here—tonight. Now hurry and get dressed."

She scooted back against the wall. "No. I won't go."

Chapter Twenty-Two

Grant scrubbed the back of his aching neck. It was his turn to ask, "What did you say?"

Jacelyn repeated, "I'm not going to leave. Not yet."

He threw his hands in the air, then jabbed them into the bed as close to her as he could and still look her in the eyes. "What in the hell are you pulling, lady? All you've been able to think about for weeks is escaping. You even made another dumb-assed stab at it today. Now I intend to make your wish come true . . . And you won't go?"

She nodded.

He growled low in his throat and straightened away from her before he wrapped his fingers around her slender neck. The damned woman's jaw was set at such a stubborn angle, he couldn't imagine why he'd ever thought of her as "fragile."

All at once, he bent and plucked her from the bed like a hawk swooping upon a baby cottontail. "You're goin' if I have to rope and gag you."

She kicked and beat at him, fighting with all her strength. "If you take me, the minute I see Colonel Alexander I'm going to tell him everything I know about you."

He hesitated just enough that she freed herself from

his arms and ran to the other side of the table. She triumphantly thought her threat had caused him to stop and think.

Grant was only stunned from the vehemence in her voice. "What if I don't care what you tell the Colonel?"

She sputtered for a minute. "You'll care when I tell the Cavalry you're a halfbreed and a traitor and they arrest you. They . . . If they only knew where I was, the Cavalry would come to my rescue. They would."

His eyes narrowed. Under his breath he grumbled that she'd drive a whole damned troop crazy and they'd race to give her back to the outlaws. Hell, a member of the Cavalry was trying to help her now, and look what good it was doing.

"You do your damnedest, lady." He stalked around one end of the table. "But I'm takin' you out of here while your pretty white hide is still in one perfect piece."

She moved cautiously in the opposite direction. Gradually she noticed that his eyes kept darting downward. With an outraged gasp she realized that she was only wearing Grant's oversized shirt that he'd helped her slip into just before falling asleep. Drat the man for ogling her like . . . like . . . a starving coyote. And drat him for almost convincing her that he was concerned about her. He'd proven that was a lie the other afternoon.

Grant feinted a lunge to his right, then swung immediately to the left when she made her dash. He gathered her into his arms in such a way that she was unable to strike out. "Now, I'm going to put you in those clothes—"

"No," she wailed. "I can't go. I can't."

Her sobs tore at his heart. Sitting on the edge of the bed, he set her on his lap and smoothed her hair away from her tear-stained face. "Why? sug . . . Why can't you go?"

She stalled by wiping at the moisture on her cheeks. She didn't know what to do. If she told him about the watch, he might run straight to the Kid and ruin her chances of finding out the truth. If she didn't tell him, he would go through with his plans to spirit her away.

Looking into his eyes, seeing his sincerity, she decided to trust her feelings and explain. All he could do was deepen the cut he'd already sliced into her heart.

She sniffled and accepted his bandana to blow her nose, then handed it back to him.

"Ah, no, you keep it."

"But, it's—"

"Jacelyn, you're stalling. Either give me a damned good reason for our sitting here, or get your sweet ass in those pants."

He started to rise. She whispered, "Wait." The watch lay under the shirt, resting between her breasts. She pulled it out and held it up for him to see.

His brows slanted upward.

Her voice quavered. "First, I think I owe you an apology."

He waited.

"You may have been right wh-when you said you . . . or your Apaches . . . didn't kill James." She glanced up at him between her damp, spiked lashes, then sheepishly stared at his chest.

Grant cleared his throat, urging her to hurry and continue. Suddenly he stiffened. Hell, the watch. He'd noticed at supper that the Kid had one matching hers. He hadn't known for sure she'd seen it. Scooting out from under her and away from the distraction of her lush naked bottom, he shook out the blanket and wrapped it around her waist.

"It's good of you to apologize, but it would've been better if you could've trusted me." He moved over to look out the window. There were no lights. No one was

336

moving about. Returning, he set the chair close to the bed and straddled it. "All right, tell me about the watch."

She clasped her fingers tightly about the gold filigree. "My parents owned matching time pieces. After they died, my brother inherited my father's watch, I, my mother's. We've always carried them with us. Always."

As far as Grant was concerned, the watch was just another nail pounded into the Waddell gang's coffin. He quickly rose and pointed at her clothes. "I figured something like that. It's dangerous for you to stay here, and we're getting out now." He stepped over and quickly, before his hands began to shake, stripped his shirt off of her and slipped it over his shoulders. Then, as his eyes darted to her bare breasts, he pulled the blanket up to cover every bare inch of her.

She reached out and grabbed his forearm. "Not yet."

Irritated at her obstinance, he snarled, "Why not?" and slouched back into the chair. He could hardly wait to hear what scheme her feminine logic had come up with.

"Because . . . I need to find out for sure if the Kid murdered James. He could have just found the watch, you know?"

Grant let loose a string of oaths in Apache, Mexican, and English. "Hell, lady, you've seen the Kid in action. The man's a cold-blooded killer. But you need to have *proof.*" He massaged the back of his neck. "Is that why you *think* you owe me an apology? That I *may* have told you the truth, but maybe *not?*"

She had the grace to blush, but that wasn't good enough. What did he have to do to prove to the woman he wasn't going to harm her and that everything he'd done up to now had been in her best interest?

Jacelyn's conscience bothered her. She hadn't meant to sound doubtful, but every time she thought she knew him, he turned around and did something so contrary to what she'd become accustomed, that now she was wary. She did trust him . . . in most ways . . . most of the time . . .

"So, tell me," he said, with a hard edge to his voice. "Just how do you plan to go about finding this proof?"

"I, well, I . . ."

"That's what I thought." He wedged his hands into his back pockets.

She tore her eyes from the corded muscles bulging across the portion of his chest exposed by the open shirt. Sighing, she was surprised how quickly she lost her train of thought when confronted by his lean, rangy body.

Grant's throat constricted at the hungry gleam in her eyes. He knew exactly how she felt. No matter the importance of other things in his life, she'd become the focus of too much of his attention.

"Two days," he conceded. "If we haven't found anything by then, we go." He shook his head, hardly believing he'd given in. Didn't want to think of the trouble he'd be in if anything happened to her.

Couldn't believe he had at least two more days to spend with her.

Grant wasn't surprised to find the Kid lounging near the cabin when he emerged the next morning. For that very reason, he hadn't succumbed to the temptation to crawl back into bed with Jacelyn last night. He had finished dressing, kept her wrapped snugly in the blanket and held her until she slept. But then he'd slipped out to the barn and retrieved the bedroll and supplies.

Since dawn, he'd divided his time between watching her sleep and trying to figure a way of finding damaging proof against the Kid. He arched his back and stretched, then glanced at the albino. "You're out early this morning. What time is it?"

The Kid appeared wary at Grant's cordial tone of voice, but pulled out his watch. "Almost seven."

"Thanks." Grant sauntered closer to the outlaw. "Mighty fine time-piece you've got there."

Eyes narrowed, the Kid snapped the scrolled top shut.

"Haven't seen one like it. Been in your family a long time?"

The Kid grinned and put the watch back in his pocket. "You've seen my *family*. Nothing stays with us for long."

"Too bad. Something as valuable as that watch would be pretty hard to part with." When the outlaw's expression turned suspicious, Grant rubbed his belly. "Reckon there's any breakfast left?"

"Table hasn't been set yet. "Waddy" and "Dory" *slept* in this morning, too."

Grant shrugged off his emphasis on the word "too," and walked on toward the barn. The Kid wasn't going to *offer* any information. Somehow, he'd have to find a way to search the bunkhouse to see if something else belonging to the mapmaker might turn up.

Damn it, the Kid had to be guilty. He had the watch. Why couldn't Jacelyn accept the fact and ride out of there with him right now?

Yet he had his own reasons for snooping. If the Kid had killed Jacelyn's brother, and scalped him, there could be other proof that the men he'd been searching for were right under his nose—as he'd suspected.

That would be something. Instead of blaming Jacelyn for slowing him down, he might end up thanking her.

By midmorning, Jacelyn was sick of Felipe Barraza. Sure, he was good looking, but in a sinister way, with his beakish nose, small mouth, and close-set eyes. He was entirely too charming and too solicitous for a run-of-the-mill outlaw, and he didn't dress the part.

If he held her hand or kissed the backs of her fingers one more time, she would scream. At that thought, she almost laughed. When had she sunk so low as to become irritated at a man for being too nice? She'd sure learned a few things in the past several weeks.

Finding herself free of the fancy man for the moment, she strolled lazily in the warm sunshine, uncaring whether her skin freckled or her hair blew free. It felt good not to constantly worry about other people's opinions or whether she adhered to convention. Other than the fact that she was a prisoner on the ranch, she was freer than she'd ever been in her life.

The bleak, desolate countryside had come alive. She'd learned the names of the plants and animals and had come to respect their hardiness and ability to survive in harsh circumstances. Much the same as she was learning to respect herself, to adapt to her situation and find the courage to face her problems without depending on a man.

She frowned and smiled at the same time as she conjured the image of Grant Jones. He'd been responsible for saving her on several occasions, but she'd learned that she could do things on her own, too. Like bake biscuits, shovel manure, rustle vittles, and haul water. She was proud of her accomplishments and the callouses she'd worn on her palms.

Looking around, she saw beauty in the ruggedness and wondered how she could have ever thought this country was ugly. It was most certainly different from Virginia, but was far from unpleasant.

An orange butterfly suddenly flitted in front of her, and she delightfully followed its progress to the edge of the woods. She meandered through the trees, watching black and white woodpeckers with red caps on their heads swoop in front of her.

Keeping the barn roof in sight, she wandered in the cool shade, enjoying her respite from worry. For the first time in days, she wasn't thinking about escaping, or finding James's murderer, or even of Grant Jones. She was just enjoying herself.

As she was about to reenter the clearing, she heard voices from behind the barn and stopped. At first she couldn't make out what they were saying, but they grew louder, appearing to come in her direction. Afraid of being accused of trying to escape, or even eavesdropping, she stepped back into the shadows and underneath a low oak limb.

"Damn it, Dick, that Jones asks too many questions to suit me. Why do you want to keep him around?"

Jacelyn recognized the Kid's voice. Her hands clenched into fists.

"We need 'im right now, that's why. There's another job comin' up and we'll need every man we got," Waddell explained impatiently.

"I don't like it. There's something about him that doesn't sit right. Kind of like that mapmaker showing up from out of nowhere."

Jacelyn gasped and quickly covered her mouth. He had to be talking about James.

"Jones is different, all right. But he follows orders and works hard. We'll jest keep a closer eye on 'im."

She heard one of the men strike a match and smelled the acrid odor of burning paper and tobacco. They were close. Very close. She held her breath.

"You're the one I worry 'bout, Kid. You're jest lucky Felipe ain't learned o' some o' the things ya done. Bringing that damned spotted Appaloosa here was a dumb trick. Hosses like that are too easy ta recognize."

Jacelyn's eyes rounded. APPALOOSA! Spotted

341

horse. The horse they'd given Grant to ride. A horse like the Colonel had loaned her brother.

"I told ya, Dick. The horse was wandering by the creek."

"Ya better be telling me the truth. If Felipe thought ya was disobeying his orders . . ."

Jacelyn felt a burning sensation in her chest and finally remembered to breathe as the voices of the two men faded, indicating they were moving on. Shock numbed her knees until she sagged down to lean against the tree trunk.

He'd done it again. Grant knew about the Appaloosa. Knew her brother had been riding the Colonel's horse. Had to have recognized the animal from the very beginning. But he hadn't said a word to her. Had listened to her pouring her heart out last night and hadn't volunteered the information.

Had she been right all along? Had he known about James? Had he been playing a part to gain her confidence for some diabolical reason? The rend to her heart split deeper. Tears spilled from her eyes. When would she learn? She couldn't trust Grant. No matter what her traitorous heart dictated, the man was a rogue.

In a daze, she raised herself from the ground and stumbled to her cabin. Humiliation flamed in her cheeks. How he must be laughing at her. He'd gotten everything he wanted—her compliance, her trust, her . . . virginity.

Oh, he must be very proud to think he'd seduced the naive white woman. She covered her face, startled by her own ice-cold hands. Dear Lord, she'd even initiated the lovemaking last night.

She shoved open the door to the cabin, tripped as she entered, and nearly smashed her fingers when she slammed it closed. Once she made it to the bed, she curled up in a tight ball and sobbed until there were no more tears left to shed.

Grant found her later, in bed, curled up and asleep. Looking down at her, he saw her tear-streaked cheeks and felt the dampness on the blanket she had fluffed beneath her head. His stomach knotted. Had the Kid or the dandy done or said something to cause her distress? If so . . .

He knelt beside the cot and shook her shoulder. "Jacelyn? Sugar?"

Jacelyn opened her eyes, then blinked them shut. Her head throbbed. She didn't want to face the world. She didn't want to hurt anymore.

"What's wrong, sugar? Why've you been crying?"

She roused enough to slap his hand away. "Don't touch me." Pushing herself to a sitting position, she whispered sadly, "Don't ever touch me again."

Grant leaned back at the hatred flashing from her eyes. "What's happened? What am I supposed to have done now?" Damn it, he was tired of her quicksilver changes of mood. He never knew what to expect from one time til the next.

She shoved his shoulder. "You. That's what happened. Every time I trust you, you betray me. I'll not fall for it again." She jutted out her chin and crossed her arms defensively over her breasts.

Angry and hurt that she was always so quick to believe the worst of him, he rose and walked over to stare out the window. "Are you going to tell me what this is about, or do I have to start guessing?"

"There are so many things to choose from, I'm not sure you'd ever get to it." She scooted to the edge of the bed and straightened her shirt. Spearing him with her eyes, she reminded him, "You remember that Appaloosa horse the Colonel loaned my brother, don't you? The horse I asked you about not too long ago?"

He shuttered his eyes and nodded.

"Well, it seems the horse is right here at the ranch, in the barn, in a stall that you work very hard to keep clean."

He shifted his weight from one foot to the other.

"Isn't it?"

He shrugged.

She came off the bed and squared her legs like a lioness about to spring. "Why didn't you tell me? Why'd I have to find out from someone else that the horse James was riding has been here all along? You had a chance to tell me the truth several times." A deep hurt thrust into her heart like a dagger. "You could have told me last night."

She stalked slowly toward him. He just stared at her with no expression. He refused to answer her. The tightly wound coil of anger inside her burst loose. She doubled up her fist and socked him as hard as she could in the stomach. Her punch ricocheted off his hard muscles.

Grant allowed the one free swing, but when she reared back for another, he caught her arms and forced them to her sides. She kicked out. He swung his leg and caught her behind the knee with his heel. She went down on her bottom and quizzically glared up at him.

He leaned down until they were nose to nose. "What if I told you, sure, I knew the Appaloosa was here, but like you, needed more *proof?* Maybe the horse threw your brother and wandered off to where the Kid could find him. Did you think of that?"

She sniffed and tried to shift some of her weight from her smarting derriere. The Kid had told Waddell that same story. But for her pride's sake, she questioned, "Did you ask him?"

"No. Did you ask him about the watch?"

"No." She couldn't meet his eyes.

He straightened and walked to the door. Before he left, he turned and, in a voice of tired defeat, asked, "You don't really want to trust me, do you?"

As if he didn't expect her to answer, he spun on his heel and stalked out.

She folded her arms across her bent knees and rested her forehead in the crook of her elbow. Was he right? Was she afraid to commit herself that totally to him? Did she really, truly love him, or was she in love with the idea of being in love with an exciting, dangerous, handsome man? Someone wildly different from any man she'd ever known, from any man she'd ever dreamed of knowing.

A short time later, Grant was in the barn currying the Appaloosa. He'd cooled down from his earlier spat with Jacelyn and was also doing some heavy thinking.

Was he doing the right thing by not telling her who he was? What would she think when she found out he hadn't even told her his real name? From the way things were going between them, she'd be back in Richmond before the *real* name passed his lips.

Damn it, Virginia was where she belonged. Arizona Territory was too dangerous a place for a beautiful woman with big city ways like Jacelyn. Although, he mused, she had changed, and there were times now when she seemed to fit in. But, he argued with himself, she still put herself into situations where, if he wasn't around to look after her, she could get into real trouble. He didn't want that kind of responsibility. Did he?

A shuffling footstep sounded behind him. He instantly turned, knowing he would find *her* there. He eyed her warily as she entwined her fingers and looked past him to the horse.

"I'm sorry," she whispered.

He put down the brush and leaned his arm against the top rail on the stall. "No need to be."

"Yes, there is. It seems I am awfully quick to judge you, even after everything you've done to help me."

He shook his head and admitted the truth. "All I've done is get you in deeper trouble." Logically, he'd made the only choices he could to keep her alive. But, sometimes, it didn't seem he'd done nearly enough.

"Believe it or not, I do know that I'm alive because of you." She dug her toe into the loose straw. "I'm grateful for that."

Grant shrugged. Damn it, he didn't want her to be *grateful*. He wanted her respect and her trust and her . . . love. He wanted her to return his feelings, whether it was right, or not.

He sighed and caught her eyes with his earnest gaze. "I promise, Jacelyn McCaffery, that you will leave here in good health. These men will get what they deserve."

Jacelyn blinked. The look in his eyes was so fierce that she backed up a step. Although she questioned how he could make such a promise without getting himself embroiled with the law, she had no doubt whatsoever of his sincerity.

"Well," she released the breath she'd been holding. "I guess neither of us is any closer to finding anything on the Kid."

He pushed away from the stall. "Guess not. That only leaves us a day and a half." He took hold of her shoulder. "When the time is up, I don't want any arguments."

She swallowed and licked her dry lips. "I'll be ready."

"Ready for what, señorita?" Felipe sauntered into the barn.

346

Without batting an eyelid, Jacelyn turned and smiled. "Why, ready for supper. I missed lunch, and I'm starved."

Felipe returned her smile and offered his arm. "Come with me, then. I haven't raided a kitchen since I was a small boy, but I'd bet money we find something good in Dora's kitchen. I couldn't bear for such a lovely lady to waste away before my very eyes."

Jacelyn placed her hand on the fancy man's forearm and cast one last glance back to Grant. A secret little grin tilted one corner of her mouth at the sparks shooting from those incredible blue eyes as they bored into Felipe's back. Could it be possible that the impervious Mr. Grant Jones was jealous? What a delightful notion. She laughed gayly at whatever Felipe was saying and sashayed from the barn.

Grant followed them out into the sunlight. When the dandy bent his head and said something to Jacelyn, and she had the audacity to laugh as if Felipe were the most interesting and humorous man she'd ever met, he clenched his fingers.

Though his heart thundered in his ears, he thought maybe it was all for the best. The longer the dandy kept her occupied, the more time he would have to do what he needed to do.

Turning back to the barn, he discovered the Kid and Bob heading his direction.

"Hey, gunslinger. Dick says you're going to be taking Dutch's chores for a while." The Kid hooked his thumbs into his gun belt and puffed out his scrawny chest. With a wink at Bob, he ordered, "Fetch our horses and saddle them up. Be quick about it, hear?"

Grant grinned. Fate was looking up. With the outlaws away from the bunkhouse, he'd finally get his chance to search through the Kid's things. "Coming right up. Sure that's all I can do for you?"

The Kid scowled. "Yeah. Bob, you think of anything?"

The black man shook his head and stared at Grant.

Grant was sorry to disappoint the gents by being con-
genial, but he was willing to do *almost* anything if it
would speed their departure.

Ten minutes later, he led two horses from the barn
and handed the reins to a big sorrel to Bob and gave the
Kid the horse he'd doctored the previous week.

Bob silently took his horse and mounted.

The Kid glared at Grant and yanked the reins. The
horse shied backward. Cursing, the albino managed to
get his left foot in the stirrup and swung into the saddle.

Glancing at Bob, the Kid spurred his horse. Two
jumps and the animal tossed him to the ground. Rolling
to his feet, he spun to face Grant.

"Fill your hand, you bastard. I'm going to enjoy kill-
ing you."

Chapter Twenty-Three

Grant stepped forward eagerly. Excitement surged through his body, electrifying every nerve ending. His fingers twitched above the butt of his .44. This was as good a way as any to settle matters with the Kid. If the truth were told, he was looking forward to it.

From the porch, Jacelyn had seen the whole confrontation. Her heart plunged to her toes when the Kid yelled out to Grant. Now, watching Grant accept the challenge, her whole world spun out of kilter.

What if he were killed? What would she do? Her own life would have no value without Grant Jones somehow being involved. Her breath caught.

The Kid bent his knees and crouched, his arms spread out slightly from his sides.

Grant stopped several yards away and stood relaxed and ready, his eyes riveted on the albino.

She started down the steps. "Wait. Stop."

Felipe came out of the house and grabbed her arm. "Cuidado, señorita. Stay with me and you won't get hurt."

She spun on the fancy man, slapping at his hand. "Someone has to stop them. The fools are going to kill each other."

Felipe directed her attention to Dick Waddell, who was just emerging from behind the barn.

"What's goin' on here? Who started this here ruckus?" Waddell bellowed.

The Kid nodded toward Grant. "Jones set me up to get bucked off my horse."

Grant stood quietly, staring at the Kid.

Bob rode up with the Kid's horse and Waddell took the reins. He examined the blanket and laughed. "Reckon this's my doing, Kid."

The albino frowned. His fingers flexed. "What do you mean?"

Silent and predatory, Grant continued to stare at the Kid, whose chin and forehead were beaded with sweat.

Waddell unsaddled the horse and held up the bottom blanket. He plucked out several nasty cactus spines. "I used this the other day an' put it back without thinking."

"Jones should have checked the blanket. It's still his doings."

Grant shifted his weight to the balls of his feet and grinned again.

The Kid's Adams apple bobbed noticeably.

Waddell stepped between the two. "Cut it out, the both a ya. There's not enough o' us ta start fighting amongst ourselves."

"But—"

"If you're gonna draw on anyone, it's gonna be me since my mistake were the cause o' this here bickerin'." Waddell stared menacingly at the Kid, who seemed more and more disconcerted by Grant's readiness to do battle rather than by Waddell's challenge.

"I suppose you're right," the Kid conceded. "Wasn't any real harm done."

Grant edged forward.

The Kid held out his hands. "I'm calling off the fight, gunslinger."

Pointing toward the albino's holster, Grant said, "You made a good call."

Darting a glance downward, what little color the Kid had drained quickly from his face. Panicked, he scurried in the dust, picking up the guns that had slipped from their holsters when he'd been bucked from the horse. He spun the revolvers back into their cases and turned a look of such hatred on Grant that Jacelyn could see it from a distance.

Felipe released her arm. "My cousin does not like to be made to look the fool."

Jacelyn rubbed the tender flesh where he'd held her and thrust out her chin. "Then he should quit acting like one, shouldn't he?"

Felipe smiled and touched the rim of his flat crowned, short brimmed hat. "I shall tender that suggestion."

Grant stood his ground as Bob and the Kid mounted up. Damn, he'd truly wanted to fight the smart-mouthed Kid. His eyes shot up to the porch, where he saw Jacelyn standing beside the dandy. She seemed to be having such an animated conversation that he thought he must've been mistaken, thinking he heard her call out a warning earlier.

If only his gut didn't twist into knots every time he saw her with the strutting dandy. The sooner he got her out of this snake's den, the better off they'd both be.

He sidestepped when the Kid and Bob galloped past him and unwound his last bandana to wipe dust from his face. Watching the outlaws' backs, he recalled his initial destination and waited for Waddell, Jacelyn, and Felipe to enter the house so he could take a roundabout circuit to the bunkhouse.

Soon, the Kid would have no secrets.

An hour later, Jacelyn volunteered to fetch water for Dora. If she didn't get away from sticky-fingered

Felipe, she was going to be sick. Every time she turned around he was there, touching or ogling her.

She tossed the bucket in the well and turned the crank, thinking how far she had come since that first evening when Grant had had to help her.

"Señorita, you should not do such heavy work. Stand back and let a man do that."

Her eyes narrowed as Felipe rushed to her side. She had already started to swing the bucket to the stone ledge and accidentally—on purpose—avoided catching it. It tipped precariously and, with just a tiny push, spilled water all over the fancy man.

Trying to conceal the devilment in her eyes, she covered her cheeks with her palms. "Oh, my goodness, just look what I've done. I'm so-o-o sorry." She pulled out the bandana Grant had left with her and dabbed at the wilted ruffles adorning Felipe's shirt. "How clumsy of me," she added merrily.

Felipe eyed her suspiciously. "It was an accident."

When she conscientiously tried to help, he took a deep breath and allowed her a view of the shape of his chest beneath the wet shirt.

"I am terribly sorry. Can you ever forgive me?" She tried so hard to keep from laughing at his pompous expression that she choked and stepped backward. Her foot caught on the pail, twisted and she fell into a puddle. She screeched, then laughed, well aware she'd gotten what she deserved.

Felipe bent to help her up. When she tried to stand, her ankle gave out beneath her weight and she fell again.

She winced when he picked up her foot. Her tall-topped moccasin prevented him from examining her leg too closely.

"With your permission, I will remove your, ah, shoe . . . and see how badly you are injured."

She noted the question in his eyes as he regarded her footwear and shoved at his hands, insisting, "No, thank you. I'll be fine. It doesn't really hurt." To prove her statement, she curved her lips into what she hoped resembled more of a smile than a grimace.

At that same moment, Grant rushed around the corner of the house, having heard her yell. He stopped abruptly when he spied the two of them sitting in a puddle, the dandy feeling Jacelyn's leg while she smiled provocatively.

Jacelyn looked up to see Grant staring at her with hurt and confusion in his eyes. But he blinked and all signs of emotion were gone. She tentatively smiled and would've waved him over, but her attention was stolen by the fancy man's sliding his hand up her calf. Her eyes pleaded briefly for Grant to come to her aid before she had to look away and pry Felipe's fingers from her leg.

Grant scowled. Her eyes had turned violet as she tilted her head, telling him in no uncertain terms to get away and leave them alone. Damn it, it would serve her right if he marched over and plucked her away from the dandy. But, if she didn't know better than to act like a brazen tease to a vicious outlaw, he owed it to her to let her learn what kind of trouble she could incite.

Besides, if he went over there, he couldn't be responsible for what he might do, to either Felipe Barraza or Miss Jacelyn McCaffery.

He felt like a damned fool. If ever a woman needed to be turned over a knee and taught a lesson, it was Jacelyn.

Slowly he backed away, then turned and hurried to the barn.

Jacelyn realized Grant was just going to leave her in her predicament. Why? Every other time she'd needed him, he'd been there for her. Why would be desert her

353

now, when another man was being so free with his dratted hands?

"Quit that." She slapped Felipe's hand again. "I told you I'll be fine, Mr. Barraza."

"Felipe, my dear. Call me Felipe."

She sighed. "I'll make a bargain with you. You help me up, then take your hands off me, and I'll think about calling you Felipe."

He frowned. "That is not so good a bargain."

"It's the best I can do."

With his right hand over his heart, he grinned ruefully, clambered to his feet, and held out his left one.

She placed her fingers in his, thinking that he truly had to be one of the most charming men she'd ever met. Too bad he was wasting his life as an outlaw. Too bad he was wasting his time on a woman who'd given her heart to another, even though the other man was also a desperado.

When she was finally on her feet, she gritted her teeth and managed to take a step without showing how terribly it pained her. "See? I told you I was fine."

"Ah, and I suppose now I am expected to keep my end of your . . . bargain?"

She nodded, trying not to grimace as she took yet another step away from him.

"Since I am an honorable man, I shall keep my word . . . for now." He gallantly bowed, but kept his eyes on her face.

"Th-thank you. I'm pleased to know there's at least one gentleman around."

Felipe picked up the bucket, dropped it in the well and refilled it. "Since you are determined to be alone, I will take this to Dora. Perhaps she will reward me with a slice of warm bread." He smiled like a mischievous boy.

Jacelyn wasn't a bit fooled. She released a long, relieved breath. "Perhaps."

When he finally turned and went back to the house, she sagged against the well and held the weight off her ankle. Glancing toward the cabin, she thought it looked two miles away. How would she ever get that far?

"You are sure you are all right, señorita?" Felipe called from the doorway.

She waved, straightened, and started toward the cabin. Several yards later she glanced over her shoulder. He was still watching her. Sweat broke out on her forehead and trickled down the back of her neck as she stepped on her sprained ankle time after time. She concentrated on placing one foot in front of the other until her eyes blurred with pain.

"Where's your fancy gentleman? Surely a *real* gentleman wouldn't stand by and watch you endure that kind of pain."

He'd come up so quietly that Jacelyn jumped. Her ankle bent the wrong way. She gasped and would have fallen if Grant hadn't reached out and scooped her into his arms. He quickly lifted her and carried her through the cabin doorway.

As soon as he'd set her in the chair, she swatted at him, but found her fist trapped in his iron-hard grasp.

"What's that for?" he demanded in all innocence.

She jerked her hand free. "For running off and leaving me with that ... that ... *damned* centipede of a man."

"I thought you liked him pawing you."

Her eyes widened. "You thought ..." She leaned down and rubbed her throbbing ankle, then peered up at him and said, "You were jealous."

Caught by surprise at her blunt statement, he tried to see her eyes but they were hidden beneath the thick fringe of her lashes. "Of that bastard?" he blustered.

She nodded.

He knelt down and brushed her fumbling hands away from her moccasin. Pulling it off, he felt the swollen joint. "What happened?"

She recalled the priceless expression on Felipe's face when the bucket of cold water sloshed over him. She smiled and said only, "I tripped over the bucket."

So, that was what the dandy was doing, looking at her injury? Or trying to. Now that he'd calmed down, Grant remembered seeing Jacelyn push those long-fingered, uncalloused hands away. But the man hadn't wanted to take her hint. Grant's gut clenched.

His own fingers moved gently over her ankle. "It'll be sore a few days."

She nodded.

"I'll see if I have something to put on it."

"Thank you."

Suddenly, they didn't seem to have much to say to one another. Feelings were too hard to control or hide— too easily read by the other.

Grant cleared his throat. "When I, ah, saw you earlier, I was coming to tell you that I searched the bunkhouse."

She eagerly scooted forward on the chair, momentarily forgetting her ankle.

"If the Kid's kept anything besides the watch, I couldn't find it."

Her face fell. "I'd really hoped . . ."

"Yeah."

Another silence stretched between them until Grant realized he still held her foot in his hand. He gently set it on the floor and trailed his fingers up her smooth arch as he rose.

"I'll be back in a while."

She nodded. As he went through the door, she asked, "Would you have killed the Kid?"

He looked her in the eyes. "Yes."

She shuddered and stared after him. He walked with such agility and grace, something no finishing school had been able to instill in her. His movements were sure and confident, and she had no doubt he fully believed in himself.

Tall, dark, handsome, dangerous. She wrapped her arms around her waist and hugged the thought that he'd been jealous. Yes, the virile rogue of a man had been jealous of another man touching *her*.

About an hour later, Grant returned with a small jar.

Jacelyn had propped her foot up on the trunk and he nodded his approval. Removing the cork from the jar, he sat on the edge of the bed and pulled her foot over to his lap.

He poured some liquid into his hand and began to rub it into her ankle. She flinched. "What is that?"

"Liniment." He set the jar on the floor and rubbed with both hands, creating friction and heat. He glanced up, hoping she didn't notice how much he enjoyed the feel of her soft skin and dainty bones.

Jacelyn felt the effect of his ministrations in every sensitive part of her body. She closed her eyes and concentrated on anything that would take her mind off Grant and the warmth flooding through her.

"Liniment. Is that the same stuff you put on horses?" She wrinkled her nose at the strong odor and attempted to pull her foot from his grasp, more from needing a moment to collect herself than from distaste of the liniment.

"I use it on animals, but it's for people, too." Grant released her foot. He was short of breath and needed to put some distance between them. Hell, he hated feeling so confused and unsure of himself. They were emotions he hadn't experienced since he was a young boy. Yet all it took was this one woman to call forth all of his insecurities.

When he hesitated and stopped rubbing her ankle, she straightened in the chair. "Well, thank you. It feels much better."

He stood quickly and backed up a step. "Yeah, just stay off of it as much as you can."

Damn it, what was he doing pussy-footing around when all he wanted to do was grab her up and make wild, passionate love. He glanced down at her, then darted his eyes to the door. From the taut nubs of her nipples stretching the flannel shirt, she had much the same notion. So why was he holding back?

He rubbed the back of his neck. Because she was as timid and frightened of her feelings as a flighty filly. She had grave doubts about him, and he couldn't blame her. All he hoped was that once this was all over, she'd give him another chance.

His eyes hooded as he took two steps back. Another chance. Did he really want that? Yes, damn it, he did. She was the first woman he'd met that he could dream of growing old with.

But dream was all he could do. Besides her thinking he was an outlaw, she was terrified of his Apache heritage. A *lady* such as herself would never lower herself to be seen with a *halfbreed*. He'd only set himself up for a world of hurt if he didn't back off and let things cool off between them.

Jacelyn lowered her lashes, also hurt and confused. Grant acted as if being near her was distasteful. She'd hoped her explanation of the happenings at the well would be enough to put things right between them. What had happened?

Keeping her eyes downcast, she was afraid he might pull his mind-reading trick again, although he hadn't done too good a job lately. "I think I'd like to lie down now."

Grant's head snapped back like he'd been slapped. So, she was dismissing him, was she? Like some misbehaving school boy. Good.

He spun on his heel and stalked angrily out the door. Jacelyn cursed the wet droplets that fell on her shirt sleeve. For a person who never used to cry, lately she could have filled a dry creek bed.

The next morning, Jacelyn hobbled up to the house. The night had been horrendous. Grant had once again slept on his bedroll. Which made her wonder how it had mysteriously reappeared. She had huddled under her blanket, trying not to jar her ankle and listening for his every breath and movement.

A pair of strong arms to comfort her would have been a blessing. But . . . not his arms. She would have been even more restless in *his* arms.

He'd tossed and turned and groaned in his sleep, until she thought there must be cactus spines in his blanket. Then he'd left before daylight. Soon after that, she'd heard the sound of hoofbeats. He'd left the ranch without a word to her.

Dejected, she'd gotten up, dressed, and was on her way to see if Dora needed help. The quiet dawn rose around her, and she realized there was no one in the world to stop her if she was of a mind to escape. Strange how the passage of just one day could change a person's outlook.

Today was the last day. If she and Grant didn't find proof of who was responsible for murdering James, they would probably leave tonight. She looked down the road, wondering where Grant had gone. If he wasn't here to help her today, fine. She would do it herself.

Dora looked up from her bread dough when Jacelyn came through the back door. "Gawd, Missy, ya look about as pert as a duck in the desert. What's botherin' ya?"

Jacelyn sagged into the nearest chair. She gazed at Dora through burning eyes. She needed someone to talk to so badly. It had been years since James had left Virginia and she'd had anyone at all to confide in. Though events had proven she didn't truly know the woman as well as she'd thought, Dora had been kind once they'd warmed up to each other. She'd even acknowledged the fact that Dora *might* have been looking out for her when the woman yelled to stop her escape.

"It's that man, ain't it?"

Jacelyn blinked, trying to hold the threat of more tears at bay. She'd suddenly lost her desire to talk.

"Here now, ain't never been a man yet worth sheddin' a tear over."

"It's my ankle."

"Shore 'tis." The side of Dora's mouth pursed with unspoken doubt.

Jacelyn wiped a hand over her eyes, hoping to hide her true feelings. "Can I help you do something?"

"With a sore ankle? Ya won't be wantin' ta stand over a hot stove." Dora grinned mischievously and gestured toward a nearby basket. "Why don't ya check the chicken coop an' see if the hens left me more eggs."

She watched Dora turn back to the bread dough. The woman was baiting her, making the point that it wasn't a sore ankle that had caused her tears. But a chance to gather eggs—probably non-existent eggs since Dora usually did that very early—was a chance to check out the barn. At the risk of proving Dora right, Jacelyn decided to take her up on her offer.

"If gathering eggs will help you, that's what I'll do." She stood and reached for the basket Dora had indicated. Stepping gingerly, she left the warm kitchen and Dora's answering chuckle behind.

The sun warmed her back as she made her way to the coop and found a single egg. As she was leaving, she paused at the corner of the small structure and glanced around. The Kid, with his saddlebags thrown over his shoulder, was skulking through the trees west of the barn. He glanced furtively around and hesitated only a moment when he saw her, before disappearing through the door and into the blackness. A few minutes later, he emerged without the saddlebags.

She met his eyes as he briefly glared at her, then followed his progress as he headed back to the bunkhouse. Why was he being so sneaky? Was it something in the saddlebags? Why would he want to hide them from the others?

Leaning against the railing, she waited until he was inside the building and wouldn't be watching her. Then she slipped around the coop and ran for the barn— grimacing with each step. Walking quietly, she heard footsteps coming from behind the barn. Quickly, she ducked inside, hiding at the back of the first stall.

"Gonna rain fer sure."

At the sound of Waddell's voice, she held her breath.

"Cain't do much, so the Kid wants we should go ta the bunkhouse an' get up a game o' poker."

"I might sit in on a hand or two before I talk to our Miss McCaffery."

She heard a yawn and could picture Felipe's bored countenance.

"Why ya wanna jabber with her?"

"She knows more than she let on about Mr. Jones. If I keep pressuring, she might let something slip."

Their voices faded and Jacelyn released her breath. She counted to one hundred then moved out into the aisle between the stalls.

Her hand trembled as she ran it through her hair. From what they'd said, they were hoping she'd incriminate Grant in some way. She'd have to be careful whenever she spoke with any of the men.

Now, more than ever, she wanted to find the Kid's saddlebags, find the proof they needed, and leave with Grant.

With her hands on her hips, she surveyed the inside of the barn. She'd have to be quick. Where would the Kid put a pair of saddlebags?

Her first instinct was to search the stalls and the stacks of hay. By the time she found out the bags weren't in those locations, her eyes watered and she stifled give-away sneezes.

She dug her fingers into the grain bin and nearly screamed when a tiny mouse scurried over the back of her hand. The mangers held only hay. Scraps of leather and other repair items for saddles and bridles filled the only trunk.

She looked over the racks that supported the saddles. Sniffing back a sneeze, she savored the fragrance of leather and hay, scents she'd come to associate with Grant. The persistent ache in her chest suddenly worsened.

Thunder cracked and she jumped. The barn darkened. A sinister sense of foreboding weighed heavy on her shoulders.

Distant lightning flickered across the door and the window above the saddles. The flashes and booming thunder rolled over one another. She took advantage of the added light and noise to feel the blankets thrown protectively across the saddles.

She stopped abruptly when she found something bulky beneath a blanket, reminding her of the one that had almost caused the gunfight between Grant and the Kid. The Kid. Her heart thudded in rhythm with the blustery storm. Slowly, yet determinedly, she slid her hand beneath the blanket. She felt something smooth and thick and pulled it into the open. Saddlebags.

Kneeling on the floor, she lugged the bags onto her lap. Were these the Kid's, or someone else's? And, why, after days spent searching for the truth, was she suddenly afraid to open them?

Taking a deep breath, she unconsciously jutted out her chin and untied the leather thongs closing the left pouch. The flap opened and several items tumbled out. A tin of matches. A sheathed knife, cartridges, and jerky.

She shook the pouch and loosened a folded piece of paper.

Clearing the straw from a place on the floor, she spread the parchment. A soft gasp escaped her lips. A map. And she immediately recognized James's work.

Since her parents had also been cartographers, she was fairly adept at reading the symbols. The map was of the Waddell ranch. In the upper right corner were notes of James's suspicions of the activities at the place. He'd seen calves with doctored brands. The men came and went at the same time, unlike a working ranch where cowboys went alone or in pairs to handle the chores.

No matter whose saddlebags she'd found, this was what she and Grant needed to prove that the gang, or someone in the gang, was responsible for James's death. That someone must've seen this map and been willing to kill to get it back.

With trembling fingers, she put everything back into the pouch. Her hand hovered over the other bag's ties. She was afraid to see what it contained. A horrible odor drifted out when she untied the strings. Furry objects dropped onto her lap. Picking one up, she wrinkled her nose and fought off shivers at the shriveled feel of the stuff.

Most of them were dark and some were longer and stringier than others. And there was a red one, with highlights and streaks of . . .

Jacelyn screamed. She threw the bags and the . . . scalps . . . off her legs. Leaping to her feet, she frantically wiped her hands on her trousers. Creepy, crawly tingles slithered up and down her spine and in the tips of her fingers.

Scalps. Oh, dear Lord. Scalps. And James . . . She blinked rapidly but couldn't stop the flow of tears. Grant. Where was Grant? She had to show him these. She gulped. That meant she had to put the things back into the bags and hide them.

Chill bumps crept over her skin. She swallowed gritty revulsion and searched until she found a rag. Tiptoeing to the bags, she gingerly knelt and picked up each piece of hair with the cloth and quickly filled the pouch. She shuddered harder with each one, and gagged over the red-haired one, unsure she could touch it again.

All at once, she heard running footsteps coming closer and closer. She grabbed the red scalp and replaced it in the saddlebag. Panic constricted her chest and numbed her legs as she stumbled to the back of the barn and into an empty stall piled high with fresh straw, saddlebags in hand.

"Damn it, Kid. I told ya ta keep them damned bags o' yours where no one'd find 'em."

"That's what I did, cousin. Knowing Felipe would come to the bunkhouse for the poker game, I hid them in the barn."

"I done told ya ta quit hangin' on ta that stuff. My Gawd, it ain't right."

"You saying I'm crazy, Dick?"

Jacelyn sank deeper in the straw. The Kid sounded threateningly unbalanced and dangerously paranoid. As far as she was concerned, he was sick in the worst way.

Her eyes narrowed and sweat slicked her skin. And he'd killed James. In a cruel and hideous way. She knew that now for sure.

Revenge burned in her mind. She wanted him to die—slowly—painfully. Like in the stories she'd read in *Harper's Weekly*. But *she* wanted to do it. She wanted the pleasure of seeing him suffer and hearing him beg for mercy.

She covered her face with her hands. Good heavens, just listen to her. She was as bad as the outlaws.

A string of curses shattered the stillness. She heard the thud of heavy leather hitting the ground. Then there was a scuff, like someone kicking away straw and manure.

"They were right here, on top of my saddle. Someone's stolen them."

"Gawd, who'd wanna steal somethin' like that?"

There was a prolonged silence. Jacelyn held her breath.

"That woman. She watched me come in here. She's the only one who could've taken them."

"She's probably up at the house with Dory. C'mon, we'll go an' find out. But if'n she ain't the one, we got our tails in a trap shore as shootin'."

Jacelyn was glad to hear the despair in Waddell's voice. She hoped they all got what they deserved. In fact, she'd see to it herself.

As soon as their footsteps faded, she buried the saddlebags under some straw and crawled from the stall and to the back door. Outside, the storm was coming closer, whipping up the wind and swirling dust and sand in small whirlwinds.

But the storm inside Jacelyn was already raging. Feelings of hatred, disgust, fear, and outrage warred for dominance as she ran toward the chicken coop, then headed for the house.

The kitchen door slammed behind her and she turned a smile on Dora as she displayed the basket. "Found one."

Dora chuckled and bent to pull freshly baked biscuits from the stove.

Jacelyn slumped into the nearest chair and buried her head in her shaking hands. Had the Kid and Waddell come looking for her yet? She shivered and brushed away a tear.

"Yore ankle a painin' ya again?"

Jacelyn looked up to find Dora watching her with sympathetic eyes and a playful smile. "No ... uh, yes ... It hurts."

"What hurts most is likely a might higher'n your ankle." Dora clicked her teeth together and laid a hand on Jacelyn's shoulder. "Like I told ya afore, ain't no man worth your tears."

With honest warmth, Jacelyn patted Dora's hand. The older woman would never know how grateful she was after her discovery in the barn to have someone to talk to and something more normal to talk about.

Looking into the living room and then out the back door, she concentrated on Dora's words. "But ... how can you say that? Didn't you cry when Wad ... Mr. Waddell made you give up your child?"

"Shore. But that were different."

Jacelyn stared blankly at the woman.

"Ya see, I knew Waddy loved me, an' that it was fer the gal's well-bein', more'n our own, that he wanted ta do it."

Jacelyn wasn't sure she believed Dick Waddell could be that noble. "How ... how do you know if someone loves you?"

Dora wiped flour from her hands and went over to sit down across the table from Jacelyn. "Ya kin jest tell." Her eyes turned dreamy. "A man'll look at ya with a fire in 'is eyes. He'll touch ya real soft like, an' trail 'is fingers down your cheek ..."

When Dora hesitated, Jacelyn interrupted. "And Waddell does that to you?"

Dora smiled. "Oh, darlin', he does a lot more'n that." She patted droplets of perspiration from her neck. "An' I've seen shore-fire signs from that good-lookin' Jones fella."

"Signs?" Jacelyn's breath caught. "What kind of signs?"

"He's a followin' ya around like a hungry pup."

Jacelyn stared open-mouthed, too stunned to respond.

Dora leaned close and whispered, "He's fallin' harder'n a bear from a honey tree." Finally, Dora laughed and pounded Jacelyn's shoulder. "He loves ya, ya ninny."

"Oh, no. No. He couldn't." Her heart beat faster than a trip-hammer. He didn't—couldn't—love her. Could he? She focused blurry eyes on the older woman. "Do you really think so?" She cocked her head, listening for sounds from outside the kitchen.

Dora nodded.

"But he doesn't act like it. At least ... maybe he does sometimes ..." She swiped a loose tear from her cheek. "But then ... he's so cold."

"He's scared, child."

Jacelyn shook her head vehemently. "Oh, not Grant. He'd never be afraid of anything."

Dora arched a thin brow.

"Really. He's the strongest, bravest man I've ever known." She thought back to the first time she'd seen him, and then again that same evening. He'd been so dark and handsome, his muscled chest bared, as he headed for the Indian camp. "And he's as fierce and dangerous as his Apache friends."

"What?" Dora gasped.

Caught up in her praise of Grant, Jacelyn raced on. "Oh, yes. He's part Apache, and . . ."

A chair scraped the floor in the next room. Jacelyn started and turned to see the black outlaw, Bob, striding quickly through the living room and out the front door. She looked at Dora and saw the woman's alarmed expression turn to one of sorrow.

"Aw, Missy, I liked your man. Wish ya hadn't a gone an' let on about 'is red blood."

With heart-stopping horror, Jacelyn realized what she'd done. She'd betrayed the trust Grant had placed in her.

She leaped to her feet, ignoring her ankle, and ran through the house to the front door.

Too late. Bob was gesturing and talking animatedly with Felipe and Waddell. Slowly, they all turned to look at her.

Chapter Twenty-Four

It was clear now why the Kid and Waddell hadn't come after her. Felipe had intercepted them and Felipe wasn't supposed to know about the saddlebags. Jacelyn shrank back in the doorway and bumped into Dora. Before she could move around the woman, clomping boots announced the men's arrival on the porch.

"Señorita, por favor. A moment of your time."

Jacelyn looked at Felipe who, for once, had no disarming smile.

"Bob has given us some distressing news."

"Yeah. When'd ya find out Jones is Apache?"

She backed up and found Dora had made room for her retreat. "I-I'm not all that sure he is." Dear Lord, she prayed, please help her think of a way to get Grant out of the hole she'd dug for him.

Felipe crossed his arms. Waddell moved to stand behind her. Bob blocked the door.

"Señorita, this is very important. I have heard the name Grant somewhere. What is this Grant's last name?"

She spread her arms and hunched her shoulders. "Jones. That's all I know."

Felipe looked to Waddell. "Hmmmm. Perhaps his name *is* Jones." His eyes bore down on Jacelyn. "But why do you say one minute he is part Apache, and the next say you do not know for sure that he is?"

Jacelyn gulped. "Because . . . he's always trying to frighten me."

"So you think he just said he was part Indian to make you believe he'd take your scalp?" Felipe asked, his slimy smile back in place.

She inhaled deeply and nodded. "But . . . he certainly doesn't look like an Indian."

Waddell snorted at Jacelyn, then faced Felipe. "Who's this Grant fella s'posed ta be?"

"Grant Ward. I've never seen him, but I've heard his name at the fort. If he is the same man, he is the Chief of Scouts."

Jacelyn narrowed her eyes, trying to take in everything at once. Grant *had* been at the fort. She'd even seen him in the Colonel's office. But was he really connected with the Cavalry? He'd certainly ridden to her rescue a few times . . . No, he would've said something to her. Felipe had to be wrong.

"He could be dangerous," Waddell added, "if he found out our plans."

Just what were their plans? Jacelyn wondered.

Waddell scratched his chin. "Don't reckon we kin afford ta take chances. But there still ain't no way he coulda been the one set the Cavalry on us the other day."

Jacelyn was strangely disappointed. Grant hadn't warned the Cavalry.

The Kid sauntered into the living room. "I knew there was something about that gunslinger." He lovingly ran his palm over his knife handle. "Apache, huh?"

Jacelyn spoke up. "Maybe not."

The Kid just grinned. The outlaws looked somberly at one another.

Jacelyn knew it didn't matter what she said. The suspicion was planted. Grant's life was worthless. And it was her fault. Somehow, she had to warn him before he rode innocently into the headquarters and was trapped. Her hand shook as she corralled a loose lock of hair behind her ear.

The Kid leered at Jacelyn. "Who's going to watch the woman now?"

The men just looked at each other.

"I can do it. And when the gunslinger gets back, I'll have a little welcoming party ready for him, too." He curled his fingers around the butts of his guns.

Her eyes wide with horror, Jacelyn took another step back. Not the Kid. Surely they wouldn't leave her alone with the very man who killed her brother. She covered her mouth with her hand to keep from screaming out her fear.

Felipe waved his hand. "I've got other things for you to do, cousin." His eyes narrowed on Dora. "Keep her with you until I say otherwise."

Dora swallowed and said, "Shore. I'll watch after her."

With the Kid still arguing, the outlaws left the house. Jacelyn breathlessly sank onto the edge of the table.

Dora walked slowly over and touched her shoulder. "What're ya gonna do, Missy?"

"I don't know." Jacelyn glanced warily at the woman, but saw only compassion and concern in her light eyes. Dora certainly wasn't responsible for what had happened. She had no one to blame but herself.

"I have to warn him. Somehow." But Dora had stopped her once before. Would the woman let her go this time?

"Ya love him, don't ya?"

Jacelyn felt an awful scratching in her throat. She nodded.

"It's gonna be all right. He'll get ya outta this."

"But, Dora, I've been dependent on men all my life. *I'm* the one who messed everything up, and *I'm* the one who has to straighten it out." And get away with the saddlebags before the Kid gets to me, she added silently.

Dora paused, apparently recognizing the determination in Jacelyn's eyes. "Mebbe ya kin, at that," she conceded.

"The first thing I have to do is get to Grant before the Kid or the other men. He's got to know what I've done and at least have a chance to defend himself."

"With your weak ankle? How?" Dora glanced over her shoulder toward the kitchen. "I might need your help in the barn." She crooked her finger under Jacelyn's nose. "If I'm ever gonna do anything, it be now. C'mon."

Jacelyn shook her head. "No, Dora. I won't get you involved. It could be dangerous."

"Missy, ma whole life's been one mistake after another. It's time I did somethin' ta make shore someone else don't have ta do the same things I done."

"Thanks. It's kind of you. But this is something I really need to do myself. You know?"

Dora nodded. "But ya need help gettin' outta here."

Jacelyn walked to the front door and stood looking out. Grant. Where are you? Who are you? Just . . . please . . . be careful.

Finally, she turned and solemnly regarded the older woman. Dora was right. She did need help. "All right. But just help me find a good gentle horse. If anything happened to you because of me . . . I . . ."

"Pshaw. Ain't nothin' gonna happen ta me." Dora walked to the back door and looked out. "Now, c'mon, before Felipe changes his mind an' sends the Kid back."

The two women cautiously made their way to the barn. Jacelyn leaned into the howling west wind and blessed the rumbling thunder for covering the noise she made as she limped along.

Once inside the shelter of the darkened enclosure, Dora worked swiftly. She led a sorrel gelding from its stall and had it saddled and bridled by the time Jacelyn retrieved the albino's saddlebags.

Dora eyed the bags questioningly. When it didn't appear Jacelyn was going to explain their significance, she shrugged and secured them behind the cantle.

Jacelyn climbed stiffly into the saddle and looked down at Dora. "I don't know how I'll ever repay you for this."

Dora patted the horse's neck and handed Jacelyn the reins. "Jest be mighty careful an' find that man o' yours."

Jacelyn sniffed. This was probably the last time she'd see Dora. She took a deep breath and clamped her legs to the saddle fenders. Kicking her heels against the horse's sides, she glanced back one last time at the small, sad woman. She blinked rapidly when Dora raised her hand and waved, then returned the salute and headed the animal for the door. "Bye, Dora," she whispered.

But her words were drowned as lightning flashed and rain poured down in driving sheets. Jacelyn ducked her head and urged the reluctant horse into the storm.

Santana's black eyes glittered. Grant put out his hand to stay the Apache. "No, don't do it. We must be patient."

"They must be taught a lesson."

"We have to be sure first," Grant argued.

"They are guilty."

"Yes, of many things. But we need proof of their involvement with the holdups and murders before the

373

Apaches and all of you scouts will be declared innocent by the whites living in this area."

Santana just stared at Grant, who refused to back down and allow Santana to have his way. "We may never find anything if they think someone is watching them."

"And who is just going to *watch?*"

"Damn it, man, you do any more and you'll ruin whatever chance we have."

The Apache folded his arms over his chest. "You leave tomorrow?"

"I have to get her out." Grant's chest heaved as he sighed. "Look, give me three days. Nobody's going anywhere and it'll give me enough time to take the woman to the fort and get back. Then we'll see."

Santana nodded once.

Relieved, Grant untethered his horse and warily regarded the dark, rolling clouds. Thunder vibrated the ground beneath his feet and lightning splintered the heavens. He shouted, "I'll meet up with you in three days."

Jacelyn could hardly see as far as her horse's ears, it was raining so hard. She wiped dripping strands of hair from her eyes and squinted ahead, trying to see something familiar.

The gelding snorted and sloshed on through puddles of water and mud. She leaned over and patted the animal's soaked neck for encouragement—as much for herself as for the horse.

Lightning spiraled through the mass of roiling clouds and she flinched. But with the sudden illumination, she saw something off to her left that caused her to sigh with thanksgiving. "Look, boy. It's the big oak. We're at the creek."

A loud snapping noise sounded in the distance behind her, followed by another. She craned her neck, but the rain fell too hard to see. Could it be Grant? Her pulse accelerated with mingling hope and trepidation. It could also be someone from the ranch who'd already discovered her missing. She gripped the saddle horn with icy fingers. Or, she thought hopefully, it might just be a deer, or some other forest creature.

Deciding not to take any chances, she quickly slid from the saddle and fought the damp leather strings until she was able to remove the saddlebags. Slogging through water and mud, she made her way to the big tree. The wet saddlebags bit into her shoulder, but she wasn't about to put them down until she found a safe place in which to hide them.

Grant. Please let whoever was coming be Grant, she prayed. I need him. She clambered down the bank and through the tangle of roots. Swiping hair from her cheeks and eyes, she peered under the overhang. Just as she'd thought, a small cave had been eroded beneath the wood and grass and shrubs.

She crawled up under the roots, and reached up as far as she could until she found a strong, crooked indentation that would hold the bags. At least they'd be out of the water if it continued to rise.

It might not be the safest place to put them, but it was the best she could do.

Backing out of the small enclosure, she climbed up on the bank and tried to brush leaves and twigs and dirt from her wet hair and clothing.

A hand encircled her upper arm. She gasped and tried to draw away, but the long, womanly fingers bit into her skin. "Ah, señorita, did I startle you?"

She felt like sobbing. So, it hadn't been Grant coming, or even a woodland creature. Mustering her courage, she stiffened her spine and faced Felipe. Worried about what he might have seen just now, she snapped, "What do you think?"

"I *think* you are too far from the house. Surely you were not *thinking* of leaving us?" He allowed his statement to turn into a question.

She jerked her arm free and bluffed, "I thought of it, all right. B-but of course I wasn't escaping."

Felipe looked at the saddled gelding. His smile didn't reach his eyes. "Of course not."

The rain continued to fall steadily, molding her shirt and trousers to every curve and hollow on her body. She felt like his eyes literally stripped her bare.

He suddenly reached out and jerked her into his arms. His lips found only her nose and chin and cheeks as she struggled to prevent him from kissing her. His arms were everywhere, and she couldn't get a hold on his hands.

"Stop. Please. Don't touch me—"

"But you have wanted me, Jacelyn McCaffery. I have seen the desire in your eyes."

"No! Let me go." She kicked at his shin, but missed. If she could only . . .

"You heard the lady. Let her go."

She gasped and nearly fell when Felipe cursed and threw her from his arms. Grant. He was really here. But he didn't know—

"You. We thought you had turned tail and run like the Apache cur you are," Felipe snarled.

Grant dismounted and stepped away from the Appaloosa. He glanced at Jacelyn in a flash so quick that she thought she might have imagined it, except for the disbelief and hurt she'd seen in his glittering blue eyes. Her heart ached. Could she ever make him understand?

Refusing to take Felipe's bait, Grant stood silently regarding the dandy. He held his arms to his sides, right hand inches above his gun, waiting to see what the dandy would do next, trying to ignore the bedraggled woman and her huge purple eyes.

Jacelyn stood stunned and immobile. Felipe reached out and grabbed her arm, drawing her close to his side. "Did you perhaps come back for the woman? I think you wasted your time, no? She is colder than a block of ice."

He touched Jacelyn's breast and laughed when she slapped at his hand. Then he wound his fingers painfully in her hair, tilting her head so she couldn't avoid his lips. His back was now to Grant.

Jacelyn whimpered. "No . . ."

Felipe's lips did not touch hers. He was suddenly caught by the collar of his short bolero jacket and flung aside as if he were no more than a flea on a pedigreed dog's tail.

An enraged growl erupted from Felipe's throat. He jerked his gun and fired, but he was too anxious. The bullet ripped into the ground five feet in back of Grant.

Grant didn't take the time to draw. He launched himself at the cursing Felipe. His momentum carried them both to the ground, with Felipe taking the brunt of the fall.

Jacelyn covered her mouth and sidestepped the pair as they rolled toward her, arms flailing, legs twisting, each trying to gain a toe hold to get the better of the other.

Felipe managed the first advantage and ended up on top of Grant.

Jacelyn shouted, "Get up, Grant. Don't just lie there." Over Felipe's shoulder, she saw Grant raise his head far enough to glare at her. "Come on."

A rumble started deep in Grant's chest and worked its way up as he grabbed hold of the dandy's jacket with both hands, levered his knees up, and flipped him head over heels.

In less than a heartbeat, Grant was on his feet, arms spread wide, balancing on the balls of his feet. He curled his fingers, opened and curled them again, urging Felipe to come and take him.

Felipe rolled to his feet and regarded his opponent with more respect. He charged forward, feinted with his right fist and swung his left. Grant ducked under Felipe's arm, but a rock slid under his right foot and he stumbled down into the swirling, rushing water.

Climbing to solid footing, he looked up to see Felipe turning with his gun in his hand. Grant reached for his revolver but mud coated the thong on his holster and his fingers slipped. He heard Felipe's hammer lock. His gut clenched. He hadn't thought it would happen like this. Jacelyn. What would happen to Jacelyn?

A movement behind Felipe caught Grant's attention. He fought to keep from indicating with his eyes what was happening, but it was difficult when his instinct was to shout and stop her. The spitfire was creeping up behind the dandy. His heart skipped a beat. A huge chunk of wood swayed in her hands. She repeatedly had to blink water from her eyes as she carefully placed one foot in front of the other.

Grant yelled and lunged forward as she brought the piece of broken limb down hard on Felipe's arm. The crack of a gun report from several yards behind them sounded, and a sharp, searing pain lanced his head. He desperately looked for Jacelyn even as he staggered backward. An eternity passed before he splashed into the roiling water.

He groped for a handhold. Anything. The water tugged and enticed, smothering him in its murky depths. He had to keep from being swept downstream. Jacelyn. He couldn't leave her like this. His fingers scraped a long, thick root. He clawed to catch it, but his hand slipped. Gulping for breath, his strength fading, he grasped again and again and came away with nothing but slick, heavy leather.

Blinking, his feet kicking the water, trying for a foothold, he gaped at the things in his hands. Saddlebags? What the hell?

Damn it, he needed something to pull himself up. He kicked again, but the creek was running too deep and fast.

A wave of water hit him full force, washing him farther away from the bank. Tree limbs, swept along with the flood, caught at his shirt, dragging him down. His energy drained. His vision blurred. One last surge of effort afforded him life-sustaining air before his head went under.

The air seemed thick and electrically charged. Lightning arched jaggedly and slanted downward striking a nearby tree, leaving behind only the scent of smoking wood. The Appaloosa nickered and shied, then spun and galloped downstream.

Felipe yelled at the men coming up to catch the other horses.

Jacelyn screamed and ran to the edge of the creek. Water washed over the toes of her moccasins. She tried to go in after Grant, but the Kid grabbed her arm.

"Come back here, woman, before our ransom winds up floating all the way to Tucson." He tipped his head. Water poured from the brim of his hat as he reholstered his pistol.

She jerked her arm but couldn't gain her freedom. "No. No, we have to help him." Frantically she struggled, but found Waddell on her other side. Between them, the two men forced her back to solid ground.

"He's gone where all good Injuns go," Waddell cheerfully told her.

She sobbed. She stared at the spot where she'd last seen Grant sinking beneath the water. A flash of white shirt lifted her hopes, but they were dashed when the white disappeared beneath frothy, muddy brown waves. She strained against her captors, searching, praying, hoping beyond hope he'd break the surface and come charging back for her.

Nothing. She looked everywhere. Her heart lodged in her throat, choking her voice. She couldn't tell where the tears left off and the rain began as water trickled down her face. Grant? You can't leave me. Not now.

Felipe stalked over to stand directly in front of her, holding his injured arm against his side. "I believe, señorita, we have unfinished business."

Chapter Twenty-Five

Jacelyn was so stricken with grief over Grant's death that she didn't register Felipe's threat.

"Leave the gal be." Waddell directed his words to both Felipe and the Kid. "We ain't got time fer this foolishness now. Jones is dead an' we got plans ta make if we're gonna collect on the gal an' git that Mex silver, too."

Dully, Jacelyn noted the other men's agreement. She limped along docilely beside Waddell as he led her back to her horse. In silence, she was escorted back to her cabin. She flinched when the bar slammed into place, locking her securely inside, but she couldn't summon the anger she'd once felt.

She couldn't feel anything. Just a numbness that seemed to have settled over her entire body—except her heart. Her heart. The last time she'd seen Grant, blood pouring down the side of his face as the water claimed him, her heart had broken.

She rubbed at the back of her neck, a gesture she'd come to associate with Grant. Once again the man had come to her rescue. He'd gotten himself killed for his effort. She hadn't even gotten to say goodbye.

Collapsing onto the bed, she buried her face in her hands. Her wet clothing soaked the blanket and bed clothes. She hardly noticed the chills that shook her body as she sobbed deep, racking sobs that hurt clear to her soul.

He was dead. Though she'd seen it with her own eyes, it was hard to believe. Grant Jones had been too vital and healthy a man to be struck down so quickly and permanently with a tiny little bullet.

She didn't know how long she lay curled on the bed before the bar was lifted and someone entered the room. She didn't bother to rouse. Life suddenly held little interest.

"Missy?"

Jacelyn burrowed into the bed.

"C'mon, Missy. Ya gotta get off that bed an' change into some dry clothes. An' I brung ya some venison stew."

"I'm not hungry."

"All right, but get outta them wet clothes before ya catch your death—"

"I don't care, Dora," Jacelyn sighed. "I just don't care."

Dora reached over and shook Jacelyn's shoulder. "Well, I care, damn it. Now git up an' do what I tell ya."

Jacelyn hiccuped. She stretched her chilled, aching muscles and turned her head until she could see the other woman. Shock stole her breath away. Dora's face was swollen, one eye and cheek badly bruised, and her lip was split. One arm was cradled in a makeshift sling.

"Ya heard me, child. Get up."

Numb with guilt and fear, Jacelyn rose to a sitting position. She wrapped her arms around her shaking body. Her teeth chattered violently. Dora's injuries were her fault. First Grant. Now Dora.

"Wh-who hurt you?" Jacelyn stuttered.

"It don't matter. Don't ya be worryin' none about me."

"But this happened because you helped me, didn't it?"

"Don't ya go takin' the credit. I made my choice. This weren't your fault. It were only a matter o' time before somethin' like this happened."

Jacelyn wiped her sleeve under her nose. "I'm so sorry."

Clucking her tongue, Dora yanked the blanket from beneath Jacelyn's soggy body. Using a dry end, she rubbed the younger girl's hair none too gently with her good arm. "Shuck them clothes, so's I can wash 'em up for ya."

Jacelyn fell into her old habit of blindly obeying orders yet, for once, was glad to have someone directing her movements. It meant she didn't have to think, or plan, or worry. At least for a while.

"Sorry about your man," Dora said as she handed Jacelyn a change of underclothes and one of the dresses from the trunk.

"He wasn't *my* man. I keep trying to tell you that," she insisted on arguing, though she couldn't have been more devastated at his loss if they'd been married twenty years. In fact, it was some solace to think that, for a while, he *had* been her man.

Automatically, she peeled off her wet things, then found herself feeling odd in the long dress. She'd become used to the pants and the freedom they afforded.

"Whatever ya say," Dora added doubtfully. She picked up the brush and ran it through Jacelyn's damp, tangled hair.

"He was just another outlaw, you know?" Maybe, if she thought of the bad things about him, it wouldn't hurt so much. But tears welled up anew as she remembered the tender way Grant had combed her hair once. The gentleness in his large hands had amazed her from the very beginning.

"Do ya really believe that, child?"

Jacelyn blinked at the question. Did she? Really?

He'd always been a gentleman. Always protected her. "I . . . don't know."

Dora harrumphed. "Waddy's feelin' a might low ta think Jones suckered him so bad."

Jacelyn looked hopefully at Dora. "What do you think?"

"I don't know either, Missy." Dora set down the brush and pointed to the bowl and spoon on the table. "Now, git your bottom over there an' eat."

"Yes, ma'am." Feeling a deep bond with the rough, but good-hearted woman, Jacelyn quirked her mouth into a rueful half-grin.

Miles downstream, Grant coughed and sputtered. His eyes blinked open, but the blinding pain in his left temple caused him to close them again. His body moved slightly as the water lifted his hips and washed him against a boulder.

He concentrated as hard as his throbbing head would allow on his surroundings. He was lying in a bed of rocks with only his lower body in the water. The flood waters had receded, which had more than likely allowed him to survive. That, and the fact that a pair of saddlebags supported his chest and protected his back. The rest of his body felt so battered and bruised it hurt to even flex his muscles.

Saddlebags. He remembered now, when he'd grabbed for a tree root, he'd clutched them instead. Who did they belong to? And why had they been hidden under the big oak?

Groggily, he pulled himself from the water. He crawled to a grassy, debris-strewn bank on his hands and knees and tried to heft the bags from his shoulder. His vision blurred. His temples pounded. One word hissed through his cracked lips as he sagged to the ground. "Jacelyn . . ."

Jacelyn hadn't slept well. When the bar scraped and the door opened the next morning, she lay still with her eyes closed. Heavy boots tread across the floor. This wasn't Dora.

She looked up to find Felipe peering down at her. Gripping the blanket tightly, she was thankful she'd slept in her clothes—something she hadn't felt was necessary when Grant was alive. Grant . . . His handsome image flickered to life in her mind's eye and her breath caught momentarily.

"You are surprised to see me, eh?"

Felipe bent down, placing a hand on each side of her, as if to trap her beneath the blanket, but she quickly scooted up. When he frowned at the sight of her dress, she felt a small measure of triumph.

"Not really." She swallowed her sorrow and tilted her chin up. "I've seen a lot of snakes around here."

And his belly dragged on the ground as low as any of the rest. Last night her heart had been so heavy that she hadn't expected to crawl out of bed ever again. Yet at the sight of the slimy Felipe, she found the strength to get up and fight. For Grant's sake, she would do anything it took to get back to Fort Huachuca. He'd risked and given his life to help her find her brother's murderer and, now that she knew, she had to see the albino, Felipe, and the Waddell gang punished. They'd all preyed on innocent people far too long.

Felipe rubbed his bruised forearm, then ran his index finger from the base of her neck to the tip of her defiant chin. "Perhaps one day soon, you will learn to appreciate 'snakes'."

She lifted her shoulders and dropped them dramatically. "I don't think so. All the snakes I've known are sneaky and cruel. I can live without them."

He grinned. "Then again, perhaps you will have to learn to live *with* them, no?"

"No."

He scowled and straightened. "Enough of the games. It is good you are dressed. We will leave as soon as you eat breakfast."

Her eyes widened. "Leave?"

But he'd already turned and walked out the door. She swung her feet over the edge of the bed and just sat there for a moment. Leave? And go where? Why?

Her stomach grumbled at Felipe's suggestion of food. She hadn't eaten anything but a biscuit and part of a bowl of stew yesterday. From the sound of things, she might have to keep her strength up, depending on what the fancy man had in mind for her.

She brushed her hair and washed her face before trudging to the house. All the while she marveled at the freshness and life around her despite the tragedies.

When she walked into the kitchen, Dora handed her a pair of pants and a shirt, washed, dried, and folded.

"Th-thanks, Dora."

Dora couldn't meet her eyes. "Thought ya might wanna wear those since ya gotta ride a spell."

"Do you know where they're taking me?" A tinge of fear crept into her voice.

Dora shook her head.

"Will I ever see you again?" Jacelyn gulped.

The older woman's weathered face crinkled. She sniffed. "Reckon I don't know, Missy. Eat now, while you have the chance," Dora insisted, pushing a hot biscuit into Jacelyn's hand.

Impulsively, Jacelyn threw her arms around Dora's neck. "Whatever happens, I want to thank you for everything you've done."

Dora wiped her shirt sleeve under her nose. "Pshaw. I ain't done nothin' 'cept cause ya misery."

"You've been a friend when I needed one most," Jacelyn said in all sincerity. "And I haven't had many friends."

Before Dora could reply, Felipe swaggered into the kitchen and hooked his thumbs in his belt. "Are you ready?"

Jacelyn looked at Dora, then once again reinforcing her own determination, she jutted out her chin. "If we have to go, I'm ready."

Dora followed them to the front room and helped Jacelyn stuff her shirt and trousers into a saddlebag. She leaned close and whispered, "You take special care o' them duds, ya hear?"

Brows furrowed at the strange request, Jacelyn nodded. She followed Felipe outside and saw only two saddled horses. A chill of dread skittered up her spine. It appeared only she and Felipe were leaving.

"Wh-where are we going?" she questioned warily as he handed her a canteen and helped her to mount.

"You will see when we get there," he replied evasively.

"The others? They aren't coming?"

"Not right away, señorita." He thoughtfully rubbed his chin. "Why? Have you come to like our company so much?"

"Not exactly," she muttered as they rode from the headquarters.

One last look over her shoulder showed Dora still watching. Jacelyn gave a tentative wave, then faced forward. A surprising emptiness filled her chest. Even as she pushed the more gruesome parts of her captivity from her mind, she realized that there had been things she liked about living at the ranch. A single tear escaped. What she'd liked best was the time she'd shared with Grant.

Thank the Lord she had memories. Wonderful memories.

Perhaps she'd had a premonition during their lovemaking when she'd vowed it would have to sustain her for a long, long time.

They rode hard all day, exchanging few words, much to Jacelyn's relief. As the afternoon wore on, though, they passed more mines and saw evidence that someone lived on several of the claims. Once, a disgruntled miner shot over their heads, warning them away in no uncertain terms.

By evening, with most of their water gone, they'd entered a dry, rocky arroyo. Off to the left stood a ramshackle cabin, and Felipe reined his horse over to the hitchrail. When she followed his lead, he waved his hand toward the weather-beaten shack and mounds of ore pilings. "What do you think of it, my dear? This will be 'home' for the next few days."

"It's a pig sty." And it was. Trash and junk littered the entire area.

He smiled congenially. "Then you will learn to live like a pig." Dismounting and walking briskly to her horse, he held up his arms to help her down.

She managed on her own, deftly avoiding his groping hands. "Why did you bring me here?"

Placing his hands on his hips, he regarded her thoughtfully. Then, as if deciding there was nothing to fear from speaking openly, he admitted, "We did not think it safe to keep you at the ranch any longer." He spread his arms and turned his palms up. "Just in case your friend Grant what's-his-name was someone other than he claimed."

His stress on the word *was* caused her lips to thin. Whoever Grant was, it had ceased to matter when the swollen waters of the creek pulled him under. Hatred for the Kid and all of the outlaws burned in her soul. But especially for the Kid. Besides brutally murdering her brother, the albino had shot and killed the man she loved.

For the first time in her life, she thought she actually could end a human life.

Felipe hesitated, but added, "It would be a shame for the law to find you before we collect our fortune."

She shook her head. "I'm afraid you're going to be sadly disappointed."

He frowned. "You are not wealthy?"

"Well ... Yes, I suppose." But she certainly wasn't going to explain the complications of her inheritance and the qualifications to her access to the money. He would find out soon enough.

All at once, the hairs on the back of her neck stood on end. When he *did* find out, her life would be worthless. There would be no reason to keep her alive. Now she understood why Grant had used that ruse in the first place. He'd been thinking of her, first and foremost.

Felipe handed her the saddlebags Dora had packed and motioned for her to precede him into the cabin. Stunned by the absolute truth of her revelation, she grabbed her canteen and went without making a fuss. She squinted and looked around the filthy, musty interior—without feeling the urge to clean.

Grant awoke to a stinging sensation in his left temple. He reached to touch his head but steel-hard fingers gripped his wrist. Twisting his neck, he winced when the throbbing started up again, but slanted his gaze to see Santana sitting cross-legged by his side.

"So, my brother has decided to join me." He held a gut jug out to Grant, who shook his head and, once again, regretted the action. "Don't think my stomach could hold your Apache rot-gut right now."

Santana grinned and took a deep swallow of tizwin, the Apache version of homemade liquor.

Slowly, Grant pushed himself to a sitting position. "How'd you find me?"

The Apache gestured behind him and Grant saw the Appaloosa tethered next to Santana's horse. His brows furrowed. He'd left the horse ground-tied where he'd found the dandy man-handling Jacelyn. No telling what had happened to scare the horse.

"I saw horse, saddled, no rider. Found you not far away." Santana laid his tizwin aside. "What happened? You have bullet wound."

This time the Indian didn't stop Grant when he reached up and gingerly felt his temple.

"Your head is too rocky to be hurt by a bullet," the Apache teased.

Grant chuckled. "You mean too *hard,* but either way, you're right." His fingers probed a short, shallow gash just behind his left temple. He'd been a lucky man.

Shifting his hips, he brushed against something that moved with him. Glancing down, he noticed the saddlebags. Damned bags. If it hadn't been for them getting in his way, he might've been able to grab hold of that root and . . .

He mentally chided himself. Then he'd have passed out right there where the Kid could've finished the job. The Kid. Where had he come from? But just as he'd been propelled back into the water, he'd seen that pale, grinning face.

He picked up the bags. Maybe they'd done him good after all.

Santana pointed at the soaked leather. "When I found you, you wouldn't let go. They are important?"

Grant shrugged. "Let's find out."

He opened the flatter side first and spilled out a match tin, knife, and a few other items. But it was the soggy piece of folded paper that arrested his interest. It was the same kind of paper James McCaffery had used for his maps.

He painstakingly unfolded the parchment and breathed with relief when it opened without falling apart. The markings were slightly blurred, and had smudged onto the folded layers, but he could make out the ranch and the creek and even a few of the words in the top corner. The map had definitely belonged to Jacelyn's brother.

He looked more closely at the knife, certain he'd seen the Kid using the bone-handled blade. His brows drew together. If it was the Kid's knife, what was it doing in the saddlebags and why had the bags been hidden by the creek?

He untied the thongs on the other side, and dumped the contents onto the ground next to the first items. He heard the hiss of Santana's indrawn breath. His own breath clogged his throat as his gut contracted.

Scalps. Damnation. Too many scalps. This had to be the work of a demented person—the Kid.

And Grant now suspected that the bags had been hidden in the roots of that big oak. But by whom? Jacelyn was looking for proof which would convict a murderer. And it was near the oak where she'd been confronted by the dandy. The more he thought about it, the more sense it made. Damn.

Did Felipe and the Kid know about the bags? he wondered frantically. No one had tried to retrieve them. And Felipe Barraza hadn't known what Jacelyn was up to or he would've been doing more than trying to steal a kiss.

"What are you doing with those, brother?"

Grant had become so lost in thought he'd almost forgotten Santana's presence. He glanced up to see an expression of pure horror on his half-brother's face as the Apache stared fixedly at the locks of hair.

"This is the proof we've been looking for, Santana. I think these saddlebags belong to the pale-skinned man at the ranch. And I'd bet my next month's pay that he's the one who's been causing you and the other scouts so many problems."

Santana growled low in his throat. "You sure?"

Grant nodded.

"We go now."

"Wait!" Grant started to rise, but sat back down heavily. He tried again, more slowly, and didn't experience the dizziness. "Santana, stop," he commanded, as the Indian swung onto his pony's bare back.

"We go."

"Not we. *I* will go."

Santana scowled.

"You go to the fort and tell the Colonel it's time. I'll go back and watch the gang."

"You cannot." The Apache pointed to Grant's head.

"I don't plan to show myself. But I'm afraid for the woman."

"Ah, the woman," Santana nodded knowingly.

Grant cautiously held the repacked bags up to Santana.

The Apache backed his horse up and gazed at them warily.

"You'll need to give these to the Colonel. Tell him they belong to one of the outlaws at the ranch. The only name I know him by is, 'The Kid'."

Santana's black eyes glittered. "The pale-skinned one."

Grant nodded. He didn't particularly like Santana's vengeful expression, yet he couldn't blame the man. The Kid, and the man giving the orders, had caused a lot of trouble and grief for the Apaches.

Images of Felipe Barraza rose to the forefront of Grant's mind. Felipe was the one Grant wanted, even more than the Kid. Whereas the Kid was mean and crazy and acted on impulse, the dandy planned every action to the smallest detail. To Grant's way of thinking, that made Felipe the more dangerous and devious of the two.

Santana held up two fingers. "We meet two suns."

Grant nodded as the Apache spun his horse and disappeared into the forest. That would mean hours of hard riding for the scout and then the Colonel and his troops, but he didn't doubt Santana's ability or his word.

Mounting the Appaloosa, Grant got his bearings and rode toward the ranch as the sun sank low on the horizon. The more he thought about Jacelyn, the more worried he became. He needed to *see* her, to assure himself she was all right.

If Felipe Barraza had harmed her in any way . . .

Jacelyn's stomach growled. She hadn't had a bite of food all day except for one of Dora's biscuits early that morning. All Felipe had to offer was jerky and tasteless hardtack.

"The least you could have done was have supplies on hand if you knew you were bringing me here," she complained.

Feliped slapped the table, leaving finger prints and raising a cloud of dust. "Enough. All you have done is complain since we arrived. Now I see why the others kept far away from you. Your venomous tongue overshadows your beauty."

She lifted her chin. "Insult me if you must, but I'm hungry and tired and thirsty." If being churlish was all it took to make him sick enough of her to leave her alone, then she wanted to do a bang up job of being unpleasant.

Felipe shot to his feet. "All right. I'll get you water, and you can sleep on the cot." He pointed to the lone bed. "But the food will have to wait until I go into town tomorrow." He tossed her a strip of beef jerky and a hard biscuit, then stalked from the shack.

She sighed and gnawed on the strong-smelling meat until she was able to break off a bite. Hope welled in her chest. Felipe was going into town. He wouldn't dare take his hostage. Perhaps she would finally get her chance to escape.

It was after dark when Grant reached the big oak with the roots clawing out into the creek. Only the debris-strewn bank gave evidence to the violence that had taken place there yesterday afternoon. It was still hard for Grant to believe he'd survived the gunshot, the storm, and the raging flash flood.

Now, if he could just find Jacelyn and see that she was in good shape. Since he hadn't been there to protect her, he was worried about what the Kid and the dandy might have done.

He tethered the Appaloosa on a long rope so it could graze, then made a careful circle of the headquarters. Silent and stealthy, he came within a few feet of Bob when the black man stepped into the trees to relieve himself.

Disappointment weighed heavy in his chest when he came to the cabin and found it dark and empty. A vague unease hastened his steps. As he passed the barn, he saw the Kid and Waddell inside feeding the horses. By the time he reached the well outside the kitchen, he had still seen no sign of Jacelyn or the dandy.

Through the open door, he saw Dora's shadow moving around. He settled down to wait for an opportunity to speak with her.

Sooner than he expected, the door slammed and she walked directly toward him, carrying a bucket. She stopped a few feet away, just staring into the heavens, holding one arm close against her as if it was injured. He crept around the rock and adobe structure and eased up behind the woman.

"Dora." He quickly covered her startled yelp with one palm. He wrapped his other arm around her waist to keep her from bolting back to the house.

"Shhh. It's . . . Jones."

Dora shook her head as hard as she could with him holding her mouth. When he finally released her, fearing he was smothering her, she was shaking uncontrollably. "N-naw. Ya cain't be. J-Jones's dead." Her pale eyes were wide and horrified. "Ya ain't real. Ya be a haunt, or a figment. But ya ain't Jones."

Grant stared at the evidence of the beating Dora had suffered. His fists clenched at his sides. Who had done this? And why? Before he could get any answers, though, he'd have to convince her he was no ghost.

"Yes, ma'am, I am. Look at me."

She closed her eyes and continued to shake her head.

"Dora, stop it. Listen to me. I know things that only Jones could know."

She continued to deny him.

"I know about Shiloh." He glanced upward, thanking the spirits that during one of the few times he and Jacelyn had had a normal conversation, she'd told him about the woman's daughter.

Her eyes flew open. She suddenly stopped shaking, but backed up a step. "You're a ghost. I knew it. How else would ya know—"

"Jacelyn told me," he hissed in exasperation.

"Jacelyn?" she rasped.

"Yes. Your Missy."

She placed one hand over her heart and tentatively touched Grant's arm. "My Gawd. Missy said ya be dead. She saw ya die with 'er own two eyes."

"Where is she, Dora?"

Dora's fingers gripped his forearm. "I cain't believe it. You're really alive."

Grant took her hand and squeezed it—hard. "I have to find her, Dora. Is she in the house?"

Dora shook her head, pulling her arm close against her chest and massaging it.

He gritted his teeth in frustration. "Where, then? Where is she?"

"She ain't here."

He sighed. "I've figured that much out. But she isn't in the cabin, either. So, *where is she?*"

The woman wrung her hands. "Felipe, he took 'er."

His brows slashed together. "Took her?"

Dora nodded. "He feared ya mighta been the law an' that someone'd come snoopin' around."

A sinking sensation tilted his stomach. "Do you know where she is?" He looked toward the light in the bunkhouse. "Does anyone know where he took her?"

"I don't, but Waddy an' the boys plan ta meet up with Felipe an' your woman soon."

"Damn!"

Chapter Twenty-Six

Dora patted Grant's shoulder. "Sorry, Jones. Don't know where he mighta took 'er. An' I don't reckon Waddy does, or he woulda said."

"Damn." Grant spun and walked several yards away, then strode back to Dora. "Can you ask? Just in case? It's important. Her life could be in grave danger."

"Yep. Jest bein' alone with that Felipe be dangerous enough."

He gazed up at the stars and said a silent prayer to the spirits. She had to be safe. She *had* to be.

"I'll see if'n I can git somethin' outta Waddy tonight. But, I ain't promisin' nothin'." She glanced worriedly toward the house.

"I'd appreciate anything you can do. Just don't put yourself in jeopardy." He took hold of her slender shoulders and looked her in the eye until she nodded.

"I love my Waddy, don't get me wrong, but it warn't right fer 'im ta let Felipe jest up an' take Missy off like that. Or fer 'im ta let Felipe beat me. An' I told 'im that, too."

"Felipe will pay," Grant promised her. He took the bucket and filled it, then paced beside the well, rubbing the back of his neck. "Just who is Felipe? I mean, I know he's Waddell's half-brother, but just what does he do for this outfit?"

She shifted her weight from one foot to the other and darted her eyes to the house and back. "All I know is that ever once in a while, he either comes or sends word, an' the boys go off fer days at a time. An' then when Waddy has a bunch o' valuables collected, he gits 'em ta Felipe and Felipe gits lots o' money fer 'em."

Grant nodded. Felipe was their fence. And with his smooth charm and manners, he'd probably ingratiated himself with the politicos around the area and was privy to information about payroll and silver and gold shipments. The gang was better organized than even Grant would have thought.

He stared at Dora's pale features, illuminated in the moonlight, and said, "If it's all right, I'll meet you here tomorrow night a little after sundown. You can let me know then if you've found out anything."

She turned to leave, then hesitated. "Ya be careful a sneakin' 'round here. The boys've been a might nervous since they took ta thinkin' ya might be law." She tilted her head. "Are ya the law?"

He shook his head. "No." He debated being honest and telling her that the Waddell gang would soon be history, but decided he'd trusted her enough for now. He'd soon find out if he'd made a mistake if the gang suddenly started searching the grounds for him.

Dora looked at him long and hard before finally seeming to make up her mind. At last she nodded, took the bucket in her good arm and lugged it to the house.

Grant made another circle of the headquarters before going back to the Appaloosa and retrieving his bedroll. When he finally unrolled it on top of a pile of pine needles he'd scraped together, he fell onto it gratefully.

Worry caused him to shift restlessly. He could probably track Felipe, but he wasn't in the best condition.

What would happen to Jacelyn if he lost the trail and wasted a lot of time? It would be best to play it safe and follow Waddell and the others to her.

Damn but he despised the weakness in his limbs and the throbbing in his temple. He rolled onto his side. Rest was an important factor now. And he was sure Dora would let him know if any plans changed. But he felt useless. Is this what one woman from Virginia had brought him to—playing it safe?

His eyes blinked closed. The last thing he remembered was the Appaloosa softly clearing its nose.

Grant met Dora after sundown the next evening. He'd done little but scout the perimeter and doze all day and felt good. The crease in his head had scabbed over and only ached dully now and then. The bruises on his body were tolerable and he could move without hurting.

Now, if he could just find Jacelyn.

Dora approached the well with caution. She glanced over her shoulder, then whispered, "Jones." Stepping quietly forward, she called again, "Jones. Ya be here, Jones?"

Grant also surveyed the area carefully before showing himself. "I'm here."

She hurried to him. "Thank Gawd. I's afeard somethin' happened to ya."

"I've been around."

She handed him a towel-wrapped package.

He sniffed bread and beef, and grinned. "Thanks." He was pleased to see her looking a little better.

"Pshaw, ain't nothin'. Figured ya'd be a might hungry by now."

"You figured right." He unwrapped the food and immediately began to eat.

Looking over her shoulder again, she told him, "I

didn't find out much. Waddy'n the boys be leavin' in the mornin', but he didn't say nothin' 'bout where Missy be."

"Hell, he probably doesn't know," Grant said more to himself than to Dora. "Did he say where they're goin' tomorrow?" He watched Dora's expression close. "Nevermind. You've done enough. And I thank you."

She shrugged. A look of resignation settled over her features. "Don't know that it'll make any difference, but wherever they be goin', Felipe set it up."

Grant cocked his brow. "Felipe, huh? Dora, you're a sweetheart." He leaned over and gave her a quick peck on the cheek.

"Aw, pshaw." She blushed and wiped at the spot his lips had touched.

He whispered, "I'll come back and check on you after all this is over."

She sniffed and nodded and walked dejectedly to the house.

Grant watched her go and sympathized. She knew something was about to happen to change her life. She knew. And he felt truly sorry for the pain and uncertainty facing the woman in the days ahead.

Jacelyn had thought being locked in the cabin at the ranch was bad, but when Felipe rode out that morning, he'd gagged her and tied her to a chair. Hours later, she was tired and miserable and still tied and gagged. She was incredibly thirsty. Her arms felt like they were frozen in their sockets. Her wrists were chafed and bleeding. Her fingers were numb. Her shoulders ached and burned. And her bottom was so sore she thought she'd never sit again.

She dropped her chin to her chest. All day long, with nothing to do but look at the dirty insides of the horrid little shack, she'd found herself thinking of Grant Jones. The tingling of tears still prickled her cheeks. For some reason, she couldn't think of him in terms of being dead. Over and over, she reprimanded herself, forcing herself to visualize his body falling back into the raging current and sinking from sight.

But it was the look on his face when he'd last glanced at her, like he was apologizing for failing, that caused her to blink rapidly and take deep breaths. As he was dying, he'd thought of her. It was a humbling notion.

The shack grew dark. Outside, she heard scurrying noises and the bark of a coyote. She shivered and her stomach growled its displeasure at being neglected for so long. How she'd love one of Dora's biscuits about now. She swallowed and instantly realized it was a mistake. That coyote might even taste pretty good.

She suddenly cocked her head. The clip-clop of hooves stopped just outside the door. She sucked in her breath and glued her eyes to the door. She didn't know what would be worse, to see Felipe when the door opened, or someone else.

Just then the door slammed back against the wall and bounced, swinging back to crash into the man in the doorway. He cursed and stomped inside. Jacelyn grimaced at the sight of Felipe. His usual impeccable clothes were dusty. His white shirt was unbuttoned and the tail hung out beneath the short, black jacket.

He stumbled into the room, unsteadily set a half-empty bottle on the table and belched. She wrinkled her nose at the smell of stale liquor.

"Hic. S'nice ta see you-u-u waited up, my . . . hic . . . dear."

Her eyes narrowed. "You're drunk," she choked around the gag.

"Hic. Sho I amm-m-m."

She shrank back when he came closer, and silently cursed at being trapped and helpless. A shudder rippled down her spine when he grabbed her chin and made her look him in the eyes.

"You knew, didn't you-u-u?" He squeezed her jaw.

Fear constricted her throat. "Kn-knew what?" she mumbled, her lips and tongue sticking to the disgusting cloth.

He cursed, yanked the gag from her mouth, then shoved, sending her and the chair toppling over backward. With excruciating pain, her hands and arms hit the floor, bearing the weight of her body and the chair. In agony, she groaned. Every muscle and tendon felt stretched and torn.

With a maniacal laugh, Felipe hovered above her with a knife in his hand. She screamed and tried to scoot the chair on the warped board floor.

The blade flashed before her eyes and she lowered her lids, waiting for the knife to plunge into her flesh. Instead, she heard a snapping sound and the rope binding her arms and wrists loosened. But when she tried to move, she couldn't. Her arms felt like lead weights.

Roughly, he lifted her to her feet. She hissed at the burning sensation as blood rushed to her fingertips.

"You bitch," he shouted, then staggered. "There will-l-l be no ransom." He stepped forward, backing her to the wall. "You had to . . . hic . . . know we were digging a dry well. Hic."

"I—"

His hat fell back off his head and the string dug into his neck. He grabbed her arm and threw her toward the bed. She tripped and landed on her side. He followed quickly, pressing her down into the smelly, lumpy straw mattress.

"If I can't get what you're worth . . . in cash, hic . . .

I'll get it this way." He wound his fingers in the front of her dress. The light material ripped easily.

She struggled, but her aching hands and arms were slow to respond to her brain's commands. He pinned her beneath him and pawed at her camisole-covered breasts, cursing again when his increasingly clumsy efforts couldn't immediately rend the silk.

He slobbered over her neck and up her jaw even as she twisted her head and did her best to throw him off. She grasped his wrist as he worked her skirt up her leg, but her fingers couldn't hold the grip for long.

"No . . ." She bucked her hips, trying to dislodge his heavy body.

He chuckled and whispered the obscene things he would do to her body.

Shuddering, she curved her fingers into claws and raked them down his back as memories of Eloy flooded her terrorized mind.

He growled and slapped her hard, then corralled her wrists in one of his hands. She yelled out when his fingers abraded her rope-burned flesh.

"Oh, God . . ." She closed her eyes, also closing her mind to what was about to happen. "Grant. Grant I need you," she pleaded.

She took several deep breaths, steeling herself. Her heart thundered in her ears. But his assault slackened. His hand still clutched her skirt, but had stopped moving up her thigh. His fingers held her wrists, but not as tightly. She lay trapped beneath him, but his suggestive hip movements ceased. His breath was steady and deep. Then he snored.

She stared through a space between the boards on the roof. "Thank you," she offered through parched lips.

* * *

The sun had been up for quite a while to Jacelyn's estimation before Felipe snorted and rolled off her. She heaved a sigh of relief. All night she'd tried to slide out from under him, but he'd had just enough of a hold on her to make escape impossible. Things were different now. And she planned to take advantage of this chance.

Gripping the torn bodice of her dress in one hand, she carefully eased her skirt from beneath his leg. Inch by inch she scooted toward the foot of the bed, trying to move without causing the rope meshing holding up the mattress to creak, or jiggling Felipe hard enough to awaken him.

At last her feet touched the floor. She looked toward the door, anticipating freedom. Excitement sang through her veins.

Suddenly, fingers twisted in her hair. She reached back and grabbed the tresses from his grasp, but found her wrists captured. He jerked her back onto the bed. Her scalp burned and tears of pain blurred her vision. He was on top of her thrusting his tongue between her lips. She gagged as his foul breath filled her nostrils.

All at once he rolled to his feet, leaving her sprawled atop the bed. She started to rise, but he snatched pieces of rope from the overturned chair and shoved her down again. Before she knew what was happening, he'd gripped her wrists and secured her hands above her head to a bedpost with the hard, scratchy rope. She gasped as the rough fibers bit into her scabbed wrists.

He easily grabbed her feet when she kicked out at his hands. Once she was helpless, he stood over her, grinning.

The harder she struggled, the wider he smiled. "Ah, pretty señorita, it is a shame I do not have the time to tame you this morning. But when I return . . ." He leered at her as a tear trickled down her cheek and into the thick mass of hair at her temple. "I promise not to

404

leave you again for a long, long time. Felipe will make you a woman, eh?"

She gritted her teeth. If he was truly leaving, she didn't want to say anything that would cause him to change his mind.

"I bought supplies . . ." He scratched his chin. "But I must have left them in town."

"T-town?" she stammered, quickly quelling the upheaval of hope that swelled in her chest.

"Yes. I will take you to Tombstone soon." He eyed her body appreciatively. "The men there will like you, and you will earn much money for Felipe. Mucho dinero." He rubbed his hands together.

Horror narrowed her eyes. A chill of despair swept over her.

Without pausing to tuck in his shirt or smooth his unruly hair, he strode to the door. Hesitating, he glanced over his shoulder at her helpless position. "Save your energy, señorita."

The door closed on his eerie chuckle and Jacelyn shuddered. The albino. Felipe. Insanity ran rampant in the family.

A bar clattered into place outside the door and she struggled in frustrated despair. Somehow, she had to free her hands and feet. She had to get out of here before he returned. Somehow.

At the same time Felipe Barraza left the shack, Grant Ward followed the Waddell gang west from the ranch toward the Dragoon Mountains. He hoped Santana found the message he'd left in the big oak and that the scout and the Colonel wouldn't be far behind.

By mid-afternoon, and after miles of hard riding, the gang and Grant crossed the road between Tombstone and Willcox and wound into the nearby foothills. Grant hung back, riding well behind the gang, even though they seldom sent anyone to watch their back trail.

He smelled the smoke from their campfire long before he saw the orange glow of flames. Riding closer, he dismounted, tethered the Appaloosa and slipped up through the mesquite and chapparal to settle in on the opposite side of the camp from the horses.

Waddell, the Kid, and Bob set up a camp which, it appeared, they planned to use for several days. Though he knew it was important to know where the gang was and what they were doing, Grant had the frustrated feeling that he was wasting time—time he didn't have to spare.

About an hour after the men cleaned up their supper mess, while they lounged around the fire, Grant went back to the Appaloosa for his canteen and the last biscuit and slice of beef he'd saved from the food Dora had given him. To supplement his meal, he added a few piñon nuts and wild onions and an apple he'd stolen from the orchard.

Moving silently back to his spot near the camp with his saddle blanket under his arm to keep off the before dawn chill, he stopped abruptly at the sound of approaching hoofbeats.

He sank down and wriggled on his elbows and knees to the site he'd selected from which to view the camp. His gut knotted when he saw the dandy, Felipe Barraza, dismounting near the fire. Hope and fear nearly drove him to his feet, but he remained concealed. All he saw was the dandy. No Jacelyn.

He left the blanket in his spot and crept beneath a wide, low-limbed oak, placing himself close enough to hear the conversation.

" 'Bout time ya showed up," Waddell exclaimed.

"Yeah, we thought you might have decided to make off with the heiress and forget about us no accounts."

Felipe snarled at the Kid. "I'd love to forget *you,* cousin. But, unfortunately, you continue to make that impossible each time you open your mouth."

Bob poured another cup of coffee and blew on the tin rim before taking a drink.

"Where's the gal? Ya didn't lose 'er, did ya?"

Felipe strode casually to the fire. "She is . . . safe."

Grant wished he could believe the slimy bastard, but he had a gut instinct that no one connected with Felipe Barraza would ever be safe. Hell, what he wouldn't give to be able to charge into that camp, jerk the dandy up, and beat him until he confessed to what he'd done with Jacelyn. But, instead, he took a deep breath. There was too much else at stake.

"Damned well better be." Waddell poked the fire with a stick, and yanked his hand back when a spark leapt out at him.

Something wasn't right, Grant thought, as he studied the dandy. Felipe's eyes never rested long anywhere and his body looked taut as a coiled spring, which also caused Grant to tense. His instinct told him Jacelyn was the reason.

The Kid spoke up smugly, "Where's all the men you were going to bring to help us with this job?"

Felipe paced in front of the flames. "I decided we didn't need more men. It would only mean less money for each of us."

Grant watched the other three outlaws look at each other and then back to the dandy. It was plain they weren't so damned sure. Whatever the job was, it must be dangerous.

"Ya find out yet how much them Mex's is haulin'? An' about when they be comin'?"

Felipe walked over and unsaddled his horse, then threw the reins to a startled Bob, who finally rose and led the animal over to tie it with the other horses.

As the dandy prepared his bedroll, he glanced at each of the gang members. "Don't worry about the details. I will tell you in plenty of time what you need to know."

The Kid scowled.

Waddell cursed, but stretched out near the warmth of the fire.

Bob slouched back to his silent watch.

Grant worried, wondering how close Santana and the Colonel were. And he thought of Jacelyn. How was she faring through all this?

Damn, Felipe. What had he done with her?

The light inside the shack faded. And with the loss of sunlight a chill settled on Jacelyn's sweat-soaked clothes. Her throat hurt when she swallowed. And even though the canteen was practically empty, just seeing it beside the saddlebags was a form of torture.

Her stomach gurgled and growled and gnawed at her backbone. She was thirsty, starved, helpless, and desperately in need of relieving herself.

Her arm sockets ached from her hands being tied above her head. Her legs were numb and cramped. She rolled her hips and managed to move her right foot. When she did, she felt a lessening of pressure on the leather moccasin protecting her ankle.

There was suddenly enough leeway to bend her knee slightly, easing the strain on her lower back. Encouraged, she tried to move her other foot . . . and succeeded. She choked out a chuckle, lifting one leg and then the other, much like a small child exuberant over a first step.

Somehow, during her day-long struggles, the rope had loosened. When she turned her foot just right, she pulled free of it completely. She sighed and closed her eyes. It felt wonderful to be able to move her lower extremities. If only she could free her hands.

She tried again and again. Her luck didn't hold.

Her energy gave out and she stopped struggling. She tried to think, but her lids kept drooping. Surely there was something else she could do. She was so close to being free. So close . . .

Grant yawned as he saddled the Appaloosa. Waddell and Felipe and the gang had already saddled up and ridden into a sandy arroyo winding back toward the road. He wanted them to have a good lead, so was in no hurry.

Mounting, he paralleled the arroyo, staying just the other side of a low ridge. Every once in a while he heard the click of horseshoes hitting stone and pulled the Appaloosa to a slower gait.

He wound down and through a dense cover of chapparal. A whippoorwill called, but he was so absorbed in watching the ground ahead—and worrying about Jacelyn, wondering where she was, what she was doing, if she was still alive—that he didn't react until Santana materialized from a small mound of sand.

The Appaloosa shied. Grant cursed and pulled the animal under control.

Santana shook his head. "My brother has been too long with the white eyes." He imitated taking aim with a bow. "Had I not been a 'friendly' foe—"

"I know." Grant waved his hand. "I know. I was busy."

"Thinking about the woman."

Grant scowled, but couldn't dispute the accusation. "Only one man knows where she is, and he's with the gang. I can't let him get away."

409

The Apache arched a black brow. "Lately, you lose herd of elk, let alone one man."

Sighing, Grant nudged his horse onto the ridge. All he could see of the gang was the crown of Waddell's hat. "Let's go. I don't want them to get too far ahead." He gritted his teeth at Santana's grinning countenance. Where was the "stoic" Indian when you wanted him?

After Santana mounted his pony and caught up, Grant asked, "Where's the Colonel?"

The Apache gestured to the southwest. "Maybe two miles."

"Good." Grant saw the road ahead and reined his horse behind a crumbling wall of boulders to see which direction the gang took.

"Evan have any idea what the outlaws might be after?"

Santana shrugged. Grant knew the feeling. There were too many temptations and opportunities for the lawless elements in this territory to narrow the choice down to one. He guessed they'd all just have to wait and see what happened next.

When the gang stopped in a stand of oak and seemed to be settling in, he turned to the Apache. "Bring the Colonel and his troop in closer." Suddenly he remembered something Waddell had said last night. "Watch for a Mexican wagon train."

The Indian nodded and regarded Grant somberly. "Watch your back til I return."

Grant's brows slashed together. "You don't need—" But the Apache was gone. Irritated that his lack of concentration caused Santana to doubt his abilities, Grant determined then and there that as soon as this fiasco was over, and the woman left for her home in the East, he would work on his skills until Santana, or anyone else, would never have reason to question his ability.

In the meantime, he pictured Evan and the Cavalry troop moving in, and imagined Jacelyn's delight to think they were coming to her rescue.

Another thought crossed his mind. What would she think when she found out the truth? That he was a member of the United States Cavalry. That his last name was Ward, not Jones.

After the last fit she'd thrown when she'd accused him of lying to her, what would she do when she found out he'd left out several more details? She would hate him all the more. And his heart ached at that notion.

He rubbed at the back of his neck and spat a stream of curses at the muddle of circumstances plaguing them from the first moment they met. Although he knew it was hopeless, he couldn't help but wish once they returned to the fort—if they returned—that he'd have the opportunity to set things straight.

An even crazier thought occurred to him. What if she felt the same as he? What if—deep down—she loved him? What if he were able to persuade her to stay, to see if they could make a life together?

All at once, his face turned to chiseled stone. What in the Great Spirit's name was he thinking? He'd never, ever, considered settling down and making a life with a woman. And to choose a woman like Jacelyn McCaffery? He was as crazy as the Kid.

A gunshot rang out. His last thought dropped like a deer hit in the heart. He climbed to the top of the boulder and peered down on a line of Mexican wagons and mule-driven carts. He knew immediately that the train carried silver and other valuables the Mexicans smuggled across the border for trading. Somehow, Felipe had gotten wind of their coming.

"Damn," he cursed as he slid down the rock and onto

the Appaloosa. He just hoped the dandy didn't get killed before telling him what he'd done with Jacelyn.

With a spray of dust and gravel, Grant spurred the horse down a slope toward the rapid staccato of gunfire.

Chapter Twenty-Seven

Grant charged along the outskirts of the ambush. The gang members, scattered along both sides of the road, fired on the ten or so Mexicans armed with a few good rifles and pistols. The acrid smell of gun powder filled his nostrils. The panic of whinnying horses and startled cries of pain echoed in his ears.

A bugle call preceded the sound of galloping hooves. Curses erupted from the outlaws and their victims. The outlaws couldn't believe they'd been foiled yet again, and the Mexican smugglers didn't want their supplies confiscated.

A movement behind a thick-branched cholla cactus caught Grant's eye. Dick Waddell stood and turned toward the horses. He'd no sooner started moving than a bullet took him square between the shoulder blades. He pitched forward into a mormon tea bush.

In front of him, Grant heard the Kid and Bob calling to each other just as the Colonel and his troop rounded the bend into the range of fire. A horse whinnied to Grant's left. He spun the Appaloosa just in time to see Felipe Barraza swing into the saddle and spur his horse into a full gallop.

Indecision warred with Grant as he watched Felipe riding away. He quickly scanned the road and saw the

Cavalry troop surrounding the Mexican caravan. The Colonel and two soldiers had their guns leveled on Bob, who stood quietly with his hands raised. Timmy B. was running fast behind the frantic albino.

Knowing that everything was under control there, Grant urged the Appaloosa after Felipe. He thought fast. Would it be best to catch up to the dandy and force him into telling where he'd hidden Jacelyn, or just bide his time and trail Felipe, hoping the outlaw would lead him to her?

Grant chose to track the snake, afraid that if he caught up to the man, he'd beat him senseless—or worse—before he got the information he needed.

Once, the hairs on the back of Grant's neck stood on end as Felipe straightened in the saddle and reined in his mount. Instantly, Grant turned the Appaloosa and halted it behind a thick stand of manzanita. Felipe shifted and looked searchingly back over his shoulder. When the dandy faced forward again and spurred his horse on, Grant was sure the outlaw hadn't seen him.

Suddenly, Felipe pulled his horse down to a slow lope, much to Grant's relief. With the long ride after Waddell and no sleep the night before, his head felt as light as a feather floating on the breeze.

Grant began to feel better after the pace eased, and settled into the saddle and smooth gait of the horse. No matter how far, or how hard, he was determined to trail the dandy.

Jacelyn had better be unharmed, or Felipe Barraza would suffer—in ways only the Apache knew to make a man suffer.

Jacelyn blinked her eyes open, saw that it was daylight and blinked them closed again. What was the use of waking? She would only feel the pain, the thirst, the hunger, the despair.

Her eyes burned and scratched as if cactus thorns had blown into them. Her lips were cracked and sore. Every inch of her throat burned. Her angry tears from yesterday had dried. Now she knew she couldn't even shed one. Water was her greatest need.

But escape was her greatest desire. She found herself rethinking her escape attempts at the ranch, about how foolish she'd been and the understanding way Grant had reacted—as if he was almost sorry she hadn't made it.

Outlaw, scout, whatever; deep down he was a good man. Even a man on the wrong side of the law could have good qualities.

In the West, there were no absolutes. A person *adjusted* to do what had to be done to protect themselves or their loved ones. They *survived*.

But Grant hadn't survived. And if it weren't for her, he might still be alive.

She shook her head, unable to think about being the cause of his death. She moved her left calf up and down her right shin trying to scratch an itch. In doing so, she felt, and suddenly remembered, the knife. The one she'd stolen, lost inside the cabin at the ranch, then finally found and hidden inside her moccasin.

Suddenly, her eyes shot open, scratchy or not. A knife. She had a knife at her disposal. All she had to do was find a way to get it from the moccasin into her hands, then cut the ropes with her hands still tied together. That wasn't asking for much.

Sweat popped out on her forehead and upper lip when she saw a glimmer of hope. The tops of her moccasins were folded halfway down her calves. The knife hilt was just barely hidden. She could do it. Couldn't she?

Contracting her stomach muscles, she pulled her

knees up to her chest and raised her legs. No, that wouldn't put the knife anywhere close enough to reach.

She lowered her legs and tried again. This time, curving the small of her back. Almost. The third try brought her knees almost to her head. Grunting, she gasped for breath as her skirt fell around her head, partially covering her face. She couldn't see and could hardly breathe, but her feet were close to her hands. Levering her body until she felt like she was folded in half, her fingers inched inside the top of her moccasin.

But her hands were so numb she could barely feel the handle, let alone grip it. And if she dropped it . . . It was either try, or steel herself to being Felipe's slave or . . . whore . . . forever—or until he tired of her, as he so quaintly put it.

Determination surged through her body where blood couldn't. She took hold of the knife and drew it from the moccasin. Her lower body uncurled, taking the pressure from her chest so she could breathe. She was still blinded, however, as there was nothing she could do about the skirt.

Her heart thrummed in her fingertips as she clutched the knife in a death grip. Now, unable to see, with her hands above her head, she had to twist the hilt so the blade faced the ropes. Fear lent strength to her hands. Desperation guided the blade. Her wrists throbbed from the added bite and pressure as she turned her hands, trying to find a way to cut the rope.

Finally she worked the handle into her right hand and curved the fingers of her left around it to add support. Gulping down a cry of pain as the rough fibers tore into her flesh, she slowly and awkwardly sawed the blade across the rope just above her wrists.

At first, she wasn't sure she was using the sharp edge, until it slipped off the rope and she heard it slice into the straw mat. She sighed in relief that it hadn't been her arm.

Again she lifted the knife. Again she worked the blade until she felt her own blood trickling down her hand. The process was agonizingly slow. She was about to give up when one cord of the braided rope finally snapped.

Her fingers had little more feeling than stubs of hard wood, but she managed to keep them wrapped around the handle. Another cord snapped. Her hands sagged. It felt wonderful, but would she be able to keep the rope taut enough to move the blade across it?

She scooted down, drawing her wrists tight, forcing the cruel rope into her open wounds, until she bit into her lower lip to keep from crying out. She cursed instead, wondering why she tried to be brave. There was no one to hear her rant and rave.

The last piece of cord surrendered strand by strand but, though it was progress, she could hardly bear any more pressure on her wrists. Her fingers were contorted so badly that they'd ceased to ache, ceased to follow simple commands.

Tears pooled at her temples. Defeat threatened. But then the image of Grant falling backward into the water flashed before her eyes. Her chin lifted until the tendons in her neck stood out. For James. For Grant. For herself. She had to do this. Someone had to be told about the Waddell gang and about the grisly find she'd made in the albino's saddlebags.

She shoved the knife hard. She held her arms steady though her muscles trembled like a horse that had been ridden too long and too hard. The last thread popped. Her hands fell to the mattress. The knife clattered to the floor. Her breath came in rapid gulps, as if she'd been running for miles and miles.

A cry finally escaped her lips as she brought her arms

to her sides. Burning sensation flowed into her fingers. After several minutes, she roused to a sitting position, knowing she needed to find something to stop her wrists from bleeding.

Just to have something of Grant's, she'd kept his bandana. Right now it was folded in her pocket. Grant. How many times had he held a bandana to a cut or to wipe the dust from her face? She cringed as she tore it, but she needed two pieces of cloth.

Wrapping her wrists, she stood and walked unsteadily over to the door. She pushed. It wouldn't budge. She was still trapped. Her brows arched. Trapped. But not helpless. At least now she would have the element of surprise on her side when the lizard returned.

She swallowed, winced at the pain and looked down to see her bodice hanging in shreds. The first order of business was to find out how much water was left in the canteen. Then she'd change into the pants and shirt Dora had sent. Then she'd find something to eat. She was famished and weakened from hunger and thirst as much as from her ordeal.

She snatched the canteen, gleeful at the sloshing sound of water, yet profoundly disappointed at the empty feel of the container. Unplugging the opening, she hesitated a brief second, closed her eyes, and brought the canteen to her lips. Life-giving liquid seared her throat. One swallow. Two. She choked and clutched her neck. Sighing with regret, she gulped the last droplets. She'd consumed just enough to crave much, much more.

Tossing the empty canteen aside, she fumbled with the thongs on the flap of the bag, but finally got it open. It was surprising how excited she felt to be putting on trousers again. Stripping off the torn dress and petticoats, she shook out the shirt and yelped when something hard fell on her foot.

After buttoning the shirt and trousers, she bent to see what could be so small, yet heavy enough to break a toe. Her hand hesitated over a small gun. She'd seen a picture in *Harper's* and believed they'd labeled it a hide-away gun, or a derringer.

Very carefully, she picked it up. Elation welled in her chest. Here, in her inexperienced hand, lay her means of escape. One bullet. One chance. She would make it count.

Her stomach grumbled as she laid the gun on the table. With shaking hands, she opened the other side of the bags and literally fell into the creaking chair when she pulled out a towel wrapped around two biscuits and two thick slabs of smoked ham. Bless Dora.

She ate so quickly that, for a moment, she was afraid she'd throw it all back up. And her throat was so dry she didn't think she could swallow the last of the biscuit.

She knew the only other liquid, Felipe's whiskey, sat opened on the other side of the table. No basin of water. No second canteen. Nothing. She reached over and picked up the bottle, wrinkling her nose at the smell. But it couldn't stop her from taking a healthy swallow. After all, it was liquid. Men loved the stuff.

Her throat burned. Her eyes watered. She gasped and coughed as the whiskey scraped the hide from her insides all the way to her belly. Quickly, she ate the last two bites of food. They promptly stuck in her throat and she had to take another drink.

But this time she sipped and it went down much easier. She even liked the warm feeling tingling through her body.

Once she had satisfied her initial hunger and thirst, however, she had one remaining need. She searched the small interior, knowing there was no privy. To take her mind from that certainty, she retrieved the small, but valuable, knife and replaced the weapon in its hidden slot in her moccasin. Finally, feeling very much like one of the Apache scouts she'd seen at the fort, she tucked her trouser legs inside the moccasins.

Then she walked over and gingerly picked up the little gun, turning it over in her hand, testing to see if it fit the palm of her hand, wondering if when it came down to it, she'd be able to shoot Felipe Barraza.

Grant had admitted that he would have been able to kill the Kid. But Grant was . . . Grant. She'd never held a gun, let alone pointed one at a man. Yet when Felipe had been about to force himself on her, she'd had murder in her heart. Now, she held the means in her hand.

Moving the chair around to face the door, she sat down. Intuition told her that *soon* she would find out just what she was capable of doing to protect herself.

Felipe Barraza breathlessly rode his horse into the arroyo and up to the tiny mine shack. He dismounted without a backward glance at the sorrel, and without taking the time to tether it.

Stumbling up the step, he slid the bar from the door, flung it open and rushed inside. He stopped dead in his tracks. The woman, dressed once again in her men's clothing, stood aiming a small gun directly at his chest.

Jacelyn tried to inhale several deep breaths inconspicuously to calm her shaky nerves. The moment had come, but she hadn't planned on the wild racing of her heart or the weakness setting her knees atremble.

"Ah, señorita, you do not wish to shoot Felipe." He moved forward cautiously. "Give me the gun. Now."

She backed up. "No. I want you to move away from the door. Now."

"But I cannot. It is dangerous for a woman alone. Es-

420

pecially a beautiful woman." He moved more purposely when he saw the indecision in her eyes.

Jacelyn was frightened out of her wits. She momentarily held the upper hand, but he'd just called her bluff. He wasn't going to let her go. She had to make up her mind either to shoot or let him have his way with her. It was that simple a choice.

Felipe moved suddenly. His left hand struck Jacelyn's wrist as she pulled the trigger. The bullet lodged harmlessly in the wall as the gun fell to the floor.

"You should not have done that. Now Felipe will have to teach you a lesson."

She darted to the left in an effort to dash past him to the door.

He lunged after her. His right arm circled her waist, but she spun out of his grasp. In desperation, he threw himself at her legs, tackling and throwing her to the floor.

She grunted as air whooshed from her lungs, and tried to kick out as he clawed at her trousers, pulling her beneath him for a better hold.

A dark shadow suddenly filled the doorway.

Jacelyn screamed and kicked at Felipe's chest.

Felipe looked up and froze. Jacelyn continued to kick and squirm until she managed to free herself from the dreadful beast. Only then did she look toward the door.

Her mouth fell open. Her thundering heart reverberated in her ears. It couldn't be ... Grant was dead. She'd seen him drown with her own eyes.

Afraid that he'd arrived too late, Grant's chest heaved as he drank in the sight of Jacelyn crouched like a cornered lioness prepared to fight for her life.

Felipe took advantage of Grant's distraction to dive into his legs, knocking him into the door. Grant reached out his free hand to catch himself and found his gun

421

hand locked in Felipe's grasp as the outlaw rose from the floor.

Growling deep in his throat, Grant regained his balance and struggled for control of his pistol.

Felipe curled his upper lip. "The woman is mine, halfbreed."

"You're not man enough to take her," Grant rasped.

The outlaw hooked a leg behind Grant's knees, startling him off balance and leaving him nothing to grab onto. He tumbled to the floor, striking his left temple on the chair, reopening his wound. He felt the sticky warmth of blood. Felipe's boot flew up, and Grant threw up his hands just in time to catch the outlaw's foot, intended to kick him in the face.

The pointed toe of the dandy's boot caught Grant in the wrist, sending his gun clattering beneath the bed.

Jacelyn watched blood flow menacingly from the gash in Grant's head. Horrified at Felipe's brutal attack, she rushed up behind the outlaw, pounding on his back and shoulders, as he pinned Grant down.

Felipe swung his elbow, catching Jacelyn square on the nose. She yelped and fell back. Grant heard Jacelyn's squeal and found the strength to swing his fist at Felipe's unprotected jaw. He felt bone give and heard a loud crack. He surged to his feet, hitting Felipe with a punch to the belly. But the loss of blood and the blow to his head sapped him of energy.

Staggering, Felipe grabbed hold of the back of the chair, then swung it as Grant stepped forward. Seeing the chair coming, Grant warded off the blow with his forearm. The outlaw drew the chair back and swung it again, abruptly letting go of the wood as it flew into Grant's rib cage. The momentum carried Grant to the floor.

Jacelyn knew she had to do something fast. Even she could tell Grant's strength ebbed with each pulse of fresh blood. She crawled to her knees just as Felipe went for his gun. Her heart stopped. Grant's gun was under the bed. She was too far away to get to Felipe in time to stop him.

The knife. Quickly, she reached into the top of her moccasin and drew it out. "Grant. Here." She slid the knife across the floor, gulping down her terror.

Grant's eyes followed the progress of the weapon. He held his breath when it bounced over a warped board and almost clattered to a stop. At last he reached out and wrapped his fingers around the hilt just as Felipe's gun cleared its holster. With the agility of years of practice, he threw the knife, burying the blade deep in the outlaw's breast.

Grant released his breath, watching Felipe's eyes widen with shock. The dandy's finger squeezed the trigger. A bullet plowed into the floor near Grant's thigh. Grant rolled to the side when Felipe raised the pistol barrel to fire again, but the outlaw's eyes rolled back in his head and he toppled to the floor like a felled tree.

Jacelyn sighed her thanks to the heavens and immediately raced to Grant's side. Untying the bandana from around his neck, she wadded it into a pad and held it to his temple to staunch the flow of blood. At the same time, she ran her free hand over his face and chest, still not quite believing he was real.

Grant reveled in her touch for a moment before reaching up to lightly brush the tip of her bruised nose. Horrendous guilt consumed him.

The thoughts he'd entertained about possibly keeping her out here with him were now out of the question. How could he swear to protect her when he couldn't even protect himself?

"Grant, are you all right? Please, darling, look at me." Jacelyn tried to hold back her joy, but the tears fell anyway.

When he finally looked up, she stared into those pale blue eyes, choked on a sob, and lifted his head into her lap. "T-thank the Lord. I still can't believe it. I thought you were dead."

Grant cupped her cheek in his palm. He sighed and assured her, "I'm fine."

"You aren't either fine. Just look at your head." She clicked her tongue and lifted the pad to see if the bleeding had lessened. It had. Then she tore a piece of material from her shirt tail and wiped the blood from his cheek and neck.

Grant saw the piece of bandana wrapped around her wrist and caught her hand. "What happened?"

She blushed. "H-he . . . Felipe . . . bound me to the bed when he left yesterday . . . or whenever . . . it seems so long . . ." She saw his worried expression and hurried to explain. "The rope burned my wrists when I freed myself."

He intently studied her eyes and every dear feature on her face, then turned his head to scowl at Felipe's still form. "You're a brave woman, Jacelyn McCaffery." He was very proud of her. He knew of few Western women who could've held up under the circumstances she'd survived over and over again. It almost made him think . . .

Hoofbeats pounded the ground outside the shack. Bridles jingled. Horses snorted. Sabers clattered. Grant regretfully pushed himself out of Jacelyn's soft lap and rose unassisted as a soldier called out, "Troop . . . Halt. Troop . . . Dismount."

Grant met Evan Alexander in the doorway. "Damn, it's about time. This lady's been waiting a lifetime for the Cavalry to charge to her rescue. You're late."

Colonel Alexander stared at Grant's head and the fresh blood congealed on the gash above his ear. "Yes, I see that." He glanced past Grant to the still body and then to the young lady standing in the middle of the room looking wide-eyed and gape-mouthed at his Chief of Scouts. "Good day, Miss McCaffery. I'm pleased to see—"

"You *do* know him." She pointed at Grant.

"Why, of course—"

She mentally kicked herself. Of course they knew each other. She knew that. Interrupting the Colonel, she amended, "I mean . . . He does work for you."

Evan looked worriedly at Grant, who suddenly seemed unable to meet his eyes. "Yes, Grant Ward is—"

"Grant . . . who?" She felt her face flush. Her stomach roiled. Oh, Lord, had Felipe and Waddell been right? Had she given Grant her trust when they made their pact to find James's killer, only to have him withhold his? There had been many times when he could have admitted the truth. But . . . he hadn't.

She gasped. Of course, he'd been right. She'd given away the secret of his being half Apache. She'd very nearly gotten him killed. But it hurt to think, after all they'd shared, he'd still kept the truth from her.

Evan felt it his duty to brag on his best Chief of Scouts. "I thought you'd been introduced at the fort, but . . ." He chuckled. "I guess we never got that far that afternoon, did we?"

She sadly shook her head.

The Colonel, oblivious to the undercurrents slicing through the small room, slapped Grant's shoulder. "Good work, boy." He motioned two soldiers inside to remove Felipe's body. "Cleaning up the Waddell gang will put an end to most of the accusations against your scouts in particular, and the Apache people, in general. At least in this area of Arizona Territory."

Grant nodded.

"Say, you haven't seen your boys, Santana and Timmy B., in the last few hours, have you?"

"Ahem, no I haven't." Grant kept glancing to Jacelyn, who met his eyes only briefly before gazing longingly out the door. Grant sighed. He felt a little trapped himself at the moment. He turned to the Colonel, who regarded him with puzzlement. "Ah, why?"

Evan scratched his chin. "Last time I saw them, they were after that pale outlaw. We corralled all of them but that one, and I was curious to know if they finally caught up with him."

Grant glanced at Loco Nick, one of his scouts. No expression. But Grant didn't need confirmation. Santana's continued absence was proof enough. "I, ah, doubt we'll have to worry about the albino, one way or the other."

The Colonel grinned. "I suppose you're right. With those two hot on my heels, I think I'd be plumb out of the territory by now."

Grant arched his brow. "Uh huh."

"Well, my dear," Evan smiled and crooked his elbow toward Jacelyn. "How does a nice hot meal, a bath, and a clean bed sound?"

Jacelyn swallowed, darted a glance toward Grant's suddenly implacable features and tentatively placed her hand on the Colonel's arm. "It sounds ... heavenly. Thank you."

Evan patted her fingers and looked over his shoulder. "We need to get that gash taken care of, son."

Grant hung back. "I will, soon's I get to the fort. But first ... There's something I've got to do."

Standing on the tottery excuse of a porch, Jacelyn looked out over the sea of soldiers and spotted Bob. And then she spied Felipe's and Waddell's bodies draped across their saddles.

She shuddered and squeezed the Colonel's arm. "Waddell?"

Grant heard her question, saw that she was looking directly at him, and nodded.

"You're going to the ranch, aren't you?"

He nodded again.

"Poor Dora." She twisted her hands. "C-can I go with you?" She met his eyes, then glanced away.

Drat it, she wanted nothing more than to run to him and throw her arms around him; to tell him how glad she was that he hadn't been killed; to explain that she'd come to terms with her feelings and that she loved him, even thinking he was an outlaw. And she did love him. More than ever. But if he didn't trust her with something as basic as his true last name, he certainly couldn't return her feelings.

Grant watched the emotions flickering through her eyes. Compassion. Sorrow. And something else he couldn't quite read.

"Ah, no, I think you'd be better off with the Colonel and the troop."

Evan smiled and led her toward the horses. All at once, he saw his Appaloosa. His eyes speared Grant, then sought Jacelyn's. "Oh, no. I've forgotten to tell you how sorry I was to hear . . ."

Jacelyn gulped and nodded.

"My dear, I really am so very sorry." He frowned at Grant. "Hurry along. I want a full report as soon as you return to the fort."

"Yes, sir." He pulled the Colonel over a step or two and quietly conversed with him so that Jacelyn couldn't hear.

Grant had barely released the Colonel before Jacelyn grabbed his arm and took him aside while the officer located a horse for her to ride. She glared and whispered, "Yes, do hurry. You, Mr. . . . . Ward . . . and I, have some talking to do."

Grant's eyes widened. "Yes, ma'am."

Chapter Twenty-Eight

Two days later, Jacelyn could hardly believe her eyes when Grant rode toward the Colonel's office with a dejected Dora at his side. She ran from the guest house and intercepted them.

Gasping for breath, she pointed at Grant ... Ward. "You arrested her, didn't you? How could you? She didn't—"

"Missy, fer Gawd's sake, hush yore caterwalin'. Your plum makin' a spectacle o' yourself," Dora hissed.

Jacelyn blinked and glared from Dora to Grant. "Well ... What are you doing here if he didn't—"

"He *asked* me ta come. Says he wants I should see somethin'."

"Oh." Jacelyn backed up a step and let them proceed, but followed along beside Dora's horse. She slid her eyes toward Grant now and then but could tell nothing of his feelings from his granite-hard profile.

In fact, after one wary glance in her direction, he hadn't looked at her again.

When they drew their horses to a stop in front of the adjutant and dismounted, Jacelyn spread her hands on her hips and glowered at Grant. Well, what did he expect? Since he never told her about *anything,* of course she had thought the worst. Dora was, after all, a part of the Waddell gang.

Colonel Alexander walked out of his office, followed by his daughter. Jacelyn and Miss Alexander exchanged smiles, for they'd run into each other several times during the past few days.

Dora silently gazed at the pale-haired girl. She stood immobilized, even when Grant encouragingly put his hand in the small of her back and pushed. "Dora, I'd like you to meet Colonel Evan Alexander, and his daughter . . . Shiloh."

"Shiloh."

Jacelyn cocked her head when Dora and Grant spoke the girl's name in the same breath. And then it dawned on her. Shiloh. Dora had named her daughter Shiloh. "Oh, my . . ." she whispered.

Evan hadn't yet noticed the resemblance between the two women or seen the stunned expression on Dora Waddell's face. He offered his condolences. "We're very sorry about the death of your husband, Mrs. Waddell. I had no idea that he was . . . I mean, the times I'd seen him around the fort, he'd been . . . well . . . a likeable fellow."

Dora dragged her eyes from the girl. "Y-ya'd seen 'im here? Waddy?"

The Colonel cleared his throat. "Why, yes. Quite often."

"That low-down, dirty sonofa—"

"Ah," Grant cut in. "Evan, there's something you . . ." His words faded as he watched Shiloh stare at the older woman and touch her own freckled face.

Even Evan had by now noticed something about Dora that caused him to turn and stare at his daughter. "My God."

Dora swallowed. "My thought exactly, Colonel."

"Well, ah, I think we, ah, should go inside and, ah, talk."

Before she followed the Colonel and her daughter, though, Dora gave Grant a big hug. "I jest cain't believe it, Jones . . . er, Ward. Ya didn't have ta do this fer me."

He shrugged and motioned toward the Colonel, who was holding the door for her.

Jacelyn dropped her hands to her sides, almost forgetting why she was so angry, except . . . "This was something else you knew all along, wasn't it?"

Grant reluctantly nodded. He hadn't thought his gesture toward Dora would be just another thing to distance him from Jacelyn.

She sighed. "You did a very nice thing." Her shoulders drooped as she turned and headed back to her room.

He put out his hand. "Wait." He wanted to look at her for a while longer. Talk to her. "I didn't . . . I mean . . . Dora was kind to us . . . to you . . . She deserved to know."

"Why couldn't you have told me?" Hurt racked her voice.

He held his hands out. "I thought you'd be safer *not* knowing everything."

Jacelyn knew he was talking about more than just Shiloh. But she was tired of always being protected, of being judged untrustworthy and incapable of knowing her own mind. "I never told Waddell you are part Apache. Bob overheard me talking to Dora. It was an accident. You really could have trusted me."

Grant's brows drew together. So that's what all that had been about down at the creek. Why the Kid had shot him. And now she was blaming herself. "It's not that I didn't . . . don't trust you. Someone was bound to find out sooner or later. I . . . you were *safer* not knowing. That's all."

She kicked up dust as she paced. "Why is it you men always think we women need to be protected?" She hesitated a moment, thinking, then admitted, "Well, sometimes we do. But, I'm sick to death of being dependent on a man. I'm a person. I have strengths, along with weaknesses," she added quickly. "I need to feel I can share work, or pleasure, or confidences, or responsibilities."

Grant summed up his opinion of her declaration in a few words. "You're a woman." Shaking his head, he said, "A man looks after his . . . woman. That's the way it is." And it still tore at his gut that he'd let her down.

She stopped pacing and fisted her fingers. "Well," she spat, "if you're hardheaded enough to believe that, then I guess that *is* the way it is." She spun and stalked away from the mule-eared jack ass.

Grant was dumbfounded by her attitude. Rubbing the back of his neck, he stormed off toward the stables.

A man wasn't a man if he didn't . . . couldn't . . . take care of his woman.

Jacelyn had been back at the fort a week when Colonel Alexander asked to see her in his office. The Corporal, with whom she'd been so upset the first time she'd charged through the door, was polite and courteous, somewhat easing her attack of nerves.

"There you are, my dear. Come in. Come in." The Colonel held the chair in front of his desk. "Have a seat, Miss McCaffery."

Her cheeks flushed as she gracefully sank into the proffered seat. "Please, Colonel, you may call me Jacelyn."

"Ahem, yes, all right."

As the Colonel walked around the desk and took a longer amount of time than she thought necessary to make himself comfortable, Jacelyn became uneasy again. She had no idea why the Colonel wanted to see her, but it didn't appear to be good news.

"I'm trying to think of how to tell you this . . . Jacelyn."

She narrowed her eyes.

"Grant, er, Lieutenant Ward, and I . . . we presumed to take it upon ourselves to send word of your brother's death to your home in Virginia."

When she just sat there and stared, Evan cleared his throat again and continued, "And I have received a telegram—to you—from Richmond." He held the paper out to her.

Her hand shook. The missive had not been opened. She couldn't believe Grant's gall—yes, she knew this had been Grant's doing—in taking it upon himself to solve what he must have considered yet another one of her problems.

He'd done it again. Taken away her independence. But a guilty twang rippled through her stomach. No telling how long she would've waited to do the same thing, and no telling if McCaffery Textiles would have even acknowledged her wire.

She opened the telegram and was surprised to read condolences from the board. They then announced she must return to Richmond immediately for a meeting to discuss what would become of McCaffery Textiles now that she was sole heir.

Her chin lifted dramatically. What would "become of" McCaffery Textiles? Why, it would "become" one of the most profitable mills in the country under her direction. What did they *think* would "become of" it? She could hardly wait to prove to those old buzzards . . .

It suddenly occurred to her that her attending a board meeting meant she would have to leave Arizona Territory. Have to leave Grant. The backs of her eyes burned. Was that why he'd contacted the company? To make sure she left soon?

She'd hoped, by staying for a time, he'd finally realize he cared for her and admit his feelings. But he'd worked very hard at avoiding her since he'd returned with Dora. Could she have been so wrong? Was she truly that poor a judge of character?

Despair sank her heart. If she were truthful, some of the decisions—most of the decisions—she'd made since embarking on this adventure to independence, had been poor ones. But she was positive the man returned some of her feelings. How else could he have made such beautiful, glorious love to her?

Or were men different than women? Perhaps they could do that without having special feelings.

"Miss . . . Jacelyn? Are you all right? There isn't anything wrong, is there?"

She jumped. She'd completely forgotten the Colonel sitting quietly across the desk. "Oh, no. Fine. Yes, everything is fine."

She quickly stood and smoothed a wrinkle in her skirt. She'd been trying to get back into the habit of wearing lady's clothing again. "I-I'm wanted in Richmond." Wanted? Was she really wanted anywhere? She didn't think so. Not anymore.

"My dear?"

"It's all right. Really. I must attend a board meeting. Perhaps I'll finally realize my dream." She blinked rapidly.

Colonel Alexander came around the desk and escorted her to the door. "Is there anything I can do?"

"Ah, yes, please. Will you make the travel arrangements for me?"

"Certainly. How soon would you like to leave?"

She gulped. "As soon as possible."

433

* * *

That evening, Dora stood in Jacelyn's bedroom doorway, proudly wearing the altered grey gown. The two
women had shared the guest house since Dora's arrival,
but had had little time to chat as Dora spent most of her
time with her newly found daughter.

"So, you're leavin', huh?"

Jacelyn finished brushing her hair, then laid down the
brush. The same brush they'd found in the trunk. The
brush Dora had been thoughtful enough to bring from
the ranch, though she'd been suffering her own terrible
loss.

"You're runnin'." Dora sauntered into the room and
eased down on the foot of Jacelyn's bed, being careful
not to wrinkle her skirt.

Jacelyn's eyes rounded. "I beg your pardon?"

"Don't go an' git all uppity with me. You're runnin'
from your man."

Jacelyn threw her arms in the air. "I keep trying to
tell you, he's not *my* man."

"He could be." Dora glanced slyly at the younger
woman.

"No, he couldn't. He's too ... domineering. I want
some control of my life."

"Aw, he ain't that bad."

"Dora, you've spent the last who-knows-how-many
years of your life hidden from the world. You don't
know any better." At the hurt on Dora's face, Jacelyn
rushed to her friend. "I'm sorry. It's just ... I've learned
to do things on my own. I may make mistakes, but
they're *my* mistakes. I feel good about myself. Do you
understand?"

The older woman patted Jacelyn's hand. "Yessum,
Missy, I think I'm beginnin' to, at that."

Jacelyn looked deep into Dora's pale eyes. "Will you

be all right here? You could come to Richmond with me." Actually, Jacelyn prayed Dora would accept her offer. She would be terribly lonely back home.

Dora chuckled. "Lawdy, Missy. I couldn't do that. But it were sweet o' ya ta ask."

"Are you and Shiloh getting along all right now?"

"Yep. The Colonel's been right nice about lettin' us git acquainted like. He'n 'is poor dead wife done right fine by my baby. She's gonna be a fine woman."

"I'm so glad. And I'm especially glad you have someone . . ."

Dora smiled a little ruefully. "It ain't been easy, learnin' the man I gave up my life fer was a no good liar."

Jacelyn swallowed the thought that *liar* was the nicest of the names she could call Dick Waddell. But Dora didn't need to hear that.

Rising from the bed, Dora glanced anxiously at Jacelyn. "Nothin' I kin say ta make ya stay?"

Jacelyn shook her head.

"You're makin' a big mistake. Ya love that man."

"I know." She wiped a tear from her cheek. Then another.

"Well," Dora shook her head. "We'll miss ya, child."

"Thanks, Dora."

Making one last appeal, Dora pleaded, "Don't ya reckon ya oughtta at least wait til he gits back an' say goodbye?"

"I . . . can't." As soon as she heard Dora's bedroom door close, Jacelyn shut her own door. She barely made it back to the bed before collapsing and curling into a tight ball of misery.

She couldn't stay and see the truth in his eyes. She'd already made a big enough fool of herself by revealing too many of her feelings.

"I can't."

* * *

Reining up on a ridge overlooking the fort, Grant pushed his hat back and wiped the sweat from his forehead as he watched the rocking progress of the afternoon stage to Benson. Folded in his right fist was a gold filigree time piece. It was the matching, masculine version of the watch hanging around Jacelyn McCaffery's neck. With a barely perceptible nod of his head, he slipped it into his pocket.

"My brother is afraid, yes?"

Grant scowled at Santana. "No."

"Then why you wait?"

"Wait? I'm not waiting. I'm . . . resting."

"Ah, resting. So that is what you call it."

"I'm warning you . . ." Grant growled.

Santana held up his hands. "You get angry. Good. Now go tell woman she belong to you."

Grant's brows shot up. "She is *not* my woman."

Santana stared fixedly at Grant.

"She doesn't like Apaches. She needs her independence. She dreams of running that damn company in Richmond."

"You tell her you're in love?"

"Damn it, no. And I won't. She needs to be back in Virginia where it's safe."

"No bad man, no runaway stages in Virginia?"

Grant silently cursed his friend's astuteness. "Probably. A few. I guess."

Santana nodded, satisfied he'd made his point.

"I refuse to be responsible for getting her hurt or killed. Hell, man, she had to save *me* from that damned dandy."

The Apache grunted. "You half white. You half Apache. You have bad omens both."

Grant frowned. "You mean *traits?*"

Santana shrugged. "Whites worry about man being man. Woman only make babies. Cook."

"Yeah, so?"

"Apache man let wife build home, do babies, even fight battles."

Grant almost grinned as he thought of the way Jacelyn had jumped on Felipe's back and then slid the knife across the floor. Her face had been filled with excitement and determination and . . . passion for life. Yes, passion. She wasn't cowering and fearful; she fought for life with exuberance.

And she'd fought for *his* life. "My God."

Santana put his hand on Grant's shoulder. "So, what does my brother do now?"

Grant had already kicked his horse down the slope. He called back, "Ride like hell and fight for my woman."

Grant slid his horse in front of the guest house and swung out of the saddle before the animal skidded to a stop. He took the porch steps two at a time and pounded on the door.

When Dora opened the door and gaped at him, he grinned and asked, "Where's Jacelyn? I need to talk to her."

"Sh-she's not here. I—"

"If she comes back before I find her, tell her to wait here."

"But—"

"I'll explain later. Right now, I've got to find my woman."

"Wait."

But Grant hurried down the steps and scooped up the reins to his horse at the same time he swung into the saddle without bothering to use the stirrups. Lord, but it felt good to announce that Jacelyn McCaffery was *his* woman. His woman . . . His heart thudded against his chest. Now all he had to do was convince *her.*

After searching the fort for her, he dismounted in a cloud of dust and rushed into Evan Alexander's office, brushing off the Corporal like a pesky flea. He felt the unfamiliar tug of a smile on his lips and tried to straighten his mouth, but knew he'd failed miserably from Evan's startled expression.

"Grant? What are you doing back? We thought you'd be gone at least another couple of days."

"We cut the renegades off before they got into Mexico this time. Didn't take as long as we thought." He spread his hands and looked around the room in disappointment. "So, here I am."

"So I see." Evan steepled his fingers. "What can I do for you?"

"I'm lookin' for Jac . . . Miss . . . Jacelyn McCaffery. Can't seem to find her anywhere."

"Hmmmm. No, I don't suppose you can."

"Damn it, Evan." He slapped both palms flat on the shiny desk top and leaned nearly nose to nose with his commanding officer. "Do you know where she is, or not?"

"Yes, I do." The Colonel stared the younger man in the eye without blinking.

"Well, hell, man, tell me." Frustration gripped Grant and he scrubbed the back of his neck. What had gotten into everyone on the post? Even the usually chatty Shiloh had been close-mouthed when he'd tried to talk to her about Jacelyn.

"She's gone."

Grant snapped to attention, then shook his head. "Gone. What do you mean, gone?"

Evan sighed and spoke very slowly. "She left on the stage over an hour ago."

438

A frown furrowed Grant's brows. She'd always talked about going back to Virginia but, he hadn't thought she would really do it. At least not this soon. Not before he had a chance to ... talk ... to her.

For days he'd avoided her every time she'd started toward him. And to postpone the inevitable, he'd jumped at the chance to lead the scouts after the renegades from San Carlos Reservation.

So, she'd gone.

The Colonel watched Grant closely. "The first day you were gone she received a telegram from Richmond. Something about a board meeting. Your idea about showing she was the only living heir to McCaffery Textiles paid off."

Grant's stomach sank. "Th-that's swell."

Evan hooded his eyes. "And she came up with some really good ideas to present at that meeting."

Grant stared out the window.

Evan continued as if Grant had shown great interest in what he was saying. "It seems Jacelyn thinks the Apache women could add some mighty fancy beadwork to her fabrics. Even thinks some of their basket work would sell back East."

Grant had been listening. Closely. He was shocked. Here he'd thought his Apache heritage would be the biggest obstacle to overcome, but Jacelyn's rejection of the Apache seemed to be working itself out. That was good. Very good.

He rose stiffly, like an old man, and walked dejectedly to the door.

"Ahem." The Colonel hid his mouth behind his hand as if covering a yawn. "You can use my Appaloosa, if you want."

Grant slung a look over his shoulder. "Use your horse? Why would ... Oh! Yeah. Thanks, Evan," he hollered as he bolted through the door. "I owe you."

Evan grinned and patted his belly. "Yes, my boy. I'd say you do."

The stage jolted over ruts in the road, throwing Jacelyn against the window frame. She righted herself, thinking for the hundredth time that whoever invented the stagecoach as a means of transportation had a macabre sense of humor—or a plain mean streak.

She looked out the window and marveled at the change of attitude she'd undergone in the past weeks since her arrival at Fort Huachuca. She was actually going to miss the unwieldy-looking yucca and the forbidding cactus. Though it seemed every plant in the desert possessed some form of prickly defense, they held a certain beauty that could never be duplicated.

She sighed and leaned her head back, glad that she was the only passenger until Tombstone. She closed her eyes, trying not to think about anything. Heaven knew, she'd done plenty during the last several days.

Still, she couldn't help wondering if she'd made the right decision in leaving before Grant returned. It had been easier, in a way, not having to see him again. Yet it felt like this chapter in her life was incomplete. Like something important had been left dangling like a broken limb on an Arizona cypress.

Oh, well. What was done, was done.

Suddenly the stage lurched. Gunfire rent the stillness. She clutched her borrowed reticule, feeling the reassurance of the derringer Dora had insisted she keep.

A bullwhip cracked. The driver called to the team. Jacelyn bounced from one side of the coach to the other. Her heart tripped over itself as she recalled another stage holdup.

"Whoa!"

She cringed at the word. Grasping the gun, she pulled

it from the purse and would have stuck her head out the window to urge the driver on, but the back right wheel dipped into a hole and tossed her to the floor like a helpless sack of potatoes.

Sputtering, she fought her skirt down from her face just as the stage door creaked open. Though still blinded, she pushed at her skirts, pointed the gun toward where she thought the door should be and shouted, "Stay back, or I'll shoot. I mean it."

There was absolute silence. No snorting horses. No jingling harness. No curses from the driver. Just silence. A chill raced down her spine.

At last she shoved the skirt and petticoats out of the way and scooted up to where she could see. Stunned at the sight before her, she felt her mouth gape open but couldn't seem to stop it.

"Meeting like this is getting to be a habit, eh, sugar?"

"Grant," she whispered. Her eyes literally devoured him, dressed in tall moccasins, blue skin-tight Cavalry pants with a yellow stripe down the seams, dark tanned chest, and a blue bandana holding back his shaggy black hair.

He'd shaved and trimmed his moustache and sideburns, but two features warred for her attention. A brilliant smile and laughing blue eyes. Her heart skipped three beats while she struggled for composure.

Grant had hardly been able to believe his eyes when he opened the door. All he'd seen was a jumble of white silk and lace and a pair of dainty, moccasined feet sticking almost straight in the air. And a behind that tempted his hands to stroke and cup its firm roundness.

And then she'd threatened the ceiling with that little toy of a gun and poked her head up, with her hair all atumble and her hat askew. He'd never seen anything so adorable in his life. It felt as if his heart smiled just to look at her.

"Hello, sugar."

She wanted to throw herself into his arms, but restrained the need at the last second. "Wh-what are you doing here?"

"I hurried back to the fort to tell you something very important, but you were gone." His smile faded. "You didn't even say goodbye."

She covered her burning cheeks with icy palms. "I—I didn't think you'd care—one way or the other."

Suddenly he reached into the stage and hauled her, squealing and kicking onto his shoulder. He slammed the door and called out, "All right, Horace. Just send any baggage back on the next stage."

Head hanging down his back, she pummeled his buttocks and the backs of his thighs with her fists. Drat. She'd dropped the derringer when he'd taken her so completely by surprise. His shoulder dug into her soft belly. His body vibrated beneath her. The rogue was laughing, enjoying her outrage.

She let her body go limp and refused to assist when he tried to slide her off. A yelp strangled in her throat when he gave up and just dumped her in the dirt. Shoving her hat out of her eyes, she rolled to her knees and scrambled to her feet. To her mortification, the stage was nearly out of sight, hidden behind a wall of dust.

Turning on Grant, she fumed, "What is the meaning of this? How dare you—"

He closed the distance between them and pulled her into his arms. Like an avenging hawk swooping on helpless prey, his mouth took hers in a mind-boggling, body-searing kiss.

Finally lifting his head, his lips brushed hers provocatively with every word he spoke. "Now, what were you saying, sugar?"

"I . . . can't . . . remember." Her breasts were crushed against his chest so tightly she could hardly breathe, but

442

she didn't attempt to push him away. On the contrary, her arms wrapped around his neck and she pulled his head down for another deep, tongue-tangling kiss.

"Sugar," he chuckled. "Don't you think you ought to wait till we get off this public road to attack me?"

She lifted her head, then buried it in his shoulder at the clip-clopping sound of hooves coming up behind them.

Grant's chest rumbled beneath her ear as he called out a greeting. "Howdy, Private."

She tried to burrow under his skin when two men laughed and returned his greeting. They even called her by name. She tried to nod, but couldn't turn loose of Grant long enough.

When all was quiet, she pushed him away and stood unsteadily in the middle of the road. "You ..." Heat rushed to every nook and cranny in her body. "You could have said something."

"Why?"

Her eyes flashed fire. "Why?" She spun and pointed after the soldiers. As she turned back to him, her mouth worked, but nothing seemed able to force its way past the constriction in her throat.

Grant sauntered over to pick up the Appaloosa's reins. "Nothing wrong I know of, a man kissing his future bride."

She stood dead-tree still. "Wh-what? What did you just say?"

He kept his body turned to the side, but shot her a glance beneath the cover of his lashes. "Thought after all we'd been through, you'd want me to make an honest woman of you."

Her stomach knotted. Her heart thudded slowly, painfully against her breast. For a moment, she'd thought ... perhaps ... maybe ... "I never expected ... I mean ... You don't have to."

Mounting the Appaloosa, he rode over and looked down at her. He held out his hand, and it shook only slightly as he said, "I love you, Jacelyn McCaffery. Will you marry me?"

She gazed into gorgeous blue eyes that irresistibly attracted her. They had so much to talk about. Differences they would have to work out.

"Please, sugar?"

Her heart pounded joyfully. She looked at his muscular thigh encased in his blue-striped trousers and remembered always wishing a troop of Cavalry would come charging romantically to her rescue.

She'd wager this one man had accomplished more than an entire division, or whatever, of Cavalry could have. *He* was all she'd ever need.

She held up her hand.

He grinned and lifted her to sit across his lap.

Wrapping her arms around his neck, she snuggled as close as she could get and felt the rise of his manhood against her thigh. Blowing her breath softly in his ear, she whispered, "I love you, Grant Jo . . . Ward."

He growled and urged the horse off the road, down an arroyo and into a stand of oak. Overhead, a hawk circled lazily, soaring above delighted squeals and husky chuckles.

The breeze carried whispers of, "The ranch? You bought it from Dora?" and "You could run the company from here, couldn't you?"

A creek gurgled merrily past groans of, "I adore you, sugar," and, "I love you, Grant."

Around them, the desert stood stately guard.

WHAT'S LOVE GOT TO DO WITH IT?

Everything . . . Just ask Kathleen Drymon . . . and Zebra Books

CASTAWAY ANGEL	*(3569-1, $4.50/$5.50)*
GENTLE SAVAGE	*(3888-7, $4.50/$5.50)*
MIDNIGHT BRIDE	*(3265-X, $4.50/$5.50)*
VELVET SAVAGE	*(3886-0, $4.50/$5.50)*
TEXAS BLOSSOM	*(3887-9, $4.50/$5.50)*
WARRIOR OF THE SUN	*(3924-7, $4.99/$5.99)*

HISTORICAL ROMANCES BY PHOEBE CONN

FOR THE STEAMIEST READS, NOTHING BEATS THE PROSE OF CONN . . .

ARIZONA ANGEL	(3872, $4.50/$5.50)
CAPTIVE HEART	(3871, $4.50/$5.50)
DESIRE	(4086, $5.99/$6.99)
EMERALD FIRE	(4243, $4.99/$5.99)
LOVE ME 'TIL DAWN	(3593, $5.99/$6.99)
LOVING FURY	(3870, $4.50/$5.50)
NO SWEETER ECSTASY	(3064, $4.95/$5.95)
STARLIT ECSTASY	(2134, $3.95/$4.95)
TEMPT ME WITH KISSES	(3296, $4.95/$5.95)
TENDER SAVAGE	(3559, $4.95/$5.95)

LET ARCHER AND CLEARY
AWAKEN AND CAPTURE YOUR HEART!

CAPTIVE DESIRE (2612, $3.75)
by Jane Archer

Victoria Malone fancied herself a great adventuress and student of life, but being kidnapped by handsome Cord Cordova was too much excitement for even her! Convincing her kidnapper that she had been an innocent bystander when the stagecoach was robbed was futile when he was kissing her until she was senseless!

REBEL SEDUCTION (3249, $4.25)
by Jane Archer

"Stop that train!" came Lacey Whitmore's terrified warning as she rushed toward the locomotive that carried wounded Confederates and her own beloved father. But no one paid heed, least of all the Union spy Clint McCullough, who pinned her to the ground as the train suddenly exploded into flames.

DREAM'S DESIRE (3093, $4.50)
by Gwen Cleary

Desperate to escape an arranged marriage, Antonia Winston y Ortega fled her father's hacienda to the arms of the arrogant Captain Domino. She would spend the night with him and would be free for no gentleman wants a ruined bride. And ruined she would be, for Tonia would never forget his searing kisses!

VICTORIA'S ECSTASY (2906, $4.25)
by Gwen Cleary

Proud Victoria Torrington was short of cash to run her shipping empire, so she traveled to America to meet her partner for the first time. Expecting a withered, ancient cowhand, Victoria didn't know what to do when she met virile, muscular Judge Colston and her body budded with desire.

Available wherever paperbacks are sold, or order direct from the Publisher. Send cover price plus 50¢ per copy for mailing and handling to Zebra Books, Dept. 4397, 475 Park Avenue South, New York, N.Y. 10016. Residents of New York and Tennessee must include sales tax. DO NOT SEND CASH. For a free Zebra/ Pinnacle catalog please write to the above address.